JUST PRETEND

ALESSANDRA THOMAS

CHAPTER 1

TOBY

ANY GUY who wore a worn-out striped shirt and a shaggy beard for a professional picture was a guy I was never, ever going to date.

I'd dated pretty much every type of guy you could imagine. The workout obsessed. The health-nut guru. The rocker. The investment banker. The druggie. The frat boy. The nerd. But this guy? The one who quite obviously gave zero shits about his appearance, so little that he consented to be photographed in a dingy shirt and scraggly beard for an ad for his own radio show?

Never.

I'd been sent a packet containing my assignment in the mail. I squinted at the flyer that had come with it. Mark Mahler would be the perfect new co-worker for me; he wasn't that interesting, I wasn't attracted, done and done. This way, I'd be able to really focus, maybe start to make a name for myself in a field I was starting to get really, really good at.

Six years ago, when I'd started college, I had no clue what I wanted to do with my life; fine by me. The world was my oyster. My parents, whose affection manifested via cash payout ten times more often than hugs and kisses, had gladly sent me to

Stanford, with little to no conditions or instructions on what I was supposed to do with my time there.

I never would have thought that I'd end up in the Master's program for Sound Engineering at UPenn, but here I was. Loving every minute of it.

The feeling of finding my passion was so empowering that I'd decided that maybe I needed to just be me—me, alone—to finally try to figure out who I was. No dating for a good, long while.

I peered through the glass-block windows of the small store-front that housed Sonic Wave Studios, then twisted the handle and walked in. *Shoulders back. Stride confident. This is your new place, and you will own it.*

If you didn't think like a queen, my mother had always told me, you'd never rule at anything.

The front room of the studio was flanked by clean and comfy couches and a freestanding desk that held only a business card tray, a small pad of paper, and a container of pens. I waited a few minutes, finally getting bored enough to spin around on my heel, when the door at the back of the room opened and a guy wearing a polo shirt with dark hair stepped through.

My brow furrowed. "You're not...?" I reached into my bag and tugged at the corner of the shiny show flyer.

"Mark?" The guy chuckled. He was about my height, which made a lot of guys uncomfortable. But not this guy. He oozed confidence, maybe too much. "No. He wishes." Ah, there it was. The cocky bastard. An easy grin spread over his face. "I'm Ethan. Mark's co-host, though lately he's been more like *my* co-host. He's been a little pre-occupied with . . . life. Anyway."

I cleared my throat. "Well, I'm Toby. The new sound girl?" He took my outstretched hand and gave it a light handshake, something that drove me nuts. I was female, not avian. Nobody was going to break the bones in my hand.

"Oh. You're Toby. We thought you were a dude."

I just smirked. I'd almost come to expect that.

"Hey, do I know you from somewhere?" He peered into my eyes, leaning in an inch or two.

I fought to keep from rolling my eyes. It was a common line, especially among grad students. Of course, most of them had seen each other around campus. "No," I said decisively.

"You're wrong. I do. You work out at Natalia's gym. The Knockout?"

"Oh. Yeah." I deflated a little in shame for being so quick to judge him. "I do. Nice to have another woman to spar with."

"*She's* amazing," Ethan responded, and with that, I relaxed a little. He was clearly smitten with the girl who had just taken over the gym where I liked to spar, which was cute, if not tragic. I couldn't see her ever being interested in a straight-laced guy like this one, but whatever. It meant that there probably wouldn't be any weird vibes between me and Ethan, which was exactly the way I wanted it.

"So, Shari asked me to get you settled when you came in. I'll show you where the sound guys—uh, girls, in our case—sit. Shari'll be glad you're here. Do you have any experience?"

"With..."

"With a studio like this," Ethan said, looking into my eyes now, as if checking that I was all there. Mentally.

Time to get it together, Toby.

"Um, a bit. This is my second year in the sound engineering program, and our first year was a lot of theory."

"And being Professor Hawley's bitch?"

I grimaced and Ethan chuckled. "Yeah. I've heard that. You spin at all?"

"I have, but I'm not great at it. Also don't love being in front of a crowd. So this job is kind of perfect, especially if there's a good amount of music on the show."

Ethan led me through the door and to a small dark hallway, where another two doors were located. The control panels took up an entire large desk, visible through a window.

"I've seen a couple programs and dabbled in computer mixing. Never really had the chance to use a machine like this." Though I'd been itching to. I knew it would seem strange to most people, but I loved having the understanding that every second of sound we hear over the radio or through speakers was made up of dozens of intricately balanced components.

Ethan nodded. "This is a whole different world, from what I understand. Shari's a great teacher. You'll be in the room to the left, and my buddy Mark and I are to the right. Hope you have fun." With a crooked smile and what I would swear was a brief pursing of his lips, Ethan left my side and went in through the other door, leaving me with Shari.

Shari had jet black hair cut into a slightly frizzy bob with bangs, and bright red lipstick that most women her age—easily mid-fifties—would never be able to pull off. But hell if she didn't. She wore all black and tapped on the control board with bright red talon-length nails.

"You must be Toby," she said, beaming and leaving a bit of lipstick behind on her teeth.

"Yup. Short for Tovyah," I replied, stretching my hand out. She reminded me of my high school friends' moms, the friends with normal moms, unlike me.

She nodded. "That's right, your cover letter mentioned that. I'm glad you're here," she said, sitting back down in a spinning padded office chair. "Take a seat." She gestured to one beside her. "Do you recognize this system?"

"A bit," I said. "In theory."

"Fine," Shari said. "So, today, you'll just watch. Jot down your questions and we'll take a few minutes to answer them after this session. Then next week I'll give you a few aspects to take over all on your own. We learn fast and furious here, but we do a great job."

"Oh, I know," I said. "I've seen the ranks of sound engineers you've helped train. It's an honor, really."

Shari Smith was a bit of a legend at UPenn, a star PhD who'd made a name for herself in revolutionizing national radio. She'd refused a traditional professorship at UPenn in lieu of offering hundreds of hours of hands-on apprenticeship on various local radio shows every year. I could name a handful of men and women who had interned under Shari and then come back to teach in the Engineering department. More than a few times, they'd played back tapes of their time in the studio with her as examples in class.

She owned this studio, and she contributed to the next generation of sound engineers in her own unique way. She really had a handle on who she was, what she felt was important.

That was exactly what I was after. The fact that it had eluded me this long was maddening, even if I couldn't deny just how comfortable I felt in the studio after only a couple moments. Maybe this was really it. Maybe this is where I would get a handle on what I really and truly wanted to do with my life.

"We have thirty seconds to show time, so get comfy," Shari said, her voice a clear balance between sternly instructional and encouraging.

Ethan slid into his seat on the opposite side of the glass, ducking down slightly to place his headphones and mike just so.

Shari started the ten-second countdown, and just as she drew out the final 'n' on "Nine..." the door was flung open and a surprisingly tall figure skidded through the doorway. Dressed in a button-down shirt and dark jeans, he stopped inches short of his rolling chair and dropped into it, sending the chair careening into the wall.

"Hey, Whiz Kid!" Ethan chuckled, clapping him on the back.

"Six," Shari warned, all while looking at the guy with a twinkle in her eye.

"Mark, Toby. Toby, Mark," Ethan said, gesturing back and forth through the glass.

A head of sandy hair, framed by a heavy beard, lifted to look at me. Starkly blue eyes widened in surprise as they looked into mine. Then a wide smile stretched across his lips, pushing his mustache into two fuzzy hills over stunningly perfect teeth. It forced crinkles around his eyes that somehow warmed me completely from my heart to my toes. I couldn't help but smile back. Yes, this was Mark Mahler from the brochure I'd stuffed in my bag, that much was clear, but something about seeing the real Mark, only separated by glass, stunned me. He was more than a person; he was a presence. Taller than I'd imagined, and smiling sunshine throughout the small space we occupied, he was larger than life.

It was like that time my mother dragged us all on a family vacation to the Grand Canyon, a few months after she and Dad had gotten back together again. She'd spent countless hours on the way, showing us pictures of the sights we'd see, but the moment we got out of the car and stood at the edge of the canyon, it was like the whole world stopped. The colors were vivid, every dust mote and gently passing cloud rendered in sharp focus all around me for just that moment.

For two fleeting breaths, something passed between us—something bigger than either of us—too unfamiliar to put words or emotions to. All I knew was that it was a connection, and it felt unbreakable.

That is, until a hard elbow dug into my upper arm. "Toby?

You with us?" Shari's sharp, rasping tone broke through my thoughts.

Right. I was here to work, not to think about why the unlikeliest of men had just knocked my focus off-kilter with one gleam of his eye. I let my hands skate over the controls and trained my eyes on the computer screen to my right. "Work," I muttered to myself as I listened to Shari's countdown and waited to start the show's intro.

This was going to be fine.

CHAPTER 2

MARK

TOBY EISEN WAS absolute pure brilliance in girl-human form.

And I'd been thinking she was a dude this entire time. I'd never met a girl named Toby. Just when I thought I was safe.

If I was going to get through the next several hours recording, I'd need to control my boner. Replaying the memory of my twin sister, Hannah, clipping her toenails in our shared bathroom was one of my go-to strategies, and the one I used now.

I wasn't exactly avoiding girls, I just wasn't looking to hang out with them on a regular basis. Especially not pretty girls. Most especially not girls that I'd be staring at through a glass window, doing one of the sexiest things a girl could do, in my opinion: operating the studio sound controls like a boss.

I'd just had a shitshow of a breakup with the only girl I'd ever loved. Kylie was so beautiful, so sweet. With her blonde hair, cornflower blue eyes, and sweet temperament, she belonged in the Sears catalog, modeling cardigan sets and baking blueberry bran muffins, or in a wholesome sitcom. She'd come from a good, solid, middle-class family, had belonged to a service-oriented sorority, earned an impressive

3.7 GPA in her education major, and sang with the voice of an angel.

Kylie had been everything that any guy could ever want, and I'd somehow let her slip through my fingers.

I'd be lying if I said I was anything but absolutely, devastatingly brokenhearted six months ago when it happened. At twenty-six years old, after being Kylie's one and only for four years, I figured I was less than a year out from asking her to marry me. That was just the way you did things. Met a girl, thought she was pretty, got along with her, loved kissing her and holding her hand, introduced her to your parents, moved in with her...that was the next logical step, with the most logical girl I could imagine. Marriage.

I figured it wouldn't change much about our relationship.

That's what she figured, too, and it was the main reason she said she wanted to bail.

Apparently, Kylie hadn't been happy. Hannah said I hadn't been particularly happy either. I didn't know about that, because being blindsided by getting dumped by the girl I had imagined the rest of my life with was pretty much taking up all the space in my brain. Through the years after college, while I hacked away at an MBA and tried to get my feet under me in a music career, Kylie had always been there. She was a girl I loved, one that I could count on to keep me company, help me with the housework, even heat up the sheets in our bed from time to time.

When she left me—with tears in her eyes to match the ones streaming down my face, so I had to give her that—I felt like a sad, lonely island in the middle of the vast ocean of Philadelphia. A couple weeks later, I heard through the grapevine that she'd snagged an audition for *Breathe Free*, a long-running epic drama TV show out in La-La Land. I spent that day with my head under my pillow, while Ethan rigged my computer in about ten different ways via extensions and simple hacks, to block all news of the show, and her. Said it'd be for the best.

Just because I couldn't internet stalk her, though, didn't mean she wasn't constantly on my mind.

Worst of all, I had my whole life ahead of me, and no clue exactly what I wanted to do with it, especially without the girl I'd always imagined by my side. Being with Kylie, who loved me no matter what—or so I thought—had given me the freedom to relax, let life take charge of me and not the other way around. I did know that drinking my face off and fucking anything with two legs was not how I wanted to react, despite what my co-host, Ethan, thought I should do. Forget one-night stands; I couldn't even bring myself to *think* about being with another woman.

Until now.

Now, across the glass, sat the most gorgeous girl I'd ever laid eyes on. I'd loved Kylie—still did, I was pretty damn sure—known she was pretty, but I'd never understood what people meant when they described being absolutely captivated, enchanted, knocked off their feet at the mere sight of a woman.

This woman changed all of that in an instant.

Toby's hair was waist-length, chestnut and deep sepia waves tumbling over her shoulders and catching on her elbows as she moved. Her chocolate eyes sparkled just above the most stat-uesque cheekbones I'd ever seen, which framed her eyes and formed an arrow pointing directly to her mouth. The pale pink, delicately curved pillows of her lips twitched as she watched me talk, like she was paying such close attention to what I was saying that she wanted to mirror every one of my words.

Like she was captivated by me, too.

Then, a thought unlike any I'd ever had, even for Kylie – I wanted to *taste* her.

I took a deep breath, hating how my long-suffering and

overly-sensitive crotch responded to one pretty girl who, now that I thought about it, offered me no more courtesy than any other girl coming to work with me at the studio would. If she was going to work with me for the rest of the semester—fourteen long weeks—I had to get this in check.

Maybe Ethan was right. Maybe it really was time for me to start dating again.

Dating. Not fucking. Which is what he told me to do four months ago, after I'd already spent eight weeks wallowing.

So, maybe we were making progress.

Shari's voice piped through the talkback. "Okay, boys, we're on in ten. And Mark? Sorry in advance. Ethan bribed me with coffee to let us lead with...the thing we're leading with."

The five-second theme for The Bro Show, the radio program Ethan and I had built from the ground up years ago when we were undergrads at Temple University, started playing, and I shot dagger eyes at Ethan. He just leaned back way too far in his stupid swivel office chair and ran his tongue over his stupid whitened teeth.

"Do I want to know?" I mouthed.

He just grinned wickedly.

"Heyyy, bros and bro-babes," Ethan half-sang into the microphone. We each took turns introducing the show and doing alternating segments. I liked sports, but he was obsessed with them, so he handled those topics, while I took on the music scene and general pop culture. We traded off restaurant reviews and fashion segments, though I had to admit I gave zero shits about what clothes I was supposed to be wearing. The fashion part had really taken off four months ago, when Shari dated some guy who was trying to start his own line of men's clothing. They eventually broke up, but not before Ethan and I were fitted with new wardrobes. The difference between us was that Ethan actually wore the stuffy khakis, thin sweaters, and crisp button-downs Mr. Fashion had seemed devoted to.

Soon after Kylie left, Ethan had also talked me into reviewing the Couch to 5k app, which meant that I almost gasped myself to death more than a few times in Philly's late-summer heat, and dropped almost thirty pounds along the way.

"As you know, our very own Mark Mahler has been seriously upping his career game in the past several months."

It was true, though I hadn't had much to do with how my unexpected career boost had started. My mother's best friend's seventeen-year-old son had auditioned for *Show Us What You've Got*, one of those nationally televised talent shows with a panel of C-list celebrity judges. I'd just started my talent management company, low on resources and contacts. Needing clients, I'd signed Magnus right away, expecting him to fall in the middle of the audition pack—neither good enough or awful enough to be televised.

I'd been dead wrong. In the space of five months, Magnus had charmed and stunned the audience every week, won the grand prize in *Show Us What You've Got*, recorded an album, spent three weeks at the top of the American pop charts, and been nominated for a Grammy. Now I had a plane ticket to L.A. in two weeks, and I distantly hoped to hear my name in a Grammy acceptance speech.

Yeah, life had basically smacked me in the face these past six months.

"Well, Shari, our show manager, and I have decided that it's time to push him along in the next stage of his evolution. Man was not made to be alone, and neither was Mark," Ethan snarked.

I rolled my eyes and leaned back in my chair, trying to look cool despite a creeping dread winding its way through me.

Ethan nodded in Shari's direction, and Shari nodded at

Toby, who suddenly looked super flustered as her eyes roved over the control board. After a couple tense moments, her eyes lit up as she found the button.

A peppy beat pumped through the speakers and three voices singing in harmony jumped in, "*It's Whiz Kid Mark Mahler! It's Whiz Kid Mark Mahler! It's Whiz Kid Mark Mahler, and he's lookin' for a girlfriend!*"

I narrowed my gaze on Ethan. "What the hell?" I mouthed. He knew I'd been heartbroken. He knew I couldn't even imagine myself dating again. Redness rose in my cheeks. My lips were pressed together tightly and, after being my best friend for so many years, Ethan knew what that meant.

"Now, I want you all to know that Mark is super pissed at me right now. He says he's still not over his ex, but I say he's lonely. It's been almost seven months and, ladies, he is *ready*. Not to settle down and commit, but at least to take a girl to dinner and do a little kissy-facing. So, Mark, buddy, I have a challenge for you. Are you ready?"

"Do I have a choice?" I deadpanned while trying to blink back the sting of tears. Shari shrugged in what was one of her favorite gestures. Sorry, but she wasn't sorry. I managed artists' careers for a living, and I knew this show, and the whole studio, depended on ratings. Not only that, but if advertisers liked our content, they sent us goodies on the regular. The concert tickets we might be able to get, maybe even VIP passes, were enough to get me salivating.

"Not really, bro. I mean, Shari approved the budget for a theme song, and we need to use it for at least...how many episodes, Shari?"

Shari winked at me with a smile, letting me know that nothing was locked in. She was like my surrogate mom here in Philly, and I sure as hell appreciated it, as much as I hated that she hadn't consulted me on this first. "Looks like ten episodes to keep it in budget, Ethan," Shari interrupted over the com.

"Ten. Shari says ten," Ethan said to the audience. "So, I think that means we'd like Mark to embark back into the land of living, virile men and start looking for a girlfriend. And, Mark, I'm not talking about just any girlfriend, mmmkay? I mean, you're hardly an old dog, but I think I speak for myself and everyone who knows you that you should learn some new tricks before you settle down."

Jesus. Ten weeks was three months. I had to try to get girls to...go out with me? Every week? For three months straight? "What does that mean? Exactly?"

"It means grab some new experiences, man! How many girlfriends have you ever had?"

"Um. Just one." He knew damn well it had only ever been Kylie. She'd been the only one willing to see the real me, when everyone else wrote me off as a wallflowered, socially awkward geek. I'd only dated here and there in college. A couple girls had gone out with me more than once, but it had never gone farther than that. Until Kylie. I sighed. "What sort of experiences are we talking about? Exactly?"

"Before I answer this question, I'm just going to put out the disclaimer: the Bro Show respects anyone who wants to limit their physical experience of loooove to marriage or greater commitment, but this is going to be the beginning of our brand-new romancing segment, should Mark agree to it. We're going to learn about Mark re-learning the art of seduction. He's gonna use beautiful words, plan incredible dates. He's gonna polish up his kissing skills, and his...other skills."

I pressed the heel of my hand to my forehead, barely holding back a groan.

"He's gonna have new experiences to delight the senses, man! And any local companies that want to contribute to that exploration? Well, we're all too happy to accept. For the most part."

Oh, God. Maybe it was just because I knew Ethan really well, or maybe it was the crystal-clear innuendo bleeding into every one of his words. But I was pretty damn sure he was asking for hotel rooms, condoms, and sex toys.

"And how in the hell am I supposed to find a girl to agree to this?"

"Hey, bro, calm down. It's just *you* we're trying to embarrass. It can be ten different girls. It can be the same one the whole time, if you get damn lucky. Of course, the girl or girls will remain anonymous unless you decide otherwise. The only thing 'the girlfriend' *cannot* be is your hand." Ethan punched one of the specialized sound effect buttons next to his mic. *badum-chhh!*

I rolled my eyes.

As annoyed as I was at being blindsided by this whole thing, I had to admit two things.

One: it was pretty damn clever. We'd been beating our heads against a wall, trying to figure out which new segment to add to the show. Shari had been begging us to find a way to appeal to more female listeners for over a month.

Two: Ethan was right; I was getting really tired of dating my own hand. Maybe this was just the push I needed, even though my heart twisted at the idea of touching, kissing, being with anyone like I had been with Kylie. I still missed her, dammit.

"Now," Ethan continued, "Mark has almost no experience."

I glared at him and leaned into the mic, ready to shoot back.

"No, no. Sorry, man. I mean, he has a lot of experience with one girl. But she went to L.A. to be a TV star. She wanted to experience more of life, I think she said, right, buddy?" His voice pitched up just like it always did when he did that annoying impression of Kylie.

I shot him a death glare, surprised that I didn't even feel the burn of tears at the corners of my eyes, like I would have any other time.

"Time for my man M&M to experience some shit, huh? We want him to try something new. Something he's never done before. Something fun. Those are the only parameters, and since we don't have any sponsors yet, he's gonna have to get creative. So, Mark, are you up to the challenge?"

Ethan started up the stupid Whiz Kid theme again, just the annoying first few chords. He must have programmed clips from it into his grid controller this morning, dammit. He made a motion with his hand, hurrying my answer along. He was right; I had to say something. Dead air on the radio wasn't called "dead" for nothing.

I obviously didn't have a ton of time to think, so, for the first time in a very long time, I let my gut answer for me. "Sure," I said shakily. "Why not?"

Ethan pushed another one of his annoying buttons, fake sitcom-audience applause echoing throughout the studio.

"All right ladies, you heard him. Oh, and, one more thing. Mark here is straight as an arrow. We love all our gay bro listeners, but that's just not how he swings. Right, friend?"

"Right," I said, pushing certainty into my voice. I was only interested, romantically and otherwise, in women. That, I'd never been unsure about.

Unfortunately, that was where my confidence in the dating department ended. Women were a damn mystery to me, and Kylie had made it all so easy. Huh. Maybe I *would* learn something here. My brow furrowed at the thought. Score one more point for Ethan.

"So, ladies out there, if you listen to The Bro Show, I automatically deem you acceptable for dating Mark. Applications accepted starting now. Tell us about yourself. Send a picture if you want. Don't worry, our Mark is many things, but he is not shallow. And please, girls, only someone who can teach him something new. Got it? Good."

He pointed at Toby one more time, and my gaze shifted her way. My breath hitched in my chest when I realized she was looking right at me with her head tilted slightly, like she was considering something about me. She hadn't seen Ethan point, so I gestured to Ethan and she whipped her head over to look at him, then fumbled for the right button again.

Her cheeks flushed, and she was obviously embarrassed by the fumble, even though she shouldn't have been. It was only her first day. Damn adorable, that's what she was.

So adorable that the over-the-top crooning of my name and how I was looking for a girlfriend faded away to almost nothing.

The only thing that mattered right that minute was Toby Eisen, the new sound engineer on the show where a main focus was now, apparently, going to be about me looking for a girlfriend.

Great.

CHAPTER 3

TOBY

SHARI RAN me though a few questions I had with the sound-board after the show. It was a bit different from the ones we'd worked with in class in a couple areas, but I walked out of the control room feeling pretty smug when Shari patted me on the back and said she thought I'd do just fine in this apprenticeship.

"Learning the equipment and developing an ear for good, cohesive sound is important," she said as she closed out the files from that day's recording, "but equally important is getting a feel for the personalities on the other end of the mic. Not just that, but managing how they sound together. You'll get to know Mark and Ethan better than you know most of your friends." That idea had made my stomach flip, just a little.

I'd be riding the buzz from a first day on the job gone great for a while, and my mind raced through a list of things I could do with myself until my head and my heart chilled out enough to sleep.

I loved Philadelphia's busy but slightly serious vibe, so different from L.A., where I'd grown up. It was nice being surrounded by young professionals who all seemed to be working their hearts out toward a goal, but sometimes it made it that much harder to get the rest I needed.

I let out a long sigh as I pushed my way out into the hallway, eager to take a deep breath of cool fresh air—well, as fresh as it could possibly be in downtown Philly.

"Hey. You okay?" The voice coming from the studio's front desk sounded exhausted. Beaten. I was a little surprised to see the sandy-blond head belonging to Mark Mahler, the guy who was so upbeat and good-natured on the other side of the glass just twenty minutes earlier.

"Yeah," I replied with a soft smile. "Just tired. And, not tired, at the same time. Nothing new for me."

He bobbed his head and cracked his knuckles, flicking his head to the monitor—where he'd navigated to Facebook—and clicked around halfheartedly. His long fingers, tapped softly against the mouse, which indicated calluses on the tips. He was a guitar player, then. In my experience, guitar players' fingers were exceptional at tapping against certain other things too...

The room felt very hot, and I focused on taking a deep breath, turning my attention back to Mark a second later. He hadn't even noticed my lapse, still spacing out in front of the computer. He looked like he was lost and anchored hopelessly in place all at the same time.

It was becoming very obvious very quickly that Mark Mahler was one person while doing the show, and another in the quiet, empty studio. "Are *you* okay?"

"Oh, yeah." He chuckled halfheartedly. "Didn't you hear? I'm looking for a girlfriend. You're looking at a guy about to get flooded with offers for dates."

I stepped over to the desk, plunking myself down in one of the chairs facing it. "It won't be that bad, you know. Lots of guys would probably love to be in your position."

He turned his blue eyes to me. "I'm not lots of guys." His

mustache twitched with the barest of smiles. "As Ethan help-fully told the entire city, I don't know what I'm doing. And...I don't think I really want to. I'm not ready."

I controlled my breath, bit back the words that my curiosity so badly wanted to let out. Was he still in love with his ex? Had she really dumped him as rudely as Ethan made it sound like she had? But I was curious, not rude. I wouldn't ask him those questions—not now, mere hours after we'd met.

I touched the desk next to his arm, placing just my index and middle fingers on the smooth surface next to the hand that was clicking aimlessly through his Facebook feed. "Hey, Mark, thanks for making me feel comfortable here today. I'm not usually nervous, but starting this apprenticeship was an exception."

His piercing blue eyes met mine, wide with surprise and searching for the meaning behind my words all at the same time.

"Yeah? Well...uh...I'm glad. Toby. I mean"—he cleared his throat and I fought to keep my suddenly quickened breathing from being obvious—"it's great to have you," he finished, watching me like I was a rare bird that might suddenly decide to fly away. My heart stuttered, and my hand clenched in surprise. Maybe I hadn't had enough to eat today.

"I heard everything that went on today," I said softly. "For-give me for saying so, but you didn't seem like you were fully expecting that whole 'Mark is looking for a girlfriend' segment."

He sighed and gave me a gentle, resigned smile. "I wasn't... uh, didn't, but I guess it *is* time. It's been awhile. Since...well, I don't want to bore you."

I felt my lips twitch into a smile, and realized that I still hadn't moved my hand from where it rested just a couple inches from his arm. An arm that was decently muscled, I now noticed.

"Well, if it helps, I've dated kind of a lot. My friend Liz said I should list it under 'hobbies'."

It was true. Liz and I had become friends after I tried to poach her man a year ago. Luckily, she had forgiven me for my unintended intrusion on their burgeoning romance.

Mark watched me, his expression half-dazed, half-confused.

"If you want to hang out and call it a date this first week," I clarified, "that would be fine with me."

Hearing those words fall out of my mouth even took *me* by surprise. "Nice" was not a word people ever used to describe me, and if I was generous in any area, it most certainly wasn't dating.

I had sworn off dating, but that was only so that I could focus on this internship and finish my classes with top grades. It was too easy for me to lose my head in the excitement of a new relationship, and I was grateful for that self-awareness.

But the dating I typically did and dating Mark Mahler had almost zero intersection. Right? The guys I'd always dated, by definition, were smooth and sure of themselves. Ridiculously handsome, too. I dated them because my constantly learning brain craved someone who had something to teach me, some door to open that would give me a glimpse of something new. The thought that, by dating a guy, I could discover another facet of the world, maybe find something I never knew I would love otherwise, was a turn-on for me. That was why I dated guys. Pissing off my parents with guys they didn't approve of for whatever reason was a close second.

"Oh, no," he said with a wave of his hand.

What? He was turning me down? This was a first.

"I mean, it's...I'm sure you don't...I'm not..."

I gave a cursory laugh through a tight-lipped smile. "Okay then. I'll see you Tuesday, I guess." He looked at me blankly. "For the planning meeting? I assume I'm supposed to be there?"

"Oh!" Mark practically yelled, making me jump in my seat. I held back a laugh. "Yeah. I mean, the sound guy—or, you know, girl, in your case, or, um, woman—they usually don't come to those meetings. But you should. Definitely should. Yeah."

I raised an eyebrow. "Shari told me I could."

"You could! And should. And...yeah. I'll see you then."

Okay. I stood up and turned to leave, surprised when I felt his long fingers snag mine. I turned, tugging my hand back gently. Mark's face had taken on a grayish pallor, his mouth working between half-open and closed, his eyes refusing to meet mine. "I just went through a breakup. My...um, Kylie, we were... long term."

Oh. Of course. The persona who'd agreed to date for ten weeks on The Bro Show just an hour ago was not the same as the guy sitting here. This guy was still totally wrecked by the last girl who'd been lucky enough to...oh hell. What was going on with me? Mark was exactly the kind of guy I'd never been drawn to. He was unremarkable, and sad, and aimless. And yet...

No. I had to get out of here.

"Take care, Mark. You're a good guy." My breaths felt shorter, my head a little buzzy. He was a wrecked man, but still. He'd turned me down.

Me.

For a date.

I shook my head as I burst out of the studio and breathed in the cool air. This year it felt like Philly was hanging onto winter longer than usual. The cold—just under freezing, I guessed— made the sunset seem like it was running late. It was six o'clock and just beginning to darken. This wouldn't last forever, but while it did, I reveled in it. I'd been born halfway around the world; in Israel, sunshine was more of a given than any other weather situation. I'd grown up in L.A., the land of sunshine. My blood still felt warmed and enlivened by warm rays, but walking out into the cold thrilled me in a strange way, made me feel invigorated, like I'd managed to change the course of my life, all by myself. I didn't have to live in L.A., no matter how badly my mom wanted me to. We weren't close, but that hardly mattered. It was an instinct of hers to want her family close, she always said, since her sister and both her parents still lived in Israel.

Living where the weather dropped to below freezing proved that I was adaptable, that I could live somewhere far away from my parents and still thrive. I tilted my head back, closed my eyes, and took a long, deep breath.

Normally, this weather, winter starting to break into spring, would make me feel full. Satisfied. Like I was coming out from a long sleep along with the rest of the world, ready to take on anything. But as I stepped farther and farther away from the office, my heart twisted and jumped in my chest. My brain was doing acrobatics right along with it - what had just happened to me?

I'd been turned down for a date by a guy with scraggly facial hair, who still dressed like he was in the Target weekly ad. Maybe worse, this guy had now promised every listener of The Bro Show—at least a few thousand Philadelphians—that he'd dedicate the next several weeks to dating. I looked amazing today, and smelled damn good, too. What was more, I could have sworn there was some kind of connection between us. He should have accepted. He should have been psyched to go out with me, even if it was just a favor to ease him into this whole new segment he hadn't been expecting.

But he'd turned me down. How heartbroken could he possibly be over this ex?

I headed toward the train station, determinedly hitching my bag over my shoulder even though it wasn't sliding off. *This is what happens when you say you won't date and then go back on your promise to yourself. You throw yourself at a guy who should have been a sure thing. And you get humiliated.*

Was I addicted to men, like my friend Liz said, however lovingly? Was I really that pathetic that a slight of generic male attention was setting me off kilter this much? It wasn't normally the case. I liked to think that a guy expressing he could take me or leave me, in not so many words, wouldn't bother me in the slightest.

Dammit, this was a sign that I was making the right choice. Probably. If being turned down by Mark Mahler, a guy that I genuinely thought I was doing a favor, was injuring me this badly, abstinence was probably the best decision. I needed to focus on work, anyway. Couldn't ruin this internship, or my contact with Shari.

Except I couldn't stop thinking of the flex in his forearm, those ocean-clear eyes, and the way they seemed to hide some quiet, lingering hurt that I wanted to know more about.

Maybe there was a solution.

I ducked onto the train and hooked a hand into one of the standing straps after coating my hand with sanitizer. These trains were disgusting, and I didn't want something so pedestrian as a communal virus to take me out of commission. I also didn't want to commit to buying a car in a city where parking was either prohibitively expensive or impossible to find. Plus, cars cost a fortune to ship, and who knew where I'd be six months from now? I'd been in Philadelphia for nearly two years now, and the itch to relocate had started to creep into my bones. The semester I'd spent backpacking in the Alps still held a fond place in my memory, and I'd always sort of had a hankering to immerse myself in the flashiness of Paris and Milan that I'd only experienced for a few days on a band tour I'd joined at the last minute.

Yeah, my parents had hated that one. Which was exactly why I'd done it.

I knew full well that my penchant for dating guys that pissed my parents off was good for me in some aspects and not so good in others. I'd gotten high at days-long music festivals, ridden tour buses with rockers I barely knew, backpacked through the Alps and met guys along the way, accompanied men on high-profile business trips, had sex in half a dozen public places—including the top of the Empire State Building — sky-dived, even gone on a fabulous date in a BDSM bar/club.

I'd had lots of great experiences, some incredible sex, and exactly zero lasting relationships. And I hadn't regretted it once. Every experience was part of who I was, and I was a work in progress.

I liked sex; I liked men; and I liked trying on different lifestyles. But none of my experiments over the last six years had led me to any kind of life that really felt like *me*.

I wasn't going to do that by settling down with the first guy I got along with.

My place—a townhouse that cost my dad way too much, thanks to his obsessive worrying about my safety—was my haven. Here, I was all on my own, and I didn't have to compromise a single thing—not scheduling date nights, not design, not which TV shows or movies I wanted to stream on Netflix. Everything was neat and clean and exactly what I wanted, down to the last detail. The coffee table was cleared and polished, my favorite throw blanket was folded neatly over the arm of the couch, and there wasn't a single stray shoe or article of clothing strewn on the floor. There was nothing better than walking in at the end of a long day and luxuriating in the quiet and surroundings that fit me like a glove.

Tonight, though, felt unusually still and quiet inside my four walls. It was on nights like these that I thought fleetingly about getting a little dog, or at least a cat. Every time I thought about that for more than a second, though, my better judgment piped in. *What if you want to go back to the Alps? What if you get the chance to live on a yacht for a year? What if you meet an Opera singer who wants to take you along on his world tour? You can't take a dog to those things. And a cat would starve after, like, a week.*

My better judgment won, every single time. Thank God. I was still dependent-free – free to go and do what I wanted, when I wanted.

I stared at my tiny, spotless kitchen straight ahead and thought of my giant king-sized bed. At five-foot-ten, I liked to be able to stretch out when I was alone or get some breathing room on the rare occasion a guy dozed off at my place.

Right now, I had two equally appealing options: fixing myself a big plate of pasta or collapsing face-first onto my fluffy comforter and growling my maddeningly non-specific frustra-tions of the past two hours into the soft cotton. I felt fundamen-tally wronged by something that never would have affected me several weeks ago. It was nobody's fault but my own, which somehow made it ten times worse.

The bed won.

I groaned my way up the narrow stairs, kicked off my pumps, and let myself fall into the blessed cloud of my white down comforter.

All my bedding was white, since I'd been old enough to pick it out myself. White spoke of purity, of a blank slate, of endless possibility. I'd always thought that with the right atmosphere in my bedroom, maybe my subconscious would come out to play in my dreams, tell me exactly who I was meant to be, and the next day I'd be able to fearlessly move in the direction of being a world traveler or an intrepid political journalist or a reclusive artist living in a cabin in the woods.

The closest I'd come to that feeling was the day I'd first sat in front of a sound mixing board and everything—the controls, the flow of the motion of my hands over them, the attuning myself to the beat and pitch—suddenly seemed to make sense. That day in class had been as close to nirvana as I'd ever felt, and that was shortly after a three-day silent meditation retreat with a guy named Lolan. I'd met him at the airport and switched my ticket at the last minute to join after he'd told me where he was headed, the smooth timbre of his voice and the way he described communing with nature drawing me in.

But audio mixing was on a whole different plane from simple inner peace. The chords and their progressions, the notes and their dissonance, the rise and fall of crescendos, the structure of chorus and verse seemed to unravel themselves in real time as I'd watched them in the mixing program. I'd felt like a goddess that day, like there was something in the universe, if only one thing, that I fully understood, and it was mine for the taking.

That was how I'd ended up in the audio engineering graduate program at Penn and landed the Bro Show internship. And that was how I'd met fucking Mark Mahler and ended up with these nagging thoughts about him. I didn't want to date him—that hadn't changed—but I felt like I somehow wanted *more* of him.

I buried my face in the comforter and growled, feeling the soft fabric steam up with my breath and eventually turning my face to gulp the room's cooler air down my throat. That was when my phone, which I'd managed to keep under my palm, buzzed insistently. I turned my head just enough to open one eye and peer at the screen. A call from my mother.

Of course.

I was being punished because I'd thought for a second about how my apartment felt lonely. However alone I felt, though, I rarely had the patience for a phone call with my mother.

I sighed and, against my better judgement, hit the green dot and propped the phone against my ear. "Hi, Ima," I sighed, trying to inject some buoyancy in my tone. I didn't think I succeeded.

"Oh Tovyah, my love. You sound tired."

"Yes, that's what tends to happen in Master's degree programs for Engineering," I replied, only barely keeping the snark out of my voice.

She made a clucking sound with her tongue, and I pictured her shaking her head. "You work too hard. You know we'd find you a job back home, degree or no. You're so talented, *bubah*."

I rolled my eyes. My mother had no idea of my skill set with anything related to sound engineering, she just knew she'd given birth to me, and assumed I was amazing from there. "Yeah, but I want this degree. You don't—" I caught myself mid-sentence, remembering so many conversations just like this one, and the ultimate futility of my arguments. Changing tactics, I started again with a cheerier tone. "How is everyone?"

"Daddy's fine, working like a crazy person. You always were your father's daughter. I'm getting in some good writing, but between official projects..."

A flutter of hope formed in my stomach. Maybe she was simply calling to check in.

"And I'm going over the next few months with Antoine. He's planning the menu for Passover and we need to know who you're bringing, *bubah*."

I bit my tongue. That was utter bullshit, of course. My parents' live-in chef could whip up a feast for thirty in four hours. It wouldn't matter whether I brought ten friends, one boyfriend, or an indie band I'd met at the airport. Of course, I knew my mother had zero interest in my friends and infinite interest in my love life, and this was just her not-so-subtle way of asking. I also knew, from too many years of experience, that she wasn't going to let up on this.

"I'm not sure, Ima. Probably just me this year." Again. Which was exactly the way I liked it. Guys were for dating, fun, and leaving when I got tired of them, or when they started to get clingy, or weigh me down. Why in the world would I bring one home to meet my parents?

She sighed, long and loud, and once again I wondered how much living in Los Angeles for two decades had affected her drama quotient and how much was just natural for her. "Tell you what, love. I'll check in with you next week, *b'seder*?"

"Sure," I replied, biting back my own sigh. It was easier to do this back-and-forth with her than to have the big conversation – I wasn't going to do what my parents wanted with my life. Especially because that seemed to begin with settling down with a Successful Jewish Husband.

After the requisite 'I love yous', I hung up the phone and resumed burying my face in my comforter. It only took thirty seconds for the phone to buzz again, and I growled into the mattress while fumbling for my phone.

This time, though, it was a text. From a number I didn't recognize.

CHAPTER 4

MARK

"WHAT THE HELL is wrong with me, Hawthorne?"

My grizzled, one-eyed, giant-by-all standards tiger cat released a halfhearted low growl as he jumped up on the couch beside me, then slumped into my side and purred like a fiend.

I loved my cat like crazy.

Maybe it was because he couldn't talk, or maybe it was because I didn't need him to, but he was the one creature on this whole damn earth that I felt always understood me. Even my twin sister, Hannah, who'd been my best friend since before we were born, wasn't always as supportive as Hawthorne.

Hannah had been nudging me to start dating again with renewed intensity lately. If I were a betting man, I'd put money on her planting the idea for this stupid dating segment in Ethan's head. It wasn't that I didn't want it, it was that I had no clue what to *do* with it.

Yes, I was lonely. Yes, I had an all-too-intimate relationship with my right hand lately. But working so much, between the hours I spent on The Bro Show and trying to build my business, was distracting me from even thinking about dating. That and Hawthorne. He always agreed with me. Always sympathized.

It still felt way too soon for me. I still missed Kylie. The first morning I'd woken up with her in my arms was the first time my heart had ever felt so full it might burst. Now, I doubted I'd ever have that feeling again.

I sighed and looked at the cat. "Beers, yeah? You think we should have a beer?"

Hawthorne got up from where he'd been slumped against my side and stretched his paws forward, then arched his back up. The dumb cat had more flexibility than I had at the age of twenty-six, which seemed pretty damn sad to me. Maybe I should take up a sport. I didn't think that puffing my way through a few 5ks a week counted as athleticism, no matter how much it had helped me burn off stress and coaxed my abs to come to light.

For now, though, with tangerine and salmon painting the Philly sky in streaks against a deep purple backdrop, I wanted to have a beer. While watching the sunset. With my cat.

Dammit.

Maybe I'd finally write a song, for the first time since what Hannah had deemed the Breakup Black Hole—the three weeks after Kylie had up and left my life with nearly no warning. At least none that I saw.

I wrenched open the fridge door for my pack of Stellas, something I hadn't stopped buying weekly since Hannah had brought an emergency pack on B-day—breakup day. Stellas were her drink. I'd never really been a drinker, having always been content to take care of Kylie on nights she wanted to party with her friends.

I'd loved our life. And I'd let it slip through my fingers, somehow.

She probably didn't even think about me anymore. Probably not even when she got pre-audition jitters. Whenever Kylie'd had a small local singing gig, I'd been the one to talk her down from the mini panic attack that always ensued beforehand. Maybe she'd never even really needed me for that.

I had few friends outside of Hannah and Ethan. I knew some of the guys in the bands I represented would be willing to sit at a bar with me, along with a few DJs from the clubs I was in close contact with, but the three years I'd had with Kylie had left me so dependent on her for a social life, so reliant on her for events to attend and friendships to grab hold of, that I hadn't bothered to get comfortable with any part of the Philly scene on my own.

When she left, I'd been unmoored, and completely terrified to put myself out there. I'd never been rejected like that, and thinking about being rejected again—whether by a woman or just by guys I wanted to be friends with—well, that was enough to stop me in my tracks any time I even thought about doing anything besides working, sleeping, or watching TV.

I hadn't thought I could feel less sure of myself than the day Kylie left me with tears in her eyes, sitting on my couch, one hand on the remote, one hand on Hawthorne, until today, when Toby Eisen, had maybe sort of asked me out. Or told me it would be okay for me to ask *her* out. Or maybe...

Well, I hadn't known what she'd been offering.

Which had been the whole damn problem.

Her words sounded like she was trying to do me a favor, but the sparkle in her eyes and the jut of her hip...well, she could have been flirting, or I could just be in serious need of attention from a woman.

Hawthorne trilled at me as I slumped into my lame rust-red couch, staring at the sunset and trying, just once, to feel something while looking at it. Hawthorne stretched his neck up and bumped my beer bottle with his nose, and I was surprised to feel its light weight in my hand. How had I downed an entire beer so fast?

Must have been thinking of Kylie too much again. That never led anywhere good.

The colors in the sky were quickly deepening, and most nights I would have welcomed a sleepy, heavy feeling that came after a hard days' work and a well-deserved drink. But tonight, all I could feel was restless—uncertain, but in a different way than usual.

And my thoughts kept coming back to the electricity in the small space between where Toby had trailed her fingertips along my desk and where my arm rested, my fingers flicking uselessly on the surface of the mouse.

I pushed myself up out of my chair and took measured steps to the kitchen for another beer.

A little rogue voice in my head told me a second beer might bring sleepiness or clarity, either of which would be very, very welcome at this point.

After cracking the bottle top and letting it clatter to the countertop—tidiness had never been something that marked my apartment—it bounced off my phone. I grabbed the cell, cursing myself for wanting so badly look for updates from Kylie on Facebook, knowing I'd most likely try to get around Ethan's firewalls once I was halfway through my second Stella.

It was pointless. Doing that only made me miserable. I'd be the one who made the mistake of texting her after she'd moved to L.A., pretending to be excited and interested about her auditions for *Meeting Mr. Right*, of emailing her "Congratulations" when she landed a spot on the show.

I tried shaming myself out of the resulting misery that she was doing a hundred times better after getting as far away from me as possible by telling myself I'd feel worse if she'd died or gotten married, though.

I knew that probably wasn't true. I knew this was confirmation that I, and the life I wanted for us, had been keeping her from achieving what she was always meant to. You couldn't film a pilot in Philly. No argument there.

I was such a goddamn *loser*. I took a long pull on my second bottle, already feeling the effects from the first wash through my blood stream. Ethan was right. Shari was right. I was by no means a male model, but I was pretty damn decent looking. *Evident by Toby Eisen kind of sort of asking you out today. Something you totally fucking blew by the way, you loser. Now she'll think you're a freak and never ask again.*

Well, said the voice of beer-stoked courage in my head, that just meant I would have to ask her first.

And I almost never had more liquid courage in my system than I had right this minute.

I shot a text to Ethan.

Me: Do you have Toby's number?

Ethan: Who?

Me: The new sound girl from the show. The one we met today.

Ethan: Oh you mean the totally hot new sound girl with the lips and the eyes? And the hair, and flawless skin? No, but I could get it.

Ethan: Are you asking her out?

Ethan: You're lucky I'm with Natalia or you'd have a challenger, Co-Bro.

I chuckled. Natalia had just recently stepped back into Ethan's life after a short, intense fling several months earlier. He was prone to getting pretty wrapped up with girls, but this was on a whole other level. He was clearly very hung up on her, since he hadn't even tried to find a serious girlfriend when she went wherever it was she'd gone. But, now she was back, and my buddy was sort of back to normal. He clearly liked her a lot, even though at any given time he seemed half-baffled by and half-terrified of her.

I smirked at the thought of Ethan being confused by any woman. Yes, Natalia was clearly something special, even if she wasn't the girl for me.

Me: Just get the number.

Normally I would have taken Ethan's ribbing, no problem, but I felt my wave of courage running out as my fingers jabbed at the screen, and I didn't want to lose it.

Twenty seconds later, Ethan sent me Toby's contact, and I opened a text to her.

Mark: Hi, it's Mark. I know that I was sort of a jerk before, but does the offer still stand?

It took me three seconds to regret it.

CHAPTER 5

TOBY

MY HEART POUNDED against my rib cage, a feeling I hated simply because I couldn't explain it. Who the hell was Mark, the scruffiest, most basic guy I'd ever met, to make me feel things I never felt?

And then, it hit me so hard it took my breath away. Mark. Scruffy. Basic. No big important job. No discernible ambition. Not a confident speaker. Not chasing a bright shiny future. Certainly not Jewish.

He was the ideal man. Not for the dating I'd done my whole life, no. But for bringing home to Seder? Absolutely ideal. I could just picture it now. My parents would hate him and they'd finally give up on me. They'd never ask me to bring anyone home ever again.

Before I could think twice about it, my fingers flew over the keys. I decided to play dumb, or coy. Maybe some mixture of both.

Me: What offer?

. . .

It took him one minute and forty-two agonizing seconds to reply. I stared at those damn reply dots the whole time. What the hell was this hold he had over me? He was bumbling and uninteresting. Hell, he wasn't even cute.

Not in any conventional sense, anyway.

Mark: To date me. Or show me how to date. Or to meet me or go out with me. Or hang out and call it a date. I don't know.

I grinned and sent him the blushing smiley emoji. This could work.

Mark: Help.

I took a deep breath. Here went nothing.

Toby: What if I need your help, too?

Mark: That would make me feel a lot better, honestly.

I bit my lip, hesitation making my belly flip and flutter. Passover was eight whole weeks from now. What if Mark and I hated each other by then? What if I'd met somebody new that I wanted to bring instead? But I knew both those worries were stupid. If we hated each other, it would be that much better for me to bring him home—let my parents see how truly dysfunctional I could be in a relationship. If I found someone new, I wasn't going to want to bring him home anyway; it was a given that I'd want to spare him.

Toby: I need someone to fly to LA with me in April for a family thing. My parents keep bugging me to bring someone home—want me to settle down. Which I'm not doing.

The reply dots appeared and disappeared for a solid five minutes.

Mark: Like…a pretend boyfriend?

I breathed out a sigh of relief. For as dull as Mark Mahler seemed, he was certainly quick on the uptake.

Toby: Exactly like that. Come home with me for Passover. I'll pay for the plane ticket, and in exchange, I'll be your date for the show's segment as many weeks as you want me. Sound good?

Mark: Maybe I'm nuts, but it sounds great.

. . .

I fell back on my bed, not even realizing I'd shifted to sitting while I watched for Mark's texts. My mouth stretched into a grin, which felt foreign. My thumbs hovered over the screen, uncharacteristically indecisive. Finally, I tapped out:

Toby: Maybe you are nuts. 😊 **When's our first date?**

CHAPTER 6

MARK

GOD, my stupid one-and-a-half beers had given me too much of a buzz to be doing this.

Ten minutes later, my head spun as I stared at the text exchange on my phone. I was, apparently, now Toby's fake boyfriend. At least I would be, eight weeks from now. I stared down at Hawthorne, who watched me expectantly like he knew exactly what I was texting Toby right this minute. Hell, he probably did. He cocked his head at me as if echoing Toby's question.

Damn psychic cat.

Me: I have no clue. That's why I'm supposed to date, remember? No idea what I'm doing.
Toby: Give me your address.

CHAPTER 7

TOBY

I PUSHED myself off the bed, where I'd been grinning at my phone for the past couple seconds, and ran my fingers through my hair. It was nearly waist-length now, and I kept thinking I should cut it. The impulse to hit a salon and chop it all off would hit me sooner or later, just like it had when I was sixteen, and nineteen, and twenty-two.

I told myself I was so thrilled at Mark accepting my offer because I liked a challenge. I told myself that I wasn't doing this to please my parents. I told myself that this was a great idea.

I already knew that the real reason a decent-sized part of me was thrilled was because I liked Mark. Just a little bit

I couldn't put my finger on *what* I liked about him, which was kind of annoying, since I could almost always put a label on the guy I was dating at the time: the rocker, the hippie, the stern businessman, the easygoing frat guy, the searching artist. But Mark was just...Mark. It was a little disconcerting, but a challenge. Maybe.

I just knew I liked *him*. There was a certain tension in the air when I met him, when I watched him work through the studio glass, and then when I almost touched him before I left work that day.

Before I could think twice, I'd pulled a sweatshirt over my camisole, toed into my flats and ducked out the door.

Stepping through the front door of my building into the mid-February air and mentally mapping the short walk to Mark's place made my heart flutter—something it rarely did, and almost never in response to a person.

This wasn't about Mark, though. It couldn't be. Yes, he was sweet enough, but nice guys were a dime a dozen. Especially in this city. Especially for girls like me.

Maybe I was just excited that I had plans to interact socially with another human for the first time in over a week. I hadn't made very many friends in the city, so unless I was on the hunt for someone new to add excitement to my life, I was usually alone. Liz was great, but she was busy, and had a boyfriend that she frustratingly loved to spend time with. Natalia was practically married to her job, running The Knockout, the gym I'd stumbled into to try out kickboxing a handful of months ago.

But I was not looking for "someone new", and this absolutely did not count as real plans, I told myself. The guy didn't even *want* to date anyone. Wasn't even interested. This was something new—taking charge of someone else's social life for a change. Maybe I could show him around the city, introduce him to some new movies or restaurants or forms of exercise.

Well, hell. That just had me thinking about the muscles that I'd observed twitching so enticingly in his forearms. If a guy could get muscle development in his forearms, I'd learned, the rest of his body was almost always impressive.

I texted him when I reached the door to his building. Holy hell, he really was just around the corner from me. Had he lived in the area as long as I had? Longer? While I had been sleeping and cooking and staring at the TV and walking around naked after a shower in my house for the past year, had he been not half a block away, doing the same things in his? Doing his girlfriend, even?

Of course he was, you idiot. Why do you care?

I didn't care.

My phone vibrated against the palm of my hand, shocking me out of my thoughts.

Mark: I'll buzz you up.

Oh. He'd been watching for me. Okay then.

This was one of the older buildings in the city, and it was evident in every element of its design. The woodworking was carved intricately and the carpet had paths worn into it. The paint was bubbling and chipping in places, and there was a scent of aged wood and a slight mustiness draped over everything. I wrinkled my nose. Inevitably, the thing I hated most about old buildings was...

My eyes skated over to the left, where the elevator doors were. Something metallic banged and stuttered behind the wall, and the door slowly slid open, revealing a metal grate. An old lady tugged it open with her liver-spotted, wrinkled hand, and slowly made her way out carrying a fluffy white dog in the other hand.

Nope. You would not catch me dead on one of those old clunky elevator beasts. Actually, if you did catch me on one of them, I *would* be dead, because I was convinced that those things ate humans for breakfast. You just never heard about it on the news because the city didn't want to have to replace all of those decrepit death boxes. It was one of the best-hidden conspiracies in Philadelphia.

I'd take the stairs, thank you very much.

After four flights—geez, I really needed to work out more—I hauled my gasping self to Mark's door.

I didn't think I'd ever wanted to see a guy badly enough to move my ass this quickly over to his place. But I didn't want to see Mark at all. At least, not like that. At least, I didn't think so.

The fact that this was so damn confusing should have given me pause. Instead, I found myself knocking gingerly on Mark's door. Before the knob even twisted, I heard Mark's voice clicking softly behind it. "Hawthorne, buddy. It's good. Really. C'mere."

Mark opened the door with the last word, and when I saw him, I couldn't catch my breath.

He was the same guy I'd seen a couple hours ago, of course. But he'd changed into black sweats and a white t-shirt. His hair was mussed, and his eyes were heavy-lidded. "Hey, come on in," he said, taking a step back and sweeping his arm to the side. His lips curved into an easy smile, and any tension that had laced through his muscles at the studio had melted away.

I walked past him, and when my shoulder brushed his, a shiver ran down my spine. I breathed in, analyzing his scent and coming up with the crisp trace of outdoor air and the musky tang of beer.

Well, that certainly explained things.

A Mark Mahler with beer on board was a more relaxed Mark, and that could only be a good thing after the standoffish slice of man I'd met back at the studio.

"Hawthorne, bed," Mark said, his voice low. Like, *low*. Wow.

The hulking cat, a grizzled, humungous minion of Satan, only had one eye, half a tail, and the personality of the pirate he looked like. He gave a low, halfhearted growl, and Mark tipped his chin down, giving him a stern look. Hawthorne hung his head and took slow steps to the corner, where he hopped onto a tiny couch, an exact replica of the human-sized one in the living room.

"Nice digs for a cat," I said, wrapping my arms around my waist.

Finally, Mark took a good look at me. "You're not afraid of cats, are you? I swear, Hawthorne is absolutely not a threat. He talks a big game but he's never even come close to being vicious. I swear."

"Never? Have you had him his whole life?" If I didn't like the idea of an adorable kitten sharing my space, this grizzled beast certainly held no appeal.

"No, but I fostered him for a local shelter a few years back, and never could get rid of him. I promise, he's good."

"Okay," I said, drawing out the last syllable. I did a slow turn on my heel to survey the apartment. A rust-red couch sat in the middle of the room, facing a flat-screen TV hung on the opposite wall. The rug beneath was striped in muted colors, and the coffee table was a mid-century, modern style nesting number. I spotted a couple of water marks on it, which made me shudder. I hated when people routinely left a mess in their wake.

My mouth twisted. On the other hand, maybe rings on the table was a good thing. Maybe it meant that Mark hadn't turned into a pretentious coaster-using asshole before the age of thirty. I forced myself to forget about it and kept going with my surveillance. There were tasseled blankets hung over the couch's arms, and a large potted plant in the corner. The walls had been painted in muted gray, and all of them besides the one with the TV were lined with bookshelves that held hundreds of volumes and various knickknacks. There was a lot of clutter, but at least it wasn't hoarder-status. Not yet, anyway.

This wasn't looking promising. At least until I noticed...

"Is that a Nathalia Edenmont?" I gasped. The colorful print

taking up most of one wall was so breathtaking that it was a shame all the clutter kept me from noticing it at first. Still, the recognition of an artist I loved took my breath away.

Mark softly shut the door as I crossed to the other side of the small apartment to get a closer look.

"For sure," I said, the smile spreading my lips wide. "I've seen this one. She constructed this motif out of butterfly wings, right? God, I saw a video of her working on this in one of my architecture classes, I think. It really made me think of the ripple effect in design, and sometimes even a song on my mixing board will remind me of the generative—"

I'd been babbling so loudly I hadn't noticed Mark step up right behind me, and suddenly that warm ripple of electricity danced over my shoulders.

"—generative theory of tonal reduction. Yeah."

I sucked in a breath as I turned to look over my shoulder at him with wide eyes.

"I never saw it like that before," he said, walking past me and staring closely at the print, framed in a hickory wood. "But you're absolutely right. It's almost like the no crossing branches aspect, where if an event ei is a direct elaboration of an event ej—"

"Every event between ei and ej must be a direct elaboration of either ei, ej, or some event between them," I finished. "Yeah."

He looked at me, then, and our gazes caught just above the soft, goofy smiles on each of our faces.

After what seemed like an eternity, he dipped his head. "I...uh...I never thought about it before," he repeated.. His nervousness was adorable. "But, yes, that's exactly how prolongational reduction would look as a piece of art."

"It really is gorgeous," I said, stepping beside him, letting my shoulder brush his and anticipating the warm buzz that settled over my skin at the contact. Welcoming it. "Where did you find it?"

"Oh." Mark chuckled, tensing. "I don't think I want to tell you that." Just like that, he was walking away from me toward his small kitchen. "Beer?"

"Sure," I said absentmindedly, still loving the fact that this guy had this piece of art in his apartment, by an artist I'd always loved but never been able to really talk with someone about. "But seriously, where? Did you steal it or something? Was it...did your girlfriend buy it for you?"

"*Ex*-girlfriend," he said pointedly, coming back over to me with a beer in each hand. I couldn't help it, my lips twitched up at the corners when he made sure to specify that his girlfriend was very much an ex. All I knew about her was that she'd broken up with him six months ago to audition for a TV show in L.A., and it sounded like she'd done all the breaking, considering Mark hadn't spent the last hundred and eighty days playing the field.

Even though, with his tall frame and gorgeous eyes, he could have dated. Regardless of the beard, messy clothing, and, I realized as I glanced at the shoe rack next to his door, a pair of striped brown oxford shoes with thick rubber soles that looked like they belonged on a sixteen-year-old.

"No. No stealing, absolutely nothing illegal or any trickery involved. It's just lame."

"Aw," I said, following him to his couch and plopping down with my back to the arm, facing him. I slipped out of my shoes, then brought my knee up to my chest. "Come on, you can tell me. I won't judge you, I swear."

"I got it at Ikea," he said, pressing his lips into a thin line. "Well, I first saw it at Ikea. But then Hannah had it specially printed on these acoustic panels, as a gift." He gave one of them a light knock with his knuckles. "Hannah forbade me from decorating my living room like a recording studio. Learned that pretty fast. This was our compromise."

Well, I hadn't been expecting that. Such a gorgeous painting, one that truly spoke to me, unlike most art, and he first encountered it at the most conveyor-belt of all home decoration stores. I tilted my chin down and looked at him with raised eyebrows. "Ikea. Really."

"I know it's ridiculous." He groaned. "Buying mass-produced art. I just liked it. Couldn't put my finger on why until you said something."

"Well," I said, holding my frosty beer out to him, "It happens to the best of us."

He just laughed, then gently clinked the neck of his beer against the neck of mine.

"What?" I said. "I shouldn't have said anything. Everyone gets their stuff from somewhere. And I love your apartment."

I realized as I said it that I really did love his apartment. I'd never been this easygoing about just flopping down on some guy's sofa, but now that I was here, looking around the room, I felt like I could take a deep breath, melt into this space, and feel happy and safe. I hated clutter, I hated mess, but at least this couch was clean, and something about his presence alone was so inviting.

"I'm glad you do," he said, taking a long pull from his beer. Hawthorne let out a heavy puff from his corner bed. The cat stood up, turned around, and laid back down again so that he was facing away from me. Mark laughed.

"This couch is nice," I said, running my hand over the fabric. "And the coffee tables are so cool. Vintage, right?"

Mark shook his head. "Ikea," he said, tipping the base of his beer bottle toward the table. "And Ikea," he finished, patting the cushion just inches from where my hand rested.

I shook my head as a slow smile spread over my face. "You're kidding me."

His bright blue eyes sparkled with amusement. "Nope. And the rug. And that giraffe sculpture over there. And the entertainment center, and that plant in the corner."

I clasped a hand to my chest, slightly shocked and a little injured that I could have sworn that he'd gotten that plant at the Morris Arboretum. I'd dated an entomologist who worked there for a couple weeks, and he'd told me it was the only place you could buy them. He'd given me one as a gift, promising they were nearly indestructible plants.

I'd killed it within a week.

Mark crooked his finger toward me, motioning for me to move closer. My stomach swooped—a sensation I could truly only remember experiencing when I thought I'd bombed a test or had to steel myself for brunch with my mother. Never with a guy. Not that I could remember, at least.

I leaned in, trying my hardest not to let my eyelids flutter down like they so obviously wanted to. I'd never drank with a guy one-on-one before. I'd only ever done it when we were surrounded by others, people I could trust, and never enough that I got really drunk. I prided myself on being able to take care of myself at all times, on always being in control of my own body. Now, all of a sudden, I was in the apartment of a stranger, who I wasn't attracted to, by myself, sitting on his couch, drinking a beer with him, and dying to hear whatever silly secret he wanted to tell me.

I was an idiot, but God help me, my body was telling me that I loved it.

So I leaned in, close enough to smell the beer on his breath. If I had leaned in an inch closer and he'd done the same, our lips would have pressed together. I fought to keep my breaths even for three long seconds before he said in a low, gruff voice, "And the plant is fake, too."

My eyes snapped up to his, which already crinkled at the corners with the beginning of his laugh. I let my head fall back as laughter overtook me.

And it occurred to me as I leaned back against the arm of his sofa, surrounded by the warmth of his place—however Ikea-micromanaged its design was—that I hadn't shared a genuine unexpected laugh with someone in a while. I couldn't even remember the last time I had.

In that moment, I wanted to keep it going, more than anything. So I composed myself, tossed my hair over my shoulder in a way that made my subconscious scream at me because the only reason to toss my hair like that was to catch a guy's attention. I waited a beat and said, "Okay. You've got to tell me more about Ikea, though. What explanation could there possibly be? Did the apartment come pre-furnished? Freak 90% discount sale you couldn't pass up? Sleep-shopping?"

"Oh, man," Mark said, shifting so he settled even more comfortably into his seat. "I wish the answer were even close to that interesting."

CHAPTER 8

MARK

IF I THOUGHT Toby was mesmerizing when I saw her at the studio, she was five times more so in a sweatshirt with her makeup smudged and hair mussed. Whereas guys I'd been friends with in passing seemed to recognize girls who were put together, made-up, and dressed down to accessories as top girl-friend material, I'd always found something so sexy about a girl I could imagine slotting into my home life with minimal effort.

And Lord knew that my home life had been pretty much my *only* life since Kylie had ditched me.

I'd met Kylie the same day I'd moved to Philly for grad school and learned my way through the city with her by my side. When she left, nothing about this city had made much sense anymore. It was too big now, too much for me to grasp on my own, and I hadn't felt a shred of desire to try. I'd felt even less like looking for someone to do it with me.

And now, within a few hours, Ethan had decided to start looking for me, and Toby had volunteered to be girl number one.

At least, I thought she had. It was all very unclear. But now, with her ducking into my apartment, gushing over that painting, using words I'd only dreamed I'd ever hear come out of a hot girl's mouth, , I was even more confused. On the one hand, she was behaving like a friend. On the other, she'd framed her offer as helping me with the Looking for a Girlfriend segment, which was *not* about finding friends. It was about finding a girlfriend. Most importantly, there was a tension between us, sustained by the occasional spark of intensity when our bodies touched. I was ninety-nine percent sure I wasn't imagining it, either. Sure, I'd been single for six months, and hadn't touched a girl the whole time, but that brief, slight contact with her was so intense that I would have had to be a real desperate mess to have been imagining it.

And I wasn't a *mess*. I had Hawthorne, I was growing my business, I had The Bro Show for extra side cash and exposure. I'd never felt like I'd needed or, honestly, even wanted a girlfriend since Kylie left, until this very moment.

Now, with Toby giving me that teasing, easy smile, her lips wrapping around the rim of the beer bottle in a way that made me think things I hadn't seriously thought about months, a very powerful feeling coursed through me. *Want*. Not just a desire for her body, but a desire of her goodness, her sense of humor, her brilliance in my life.

Yeah, okay, want of my fingers running through her hair and brushing under the hem of her shirt was there somewhere, too.

I didn't know what it was about Toby, but I got a strong sense that if I wanted that—if I wanted to see her sitting on this couch and hear her laughing at my lameness more than this one night—I needed to be open with her.

"So, do you really want to hear the story of how my apartment became an Ikea showroom? It's not exciting at all, but I'll tell you."

Toby shifted on the couch so that she sat on her heels, her eyes slightly higher than mine, her delectable breasts jutting out as she settled in the new position.

Do not think about Toby and positions.

"Kylie and I were together for three years. Uh, three and a half," I started. I waited for the typical slosh in my stomach, the stab of pain that usually jabbed at my insides, when I brought her up. "We, uh...we had a little place near Sansom. Two bedrooms, so she'd have an office."

Toby wrinkled her nose. "Okay."

What the hell was that look about? What girl wouldn't want a cute place on Sansom with her boyfriend and a space for her to work comfortably from home?

"One day, she came home from her internship, just so excited. She'd gotten an offer...kind of like a job offer."

"And?"

"Well, the offer sort of required her to move to LA. She's a music teacher, but she always wanted to act and sing. She talked about how she could probably make it home once every two or three weeks, and how it was such a great opportunity, and she was so excited."

"That sounds awesome," Toby said, looking at me with genuine confusion in her eyes. "Everybody's happy."

"She thought so, too. I didn't."

"Why not?"

"I don't know. I had started some stuff—work related plans—that would keep me in Philly. We already had a place here. I wanted to make plans. Life plans."

"Like...?"

"Like settling down. I...well, I had a ring."

"Oh. Oh, God." Toby squirmed backward a little, then her arm flew to her stomach, the flat of her forearm hugging her tight, like she was trying to hold something in.

Well, that was an oddly strong reaction. "And I didn't think that plan was compatible with her being in L.A. most of the time," I continued cautiously.

"I...see. I think. Did she?" Toby's brow was furrowed, and she peered at me like a puzzle that was just complex enough to disturb her a little.

"Huh?"

"Kylie," Toby said. "Did *she* think it was compatible with settling down?"

I scoffed, taking a long drink of my beer. Hawthorne sat up and tilted his head, examining me, his irises large. "Obviously not."

Toby's eyes scanned the walls, the floor, then settled on her beer, focusing on anything but me. "So you broke up. Instead of trying the long-distance thing."

"It was never really an option." I surprised myself with the admission. I'd been thinking this whole time that I'd loved Kylie enough to want to make it work, if she'd wanted the same thing. But talking to Toby about it was bringing me more clarity than a pretentious beer could, apparently.

Toby just sat there silently, nodding slowly. I jumped in, hoping to stop this new awkwardness between us in its tracks. "So I found a new place, somewhere nice enough where I could have Hawthorne, then moved in the stuff that we identified as mine from the old place. Which turned out to be just a ratty old futon, some folding chairs, and a few mismatched dishes."

Toby shook her head, finally giving me a little laugh. Relief flooded through me. "I still don't see how this became Ikea."

"Easy. Hannah," I said, leaning back and grabbing a picture of us off the side table. It was a cheesy relic from our senior photo shoot. She'd given it to me as a Chanukah present a couple months ago. "She has been responsible for keeping me from embarrassing myself with my clothing, hygiene, and other living conditions since we were born."

Toby raised an eyebrow.

"We're twins," I explained. "She lives in New York now, but

she made some stupid excuse to come visit me a couple weeks after Kylie left. I know she was checking up on me, especially since my parents didn't ask me too many questions. They, uh... never really liked Kylie as much as I wanted them to. I think they were happy we broke up. Or maybe they were giving me space. I don't know." Dad had thought she was lazy and flighty; Mom had thought she was a snob, but I thought the real reason she never liked Kylie was that she wasn't Jewish.

I leaned forward and slid my half-finished third beer onto the coffee table. I wasn't a big drinker, but I also wasn't a guy without enough bulk to handle two and a half beers in such a short time frame. I felt buzzed, relaxed, open, and happy here, sitting with Toby, telling her about my life. Whenever I talked about The Breakup Black Hole with anyone else, I sunk into a funk that lasted anywhere from twenty-four to seventy-two hours. This didn't feel like talking about Kylie, though. This felt like talking about *me*.

And since Toby wasn't here for a date, there was nothing out of bounds about it. I loved how she listened. Like I was the only important thing in the world while I was talking. Like she was taking in every detail about me in the same way she would a work of art in a gallery.

Yeah, Toby made me feel damn good about myself.

"And, let me guess. Hannah works for Ikea and hooked you up."

I laughed. "If only it had been that easy. No, she told me that I was a big boy now and I had to have an apartment that made me look my age. She even used Hawthorne against me. Said I couldn't raise a cat in a hovel that looked like it belonged to the Unabomber."

Toby laughed. "She had a point. So, she took you to Ikea?"

"No, she gave me an ultimatum. Decorate the place myself in a week, or let her do it and pay the bill. Hannah has expensive tastes. I drove up to King of Prussia, parked at the biggest store..."

"Which of course was Ikea," Toby supplied with a smile.

"Yes. Of course." A laugh bubbled up my throat. "Some nice sales girl helped me and a week later I had this beautiful master-piece." I gestured around my apartment like it was the grand foyer of some fancy hotel.

Toby laughed again. It was such a good, solid sound. Throaty and genuine. I could listen to it all day. "That's fair. If pathetic. You have to know how sad it is, Mark, that your entire apartment literally comes from the page of an Ikea cata-logue." She leaned in on the last few words, like she was giving me an intervention. When she did, her body tipped forward, sending her off balance and falling toward me. Her hand shot out and she gripped my forearm to steady herself. A wave of warmth crested through me, and I fought to take a slow deep breath instead of groaning like my body told me to at her touch.

Toby settled back on her heels, but didn't move her hand from my arm. Instead, she trailed her fingers an inch or two along my skin, toward my elbow, and then let it slowly drop. She must have been buzzed. Slow to react. There was no way she was flirting. Was she?

"So, you said your sister was responsible for your general appearance since junior high." Her smile was bemused. "Does she approve of...you know?" She gestured vaguely at the top half of my body.

"What? Undershirts?"

Toby laughed. "The beard. It's...quite something." She quirked an eyebrow at me expectantly.

I pulled my palm over one jaw, then the other. I shrugged. "She teased me when I first grew it. But Kylie never had a problem with it."

Toby wrinkled her nose. "She liked the long beard? Wasn't it kind of weird during...you know..."

Oh my God. She was talking about sex. Wondering about whether it was inconvenient, or messy, when I went down on Kylie.

There was that flush in her cheeks again, a gentle bronze pink that made her eyes light up with golden sparks. Holy crap, I'd probably pay to watch her cheeks flush all day long.

Forget about the fact that she was asking me about how my beard affected my sex life. I was going to need to pull a pillow onto my lap if I didn't keep myself from thinking about my beard interacting with Toby's body. "There wasn't much...you know," I said, only realizing how pathetic that sounded as the words came out of my mouth. "Kylie was...too tired a lot. Especially near the end. So...no."

Toby let out a long breath, and I could have sworn I heard it shudder just a bit.

"Your sister sounds great," Toby murmured, suddenly fidgeting, stretching one finger with the opposite hand, then moving to the next.

I nodded, swallowing hard. Hannah was amazing—an advertising genius with more connections than it was reasonable for a twenty-six-year-old woman to have.

"You sound proud of her," Toby said. "I have a brother, seven years older. I love him, but...sometimes I wish I had siblings closer to my age."

"She can be a pain in the ass, too," I interrupted. "For example, the Ikea apartment. She also made me start running, sort of. Had her friend bully me into weight training. Said I couldn't sit myself to death in a studio."

"Ohhh," Toby said as her gaze skated down my torso. What was she thinking, when she looked at me like that? Probably that she never would have thought I worked out. I was sure that a girl as gorgeous as her, as easy to be around, had dated exclusively models and athletes. She'd certainly have her pick of them.

"So, this dating thing, 'Looking for a Girlfriend'. Do you think she had anything to do with that?"

I dipped my head. "Yeah, I have a hunch that she did, but I haven't really had time to get angry about it. Didn't even have a chance to ask her. Got kind of ambushed by, well, by you, before I could."

The air between us crackled, the warmth of the apartment turning heady in an instant. Toby watched me intently, her eyes trained on mine. "You're not upset, are you? I mean...I thought, back at the studio, you said you'd just gone through a breakup. Thought you could use a buffer, and since I was right there..."

I licked my lips without even realizing what I was doing. "A lot can happen in six months," I said softly. My shoulders went up and down in a noncommittal shrug. Was I ready? Hell if I knew. I missed Kylie, yeah. But maybe I should try to stop. Maybe Toby, rumpled and gorgeous, sitting on my couch on a Friday night, was my sign from the universe.

Her eyes flicked down to my lips, then back up to mine. Her brows crinkled in, like whatever she was thinking as she looked at me was causing her mild agony.

And, God help me, I hated that she looked pained, or maybe I was just too damn chicken to do anything about the moment that could have existed between us, if I'd just been brave enough to reach out and grab it.

But I wasn't brave. Never had been.

I leaned to my right and grabbed my beer instead.

"I don't think I've really changed that much," I said, almost more to myself than to Toby. "Since the breakup." Nobody had asked if I was ready. Everyone just *assumed* I was and hadn't managed to find a girl to date me yet. The truth was that I hadn't bothered looking, and Toby was the first person in my life, stranger or not, to really pick up on that.

How was it that she could read me more clearly than anyone ever had?

"I still want the same things," I continued, daring to raise my eyes back to hers.

"Someone to give a ring to," Toby said. Her voice was flat, but she was still listening, still genuinely wanting to hear what I had to say.

I shrugged again. Honestly, I'd returned the ring and hardly thought about it since. "I guess? I mean, that's the goal for most people, right?"

Toby just raised an eyebrow. I kept rambling.

"But Kylie is no longer one of those things that I want. She was...she wasn't right for me, and it took her leaving for me to see that. Still, I guess I would like someone to keep me company around here."

A low growl emitted from Hawthorne's corner, and I turned to him and rolled my eyes. "Oh, stop. I love you, buddy, but it's not the same."

When I turned back to Toby, expecting her to be laughing at my crazy cat, she was reaching down to the floor to gather her bag. Her mouth was pursed tight, drawing a slight chin dimple into view, and her whole body was suddenly tense. "You okay?" I asked, alarms sounding through my body.

"Yeah. I'm fine," she said, her words short. "I just...I remembered..." She shot to standing, her twisted eyebrows and deep breaths painting a picture that was half pity and half anguish. "I have to...be home. I'm sorry. I'll see you in a few days, okay?"

"Sure. Um, okay. Yeah, for the meeting." I winced at my own words. 'The meeting?' What an idiotic thing to say.

There was a pit in my stomach as I watched her stride to the door and I hurried to catch up with her. I didn't know if it was because now I might have to work at finding someone to go out with me for the new segment, instead of having her come to me, or if I was really just afraid of losing *her*.

"Thanks for the beer, Mark. And the tour of the Ikea apartment." She opened the door, and I side-stepped out of the way before it hit me in the face, like her abrupt change of mood had. She smiled at me, but I could tell it was forced.

"Yeah, uh...my pleasure," I stammered, grasping for anything I could say to figure out what the hell had happened in the last two minutes and coming up short.

With one foot out the door, Toby stopped and turned back to me, her eyes searching my face for something her expression didn't reveal. Then she lunged for me, cupped my jaw in her hand, and planted a hard kiss on my lips. Her mouth parted for half a second, just long enough for me to get a taste of the damp deliciousness of her plump inner lip before she pulled away.

She tasted like beer and mystery, like home and the unknown, all at the same time.

She gave me one more short, shaky smile that didn't reach her eyes, and then she was gone.

Then it was just me and Hawthorne and the Ikea apartment again, quiet and still, like nothing had ever happened.

Except that the stirring in my gut and the energy coursing through my veins told me that absolutely everything had changed.

CHAPTER 9

TOBY

I HAD no idea what had come over me today. At all. When Ethan brought up the new segment, the gears started to turn, slow and heavy, in my mind. By the time Mark and I were standing alone in the studio after the show, the idea hadn't seemed half bad. Teach someone something about dating, instead of reaching for guys who could maybe teach me something, show me something new.

It wasn't like agreeing to date Mark wouldn't benefit me. I'd never brought someone home to my parents before. Maybe this would satisfy my mother until Chanukah. Maybe longer.

Unfortunately, I'd been totally wrong about all of it. Mark Mahler, who was supposed to be looking for a girlfriend, wasn't a fun challenge with a convenient side benefit. He was a freaking black hole.

It was fine for a guy to have an apartment from Ikea. I mean, entirely from Ikea. I wouldn't ever date him, not even casually, though. I needed more. I needed someone who was unique, someone vibrant and alive. I needed someone who knew what he wanted, and who knew he wanted someone like me.

I at least needed someone whose bones I wanted to jump every time I laid eyes on him.

Mark was just a bro, clomping along through life. Mark wasn't looking for a girlfriend, but he sure did miss his ex. He was looking for a fast-forwarded relationship, one that was already set in stone, there for the long haul. He wanted to be settled. He had a cat, for God's sake. What kind of a single guy had a *cat*? They were cute, for sure, but they wanted things from you. Constant care. Guarantees. Commitments. They tied you down.

No, no, and no. And oh *hell* no.

Besides, Mark's cat wasn't even cute.

Okay, he was, in a 'you-could-grow-on-me-if-I-was-in-the-right-mood' sort of way. And so was Mark.

Dammit.

I reached the bottom of the stairs, the very slight buzz I'd gotten from my beer gone in my rush to get out of there, and pressed my back against the wall just beside the exit. I was breathing heavily, and my heart was twisting, jumping and protesting in my chest.

Mark wasn't the kind of guy I could just get one taste of, that much was clear. There was no point in denying it, even if I didn't understand why.

There was one huge, glaring problem. When the little Bro Show jingle said Mark Mahler was looking for a girlfriend, it meant every stupid word. If you signed on to date Mark Mahler, you were signing on to slipping into his quiet, unassuming life, and staying there for a good long while.

And no matter how inexplicably drawn to him I was, I was just not going to do that. Not now, and not ever. I had so much more to discover about myself, and there was no way I was going to be able to do it while feeding a one-eyed cat its kibble in the middle of an Ikea catalog.

———

I couldn't sleep at all that night. I showed up to my TA section cranky and jittery from the three espresso shots I'd downed even though they'd been totally ineffective. I snapped at my students and let them go fifteen minutes early, and then sulked in my office while imagining what my evaluations would look like in thirteen weeks. Damn Mark Mahler. I wished I'd never met him.

I absolutely hated I couldn't stop thinking about how much I *liked* him. His blue eyes, his gentle smile, his easy sense of humor, the warmth of the apartment, even the ridiculousness of his cat. Who the hell named their cat Hawthorne, anyway? What did Hawthorne even write? Maybe I should read something by him...

"No! Dammit!" I hissed in a whisper. I would *not* chase after a guy like Mark Mahler, not in any way, shape, or form. I refused to.

"Everything okay in there?" JJ, the TA in the cubicle next to mine, my ex-fling, and my friend Liz's devoted boyfriend, had ears like a bat.

I groaned and leaned back in my chair. "Yes. Fine. Whatever. Boys are stupid."

"Hmmm. Liz would agree with you."

JJ's roommate-turned-girlfriend, who he was madly, annoyingly in love with, had been subjected to a Bachelorette-style dating series as part of her first year working for Philly Illustrated, a local rag that tried to imitate People magazine and did mostly a very poor job of it. They'd had a following, though, and there had been more interest in Liz's dating escapades than anyone had anticipated. I had to hand it to her, she did have a gift for writing those articles, though.

It had been dumb, too. Liz was a mostly vanilla girl who

didn't crave adventure, surprises, newness. She wasn't looking for a type. She wasn't looking for a guy to show her new things to help her find herself. She already knew who she was, I supposed. Which was a basic Philadelphia girl who was happy with the tragically unremarkable norm for her life.

No offense to JJ, but, as a PhD student, he'd morphed into a pretty typical guy. The two of them would be house hunting in the suburbs before they knew it. I'd bet money on it.

Not me. That was why I couldn't date Mark. 'Unremarkable' could have been his middle name.

Except for those eyes. I could get lost in those. Too bad my obsession with wanting to look in his eyes—wanting to kiss him —wouldn't add any adventure or discovery to my life beyond that first kiss. Okay, maybe first two kisses. Because, for reasons I still couldn't grasp, I hadn't been able to stop myself from smashing my lips against his before I left his apartment last night.

I groaned again, letting my forehead fall to my knees.

"Are you going to tell me, or just make me listen to your symphony of non-specific agony for the next hour and a half?"

I'd dated JJ half a decade ago, back at Stanford. I was damn happy when he showed up at UPenn four years after the last time I'd seen him, and even tried to tug him back into my life for a few dates—and rolls in the hay afterward. What could I say? He had an impressive package to offer, and he was the definition of geek chic besides. He wanted to be an astronaut, and if that didn't fit my "extraordinary guy" rule, I didn't know what would.

But he was all grown up and settled now, and only had eyes for Liz. *Grown up and settled.* It was like a damn epidemic.

Luckily, Liz had forgiven me for trying to horn in on her territory over the last several months, and was gracious enough to be a good friend to me. She'd even gone to Natalia's gym for the first few classes with me, and introduced me to Joey and Hawk's, two places that had really made me feel comfortable in Philly.

Jordan rolled the squeaky cracked-leather office chair from his cube over to mine. He was so tall and lanky, his bony knees pumping crazily in order to make the chair move just a few feet. I couldn't help but crack a smile.

"Toby Eisen, I have literally never seen you flustered over a guy. I mean, you came sort of close with me, but...yeah. You're a disaster."

"Thanks," I mumbled, wishing the buzzing confusion in my head would just go away. This was insane. There were guys I would date, and guys I wouldn't. No judgment either way, but no deliberation, either.

"You know how I only date guys that are...interesting," I began.

JJ raised his eyebrow. "You mean weird dudes. Is that a rule?"

"Honestly? Yes. It is." I titled my chin up a bit, determined not to let JJ make me feel stupid. Only dating extraordinary men had taught me things most people would never dream of.

Like the one time I'd dated the rocker who could play guitar with his teeth and his feet without missing a beat. Or the guy who had founded his own company with double the number of nonprofit offshoots for each of their offices. Or the guy who was designated the most beautiful man at Stanford three years in a row, or the one who had won a season of Top Chef, or the Yogi who held clinics all across the United States with girls—and guys—willing to pay three-hundred dollars for an hour in a sweaty room with him.

I hadn't had to pay a dime to spend many more hours than that all tangled up and sweaty with him. In fact, he'd bought me dinner first.

I wasn't stuck up, even though I knew I came across that way. I just valued my own time and energy enough to make it difficult for guys to get.

"You know me, JJ. I'm just trying to discover myself. Figure out where I fit in. These guys who are so outside my realm of experience, maybe they can show me something new. Maybe they'll help me figure out who I am."

"How has that worked for you so far?"

"Not too badly," I said defensively, my chin tilting up as I scuffed the floor with the toe of my sky-high heel. "Like, you, for example. I was never really into music until we spent the weekend at that music festival. You were so into those, remember?"

"I don't know. I guess. For a year or so, until I got serious with school. People change all the time. How does that affect your rules?"

"By the time they've changed, or mellowed out, in your case, I've usually finished up with them," I said without thinking. I realized how awful the words sounded as they flew out of my mouth.

JJ raised his eyebrow again. I freaking hated that.

"Listen, don't judge me, okay? I'm allowed to casually date guys. If you think I'm a bad person for that, please check your misogyny at the door."

JJ laughed and held up his hands, palms toward mine, begging for surrender. "I know that, Toby. Believe me. But don't you want to do anything more than casually date?"

I shrugged. "Haven't yet. Haven't met anyone that made me want to."

"And maybe that's because you're dating what amounts to a carefully curated list of absolute weirdos on purpose. Excluding myself, of course."

"Of course. That was years ago." I bent my fingers, one by

one, in toward my palm, cracking the knuckles with my thumb. Suddenly I remembered how mesmerizing it had been to watch Mark do just that, and I clenched that hand into a fist. "Whatever, JJ," I mumbled. "You're just smug now because you're all married to Wifey Liz. It's not like it's *normal* at this age."

"Married?" he scoffed. "Not yet."

My heart stopped. "Wait a minute. Are you two *engaged*?" I felt like I couldn't get a solid breath into my lungs. Liz and I weren't best friends, but we hung out enough for her to tell me when she got engaged. Fuck. I couldn't breathe.

"Not yet," he repeated. The movement of his hand to a small solid object in his pocket that could only be a ring box was so swift most people would have missed it, but I didn't.

"Holy crap, JJ." His grin could have lit up the entire campus, but it was just making me feel claustrophobic.

"I'm twenty-six," he said, leaning back casually. "Maybe we'll have a long engagement, maybe not. But I love her. Can't see the rest of my life without her. I figure it's as good a time as any."

My lips felt numb. "I guess," I said faintly. "I just... I mean... I have never experienced that. That level of feelings for someone."

"Do you think you might want to? That's what most people want, Toby."

"Well, I'm not most people. Obviously."

JJ shrugged. "You do you. I still don't understand why you're so torn up over this guy, though."

"Because...he's just a guy. I mean, he's cute. Not beautifully handsome, but, like...fascinating. And good at what he does. I'm working on the other side of the glass from him."

"He's a radio host? What show?"

I rolled my eyes. "The Bro Show. So pedestrian."

JJ slapped his knee. "I love those guys. Wait. Are you talking about Mark Mahler?"

I let my head fall back and groaned again. "Yes."

"The guy who looks like a mountain man?"

"He doesn't..."

JJ raised an eyebrow at me, then gestured to the flyer, which was sitting out on my desk.

"Okay, he does," I said, my cheeks heating, "but in person it's...different."

JJ stuffed his tongue into one side of his cheek, nodding in appreciation. "Toby, go out with him! You just drifted off into La-La Land for a second, thinking about this guy. For God's sake, you're *blushing*. You never blush. Don't tell me that a man that makes your cheeks go pink is not extraordinary enough for you to date. "

"Well, I kind of already said I would," I mumbled.

"What does that mean?"

"You heard the new segment, right? He's supposed to start dating again, but it's mostly for Ethan to embarrass him, I guess, and...I don' t know." I buried my face in my hands, making a long dark curtain of hair around my face. "He's so...*magnetic*," I said in a muffled moan.

JJ sat up straight. "I can't believe we're talking about the same Mark Mahler." He tapped at his phone and pulled up the station's page, then flashed the old Bro Show flyer at me. "I mean, I know you've dated a few scraggly dudes and hipsters, but...I wouldn't have guessed..."

I buried my face in my hands. "I don't know what it is about him. I kissed him."

JJ's eyebrows shot up, and then he just started laughing. "Good luck, Toby babe. Looks like you're already gone for him."

I rolled my eyes, feeling a rogue tear spring up at the corner. I fought against swiping at it. "Shut up. You don't know what you're talking about. I only suggested one date. To get him started. For the show. And then I'm done." I decided to leave out the part of the deal where Mark agreed to come home with me for Seder. That would just get JJ going more.

"Whatever you say." JJ chuckled, rolling back into his cube. I heard him stuffing his computer in his bag before standing to leave. Then he paused. "Wait a minute. You're this torn up about him and you haven't even had one date?"

"Well..." I said, slumping back into my chair. "Not technically. But I did go over to his place. And met his cat."

"And...?" JJ was loving this too much. I'd slap the smirk off his face if I didn't love Liz so much.

"And I kissed him." I groaned, covering my face with my hands.

"Let me know if you need second date ideas," he half-said, half-sang. Asshole.

I balled up a spare syllabus from my TA section and tossed it at him as he walked out. He laughed at me one more time before he ducked into the elevator.

I didn't even have to dig deep. I knew the only reason I was so pissed is that JJ was absolutely right. I couldn't stop thinking about Mark—basic, sloppy, inexplicably captivating Mark—and I'd only met him twenty-four hours ago.

I was screwed, and not in the way I wanted to be.

CHAPTER 10

MARK

NEITHER TOBY nor I had had enough to drink to not remember what had happened the night before. Hell, I wasn't even hung over. Not even a little bit. The two and a half beers over two hours were just enough to have me lulled into a deep sleep and keep me there for the entire night.

Of course, the peaceful sleep was haunted by dreams of Toby. Her lips, the way her hips curved when she pulled her knees to her chest, the throatiness of her laugh when she was truly surprised by a joke. And her freakish strength when she wanted something.

I could only assume by the way she'd kissed me last night that she'd wanted to. She'd looked like she was steeling herself, like she was jumping into something she couldn't fully understand but was determined to do anyway.

I hardly knew her, but I got the sense that was how she approached everything in life. Full-on or not at all.

If I closed my eyes now, even as I took my first sips of coffee, I could still remember how she tasted.

I wanted more.

It was the first time I'd wanted anyone—any*thing*—for as

long as I could remember. I'd loved being with Kylie, felt safe and secure and at home with her. But how long had it been since I'd *wanted* her, felt desperate to be near her instead of just mourning the absence of her?

Yes, I'd been lonely in a new place all by myself, which, I had to admit, was pretty lamely decorated. I felt Kylie's absence every day when I was cooking dinner alone or watching TV alone or folding laundry alone. But I never felt desperate to have her back—nothing even close to the way I felt about seeing Toby again. Like I was ready to crawl out of my skin just to get closer to the time we'd be in the same room again.

I was able to keep my mind clear during my run, but the second I stepped foot in my apartment again, it was like the ghost of Toby followed me with every step. For the first time ever, my apartment held the faint echo of a different girl sharing my space. I could see her on the couch, hear her laugh, remember the things she'd said that made Hawthorne growl.

He raised his head a couple inches when I opened the door, regarded me with his single eye for a couple seconds, then set his head back down and sighed heavily, as if my interruption of his nap was the most frustrating thing that had happened to him all week. Maybe it was. What a life.

I chuckled as I dropped my keys on the counter and kicked my shoes off in the direction of the mat next to the door. "You are such a lazy asshole, Hawthorne." His ear twitched but he didn't even bother to open his eye for that one.

Even though Toby had never been in my shower, though, thoughts of her followed me there anyway. As I pulled my shirt over her head, I pictured her doing the same. Her hair was so long. What would it look like cascading down her naked back? Would it brush her waistband, maybe even get in the way of her fingers as they worked the button of her jeans open?

Would Toby duck under the water first, or would she laugh

as I pulled her in after me? Would the water bead up on her lips in a way that would make me want to lick it off? Would the chill of cool air on her damp skin make her nipples pucker? What color were they? Were they rosy, picking up the blush from her cheeks, or brown, like toffee?

I groaned as my dick jumped at the thought. God, I was an idiot.

Kylie had never agreed to take a shower with me. She was a curvy girl, petite and very round in all the places I loved, and always complaining about how she looked naked, how "nobody wanted to see that ."

I'd wanted to see "that", desperately, but she'd had a strict lights-out policy for sex, and I could count the number of times she'd agreed to be fully naked with me on one hand. The one hand that was now stroking my stiffening dick while I imagined what Toby Eisen would look like without a single stitch of clothing on.

I imagined a world where Toby and I had gone out on a date and ended up back at my place, where she put my hands on her body like there was nothing she wanted more in the world, where she grabbed for me, her eyes full of feeling, like she wanted me just as badly as I wanted her.

I wasn't blind. I'd noticed the way her eyes had raked over my body, had connected with my eyes, a handful of times last night. Maybe, if she really was agreeing to go out with me, another kiss was a possibility.

And if a kiss was, maybe, someday, a shower would be.

I imagined what it would feel like to press my wet body against hers, my rock-hard cock pressing close to her softest parts, and that was all it took. I came hard with a long, satisfied groan, my forehead crushing my other fist into the shower wall.

I wiped down the shower wall, rinsed off, stepped out, and tugged some clothes on while my body was still half-wet. I needed to focus on getting ready for the show I had tickets to tonight—a set in an underground club that only opened when a new DJ impressed the owner.

As much as I hated the ambiguity in Toby's offer, and hated myself even more for kind of sort of turning her down at first, I was hoping she'd give me a second chance to accept. My hopes were high, buoyed by the memory of her lips pressed hard and fast against mine. But if I was going to make the first "Mark Mahler looking for a girlfriend" segment that would have listeners asking for more, I had to determine if I already had my first date lined up.

Which was a great excuse to text Toby now.

Me: Thanks for coming over last night.

She didn't answer right away, or even after several minutes. My fingers itched for something to do. I desperately wished I hadn't washed all the dishes. I walked around the living room, dusting off the top of the TV, picking up a t-shirt that had somehow ended up on the floor there a couple days ago.

When my phone buzzed in my hand, I about had a heart attack.

Toby: Thanks for the beer. It was nice.

Dammit. That didn't further the conversation at all. She was smart enough—and experienced enough, I gathered—to know how to keep the ball in my court.

. . .

Me: So. About what you said Friday, in the office.
  Toby: What was that?

Oh, God. She was going to make me say it. I took a deep breath and commanded my fingers not to shake more than they already were.

Me: How you could help me out with this dating thing.

The reply dots appeared for several seconds, then nothing. Then more nothing. Nothing for five minutes, then ten.

I decided to organize my drawer of graphic t-shirts. That took another eight minutes.

My shower walls probably could stand to be scrubbed, considering what I'd just done in there. I dug under the sink for a sponge and was about to tackle them when I heard my phone buzz again, from where I'd left it in the kitchen.

I practically catapulted myself across the house to get to it faster.

Toby: Yep. We hung out last night. That counts for week one.

Did it really count? We'd barely hung out for half an hour. But we *had* kissed. I could probably include that. As long as I asked her permission first. Maybe, when I talked about it, I could distract from the usual "dating" expectations of week one by making fun of my own apartment. Maybe leave the audience in suspense about whether I'd be seeing her again, considering that I was in suspense so desperate my heart felt like it would explode.

Then again, maybe she was trying to tell me something. Maybe it had been so awful that she wanted to make it clear that she would not be going on another date with me. That had counted, that was enough, thanks very much.

Just as my heart began its descent to its familiar miserable location in a sad, dark pit in my stomach, my phone buzzed again.

Toby: Still want to take your chances with me for a second week?

My eyes went wide. My hands shook as I tapped out a response before I could think twice about it. As dumb as I felt admitting it to myself, I'd really been expecting Toby to bail on the arrangement we'd made after our first date.

Me: Absolutely.

I stared at the phone. Yeah, I felt pathetic even to myself, but this girl, and the barrage of conflicting messages and feelings she caused to rain down on me, had me totally captivated. Shit. Maybe she was waiting for me to suggest some options, or plan something or...

Honestly, Kylie and I had mostly sat around our apartment, or tagged on to plans her friends already had. When Ethan said I had no dating experience, it wasn't an exaggeration. I didn't even know where to start to plan one. Should I Google "Nice restaurants in Philly?"

My palm vibrated again.

Toby: We'll be done at the studio by 7:00 Friday, right?

Me: Maybe a little earlier. Shari usually likes to get out of there even sooner.

Toby: Oh yeah? Is she a partier?

Me: Like you wouldn't believe. She didn't even want to come in on Friday when Ethan and I decided to move recording to that day, but she loves us.

The reply dots appeared and reappeared at least three times over the next five minutes, with no text actually coming through. Not that I was really counting or anything. Maybe she had plans, or at least a suggestion for what we could do. Maybe that was just what all girls did, some superpower or secret little-known ability they all had by default of their gender.

Finally, Toby sent an attachment—a screenshot from a website, its colors muted teal and pink. "Sansom Yoga Studio", it said at the top. Below the header was a class description:

Hatha Yoga, Friday, 7:30 - deep, connected stretching. A combination of muscle-lengthening poses and breathing exercises, helping bring peace to the mind and body.

I raised my eyebrows. Yoga? For a date?

My phone buzzed with one last message.

Toby: Been meaning to try this place. Wear comfy clothes.

Comfy, I liked. The inability of sweats to keep my hard-ons in check? Not so much.

This was going to be interesting.

Over the next few days, I tried to drown myself in work. In the music business, there was almost no limit to the artists you could explore, the clubs and venues you could reach out to, the business contacts you could build upon. I told myself when I started that I'd book any show but a wedding, and even though there were times I thought I'd have to do just that to make rent, I'd managed to keep myself afloat without breaking that original promise to myself.

Luckily for Mark Mahler Management, there were plenty of starving artists in Philly who couldn't quite afford to move to New York, just angling to be noticed.

I managed to pack the weekend full of shows where I scouted new artists, brunched with club owners who hadn't even gone to sleep since the previous night's show, and met up for drinks with a producer at a small record label. I didn't like to get my hopes up, but there was no denying that my efforts to get M3 off the ground were finally starting to pay off.

Before the Bro Show planning meeting Tuesday, I paced in front of my closet for half an hour, tugging shirts over my head, realizing almost every non-button-down I owned was old or stained or fit funny, tossing each one on the floor in turn.

Finally, I found a thermal long-sleeved shirt that looked decent. I vaguely remembered buying it during the week of sub-zero weather Philly had back in January. Kylie had taken our iron when she moved, so I tried to get the wrinkles out of my jeans in the dryer. It sort of worked.

I was so nervous about what I'd say to Toby, how I'd act around her at that meeting, that it was probably for the best that I didn't get to talk to her at all.

She slid into her seat four minutes late, whispering an apology to Shari with those soft pink lips, and met my eyes only a couple times while we hashed out the details for that week's show. Ten minutes into the meeting, Ethan asked if I'd managed to find a girl willing to date me yet, then collapsed into man-giggles while playing that damn "looking for a girlfriend" song. Toby looked up at me with eyes as wide as saucers, then stammered something about needing to use the restroom. She didn't come back until we were discussing Arena football.

As soon as the meeting ended, Shari pulled me into her office to go over some of the studio's financials. I'd asked her for this favor—mentoring me on the business aspect of the music business. I was beyond grateful for her help every single day, except the one day I really wanted to talk to Toby after that damn meeting. Get a read on her. Find out what she was thinking, feeling, about this whole dating thing. About that kiss. (God, that kiss.) About us.

By the time I left Shari's office, Toby had left. I didn't have the guts to text her.

After all, we had a date scheduled for Friday. That was the deal, no more, no less. What more did I want?

For the next three days, I worked like a crazy person. I must have annoyed the hell out of my clients, texting, emailing, even calling them at least twice as much as normal. I cleaned my apartment. I tried to brush Hawthorne and was bitten a few times. I went shopping and tried to cook something. I organized my kitchen cabinets. I went for run after run after run. At least that was a tried and true way to clear my head.

The first time Natalia, my sort-of trainer, had called me, bullying me to get out and pound the pavement, she told me we were going to kill time in kilometers. Of course, back then I was trying to make the hours of the days without Kylie pass by doing something other than watching Netflix and shoveling cheezballs into my mouth. Natalia had told me, matter-of-factly, that running could solve anything. She said she was going to run with me, and she did, every time, over Facetime.

In another universe, where Natalia hadn't had a fling with my best buddy, I might have developed a crush on her. Even forgetting that, it was too soon for me, and she was too terrifying besides. She was thirty percent fitness buff and seventy percent daredevil, with the muscle to prove it and a personality to match. Not that there was anything wrong with a girl who was completely ripped and craved danger, but I just was not up for the ride. Every time we ran across the Benjamin Franklin Bridge, I was afraid she was going to start scaling it and then jump into the river or something.

I liked keeping my feet on the ground, thank you very much.

I also liked running, I'd been really surprised to discover. Really liked it. Something about the way my breathing fell into a rhythm, how I was moving just a little faster than the rest of the world. How I felt like I'd accomplished something when I'd gone three or five or seven miles.

Plus, it didn't hurt that, after a few months of daily jogs, I was starting to see the very faint outlines of a six-pack on my torso. I wasn't a vain guy, but no guy I knew would be upset about seeing that in the mirror, either.

It was also something I'd started after Kylie left. Something that defined my life *after*. Running wasn't much, but it was something that I had never shared with her, and it was my first piece of proof that I could build an adult life without her.

Of course, I'd known that, intellectually, but when you've been with one person since your first year out of college, you've basically grown into adulthood by her side. When I'd found myself suddenly navigating adulthood alone, it was disconcerting, to say the least.

But, between the running and finally getting some traction on building my own business, I was getting there.

I settled onto my couch with my tablet, ready to beef up my knowledge of Jerry Z, another DJ I was shadowing who was rumored to be playing some shows on the East Coast in the next couple weeks. He was trying to break into the country-EDM fusion scene, and if he was any good, his sound would fill a mostly-empty niche in Philly. Just as I'd pulled up one of his videos on YouTube, my door nearly shook off the hinges with a sharp, rhythmic knock.

I practically jumped off my couch, spooked. My first reaction as a lifelong homebody was to stay absolutely still and pretend I wasn't even home, but then an unmistakable sing-song voice snaked through the tiny crack between the door and its frame.

"Marky Mark. I know you're in there."

I groaned, dragging my palm down over my face, realizing just how wild my beard was starting to get.

"Hannah, you did not tell me you were coming into town." I sounded more annoyed than I felt. I loved my sister more than I could say, but her assumption that I was always ready and willing to hang out was damn annoying. It only got worse when she moved to New York, since an unannounced visit to Philly also meant my twin sister crashing on my couch...unannounced.

I opened the door, bracing myself for what I knew was coming. Hannah was a five-foot-four ball of strawberry-blonde, freckled energy who tried to tackle me every single time she saw me. Today was no exception. I grunted when her arms swung around my neck, smiling as I kissed the top of her head. Something was off. I sniffed, briefly.

She drew back, her smile bright and teasing. "Did you just smell me, baby brother?"

I wrinkled my nose. "You usually smell like strawberries. Now you smell like...something else. Like a grownup."

"I changed shampoo. Also, that's creepy." Hannah grabbed a garment bag, which she'd apparently hung on the stairwell, and plastic case with a handle that held at least a dozen bottles of shampoo and other products. "Anyway, I heard that Ethan finally pulled the trigger on Mark's on the Market."

"On what?"

"You're looking for a girlfriend?" Hannah's voice was heavy with faux-innocence, and there was no way she was going to hide that sneaky little smile from me.

"I don't think anyone's calling it that..." I trailed off, realization washing over me. She'd definitely been in on it from the beginning, scheming with Ethan to figure out how to get me dating again. "You knew," I said, glaring at her. "Wait." My eyes darted to the box of beauty products. "What's all this crap for?"

"Come on, Mark. You know very well what it's for." Hannah sighed, ramming her way into my place. "You can't go looking for a girlfriend with all that hair covering your face."

"I don't see out of my chin. Or my upper lip."

"Whatever." She sighed, dropping the box onto my dining room table with a *thunk*. "Mark Mahler, prepare yourself for a wardrobe refresh and some serious manscaping. You, my dear brother, are getting a makeover."

CHAPTER 11

TOBY

IT HAD BEEN the longest week of my life.

The weekend, with that stupid, delicious kiss fresh in my memory, was hard enough to get through. Tuesday's Bro Show planning meeting felt almost impossible. I got there late and left as soon as I could, so that I wouldn't have to talk to Mark.

My house was too clean. My students, for once, had zero annoying-ass questions to keep me way too long after class. Hell, they barely sent me any stupid emails. There weren't enough seats at Starbucks for me to loiter there even a little while. My workout DVDs didn't last long enough (I did the Pilates one twice in one day). I went to The Knockout, Natalia's gym, where she managed to get close enough to body slam me within the first five minutes of sparring...and three more times after that.

Even when I was home, in the house I'd been obsessively cleaning, I couldn't relax. Whatever tension insisted on zipping through my veins since the moment I met Mark exhausted me and made me feel like running a marathon all at the same time. I binge-watched a TV show that everyone else on the planet seemed to be caught up on, screaming at the characters for their stupid decisions and searching social media for the latest fan-theories, typing out responses with flying thumbs on my phone.

Participatory TV. It was a decent time-killer.

I spent two hours on Friday getting ready, reminding myself the entire time how idiotic this all was. Yes, Mark was driving me crazy. But I had an explanation, which was that I had zero explanation for why I was so drawn to him. I always knew specifically why I wanted to date every guy I went out with. Mark Mahler was an anomaly. That was all.

It was a very good thing, I told myself as I scrubbed my kitchen sink for the fourth time that week, that I had a solution to the problem that was Mark. I would fake-date him for a while, get him out of my system, just like I did every other guy. He would come home with me for Passover, my parents would hate everything about him, which would be great, because by that point I would probably hate everything about him, too. It rarely took more than six weeks for that to happen. Yes, I had a plan, and this would all be fine.

I blew out a long, calming breath as I piled my hair into a bun that was supposed to look effortlessly haphazard, but in reality, made my arms ache from adjusting each and every piece so the whole thing didn't droop or release long strands of hair. There was a fine line between 'messy bun' and 'sloppy hair', and I wanted to be on the right side of that line. I was already wearing my favorite yoga pants—the ones that were soft as butter, clung to every contour of my ass, and were just short enough to show off my ankles without being capris. A slouchy, loose-knit sweater over my camisole and little black suede ankle boots kept this outfit solidly in the gray area between fashion-able and yoga-chic. I gave myself one last nod in the mirror and headed to the studio, taking measured breaths through my nose the whole way.

I was right on time again, on purpose. I arrived with just

enough time to situate myself at the soundboard and review the notes on what I'd need to be ready for in the first segment. Steady, deep breaths, hair and makeup on point, and I knew my board inside and out. I'd just focus on recording this one show, and *then* worry about this date-that-wasn't-a-date with Mark.

It was five minutes to showtime. I could do this.

Shari dumped her binder and papers for the show on the desk next to me, and, on the other side of the glass, Ethan strode into the room talking with some guy I didn't recognize.

They both sat down in front of the microphones, then the other guy looked up at me and—

Hel-lo.

From the tips of his slightly worn oxfords to the collar of his cozy, half-zipped gray sweater, I had never seen a finer specimen of physical perfection. He wasn't wearing skinny jeans, like half the self-absorbed male models in clubs were doing, but I could tell that his boot cut wasn't hiding any chicken legs. Solid hips sloping up into slightly wider shoulders, a neck that bore just a hint of muscle and looked utterly lickable, a jaw that was more chiseled than Mount Rushmore. He had a fairly standard haircut, trim all around and slightly longer on top, but that was the only non-gorgeous thing about him. At 6:00 PM, his five o'clock shadow had just started to show. An image flashed through my mind of what it would feel like rasping against the underside of my breasts when he teased my nipple with his teeth. The only thing that interrupted my little flash of a daydream was the startling blue of his eyes. Even through thick studio glass, their color was absolutely piercing. These were no kaleidoscopes of color, but pure, deep, rich blue. If they were this bright under harsh fluorescent bulbs, I could only imagine what they would look like outside. Maybe in a swimming pool. With him shirtless, pressed flush against my wet body.

Then, about five seconds after Adonis himself sat down, in a terrible, wonderful flash, I recognized him.

Mark.

Mark fucking Mahler, re-dressed, shaved, and impeccably groomed. Mark, who I'd convinced myself was unattractive, albeit magnetic, a week ago. Mark, who I'd agreed to fake-date just to get my parents off my back. Mark, who was giving me heart palpitations with his tentative, awkward, blessedly beardless smile right this moment.

During the intro "Catch Up with the Bros" segment, and then Ethan's recap of some local baseball drama that sounded more involved than anything I ever encountered at my Los Angeles private high school, I fought to make my breaths even. I willed my cheeks to drop the shade of pink I knew had bled through them, without having to press my chilled fingers to them.

I couldn't decide if, when the show was over, I wanted to run away from Mark Mahler forever or climb him like a tree.

Before I knew it, that damn jingle blasted through my headphones. The realization of what was about to happen hit me all at once, like an anvil on my chest. The Whiz Kid Mark Mahler who was Looking for a Girlfriend had found his first date. It was me.

He was going to talk about me, on the radio, while I could see him. While he looked like he did. And it was my job to make the segment sound flawless. I hovered my hand over the sound board. My fingers only shook a little bit. I could do this.

"So, I actually did have a date during Week One," Mark told the microphone once that infernal jingle finally wound down. His eyes flicked to mine, and there was something in their sparkle that turned me inside out and upside down.

Whatever this guy was doing to me, I needed to figure it out, and fast. Before I completely lost it.

CHAPTER 12

MARK

"YEAH," I answered Ethan's surprised arched eyebrow. "I saw her not too long after I left the studio last week. Things just sort of fell into place."

I had to admit, the sight of Ethan pumping his fist and squeezing his eyes shut in a show of victorious excitement felt pretty damn good.

"See, this bro moves fast!" Ethan crowed into the mic. The chorus of M.C. Hammer's "Can't Touch This" burst through the studio from one of the buttons on his grid controller for three agonizing seconds. "So, go ahead. Tell us what happened. In as much detail as you would like." He said the last sentence leaning in close to the microphone and dropping his voice down to a smooth bass. I could tell Shari was trying not to laugh.

I glanced at Toby through the glass, my lips pressed into a tight line. I did not want this to embarrass her, but she wasn't even looking. I felt a short burst of relief before realizing that her not looking at me meant I would have no idea of her feelings about this at all. She had arrived at the studio just before I had, right under the wire. I'd seen Shari talking to her, and felt guilty that I hadn't warned her about Shari's rule that being on time was the same thing as being late. Now, Toby was staring intently at the controls under her fingers, not giving me a single glance.

This girl was damn near unreadable. My nervousness was only compounded by not having heard a word from her since she'd texted me to wear comfy clothes, the day after she'd assault-kissed me, which was also the day I met her. She was a puzzle that I desperately wanted to try to solve, but had no clue of the first step.

"Uh, I...well, I was having a beer, and I texted her about how idiotic you made me feel on the show last week."

"Sorry not sorry," Ethan said, again in a low suggestive voice.

"And before I knew it," I pressed on, shooting him a glare, "She was at my place. So I showed her around."

"So, when you say you showed her around..." Ethan pressed another button and the opening strains of *"Let's Get It On"* arced through the air.

"Ethan. Please. I literally showed her around my place. Which was a total mess, and which she quickly realized is exclusively decorated and furnished with IKEA merchandise."

Ethan sucked in a breath, then shook his head with a low chuckle. "And her reaction?"

"I don't know. I'm guessing she thought it was pretty sad, because she left right after she realized how pathetic it is that I relied on a retail catalog to decorate my living space."

"Of course she did, because it was due to the general melancholy that was your post-breakup ass."

Great. Now Toby had that image in her mind *and* she'd have to go back and bleep out yet another curse word. "I remember how your sister threatened you to put *something* in your new place. I remember it well, but I will link to the show and the accompanying article for our listeners who don't know you quite as intimately as I do," Ethan said, waggling his eyebrows. "So, there are two things I know all our listeners want to know, though I suppose you aren't strictly obligated to give them any answers."

I chuckled. Of course I had to respond to his questions. That was the point of the segment.

"Where did you find this young woman, and will you be seeing her again?" A deep voice-over came out of the speaker, booming: *Inquiring minds want to know.*

My eyes darted to Toby, who gave me a tiny, almost imperceptible nod, with the barest of smiles on her face. Warmth flooded me. She trusted me.

"I found her," I started, using air quotes on the last two words, "through the show." Ethan's eyebrows shot up and he leaned forward to the mic, but I preempted his question. "No, I won't elaborate. And, yes, I can say definitively that I will be seeing her again. She signed us up for yoga. Tonight."

"Bro!" he crowed, slow-clapping. "You must really like this girl to let her take you to a yoga class. Have you ever even done yoga, man? It's like fancy twister, right?"

"I don't know," I said, drawing out my vowels in an effort to sound casual. "I kind of like that she knows what she wants to do on a date. She made the plans, I want to make her happy." Making eye contact with Toby right now would make this all too obvious. I knew she trusted me, but we needed to talk about whether to identify her as the girl I was dating in this whole insane segment. Instinct told me we should wait until we'd been seeing each other for several weeks, at least.

God, I wanted it to last that long.

"All right, well, I hope you learn something. Just don't pull any muscles so you can still enjoy yourself. You know, after." Ethan mashed his finger down on a button and *"Let's Get It On"* started blasting out of the speakers.

"Okay, okay. I should just say that I do not approve of

Ethan's message. It's not okay to assume that there will be anything physical happening between me and this very nice young woman I'm going out with tonight. At least, nothing that doesn't happen on adjacent foam mats in a yoga studio."

Ethan chuckled from the other side of the mic. "Chill your balls, man. Everyone knows that I am a feminist and I love the ladies in more ways than one. Respectful ways."

"Well, hopefully this segment will remind you of that. Weekly."

Shari's shoulders shook with laughter, and I finally got some eye contact from Toby. A gentle smile reached all the way to her eyes, and she bit ever-so-gently down on her bottom lip.

"Hey, bro, speaking of something physical, I am so very disappointed that this show does not live stream video. Your look is just completely different than last week—or ever before. What the hell happened to you?"

I leaned into the mic. "Listeners, Ethan means to say that I am looking very polished and dapper."

Ethan snorted. "That's one way of putting it. The Whiz Kid has put some serious effort into his appearance this week. I was shocked—*shocked*—when he walked in here, baby-faced. I haven't seen Mark's actual face-skin in—well, I haven't *ever* seen it."

"Only my twin sister remembered what I looked like clean-shaven. She was the one responsible for this, uh, manscaping, I think she called it."

"In all seriousness, it looks good, man. You've got the jaw for it. And this outfit...not wrinkled. Looks like it came from some-where other than the discount store. Nary a scuff on your shoes. An actual belt. I'm loving it. Truly."

"Thanks, friend," I said, sincerely. The only opinion I'd had to go on before now was Hannah's, and while my sister was a woman with good taste, I had to take her comments on my appearance with a grain of salt.

"What do the ladies of Sonic Wave Studios think? Shari? Toby? For our listeners, Toby is our new sound girl."

Toby leaned to the side and whispered something in Shari's ear, then grabbed for her legal pad. Both of them scribbled on a sheet of paper with markers, and then held them up. Shari's read 8/10. Toby's, 10/10.

My heart stuttered in my chest. Was she serious?

Toby's pink tongue darted out and licked her lips. The briefest of smiles twitched at her mouth, glinting in her eyes, which locked on mine.

Oh, God. It was a damn good thing I was sitting down, with the view of my crotch safely obscured.

The rest of the show passed without incident, and I even got one more look of admiration from Toby when I reviewed the latest New York Times bestselling twisty-turny mystery novel. I'd loved the suspense and clipped writing style, but hated the immaturity of the main character. The way Toby's lips shadowed a few of my syllables as I talked made me wonder if she'd read it too.

Shari was predictably out of the studio right on the nose at seven o'clock, and Ethan bustled around, closing out our show as quickly as he could. There were a couple of girls who showcased indie rock live for a full three hours after we finished taping, so we didn't have to lock up or anything. While I stopped in the men's room to change into yoga clothes, Ethan hung back, halfheartedly chatting up one of the girls. Hannah had brought me some insanely soft dark gray sweats and a pair of casual sneakers that I really liked. After waffling over it for a minute, I patted some of the woodsy-smelling lotion she'd given me along my shoulders and down my arms, plus refreshed my deodorant. I hoped this wasn't one of those sweaty yoga classes, but I'd rather be safe than sorry.

I walked out to find Ethan shuffling through some stacks of papers at the front desk. I tilted my head toward the door, silently asking him if I could duck out. He gave me a nod, smiling at something over my shoulder. I pushed the door open, and right outside it stood Toby, her long waves blowing slightly in the breeze, like some ethereal yoga-pants wearing goddess.

I could tell her leggings were soft without even touching them, which somehow just made me want to run my hands over them even more. They clung to every muscle and curve of her legs, and my God, her legs really did go on for days. I could easily get my hand halfway around her thigh, if I grabbed it. Like I would if she had it wrapped around my waist.

I was suddenly very, very grateful to my past self for deciding to wear boxer briefs under my sweats instead of going commando.

"Nice job we have here. We can wear anything we want to the studio." Her alto voice skated across the slightest bit of gravel. I couldn't figure out if she did it on purpose, or if every word that came out of Toby's mouth just sounded sultry as hell.

I swallowed and forced words out. "Got that right," I said. "Though I will tell you that Hannah expressly forbade me from wearing sweatpants out of the house when the whole makeover thing happened. She said the only time I could leave the house in sweatpants was if I was retrieving life-saving medication. Or if the place was on fire."

Toby gave one of those soft, deep laughs, then did that lip-biting thing again. I would have sold my soul at that moment to be the one biting that soft, pillowy pinkness. "So, this is a forbidden wardrobe choice, then," she said.

What the hell was going through my head? I'd never even

thought about biting at Kylie's lips. "Hannah knew about my yoga date. She gave me these sweatpants," I admitted.

She laughed, and the sound sent a shiver through me. My God. Toby Eisen was going to drive me nuts.

"Ready to go?" she said, pulling me out of my daydream. Thank God she did, because I was sure that I'd start to drool and stammer at any moment. "It's just a few blocks around the corner. Nice night to walk."

"Absolutely," I rasped out. Toby grabbed my hand as we walked down the sidewalk, showing me instead of telling me which direction we had to go. That took a hell of a lot of confidence—just trusting a guy would follow you anywhere you led him.

As we strolled in the direction of Sansom street, her long, slender fingers wrapped in mine, I was a hundred percent sure I wouldn't want it any other way.

CHAPTER 13

TOBY

I DIDN'T KNOW what made me grab Mark's hand as we walked down Sansom street. It wasn't crowded, so I wasn't afraid of losing him in a crowd. It wasn't even cold enough to need gloves.

All I knew was that when our fingers wove together and our palms pressed against each other, I felt like I could do anything. Including a mystery yoga class with a guy I should not be interested in but definitely was.

Especially now. His twin sister had put him through this incredible man-makeover, and for that, I could have kissed her myself. But why had she done it? Was it because he was suddenly supposed to be dating as many girls as he could get his hands on?

Well, they couldn't have him. At least, not until I decided to give him up.

I didn't dare to look into his eyes until we were at the door to the studio. It was small, just a fifteen-by-twenty room with a wood floor, framed by frothy white curtains. The instructor was a tiny woman with a head full of skinny dreadlocks, wearing a full-body leotard that showed off every contour of her very toned frame. When we opened the door, ringing the little bell attached to it as we did, she paused from where she'd been traipsing around the perimeter of the room.

"Ah! Company! I'm so glad."

"Is...there's a class here tonight, right?"

"Yes. Is it seven-thirty already?"

."..Yes." I tried not to look at her like she lived on another planet. "Is it not your class?"

The woman gave a soft laugh. "Of course it is. I'm the owner of the studio. I just try not to watch the time. It helps me recognize every person who walks through the door as a treasured guest." She pressed her palms together, fingers pointed up, like she was praying, and let her eyes close for a beat.

Mark glanced over at me, eyes wide, with a little smile threatening to break out. I fought to keep from giggling.

"I am Lisa," she said in a hushed voice, slowly opening her eyes. "It will be my honor to practice with you today. Did you register for the class in advance?"

I nodded, and she bowed her head one more time before busying herself with collecting yoga mats and long cotton straps out of various baskets along the wall.

"Please, choose a spot that speaks to you."

I couldn't help but notice Mark shuffle half a step closer to me, and forced the giddy energy rising in my chest to settle down. Suddenly, picking a first date activity where I'd have to stay calm and still seemed like the dumbest idea I'd ever had. Or... oh, hell, what if it was one of those crazy kinds of yoga where I ended up grunting and sweating my way through inhuman-level side planks and shit?

"Ah, I see. You're a couple. The attraction between you is almost tangible. I can typically sense auras if I concentrate, but I don't need to with the two of you. It's practically rolling off you."

I couldn't look at Mark. I wanted to, so badly, but I didn't know what I'd do with what I saw on his face. If he was looking at me with heart-eyes, I might just grab him and kiss him, right in front of Lisa. If he looked scared at the suggestion that we had a connection, I knew deep down, from the tight little ball forming in my stomach, that I'd be crushed. And being crushed over a guy just made me feel ridiculous, and then I'd feel embarrassed, and that would make me angry at myself.

Best to just do yoga.

"Uh, we..." I stuttered, trying to figure out what to say considering all the possibilities of what this *thing* was between us. But Lisa was already laying out the mats, pushing the long straps off to the side, then sashaying over to the corner, where her own mat sat next to a set of small bottles and her phone. She plucked one of the bottles from the floor, and then walked back over to us.

Lisa dropped some oil into her hand, and extended it toward my breastbone.

"What is this?" I said, flinching away from her.

"It's a blend of essential oils—jasmine, ylang ylang, rose, and sandalwood. The ideal mix for heightening senses in our practice this evening. Since we're doing a couple-focused practice today, we want to diminish the light and focus on the touch. This oil will bolster your attraction for each other while heightening the sensation of skin on skin."

Mark coughed, his face turning a little red. I couldn't help it —I giggled. Not wanting to lose the moment, I asked, "Should we undress, then?"

I'd tried a lot of different kinds of yoga, but I'd never heard of naked yoga. Well, except for tantric, but that was when the end goal was a long, luxurious roll in the hay. I was willing to bet that Lisa was not about to invite us to fuck and get off in front of her in the middle of the studio tonight.

Lisa gave Mark a patient dip of the head. "Access to the chest, abdomen, and legs are helpful for a tantric session, if you'd like to remove your shirts. But whatever you're comfortable with is fine with me." She turned back to her mat, walked a few steps, then paused and looked at us again. "I will ask you to keep your genitalia concealed, however. I haven't prepared the studio for that today."

I tried, and failed, to stifle a giggle. What in the world did preparing a studio for genitalia entail?

I turned to Mark as Lisa fiddled with her phone and turned down the lights, arching my eyebrow up in a silent dare. "Well?"

Not breaking eye contact with me, he pulled his plain white t-shirt off, slightly mussing his short-cropped hair. It was so different from those long waves he'd had just days ago, and my fingers simply itched to touch it.

I'd worn boy short style undies to the studio. Not wanting to be outdone, I tugged the waistband of my baggy pants down past my hips, letting them fall to the floor and pool around my feet. All I had left was a loose-knit sweater with a black cami underneath. He was bare-chested in sweatpants.

We looked like we'd just rolled out of bed. Or were about to roll into it.

I swallowed, hard, only then realizing my mouth was dry. I hadn't anticipated that Mark was the kind of guy who would just strip off his shirt in front of me, or that him doing so would make me want to drop my pants in front of him. Hell, the way his eyes were flashing at me now, fixed on mine instead of raking up and down my body like I'd expect from any other guy, I kind of wanted to drop more articles of clothing.

But, oh, was I glad that he'd taken his shirt off. By some miracle, the scruffy music nerd that I'd first met in Sonic Wave Studios had a well-cut torso. He had defined pecs and abs.

Closer, more tactile examination would allow me to count those abs.

Lisa motioned for us to sit down on the mats she'd laid out. Mark settled on his first, and instinctively, I sat on my mat, facing him. There was something addictive about his face, like reading a book you couldn't put down. I had a sense that something incredible was hidden behind his eyes, just underneath his smile, waiting for me to uncover it.

I pretended to be busy getting comfortable, because I just didn't trust my own self-control if I kept up that eye contact. Mark didn't seem ruffled by it at all, which was mildly annoying. As I wiggled around the mat, trying to find a position that wasn't totally uncomfortable for my bony butt, Lisa walked around the room, drawing frothy white curtains in twenty-foot square all around us. I was suddenly very aware of every little movement Mark made—the whoosh of air in and out of his lungs, the way his fingers fidgeted ever so slightly where they rested on his knees.

I would have expected a soft zen soundtrack to pipe in through the studio's speakers, but instead, low, sensuous violin music bled into the air all around us, as the room grew heavy with darkness and a scent that was a mix of orange and some herb I didn't recognize.

"I'll ask you both to turn, so you're facing away from each other. At the beginning of our practice today, we want to isolate the senses. We want to feel before we add sight. Then, Mark, I want you to move back so that you're sitting on Toby's mat." She leaned down, her hands hovering, while we did as she asked, then gently guided us to scoot back a little more.

It didn't register, exactly, what it was Lisa was asking us to do, until I was sitting with Mark's back flush against mine. Every breath he took pressed into my ribs, every whoosh of air out of his lungs prompted a shuddering exhale of my own.

"This is just a pose to get established," Lisa said, her voice low, barely there. "Slowly, we'll turn to full-facing poses. The goal for this practice is to load your senses completely with one another." Her footsteps were soft as she approached us, then crouched beside me and gently took my forearm in her hands. "We're going to do a gentle partner twist, now. Toby, turn your gaze over your left shoulder. Let your arm relax as I guide it to where it will rest for this next pose." As she lifted my arm, she slid one hand down so that her fingertips brushed my palm, then pulled it around, settling it on Mark's leg.

More specifically, on his upper thigh.

Which clenched for a half second as my fingers splayed across it.

Mark's sweatpants were soft but his thigh underneath was all muscle. I indulged the thought of exactly how those thighs could leverage to move other parts of his body in just the right way, to hit just the right spot...

"Continue the breath," Lisa said, mercifully breaking my thoughts. Mark was just a normal guy. No, he was worse than that—he was *boring*. I reminded myself that I didn't want to even think of enjoying myself with a guy who couldn't—or wouldn't—figure out how to live his life to the fullest. He couldn't even furnish his apartment without a catalog. Couldn't dress himself without his sister.

That reassurance worked to calm me, until Lisa told Mark to mirror my pose. His palm was wide and warm against my bare leg. I'd never know whether he intentionally placed it so far in, just inches from the juncture of my thighs. I didn't dare look down to see exactly how completely his large hand covered my slender upper thigh.

It was hard enough imagining it and trying to ignore the vague ache that was taking up residence inside me, just inches from where his hand lay, radiating warmth against my skin exactly where it could do the most damage.

"Just *feel*," Lisa murmured. "I'll remove myself from this space for each pose. One-on-one practice is optimal for maximum connection."

"Can we move?" Mark's voice ground out, plucking a nerve inside me that shot straight down my midsection.

"Ideally, we want to maintain this pose, but at the same time, we must go where the breath urges us. I will re-enter the room to get you settled into the next pose."

Her footsteps padded softly away, and just a few seconds later, the door closed softly behind Lisa.

We were alone. Half-naked. In the dark, touching each other's thighs.

It didn't take me long to realize we were breathing in sync, our shoulder blades pressing together with each inhale. When we exhaled, the comparative cold skittered against my skin, making me shiver.

Mark's thigh tensed under my hand again. "You okay?" he asked softly.

"Yeah, just...it's kind of cold in here."

At my words, his hand tightened the slightest bit around my thigh. He really did have very large hands. How had I missed that before today?

We'd been gazing over opposite shoulders, but when he spoke, he turned his head so that his cheek was against mine, his lips only an inch away. "Do you want to put your pants back on?"

The ridiculous, wonderful strangeness of this whole situation suddenly hit me, and a giggle burst out of my throat. But the answer to his question was clear: no, I did not want to put my pants back on. I wanted to take more clothing *off*, and I wanted his fingers to be the ones that did it, reaching under the elastic band of my panties, searching for the spot to press or flick or brush that would drive me absolutely wild.

But I couldn't possibly say this to him. Somehow, he was different from the guys on whom I'd so freely unleashed dirty words in the past. So instead, I let out a slow breath, trying to regain control of myself. "I'm okay."

We stayed like that, breaths synced, feeling the warmth and receding coolness against our skin in turn. His body against mine was heavy in a wonderful way, like a blanket on a cool afternoon. I could get lost in this feeling—a thought that terrified me.

The soft snick of the door re-opening made my breath hitch, and Lisa's calm voice asked how that had felt. I stammered a reply, and Mark did the same, which had us both laughing. Our shoulders shook, vibrating against each other. She did have a point; it was something extraordinary to feel someone's emotions when you couldn't even see them. Not in a bad way, just in a different way than I'd ever interacted with anyone.

Maybe I wasn't the only one contributing something new, here, after all.

Lisa informed us that we'd now be moving into a longer-lasting pose, then asked both of us to turn.

Mark's blue eyes looked dark and stormy in the scant light, and the change from their stark brightness in the studio earlier took my breath away.

His knees brushed mine, and I struggled to keep my shiver from being too obvious. I knew I'd failed when the corner of his lips quirked ever so slightly.

"Mark, I'll ask you to touch the soles of your feet together." He complied, while I just struggled to keep my eyes from trailing down to his crotch. "Now, Toby, you're going to do the same thing, but you're going to circle his torso with your legs.

You have lovely long legs, so you can let your soles touch at the base of his back, just to keep the energy flow moving."

"So..." My words were as shaky as my breath. "You want me to straddle him."

"It's called the Yab Yum," Lisa explained in a quiet musical tone. "Come, let's not lose the sense of peace."

So, following the pull of my body toward Mark's that Lisa had seemed to sense when we first walked in, I planted my hands on his shoulders, stepped my feet on either side of his thighs, and settled down onto his lap, facing him.

It was the sexiest thing I'd ever done with most of my clothes on.

Lisa guided our hands to rest on each other's ribs, then rubbed her palms together. "This ylang ylang essential oil blend is like magic," she explained. "It awakens desire, but more than that, encourages connection where it had been lacking."

Yeah, pretty sure our connection had already been fired up to a roar. But okay.

Her warm palms cupped the back of my head and, I assumed, Mark's, and gently placed our foreheads together. I gave a surprised gasp, and she moved her hand down to the base of my skull. "Relax, friend. Let your third eye meet his. Give in to the connection."

I wanted to open my eyes to look at Mark, but it was like an invisible string tugged my chin toward the floor. I couldn't do it. Again, Lisa padded away, and again, silence wrapped around us like a thick fog. His breath leaked out from between his lips, eddying against mine, pooling under my nose. After a few seconds, he asked, "Are you okay?"

"I think so," I replied without even thinking. "I feel..."

He lifted his forehead away from mine, and whether I hated losing the connection, or feared what his gaze would do to me, I reacted. My arm slid up his back, dimly registering the muscles there, and my fingertips brushed through his short hair, dragging his head back to mine. "Yeah, just..." I sighed when our foreheads rested together again, and he let out a soft chuckle.

"I don't know exactly what that meant, but...me, too."

"Yeah?" I didn't know either. I had no idea what to call the powerful feeling coursing through my veins, growing stronger with every second that his breath mingled with mine, but somehow, I knew he shared it.

"Yeah," he said, softly. His thumb brushed up and down an inch, right beneath my shoulder blade, so softly I might not have noticed it if the room hadn't been plunged into near darkness, if we hadn't been sitting like this, if the gentle strains of violin weren't floating through the air.

"Mark," I breathed.

"Toby?" he answered. In the very same breath, his head turned a millimeter so his nose could notch against mine, and then finally, mercifully, his lips softly brushed mine.

A desperate, needy sound, the cross between a moan, a sigh, and a whimper, opened my lips against his, and he latched on, his tongue flicking against the wet seam of my mouth. Whatever feelings had been perplexing me minutes ago were now amplified, almost unbearably, and I surrendered my body into his, feeling my hips slide forward, reveling in the press of his erection against the cleft between my thighs, which grew wetter by the second. There were three layers of clothing between us, yet I swore I could feel the ridge at the head of his shaft, brushing a long-neglected spot that now threatened to drive me wild.

My legs spread wider along with my lips, and his tongue swept along the edge of my upper lip as mine scooped beneath it, trying to taste more, savor every wisp of his hot breath.

I hadn't noticed his hand sneak up into my hair, so it took me by surprise when I felt a tug on my scalp as he wrapped a handful of strands in his fist.

I squeaked, smiling against his lips, not giving a shit that our teeth clacked together. His cock had gotten even harder, and I ground down on it, knowing somewhere in the back of my mind that I must look like a crazed animal and struggling to care. Mark gasped, answering the motion with a deep rumble from the back of his throat, and swept my mouth with his tongue again. I closed my teeth the slightest bit, letting them scrape against it as he licked out, then opened again to welcome another plunging invasion. His other hand had long left its soft resting spot under my shoulder blade to move to my ass, and the feel of his fingers digging in would drive me absolutely insane if we kept it up much longer.

I nearly forgot we were in a yoga studio until Lisa walked in once again, causing us to wrench our lips apart. It didn't matter. We were both gasping, pressed together even closer than she'd left us, and Mark had left my hair tossed in every direction and wildly snarled. I looked at Lisa sheepishly, somehow still wary of meeting Mark's eyes.

"I can help you move into one last pose, or we can end the session here." Lisa's voice was still calm, but didn't hide the amusement in her tone. I wondered how often this happened in the studio, if she knew exactly how many minutes it would take a tantric yoga session to turn into a tantric sex session. I vaguely registered a mental note to look her up once I was alone again.

"I think we should end here." Mark's tone was still gruff, but decisive. Something I'd never really heard from him until this moment. His hands moved to my waist, gripping me there, then eased my body away from his.

"Very well," Lisa said with a knowing smile. "I'll be in the back, and I'll let you show yourselves out. Thank you for practicing with me today."

I vaguely registered my feet planting under me, my legs stretching to standing. I watched Mark, waiting for him to do the same, until I realized that he might need a minute to deal with his tenting situation, especially given the sweatpants.

I really did love doing that to a guy.

I smirked as I pulled my leggings back on, not missing Mark's eyes studiously trained on the wood-grain floor as I did. Every second of that explosive kiss between us replayed in slow-motion through my mind as I gathered my bag on my shoulder and slowly stepped into my shoes, smiling with jittery excitement when Mark stood up.

He pulled his shirt back on, then shrugged into his jacket, which I held out waiting for him.

As we made our way to the door and he held it open for me, I couldn't help but notice he was the one who was avoiding meeting my eyes now.

We walked all the way to my apartment, our breaths puffing faint clouds into the chilly night air, before either of us said a word. Mark scuffed his toe against the concrete, then, finally, spoke. "Toby, that was -"

"Something new. Right? For the show?" The words shot out of my mouth. I desperately wanted to keep this kind of easy banter at the forefront of our relationship. Light and safe, exactly how I liked it. The only problem was that trying to do that with Mark after whatever it was that had just happened between us felt fundamentally *wrong*. Like there'd been some shift in me and, instead of expressing myself like I always did, I was keeping some part of me locked away.

It left a sick feeling in my stomach.

"Yep. Absolutely. Also totally nuts, way out of what I'd always assumed my natural range of motion was, and…"

He stopped, and on reflex, I turned to face him.

Mark's breathing was heavy, instantly transporting me back to just minutes ago, when our bodies had been tangled together in the name of yoga and soul connection, or whatever.

It was then that I realized that he was looking at me like no guy ever had - like I was a roller coaster and he was equal parts terrified, thrilled, and about to puke at the sight of me.

"You okay?" I asked softly, a tenderness for his entirely sweet expression warming me from the inside out.

"Absolutely," he said, clearing his throat and dipping his head. He needed a moment. I could give it to him. There was something about him that made me wait longer than my customary two seconds before making a decision about a guy.

Maybe much longer.

After an excruciating second or two, he looked back up at me. "Just...didn't you feel like you were in the Lion King?" Mark laughed, though there was something serious in his tone, the way the gruffness in his throat hugged every word. "Third eyes and connection? I wouldn't have been surprised if Lisa had blasted 'The Circle of Life' for whatever our next pose would have been."

He licked his lips, and I didn't miss the way his eyes drifted down to my lips when he mentioned that last pose. The one I'd been pretty damn disappointed that we weren't doing.

Maybe we could get back there. He just had to say the words, ask me to do what it was clear we both desperately wanted. I fidgeted, my fingers twitching at my side, still dying to reach for his.

Fuck it. There was no sense fighting something I wanted so badly that it left my whole body trembling, wedged a whimper inside my throat begging for release.

I just knew we couldn't go to his place. The one-eyed cat and the scratchy couch and the clutter on every surface would only throw a dozen wrenches in this smooth, flawless, all-encompassing need that was starting to drive me absolutely fucking nuts, a truth that I was sort of annoyed to admit to myself.

"I have a couple amazing spots for doing yoga at my place. We're close to it, too," I said, surprising even myself with the sexy grind of my own words out of my throat. Finally, I let my hand slip into his, and he took it right away. He used it to tug me to him so that our bellies pressed together, my lips hovering deliciously on level with his. God, how was it possible that Mark Mahler was the first guy in as long as I could remember that made my heart dip like that with the smallest of gestures?

Mark dropped my hand and gently combed my hair back from my face with those beautiful fingers of his. His forehead rested on mine, so gently I could have been imagining it if it weren't for his breath swirling against my lips, setting the air between us on fire.

Instead of kissing me like any other guy would have done, he spoke. "If I follow you home," he said, his eyes wide like the puppy he was making himself sound like, "I don't think I'll be able to leave without taking this a lot farther." His hands shook as they gently trailed down my neck, the tips of his fingers leaving a spine-tingling electricity in their wake.

It took my brain a few seconds to process what he'd just said. "You don't...you don't want to have sex with me." My words were flat with disbelief, for once not controlled by whatever image I wanted them to project. I had no clue what that image even was with this guy.

"I did not say that," Mark said, taking a slow step back from me. "It's...the opposite. But I'm not...I don't want this to be..." A soft growl came from the back of his throat as he pressed his lips together, shaking his head slightly. "Let me try again. I know this is supposed to be you doing me a favor. The whole dating thing. Showing me something new."

I stared at him blankly.

"For the show."

My heart swooped again. God, being so close to him practically erased the show from my mind. He'd transported me to another plane of existence where even the internship I'd snagged in the name of the career I had my heart set on was a non-factor.

"Right. For the show." I felt my eyebrows pull in. "I'm sorry, but I'm not following. I'm...I just thought...we're having fun, right? Tonight's been good?"

"Absolutely," he said with a gruff laugh. "I am. Having fun. But I haven't decided..." He blew out a long breath, and then caught my gaze again. "I like you, Toby. A lot. And we're working together, and I don't want there to be anything weird between us."

"Weird? Mark, it's okay." I laughed, relieved. This, at least, I was familiar with. A guy not wanting our relationship outside work to interfere with the job. "Listen, I'm not looking to rope you into something serious."

Mark sighed, but it wasn't one of relief. No, when he turned just enough so that the street lamp illuminated his whole face, I read his expression clearly - resignation. Regret. "Exactly, Toby. When we kissed, it was like...I'm not sure how to describe it, but I do know it didn't feel like something that was just the new thing of the week."

Oh. *Oh.* "So, you..."

"I just want to get to know you a little better, maybe, before we get carried away. If, uh...you know. If I haven't just ruined my chances by saying this."

My stomach twisted vaguely at this weird cross between rejection and proposition. He was basically asking me to promise to do this again—to put myself out there, to open myself up—so that he could decide if we were ready for something even more physical.

I didn't need time to decide—didn't *want* it. I was ready now. Mark was asking me to look into my own future, when I could barely even tell him what time I'd be waking up tomorrow or when I'd next want to travel on some random vacation out of the country.

But he looked so patient, so hopeful, so normal for a guy who was ending a date, and the memory of that kiss in the yoga studio was still sending electricity straight through me, ending in an aching between my thighs that I would have to take care of all by myself for the first time in a very long time. I wanted him. I had just a few breaths to decide whether I wanted him enough to do something I never did—predict how I'd feel about a guy, what I'd want from him, days from now.

My brain was misfiring, fighting back against the foreign idea. I had to calm it somehow, and so without even thinking, I leaned into him, pressing my lips to his, soft but insistent, cupping his jaw in my palm and giving into my hunger for him with a flick of my tongue against the seam of his mouth. He groaned and opened to me, letting me taste and giving back as good as he got.

Maybe this is as close as I could get to answering that, yes, there would be a next time.

I just hoped he'd take this yes for an answer.

CHAPTER 14

MARK

I HONESTLY COULDN'T FIGURE out whether I'd won or lost at the end of that date with Toby.

All I knew was that my dick was currently kickstanding against my sweatpants, my mind was running a mile a minute, and I was rapidly cycling through hating myself and sticking to my guns as I watched her pull her lips away from me and walk to her door. I desperately wanted Toby, but I wanted more of her than she was giving me before we slept together.

Toby was the kind of woman any guy would salivate over. She only wanted two things from me: sex, and for me to be her date for Passover just a few weeks in the future. After that, we'd be done. She didn't want to get engaged, share an apartment, hell, she probably didn't even want to share my sheets for the night. Especially for a guy like me, who'd never been even close to a chick magnet in his entire life? Well, Toby was like the pot of gold at the end of an impossible rainbow.

I knew that. What I didn't know was why I let her walk away from me.

I also knew that it was absolutely, positively the right thing to do.

My sleep was restless, even after a long shower where I jacked off twice and eventually had to let the water run cold just to calm myself down. Of course, then I couldn't get to sleep, and when I finally did, I just dreamed of Toby. Her kisses, the taste of her lips when I sucked on them, the little moans she made in the back of her throat, egging me on to taste more.

I didn't even know I was supposed to suck on a girl's lips. Kylie had a fairly set routine for seduction: grab me by the shirt, kiss me hard, stroke my dick until she made sure I was good and hard, then tell me she wanted me. The pump-and-cum portion lasted a few minutes, and then we'd cuddle and fall asleep. I'd always wondered whether she came. I never asked, and never really been too bothered by the possibility that she hadn't.

After all, she seemed happy.

Toby was different. I wanted to watch her face when she came. I wanted to make her happy, make her feel things that no other guy ever had. I wanted to take my time with her, to be completely focused every minute, from first kiss to second orgasm. I wanted her to think of me when she thought of good sex, and only me.

The problem was, I didn't know how. The number of girls I'd slept with was in the single digits, and their demands were relatively low. Toby was the kind of woman who wanted more, and the kind of woman who always demanded what she wanted. Because she believed she deserved it. I just didn't think I could do any of that if there wasn't something real between us – something deeper than hormones and weird sexy yoga.

It was thrilling and terrifying all at the same time.

When my caveman brain had finally run through all the things I wanted to try to do to give Toby pleasure, I fell asleep. The sun was just beginning to rise, and for the first time ever, I was one hundred percent relieved that I didn't have any plans for the rest of the weekend.

A pounding on my front door pulled me out of sleep, my head still groggy and my eyes blinking slowly open. My feet were hanging off one edge of my bed, freezing, while my chest and neck were cocooned in sheets and my blanket, making sweat gather at my hairline. I was stretched out across the bed diagonally. Apparently, I'd spent all my sleep tossing and turning.

Not surprising at all.

Someone pounded on the door again. My groggy head struggled to figure out who the hell it could be, banging down my front door on a Saturday. I'd paid my rent, and even if by some freak occurrence it had gone missing, my little Taiwanese landlady, at eighty-three years old, was not the type to bang on anyone's door, ever. I'd spoken to my parents a couple days ago, and besides, they had the Midwest manners of any Ohio couple, and would never even *entertain* the idea of stopping by unannounced. Hannah was the opposite, but she'd just been here, and made it clear when she left that she'd be traveling for the next several weeks.

I scooted to the edge of the bed, my freezing feet hitting the freezing floor, and blinked again as I searched for my pants. My morning woody was probably still remembering that goddamn yoga class and Toby's amazing smell and wild wavy hair and soft gentle fingers and—dammit. I was going to have to zip up my jeans if I was going to open the door, and that didn't seem likely.

More pounding.

"Just a minute!" I finally managed enough command of my voice to answer. I pulled my jeans up without zipping them, thinking about the stack of utility bills I should be tackling this weekend to get Woody to relax a little.

Just thinking about that made me hate myself all over again for not taking Toby up on her invitation. Morning erections were always kind of a nuisance, one that Toby may very well have appreciated, if only...

If only I hadn't turned her down.

Damn past-me.

Back to the bills, Mahler. This is not helping.

I palmed my phone in my back pocket and yanked it out. The lock screen showed twenty-two missed texts.

My heart sped up. Maybe she'd sent me a message. Maybe she understood. Maybe we were on the same page after all. Maybe, just maybe, I could see her again. Today.

There was suddenly nothing I wanted more.

But when I swiped the phone to unlock it, I was greeted with a string of one-and-two-word texts from Ethan.

I muttered a few curse words under my breath and scrolled through them quickly.

Ethan: Bro
Wake up
Unless
Hey do you have a girl there
I have breakfast
Wake up

Jesus. Thank God I'd had my phone on silent. There was a thirty-minute gap, and then another string of texts:

Wake the fuck up Mahler
Donuts
Bagels?

Joey Hawkins' breakfast mac and cheese?
My treat?
I need a gym buddy
Get your ass up

It was like a caveman had figured out how to do voice-to-text on a phone. Honestly, it was a miracle that this guy had as many degrees as he did. He may have had two degrees and a big-boy job, but his stream of consciousness was alarmingly sparse.

I did feel bad, though, that I'd slept past the time we usually hit the gym on Saturdays. Plus, it was hard to ignore an offer of brunch from Joey and Hawk's.

Next, there was another string of texts, time stamped an hour and a half later.

You can't keep a girl past lunch time
I'll be over at 1:00 for a debrief

More pounding on my door jolted me from staring, wide-eyed, at my phone.

At least I knew who it was now, and at least I knew he'd have bagels. Or at least some form of carbs.

Ten minutes later, I sat at my bar-height table across from Ethan, who had mercifully brought me a cup of coffee, an everything bagel, cream cheese, and lox. He polished off the last of his bagel—whole wheat with plain cream cheese, probably light; the dude took no risks on food that might compromise his physique.

He fixed a stare on me. "Okay, man. I have given you time to tell me on your own, and you have given me zero information about last night. So, I'm going to have to interrogate you. I don't see any evidence around here of this mystery lady you took on a date last night, so I'm going to assume you either stayed out late —maybe overnight—with her, ate somewhere that gave you food poisoning, or have come down with a freak flu that kept you in bed this long, in which case you can tell me now so I can get the fuck out of here. Oh, and you can apologize for not texting me to cancel our gym slot later."

Ethan was the biggest germaphobe I'd ever met. I was finally feeling awake enough to crack a smile.

"None of the above." Despite my exhaustion and the less-than-ideal way the night had ended, I lost a few seconds thinking of yoga with Toby, not even realizing that I had started staring off into nothing, daydreaming, until Ethan play-smacked me across the face.

"Who is this girl? She's turned you into Sleeping Beauty traipsing through the woods and singing to the birds, man. Listen, I knew you for half the years you were with Kylie, and I never ever saw you like this. Ever."

The sad thing was, he was right.

I took a bite of the towering bagel in my hand, buying myself several more seconds. I had no clue what was going on between Toby and me—didn't even know whether she wanted to see me again. There hadn't been a single text from her, but then again, it had only been a few hours, and that kiss...

"Gotta plead the fifth, man. It's too new."

Ethan clapped his hands together and chuckled like I'd just given all the info away. "So that means two things for sure. I know this girl, and you want to go on another date with her."

I looked at him like he was nuts. I didn't know a single person who could keep up with Ethan's mental acrobatics, but as much as I hated to admit it, he was usually right. Including right now. He knew Toby, however marginally, and I was dying to go on another date with her.

Best to bluff, though. "Now you're just pulling stuff out of your ass."

"Au contraire. First," he said, annoyingly lifting his finger in the air and moving it toward my face, "If I didn't already know her, you wouldn't care what I thought of her, because I wouldn't *have* anything to think of her, because I wouldn't know her. Second, you won't tell me who she is because you don't want me to mess it up in any way, and the only way I could do that is if I have easy enough access to her."

"Okay. Yes, you're right. Sort of," I mumbled through another mouthful of smoked salmon. I swallowed, and then thought of something. "But it doesn't mean I want to go out with her again. Maybe I just don't want you to think too badly of her."

Ethan shrugged. "Bro code dictates that I couldn't date her anyway. And I'm not a dick. I have my own brain."

I stood up, brushing my hands off and leaving a mess of seeds on the table.

Ethan stared at me as he took a long, slow drink of his coffee, then wiped every last crumb of the mess from the table. I paced around the living room, mindlessly picking stuff up and putting it back down.

Last night with Toby had been so incredible that it was hard for me to believe that today was just another normal day. Last night felt almost like stepping into another life, led by another me. The weirdness of being clean-shaven, having much shorter hair, and having scented lotion on my skin probably contributed to it.

Still, I could count the number of dates I'd call outstanding on one hand, but this one had blown my mind. Being so close to

Toby, so still, so content and so hungry at the same time...this was totally new territory for me.

"I respect that you won't kiss and tell, man. I get it. I mean, you're like Mr. Darcy, but. Whatever."

"Since when are you into Pride and Prejudice?" Ethan liked action flicks with lots of explosions. I'd seen Pride and Prejudice —in several incarnations—because Hannah hadn't wanted to read the book in high school, and insisted I watch the movies with her. I never did figure out whether she wanted a partner in crime or just someone else to validate the experience of cheating on another English assignment.

"Since I watched the movie with the most beautiful girl on the planet." Ethan's voice dipped lower as he cleaned more invisible crumbs off the table.

My eyebrows shot up. Ethan dated a lot of girls - more respectfully and certainly more carefully than a lot of guys I knew - but for him it was pure recreation. He hated being alone and kept girlfriends to stave off loneliness. To him, dating was more of a necessity, like taking his car in for an oil change. I'd never heard him talk about a girl in such sweeping, romantic terms. But just as I was about to tease him, or at least make him tell me something about her, I realized that he would be able to use it as ammo to get me to reciprocate.

Ethan was right. I didn't want to talk about Toby. Some of it was out of respect for her—she did work with us, after all—but if I was being one hundred percent honest, it was mostly to preserve my own ego. The date was so damn confusing. At one moment, it felt like we were about to have sex in a yoga studio, and in the next, I was telling her that I wanted more from her before we slept together. Most of the confusion came from me and my inexperience, granted, but...she still hadn't tried to contact me since then.

"Let me just grab a towel and some water bottles," I muttered.

After I locked up, we walked down the stairs, out the door, and out into the crisp early-spring air in silence. There were a few other people out, seeking brunch or a workout after a rough Friday night, just like I was.

We scanned our membership cards at the front desk, locked up our bags, and made it to the weight bench before I couldn't hold in my question any longer. "How soon can you text a girl, do you think?"

Ethan hefted a thirty-pound barbell in each of his hands, then let them rest at his sides as he slowly turned to look at me, a shit-eating smirk spreading across his face.

"I knew it. I knew this was a good one. How good was it? The date?"

Relief washed over me. I didn't know if it was pathetic or great, how much I was dying to talk about Toby, all the things that I really, really liked about her, and maybe more importantly, all the things that really confused me.

"Really good, man. So good I couldn't sleep."

"So you did sleep with her!" Ethan did a victorious bicep curl, then reached his weight out for me to pound with my own.

"No. No, she...we...I didn't..."

Ethan's mouth twisted down in what could only be a frown of pity. "She's playing hard to get. I get it. No problem. She's entitled to that. Makes them feel good, sometimes. Make them want it more when they finally give it to you."

I focused on grabbing my own weights. I knew it was some macho bullshit, but I still didn't want to tell Ethan that I had been the one to shut the whole thing down. Maybe I didn't want to remind myself of that fact, either.

I shrugged and started on my own bicep curls. I was glad I'd met Ethan in that business class almost two years ago, mostly because he was a good listener and the one who got my ass to the gym and then back out in normal society after Kylie and I had split. But we'd never really talked about girls. I'd always been too embarrassed to ask what he was up to with them and he'd always been too kind to tell me. We got along just fine talking about Philly sports, our families, indie music, and the best burgers in town.

"So, she didn't text you yet?"

I shook my head and grunted into more curls.

"And you really want to text her?"

"It was a good date, man. There was a connection there. I think we could really—"

"Yeah," Ethan panted into the end of his set. "Got it. Do me a favor, bro. Pull up her contact on your phone."

Geez, Ethan was a good friend. Maybe I'd get lucky and he'd type up the perfect text on my behalf.

"Delete her name if you really don't want me to see it. Or change it."

I complied, erasing most of her name and leaving just "TE." As good as I felt about us, I stood by my decision not to mention that the girl was Toby. Hell, I was on the verge of entering into a permanent weekend daydream state over her. I really didn't want things to get weird, for everyone's sakes, especially because she worked with us.

Ethan glanced at the number. "650 area code. Not local?"

"Not 'til recently," I muttered, lifting the dumbbell above my head to start on triceps.

"You'll see her again, like in passing?"

Yes. I couldn't tell if I loved or hated that fact. I shrugged noncommittally, hoping I wasn't giving it away. "Maybe. Probably. She's around."

"Great." Ethan stabbed at the phone a few times and then dropped it on the foam-padded floor beside me.

I tried not to look down at the phone, but when Ethan turned his attention back to the weights, I did.

All I saw was two words: "Contact deleted."

I dropped my own weights, felt them bounce a little as they thudded against the cushy flooring, thankful after the fact that they hadn't smashed my toes or the phone, and yelped, "What the hell, man?"

"It's for your own good, my friend. You're clearly head over heels and I cannot let you sabotage what might turn into a solid relationship, or at least a good night together, by chasing the poor girl down not twelve hours after your date, making yourself look desperate, and turning her off. It's one of the oldest rules in the book, buddy, which you obviously knew already, or you wouldn't have even asked me."

I just stared at him, my jaw slack. "What the *hell*?" I repeated with a stutter. "You could have just said 'three days', or something. I was asking you for advice. Clearly I was going to follow it."

"Statistically, my friend, seventy-seven percent of people who ask their friends for advice already know what they're going to do. They just want validation, and if they don't get validation, they make up an excuse for ignoring their friends. This way, at least I won't be complicit in fucking this up for you."

"Fu...it's...wha..." I sighed.

"Use your words, Mahler. If it's meant to work out, it'll work out."

"What the hell?" I repeated, I hoped for the last time, weakly as I took a seat on the floor. I'd do abs in a second, I told myself, so I didn't look totally pathetic.

"You said you would see her in passing. That's all you need. The right woman is like a fine wine, Mark. You need to put space between the two of you. Let it breathe."

"I think you're mixing your metaphors," I mumbled. "And it damn well had better work out. Or I'm blaming you."

I knew I was overreacting; I'd see her again on Tuesday, just three days from now, if she showed up to the planning meeting like she was supposed to. But every muscle in my body wanted to be back in contact with her again, even if it was just to say something normal like, "I had a nice time last night." How would she even know what I thought about the date?

Ethan settled at my feet, pressing them down to the floor, a nudge for me to start with the sit-ups. "You can thank me later, man. In the meantime, let's get those abs looking as cut as possible."

CHAPTER 15

TOBY

MARK MAHLER totally fucking terrified me.

That was the thought that ran through my head as I left him on the sidewalk in front of my apartment, then again as I quickly scrubbed my face and ran a toothbrush through my mouth, and continued as I laid in bed staring at the ceiling and hating that I could not stop thinking about him.

Even now, twelve hours later, the light of a new day failing to bring me a fresh perspective, walking around my apartment was like an out-of-body experience.

Something had changed, but I couldn't figure out what it was.

This was the part in the rom-com when I would go out to brunch with my girlfriends and pitifully try to tell them what was bothering me, and then they would tell me that I wanted to have sex with Mark Mahler. They'd giggle that maybe I wanted *more* with Mark Mahler. The imaginary bestie-and-or-giggly-sister-figure in my head told me that, for the first time, I was unfocused and unmoored at the hands of some guy.

"Shut *up!*" I hissed at nobody.

But even as I tried to shake the truths my gloating, teasing subconscious kept pushing to the front of my thoughts, I couldn't stop thinking about that kiss. I had never, in all the years I'd dated and all the guys I'd kissed, experienced any feeling like that before. The way he moved his lips against mine like he knew exactly what I wanted, could read every innermost wish for a nip or a lick, every desire to taste more of him. If there was a sex toy that I could program to move like Mark's mouth, I'd be set for life.

Thinking about Mark's mouth as a sex toy only made matters worse. Without meaning to, or even fully realizing I was doing it, I let my hand drift down to my breasts, brushing my nipples in turn on the way, imagining Mark's lips tickling the skin there instead of the tips of my nails. My own rapid breaths thrummed against my palms as they skimmed my ribs, then the dip of my belly, then up over the ridge of my hip bone.

For a few minutes, I was able to imagine that Mark had made a different decision about coming home with me last night, and then I drifted off to sleep again.

When I woke, it was afternoon. I turned over my shoulder to look for Mark. Part of me had wanted him to come home with me so badly that I had imagined him there, next to me, his warmth chasing away the cold of the pillow I never used.

I growled, frustrated at my own imagination. Men didn't sleep over at my place. I always encouraged them to leave shortly after our dates had concluded. When it came to Mark, however, my subconscious clearly wanted him in my bed.

Just to chase the image of a shirtless Mark smiling at me from the empty pillow next to me away, I dragged myself out of bed. Before I knew it, I was in the shower, watching the steaming water curve over my jutting hip bones.

I was thin. Like a reed, my mother had always said. Thin like her. Reeds looked weak, could even be bent almost in half, but they were so strong that they almost never broke.

Not all men liked strong women, she'd explained to me with tears in her eyes after my father and she had "taken a break" for the fifth time, maybe the sixth. I was seventeen. She made me promise, as I looked up at her with hurt confusion mingling with the tears in my eyes, that I wouldn't let that keep me from being exactly what I was born to be—unbreakable as a reed.

I was just thankful that my brother hadn't taken Dad's behavior as a model for how his should be. David married his wife, Roni, a couple years ago, and I would have swallowed my own teeth if I found out he left her side, literally or figuratively. He worshipped the ground she walked on.

It was sweet, but to be honest, I really didn't understand that either. Roni was not the kind of woman my mother would have called "strong." ." She was so dependent on Ben, but then, Ben was dependent on her, too.

When I started college, I'd made peace with the idea that maybe some couples were just like my mom and dad, moving through life in concentric orbits, only occasionally coming close enough to one another to live life in tandem for a while. If I lived my life that way from the beginning, chances are a relationship could never even come close to hurting me the way it'd hurt my mother—over and over again, more devastating each time.

The only way that would work, though, was if I knew exactly who I was, what made me the person I was, what I wanted out of life, before getting tangled up with anyone else's life. Before I let myself fall in love.

I'd made a list of things I wanted to figure out before I even considered settling down. Interests, careers, food, living preferences, music preferences, pet peeves. At the age of twenty-five, I was still very much learning who I was. So, even if I really, really liked Mark—like, *really* liked him—there was no way I could really know I wanted a life with him, if I didn't even know what I wanted *my* life to look like.

Besides, the guy had basically stepped out of the pages of a Target catalog.. A makeover from his sister was one remarkable change, sure, but how much did that change him? Not at all, probably.

That was what I kept reminding myself all day Saturday as I strategically moved my phone to stranger and stranger places around my apartment so that my itchy texting fingers wouldn't relent and send him a text.

There was something very strong between us, I'd admit that. Maybe it was just that I hadn't had a really good fuck for more months than I liked to admit. Maybe it was because I had never seen a pair of blue eyes quite like his, and I wanted to get better acquainted with them. Maybe I couldn't stop remembering the way my head had spun when he kissed me. There was nothing wrong with any of that, but none of that was real. It was all hormones, typical, physical reactions that I should not allow to dictate my life.

Unless—and this was the most terrifying option—the allure of Mark was wrapped up in the way I felt totally relaxed when I was around him, almost like I was alone, but warmer, cozier. Safer, steadier, more secure. Like I'd be happy to never shift from his side.

I'd never felt anything but relief when I went home to an empty apartment after a date. It was freedom to be one hundred percent myself. I'd worked hard to earn that freedom, and never adjusted well to sharing it with others. Not even totally delectable, thought-haunting radio show hosts.

I puttered around my house, rearranged the furniture in the living room, scrubbed every corner of the already spotless kitchen clean (even though I couldn't remember the last time I'd cooked in it), and did three loads of laundry. I tried not to think of Mark the whole damn time, while hating that I could still recall the taste of his tongue brushing into my mouth like he owned it, hating that my mind was so preoccupied with wondering how I could make him laugh again in that deep, gravely way he did when we were on our way out of the yoga studio.

I may have dreamed about that laugh a couple times last night, and woken up with my hand between my legs. Maybe.

I sighed and collapsed onto my couch, flicking through my various video-on-demand accounts, growing increasingly frustrated when not even the descriptions of any of the shows held my interest.

Maybe I should work on something for The Bro Show—a new transition, or even just tinker with the sound from the last recording so I'd be ready for Tuesday's meeting with a sparkling new observation or suggestion.

Tuesday. When I'd see Mark again. So many hours from now.

Yeah. That would have to do. Because there was no way in hell I was texting him, let alone calling him. And I really wanted to hear his voice again.

I pulled my laptop off the coffee table and onto a pillow that I rested on my thighs, opening up the program to access the files that Shari had made me an admin on. I clicked "play" on Friday's recording. When Mark and I had looked at each other through the studio glass not even two days ago, I'd had no clue how soon we'd be lip-locked, and even crazier, how much I would love it. There had to be something he wasn't telling me about his level of experience. No guy was that good at kissing without some serious hours of practice.

Well, that thought didn't help at all. I played with the mixer, listening to Mark's voice when I increased the treble, or the bass, or when I slowed it down just a touch. Any damn way I mixed it, he sounded sexy as hell.

My phone buzzed against the table all the way across the apartment, where I'd purposefully left it. I shoved my laptop to the side and dove for the phone before it could stop ringing. Maybe he was calling me. Maybe he was thinking about my voice, too. I couldn't date Mark—that much was clear—but maybe we could spend one more night together. Maybe he'd put the proposition into words I couldn't refuse.

"Hello?" I answered breathlessly.

"Tovyah! You answered."

My breath caught in my chest, then I silently cursed myself for being so stupid as to answer the phone without checking the caller ID. What had I been thinking? Literally, the only person to call me for the last several months running had been my mother.

"Hi, Ima," I said, trying to hide my disappointment as my mind raced through possible excuses for getting off the phone as quickly as possible.

"Hi, *bubah*," she crooned. She'd lived in the United States for twenty years now, making her English nearly flawless, but her Israeli accent really dripped through when she called me by my pet name. Or when she wanted something.

"What's up?" I asked, trying to make my voice sound like I hadn't just spent my entire day hot and bothered and puttering around my house.

"I am having your father book your flight today, and I wanted to make sure you didn't have any conflicts. So, six weeks from Friday, there's a flight that leaves at two o'clock..."

"Ima!" I interrupted. I'd learned over the years that once my mother started talking, it was almost impossible to get her to stop. "My flight where?" I racked my brain for any weddings or family vacations coming up, and couldn't think of a single thing.

"Home, of course."

"For...?"

Ima laughed like I'd just told her the most hilarious joke. "Oh, Tovyah. Careful, or I'll make you sing the four questions again, even though Roni swears that Sarah can do it, I don't think I've ever met a three-year-old who can really—"

"Wait. Passover is in eight weeks, right?"

"It was last time we talked, which was two weeks ago."

I groaned. Mark fucking Mahler really was consuming all my brain cells.

"Don't worry, my love. I know it's early, but it'll be warm enough to celebrate springtime in California, just like always." She gave herself a little laugh, and I normally would have humored her, but not this time. I was already anticipating her next question, the same one she always asked.

"Well, then, *bubah*, I'll tell Daddy to go ahead and book it. We'll speak soon, yes?"

"Wait!" I said. "Aren't you going to ask me if I'm bringing someone special?"

My parents were liberal as hell—hence the 'someone special' instead of 'a boy' in Ima's phrasing—but that didn't quash whatever weird Jewish cultural impulse had them obsessed with me finding someone to settle down with. All they cared about was that said person had a career path in some well-paying field and was a member of the Tribe.

I could practically hear my mother's eyebrows shooting up on the other end of the line. "Of course! Are you bringing someone special?" She was very clearly stifling a giggle. God, this was almost too easy.

"Yes, I am. If it's okay with you. I'll just text Dad his details tonight, so he can book the ticket?"

"*M'uleh!*" she trilled. *Amazing.* "How wonderful, Toby. We're so proud of you."

I rolled my eyes and fought to keep from audibly sighing. I had scored a spot in one of Penn's pickiest grad programs, but the "someone special" was what finally made my mother tell me how proud she was.

How silly of me to think that I'd ever be good enough for her all on my own.

"I'll see you soon, Ima."

I almost felt guilty as I hung up the phone. There was some unspoken rule between us that when I finally agreed to bring someone home to meet the family, that person would be someone who I intended to make *part* of the family. That person being Jewish, successful, and a serious adult weren't requirements, exactly, but I knew my parents expected whoever I brought to their table to be an actual candidate for coming back for the next holiday, and the one after that, forever and ever, until they died.

It was a little cruel that the first guy I would ever bring home would be none of those things my parents so desperately wanted for me. Mark wasn't a serious adult, wasn't on any sort of successful career path—one mention of hosting The Bro Show, and maybe playing a clip of one of the more controversial segments, would prove that. And the kicker—he certainly was not Jewish.

If this gamble paid off, he'd be the first and the last guy I'd ever bring home, which was, after all, what my parents were hoping for. Sort of.

I shot off a quick text to my Dad with Mark's first and last name and, after a quick check on Facebook, his birth date. Dad, ever the texting economist, just replied with a thumbs-up and a smile.

I sat back in my chair, stretching my arms above my head and feeling the first relief from the odd plaguing tension that had taken over since my night with Mark.

All I had to do now was keep Mark entertained on six weeks' worth of dates, so he could feed The Bro Show's demands, and keep him just interested enough in me to get him to come home to meet my parents.

I didn't think it would be that tough. Yes, some people might call me cocky, but I didn't think there was any doubt about Mark's interest in me. I liked hanging out with him, too. I loved kissing him. I was pretty sure I'd love trying to get even more out of him, too.

One side of my mouth tugged up and a little starburst of warmth spread through my chest. This was almost too easy. Win-win for both of us, and a hell of a good time. I just hoped it would work.

CHAPTER 16

MARK

THREE AGONIZING DAYS LATER, I stood in front of the mirror, trying to move one more unruly wiry hair into place. I would never forgive my Jewish relatives—all on my mom's side —for this genetic ridiculousness that made it almost impossible for me to look put together.

I hadn't heard from Toby since our date at the yoga studio. And, of course, she hadn't heard from me, since Ethan had deleted her from my phone. There was no way in hell I was going to ask Shari for Toby's number and make her think I had a thing for our new sound girl. Ethan was enough to deal with.

Especially because I did have a thing for Toby. There was no point in denying it to myself, was there? For the last two and a half days, I'd done nothing but try not to think about her and I'd failed miserably. I'd gone to the gym four times. Called my sister twice. Scrubbed my bathroom from top to bottom,again.

I did brunch on Sunday with a club owner and an up-and-coming DJ to ease their hangovers from the night before, an early dinner with a startup record label to play client demos and drinks with another club owner to drum up some business for my artists who hadn't seen a good gig in a few weeks. As much as I loved my downtime, I could act like an extrovert when the situation called for it. Most importantly, I was passionate about the work—my weekday meetings with musicians and bands were becoming more and more plentiful as word-of-mouth sent them my way. I'd already booked a couple dozen gigs for longer-standing clients in some venues that paid them more than a pittance, not bad for the six months since I'd started in earnest.

I'd kept doing The Bro Show for two very specific reasons: money, and the contacts the show would potentially keep live for me. So far, Shari had only made one love triangle match between me, a band, and a club. Something was better than nothing, though, and I knew she always had her eyes open.

Yeah, Ethan was also a factor. We'd been friends since we'd landed in the same business class a couple years ago, and he'd taken me under his wing. He'd included me in study groups at first, then trips to the bar with his friends, movies, and sports games, until I felt like I belonged in Philly just as much as I did back home in Ohio.

Even though he'd since sailed through school with an actuarial degree and had a job that paid enough money to quit The Bro Show and the pittance it paid, he loved doing it. If I quit, it wouldn't be the same. I owed it to him to stay on.

Plus, now The Bro Show had one undeniable, sharp-as-a-tack, willowy and gorgeous upside.

I couldn't wait to see her in two hours. My stomach was in knots and every vein in my body zinged with anticipation. I knew I wouldn't be doing anything physical with her at today's meeting besides looking at her across the conference room table, but, maybe afterwards, I'd have the chance to...

I shook my head, hard, and stalked to the kitchen for a drink of water. The sink was already half-full of dirty dishes – how in the world did that happen so quickly? That was one thing about Kylie's absence that I still hadn't adjusted to. It had taken me a week or so to realize that she had been the machine behind collecting my dirty dishes from around the house and washing them, just like my mom had always been when I'd lived at home. I'd never forget that first disgusting hour-and-a-half's worth of dishes I had to do after she left.

The slightly metallic taste of Philadelphia's tap water still caught me by surprise from time to time. Everything seemed cleaner, airier, more spacious, more *wholesome* back home in small town Ohio. I'd always thought that, eventually, I'd want to move back home, but in the past year, the metallic water and run-down apartment buildings had become an afterthought to the thrill of doing well in a business that was going better than I ever could have anticipated.

Besides, now there was Toby. I wasn't delusional enough to imagine her as my girlfriend, not even close. I'd never met a more skittish woman in my life, and as much as I loved kissing Toby, I knew in my gut I wasn't, never would be, the kind of guy who enjoyed casual relationships. She hadn't lied about what she wanted, so I couldn't blame her. Still, the idea of a one-night stand had always made my skin crawl, which meant I also couldn't sleep with her. Yet.

The more I thought about that kiss, though, the more I thought it was possible that I'd be the one to convince her that more kisses were worth it. Morning-after kisses. Cooking together kisses. Holding hands and napping in a meadow on a warm summer day kisses.

Okay, maybe that last one was going too far. I'd file that one away in the "pipe dream" category.

I figured I should start with looking good for today's studio meeting. Really good. I wasn't a model, not by a long shot, and I didn't have a ton of experience with women, but even I could tell that Toby was attracted to me. Couldn't hurt to play it up.

A few more paces had me across the apartment and staring

into my hole-in-the-wall closet, which was only closed off by a thin curtain on a cheap tension rod. A couple graphic tees littered the floor, along with the only jeans I really felt comfortable in, crumpled in a sad pile. Hannah had bought me a flannel button-down last winter, but I'd only tried it on once before deciding I looked like a guy who was trying way too hard.

There was no denying, however, that Toby had reacted positively to the whirlwind Man Makeover that Hannah had inflicted upon me. The way her fingers brushed over my scalp suggested she loved the cut, and my jaw did look much more pronounced without the beard covering it.

Hannah had promised me that women loved the light woodsy scent of the lotion she'd brought over. Those jeans Hannah had given me fit much differently than the worn, baggy ones I'd owned for years—the ones I had been wearing the first time I met Toby, and she all but dismissed me.

Yeah. I needed to look good for this meeting.

My eyes flicked to the other side of the closet, which dressed Business Man Me. Crisp button-downs in pale colors, flat front slacks, and polished shoes with smart squared-off toes made me fit in reasonably at most bars and clubs. It looked good, but when I wore that shit, I never wanted anything more than to change out of it and into sweatpants at the end of the night. When I'd expressed this to Hannah, she'd thrown her head back and laughed, eventually explaining to me that I'd just described how every woman on the planet feels about her bra at the end of the day.

That had made me sad. I loved boobs. I didn't want them to be uncomfortable, ever, and I was fairly certain most of the world's boob-appreciating population would agree.

Do not think about boobs right now, asshole. It was too late. I was already getting hard thinking of Toby's palm sized breasts, and the nipples that decorated them, begging to be flicked by my thumbs and tongue.

My phone vibrated in my pocket, making me jump. "Yeah?" I answered. Ethan could be an annoying-as-fuck asshole, but we were still close enough for me to be able to instinctively tell when he was going to call.

"You have another date tonight?"

"Yep. Sure do," I lied. Seeing her was like a date. Sort of. Besides, I wanted to leave my evening open in case Toby asked me to hang out.

"Seriously? Damn, I expected to be making fun of you for dropping the ball. Well done, man."

I grunted. "Trying to make myself look presentable for it. I'm a wreck."

"You want to wear that navy sweater you have that makes you look like you have pecs, and the pair of stone washed jeans you wore to the studio last time."

"Any thoughts on shoes?" I asked, trying not to let the sweater muffle my voice when I pulled it over my head.

"Black Oxfords?"

"What's an Oxford?"

"You are a child. You know that, right?"

"What's your fucking point, man?" I was dangerously close to whining. Being only minutes away from seeing Toby again was messing with my head. I'd never felt this unsettled by a girl. Ever.

"Lace up shoes with dark soles, dude. I would be shocked if Hannah didn't leave you something like that."

"You told her to bring me Oxfords, didn't you?" This would be annoying if it wasn't so damn helpful.

"Your closet needed help."

"That's creepy, that you guys were talking about my wardrobe."

"Whatever. Finish suiting up, maybe take a shot before you come in today. You're not yourself when you're mooning over a woman. Apparently."

"Big help, friend. Thanks," I grumbled. I pressed *end* and slid the phone into my pocket.

I stared in the mirror and ran my fingertips through my hair one more time, then blew out one long slow breath. "You don't need a shot. Tonight, you're going to kiss Toby Eisen, sober. With clothes on, without essential oils and mood music. And she's gonna love every second of it."

If only my lame pep talk could stop my hands from shaking and my palms from clamming at the thought.

Her eyelids were sparkling.

Toby Eisen, the most perfect woman I'd ever shared air with, was sitting across the table from me, talking to me about my show, making damn intelligent observations about how tweaks in the sound could improve the whole experience. But all I could think about was how her eyelids were sparkling.

That may have been because she was putting them clearly on display; with her eyes turned everywhere but at me, her eyeshadow was pretty much all I could see. Glittery and pale blue, it was damn mesmerizing. I was desperate to look into dark-chocolate eyes she kept so carefully tucked away beneath that makeup, though.

As Shari went through the plans for our upcoming show minute-by-minute, Toby either typed madly on the slimline keyboard attached to her tablet, tilted her head down while pressing one side of her headphones to her ear, or turned her head to Shari and asked a quiet question, nodding and jotting more notes when Shari dove into tech jargon.

Toby didn't join in on the conversations about the standard

Bro Show segments—food and restaurants, TV and movies, the fashion segment—but as soon as I mentioned the new music feature, she perked up. I'd be playing a track from an EDM artist I'd taken on as a trial, and as soon as I mentioned some of the track's details, I was rewarded with fascinated eye contact.

For a couple of free-falling seconds, I was caught completely off guard at just how much light those dark brown, nearly black eyes could hold.

"Okay, this is great. I've been wanting some more experience with EDM," I realized she was saying.

"R-Really?"

Ethan snorted. I wanted to elbow him, but also wanted to not look like an even bigger idiot in this moment.

"Yeah. Can you elaborate on a couple things for me? First, which sub-genre are we talking about? It's important for the way I'll interlace the bass lines at their start points."

I could feel my eyes going wide, then a smile tugging at the corners of my mouth. This girl liked audio engineering—obviously enough, since she was in the grad program for it and had sought out this job—but, based on her questions and how she leaned across the table toward me, listening intently to every word of my answer, she *loved* sound engineering for music.

After I'd played about thirty seconds of the track and emailed her the mp3 file for her to work with from home, she caught my eye and, God help me, caught her bottom lip between her teeth for a split second.

She was going to kill me.

"Okay, and last is the Whiz Kid Mark Mahler segment..."

"You mean the whoring Mark out to Philadelphia segment," Shari said. "Ethan, I think maybe we should re-evaluate—"

"Re-evaluate what? Do you have any idea how many emails I got about our most eligible bachelor?"

I couldn't help but notice Toby shift in her chair and her

mouth turn down into the slightest frown. I sat up a little straighter.

"Emails. Really." Shari deadpanned, raising an eyebrow when Ethan waved his phone, displaying his inbox.

"Yeah. This one says, 'Way to help a bro out!'. Thirteen separate women emailed us with a proposition for a date and a picture of herself."

"Hold on, dude. You said I could pick the girls I went out with." My eyes flicked to Toby, who was examining her nails.

"I did! I just think this is reflective of the enthusiasm for the segment. And you should go out with this one. She's hot." Ethan stabbed at the screen of his phone and then flashed me a picture of a girl with chestnut hair holding a dog, her teeth flashing white in a huge smile. "Plus, I think she actually included the phrase 'Netflix and chill' in her proposal, so..."

Toby blinked hard, then stared at her tablet like she hadn't heard a thing. Maybe she hadn't.

I glared at Ethan, and he cleared his throat. "Okay, then. You have a date tonight, correct?"

"Well...uh..." I knew what I *wanted* to be doing. Making out with Toby. Running my hands over the slight, soft swell of her hip and burying my face in her hair, and some other parts of her body, too. But she was right here—I couldn't say any of that without looking like a total perv. Plus, I'd turned her down for physical fun on our last date, something that seemed like a grave mistake when I was this close to being able to touch her.

Still, I didn't want to ruin the chance that something more, something big, could grow between us. Maybe I'd take a chance.

"I'm planning on one, yeah. But it hasn't been confirmed."

I didn't miss the answering half-second smile that flicked across Toby's face. *Yes.*

"How about meeting the parents?" Toby asked, cool as a cucumber. "Uh, for a later segment." She locked eyes with me for another split second, then turned to Ethan. "I know it's crazy, maybe, but that might make things more fun. Amp up the listeners' anticipation. Spring break is right around the corner; I'm sure there's at least one lady in Philly who would love to introduce Mark to her folks."

"Uh..." Ethan looked from me to Toby and back again. I had to admit I took some satisfaction in Toby managing to catch him off guard.

"Uh..." I echoed, my eyebrows arching up at her.

"I mean, I don't know if you still want to keep seeing the girl you saw last week..."

"Yes!" I practically shouted, shocking even myself with how loud that word came out. Watching her for a reaction was one of the most nerve-wracking moments of my entire life.

Thankfully, it was followed by immense relief. Her cheeks pushed up into a blinding grin for just a second before it condensed to a more contained, private smile. She swallowed hard, then continued. "Great. So, think about it. Serials work better than one-offs, don't they? And it would be quite a high point. I'll bet a dozen girls would be happy to let Mark ride along with her home, show off a good-looking Whiz Kid to her parents," she finished, breathing deeply in and watching me with her shoulders pushed back.

"I mean, Ethan... people could call in with advice for me, right?" I asked. I loved this idea. I wanted to help Toby, and I couldn't deny wanting to meet her parents.

He just sort of nodded. In a rare occurrence, Ethan had been stunned into momentary silence.

Shari snorted. "As long as you two don't turn this into an audio version of all those trashy dating shows, it's okay with me. Just keep it clean and keep it to the ten minutes a week I gave you for the segment. *Capisce?*"

Toby let out a shaky laugh. "It's all for the magic of radio. We're always looking to shake things up, aren't we?"

"I suppose so," Shari replied, then shook her head and muttered to herself while she made a few more notes in her overstuffed planner. "All right, crew. That does it for today. See you on Friday."

I smacked my palm against the table. "Nope. Remember, Shari, we've gotta run a classic Bro Show this week instead of taping a new one. I've got that work trip, and I absolutely have to be out there Friday morning. I can't get back until Tuesday night, so the classic episode will let us skip next week's planning meeting."

Toby's eyebrows climbed up to her hairline. I would have given anything to know what she was thinking in that moment. Was she curious? Impressed? Shocked? I wasn't the kind of guy to brag about my career. Besides, I wanted to make her ask, to see if she cared enough to draw the information about what I did for a day job out of me.

Shari nodded and said, "That's right! Glad you reminded me, or I would have been waiting here for you two on Tuesday, pissed as hell."

Ethan and I laughed as Shari gathered her things. She stood on her tiptoes and slung an arm around my neck. Her voice was emotional, but gruff, as she said, "Good things are gonna happen for you, Mark. I believe it."

Shari may have acted like Ethan and I were nothing more than pains in her ass, but we knew she loved us. "Thanks, Shari."

With that, she stood up and walked toward her office in the back of the studio, leaving the three of us still at the conference table. Toby just sat there, tapping at her phone. Ethan slapped a hand down on the table next to me, and stood up, running his damn mouth.

"So, if that date doesn't work out, wanna get wings tonight? I know you're an old man who doesn't go out on weeknights and all, but I thought..."

Finally, he caught the silent look of death I was giving him, and cleared his throat. "Yeah, just...shoot me a text. Okay."

"Sure, man," I said, my voice surprisingly low and quiet. Then I turned all my attention to Toby. Just me and her, alone in a very non-romantic, fluorescent-lit studio conference room. Still, I didn't say a word, just waited for her. Whatever was happening between us, whatever was about to happen now, I didn't want to mess it up by tripping over my own damn words like I was so prone to doing.

Her eyes danced with something mischievous, and at least the slightest bit happy. "Wanna take a walk?"

I nodded, and we stood together. I waited for her to pack up her bag, watched as the graceful lines of her body sheathed themselves in her coat sleeves, tried to memorize the swing of her wavy hair against the small of her back when she wasn't looking.

We pushed out into the early spring air, where Philadelphia had just seen another light rain. The sun was staying up later and later, and there was a tinge of fresh dewy smell to the air. I took a deep breath in spite of myself, letting myself get lost in the early sunset light draping the busy sounds of the city before I realized she was watching me.

"We didn't talk about whether we were going to tell them," I blurted. "But I figured..."

"Oh, yeah. You were totally right. I don't even want to know what Ethan would say—or do—if he—"

"Exactly," I finished. So that was settled, then. This thing between us, whatever it was, was going to be a secret, for at least the next couple months.

That didn't mean it had to stay that way once the Bro Show segment was over, though. Did it?

"But I truly do want you to come home with me for Passover. You know, if you're still up for it."

"I am. I...I really am," I finished lamely, hoping that looking into her eyes while I said it would help convey how serious I was. I still couldn't quite shake the feeling of her actually wanting me to meet her parents. After a few kisses. I supposed it'd be way too dorky to pinch myself, but I wanted to make sure this was real. So, instead, I joked. "Do you always bring guys home when you have some family function you're dreading?"

Toby let out a rough laugh. "'Dreading' might be too strong of a word. I just..." She shrugged, then let her gaze settle on nothing across the street. "They asked. They ask every year if I'm going to bring someone special with me, and I never have. You coming home with me will help me out a lot, and..." She shrugged again. "I like you."

"I like you, too," I said, feeling a small piece of my heart turn over as she received my words with a smile.

"So," she said after another dozen steps. "Out where?"

"Huh?"

"You said you have to be 'out there' by Friday morning. Where do you need to be?"

"California," I said, shrugging. "A lot goes on in California."

"So that means I won't see you for, what? Ten days? We've never gone more than a few days without seeing each other," she said, turning her teasing puppy-dog eyes and frown on me.

I barked out a laugh. "We've only known each other for, what? One week? Less?"

Her steps slowed, then stopped. I stopped alongside her.

She moved close to me, smoothed her palm up over my care-fully-chosen sweater, pressed up on her tiptoes so those rosy lips of hers were just inches from mine. "I guess it just feels like longer," she murmured. Her breath swirled in clouds through the air, but warm against my chin, and I let my forehead fall to touch hers.

"I guess it does." My voice had gone soft, too.

God, it would be so easy to let myself get lost in her, to sweep her up in my arms and kiss her senseless and carry her back to my apartment and spend the night wrapped up in her. I wanted that. I also wanted to go home with her—get to know her past a little better, figure out what she was about. See her space. But I wasn't crazy, and I remembered the conversation we'd had the last time we were alone together with crystal clarity.

She wanted sex, which was great. But for her, it was only sex, even if it was attached to a fake boyfriend for a family function.

I wanted sex, but I wanted something more, too.

I didn't need a confession of undying love, or even her toothbrush in my bathroom, but I did need a little more reassurance. Maybe I could survive one woman who wrapped my heart around her little finger and then crushed it, but I knew I couldn't handle two. Not in one year. Especially not when the second one was the completely mesmerizing Toby Eisen.

So I forced myself to take a step back from her, sighing as I did, and held out my hand for hers. "You hungry?"

I could swear I saw her pout at the non-kiss, and it made something in my blood sing.

"Yes," she said quietly, "but not for food."

I nodded, hating the part of me that insisted on holding out. I wanted her so badly, but I did not want a roll on my mattress, an awkward visit home if she hated it, then having to deal with the most awful of tense situations I could imagine sitting across the studio from each other for the next several months.

Plus, I had work stuff to focus on. The most important work stuff of my entire career, maybe. I still couldn't quite believe that an artist I managed was up for a Grammy. I'd be there, at the ceremony, in a tux. Though *winning* a Grammy was a long shot for Magnus Gunnar—this year—being there for him while he lost Best New Artist meant being there for him while he won something else, some other year. I wanted to be there from the beginning. That was my whole brand. Mark Mahler Management: 'There for You from Day One'.

"As much as I hate to say this," I said to Toby, hoping my voice conveyed the regret I felt, "maybe it's best if we don't hang out before the next Whiz Kid segment. You know, even after I get back. I want to keep the dates compartmentalized, you know? One date per show. I really do want to talk about our first date as a stand-alone."

"Making out in a yoga studio?"

"Probably just the yoga," I chuckled. "You know that was my first time, right?"

She giggled. My heart nearly stopped. "Yeah. You said. It was obvious. You're not that bendy."

"Hey," I said, feigning offense. "That's not fair. I didn't get much of a chance to show off any bendiness that I might have had in the first place. Or strength."

"That's true. You know, I could think of one thing that would allow you to demonstrate both your bendiness and strength."

Instantly, an image popped into my head. Toby, naked and writhing beneath me, one of her legs hooked over my shoulder, my biceps flexing as I worked to hold myself up while thrusting into her. I groaned. "You're killing me, you know that?"

"Hey, you're not the only one who's dying here." She was teasing me, but the seriousness in her tone was plain as day.

We arrived at the door to her apartment half a minute later, thirty seconds that felt like they stretched on into forever.

"Don't get me wrong," I finally said, "I loved our last date. *Loved* it."

She grinned. My heart soared.

"It's just that...if we hang out any more...I'm afraid we'll have such an amazing time and discuss so many deep, important topics that I'll have all this stuff to talk about, we'll end up with a twenty-minute segment, and then you'll have to edit it down to five."

"And then I'll be too busy to go out with you the next weekend."

Jesus. If she pulled her lip between her teeth like that one more time, I'd end up taking her against a brick wall in an alley somewhere. "So, besides the overbearing parents, is there anything else about Passover with your family I should be terrified of?"

She turned to me, stretched out a finger, and pressed it gently to my lips, silencing me. I wanted to suck it into my mouth and take her, hard, up against the brick wall of her building. Whatever it was that she really wanted out of this whole 'taking me home to meet the parents' thing, she would end up getting it sooner rather than later. I'd only known this girl for a week and a half and she was already making it very clear that, eventually, she got what she wanted.

And what she wanted right this moment was to kiss me. There was no universe in which I could argue with that. She pressed up on her toes, leaned in, and gave me a decisive yet soft kiss. A second later, she was climbing the stairs.

"See you Friday?" I called. "Next Friday. We could go out after we tape the show."

"See you next Friday," she agreed, as if confirming an appointment for something mildly pleasant, like a manicure. "Unless you miss me too much. Then...you know where to find me." She tugged her phone from her coat pocket and waved it back and forth.

"I thought you liked your space," I said, turning the words over in my mind.

Trying to figure out what Toby truly wanted from a guy might twist my brain into knots.

"That's the beauty of texting," she said, lifting an eyebrow. "It's typically done between people who are in two completely different locations."

Then it hit me. Ethan had deleted her from my phone. "Oh! Actually, I, uh...lost your number. So..."

"So, I guess I'll have to text you if I'm the one who misses you too much? That sounds like fun," she said. With that, she ducked inside her front door, dismissing me with a wave of her fingers.

When the door was shut, I spun on my heel and groaned into the rapidly darkening night. This girl really was going to kill me.

CHAPTER 17

TOBY

THE NEXT MORNING, I got up early to run. I tossed and turned all night, and I knew the biting cold morning air would slap me into full alertness.

I had never had less fun leading a guy on. Probably because it felt more like he was the one leading me on.

No, I didn't want a relationship right now, which I thought made absolute sense. No, I didn't even want to be roped into dating just one guy, especially not for a predetermined length of time. I knew that sleeping with Mark would make things beyond weird for the duration of my internship on the show if we were somehow incompatible between the sheets...but, dammit, I wanted him inside me so bad I could practically feel it.

Yeah. It was that bad.

As frustrated as I was, though, I kind of loved that Mark didn't have my phone number.

In the hours before I saw Mark yesterday afternoon, I'd gone back and forth on canceling the whole 'I'm bringing a guy home for Seder' thing. I wasn't an awful person—never wanted to screw with a guy just to mess them up in the head, and certainly not to hurt them—but it was time my parents were confronted with the fact that I was just never going to date someone they loved. It just wasn't humanly possible. There was no middle ground between the guys I wanted and the guys my parents wanted for me.

Mark could be my stand-in for that. There was no reason for me to feel bad about it, was there? He might still be in love with his ex, but that didn't matter, even if my eyelid did start twitching whenever I thought about the mythical Kylie. What made her so incredible, anyway?

Whatever. I was helping Mark for The Bro Show, he could help me with my parents in return, and we'd both have a ton of fun doing it. Well, maybe this particular point in our relationship could be deemed *frustrating*, instead of *fun*, but we were getting close.

We had to be.

I honestly thought I'd have a real shot at getting in his pants after this week's meeting. If I could squeeze in enough flirtations and a few dates...maybe I could break him. But now, with him saying he didn't want to spend any time with me for the next ten days, I was screwed. Or, you know...not screwed.

At least I had homework and internship work to distract me. I ordered a pizza from Marco's—with sausage and banana peppers, my favorite—peeled off the skinny jeans I'd chosen that morning that had turned out to be a little too skinny for comfort, and settled onto the couch with the assigned reading from my Vocal Production Techniques and got to work. The only good pants were no pants, I thought to myself as I snuggled under a blanket.

I was really glad I'd finally settled on a graduate degree in audio engineering. There was something soothing about the way the formulas followed the same rules every time, the way the results were predictable and manifested into something you could hear, something you could feel. Translating numbers and formulas into sounds never lost its magic. It transcended language and culture, put me in touch with people across the globe, potentially. I even loved the homework, as dorky as that sounded.

That was one thing I'd learned about myself, then, that was all me and came from no guy, and certainly not my parents. Sound Engineering was something that I knew was well and truly *me*, defining me inside and out.

Before I knew it, I'd blown through thirty pages, five home-work questions, and the entire wait time for the delivery guy. He knocked on my door and I shoved my tablet off to the side, suddenly realizing how hungry engineering homework made me.

The delivery guy leaned lazily against the door frame, the pizza supported by his forearm like an afterthought. His eyes raked down over my body, pausing briefly on my breasts and then drinking in my legs. Which I only just then remembered were naked all the way up to my cotton boy-short panties.

"Uh... just a second," I stammered as I stepped to the side to grab my purse. Even after rifling through it for a few awkward seconds, I only found a twenty, and the pizza cost nearly that much. "Dammit, sorry. I know I have some ones in here."

"You know, if you don't have any change, I'd accept a slice of pizza and a hangout as a tip."

My eyes flicked to his, annoyed.

He had long scraggly hair and a day or two of scruff, glasses, a graphic tee, and jeans that hung off his hips like they'd been made just for him. At a head taller than me, he was the height that I loved. This was the kind of guy I would have jumped at the chance to be with just a few weeks ago.

Thankfully, my fingers found a wad of ones shoved in the corner of the inside pocket of my purse. My house was always neat and tidy, but my purse, for some reason, was another story. I was paying for it now.

"Thanks, no. I've got it."

"Please, no offense, I just... sorry, ma'am," the guy stammered as I grabbed the pizza and shoved the tip into his hand.

"Yeah, yeah. I knowForget about it."

"Right." He turned to leave, then remembered something. Over his shoulders, he said, "Thank you for your business. At Marco's, we come fast, no apologies."

I winced. That tag line was bad enough, but to make the poor delivery kids say it every time? I almost felt sorry for the guy as I pushed the door shut. Regardless, there had to be some middle ground between inviting himself in for a roll in the hay and calling me 'ma'am'.

"Do I look like a ma'am? Am I starting to look like my mother? Should I ask her for some wrinkle cream?" I sighed and plopped back down on the couch, the pizza box threatening to scald my thighs even through the blanket I'd pulled over them. "And now I'm officially talking to myself. Which I guess *is* something that crazy middle-aged ladies do. Awesome."

I threw my head back and groaned when it banged the arm of the couch. This was it. I had reached peak pathetic.

Then, as if my mention of "crazy middle-aged ladies" had amplified and reached all the way to Los Angeles, my phone trilled, making me jump. I knew who it was before I looked on the screen.

"Ima," I said, pressing the phone to my ear and rubbing my face with the other palm. At least I hadn't bothered to put on any makeup that could be ruined by my pity party.

"Tovyah, my love," my mother crooned into the phone. Something clanged in the background, and I rolled my eyes. Ima never could do just one thing at a time—she was probably trying to bake something, got bored, and called me. "I'm thinking about

Passover, and I wanted to make sure your friend's plane tickets are all set up."

I barely suppressed a scoff. She knew his tickets were just fine, I would have bet my life on it. "Yes, he's all set up."

"Ah, okay, I can see here on the email." I knew damn well she wasn't at the computer. I'd just heard her in the kitchen, and it took that woman forever just to move past the screen saver. "Ah. Mark Mahler." She drew out the "ah" in his last name like it was savoring a bite of something delicious. "Do you know where his family's from?"

It was a question that would seem innocuous to most people, but I knew that this was my mother's very poorly disguised attempt at what was commonly known as "bageling"— trying to find out if someone is Jewish without actually asking if they're Jewish.

"Ohio," I answered, my voice flat. "And I know you're not at the computer."

"Bah," she replied. She was waving her hand in the air, I knew, like I'd just said the most ridiculous thing ever. "I meant I saw it before. What city in Ohio, *bubah*? Cleveland, maybe? Do you think he knows our friends the Shapiros? They've lived there for ages, and—"

"Ima, no."

"No?"

"No, he doesn't know your friends. No, he's not Jewish. He's just a regular American guy, and he's my boyfriend, so he's coming to Seder."

"Your boyfriend?" she squealed.

Great. Now I'd gone and done it. I was so damn distracted trying to figure out what Mark and I actually were to each other that one of the possible words for it must have just slipped out.

"Ima, I didn't mean—"

"In all these years, there's never been anyone serious enough for you to call him *that*. Oh, I'm so happy."

My brow furrowed. "Ima, did you hear what I just—"

"Okay, my love, I must run, the oven is beeping."

The oven, as far as I could hear, was not beeping. But there was no point in belaboring this pointless conversation any longer. "Okay, Ima. Talk to you soon."

"*Neshikot*," she trilled before hanging up.

Kisses. Yep. Great.

I sighed. I understood that she was excited that I'd referred to Mark as my boyfriend—which I was still reeling from—but how long would it take her to register the news that should have paused the whole conversation?

He's not Jewish.

God, I'd wanted to save that bombshell for the actual dinner. I sunk down into the couch, replaying her reaction. Maybe she just hadn't registered what I'd said. It was my own damn fault, since I'd so stupidly volunteered the B-word.

He wasn't my boyfriend. I didn't even *want* him to be.

What I did want, desperately, was for him to be here right now, distracting me with those delicious lips of his.

Stop thinking about that. I couldn't remember the last time I'd wanted a guy lounging around on my couch, like he lived there, like he was some seamless part of my life. Put Mark and I together on a couch eating pizza and we might as well be a married couple, or at least live-ins.

I didn't want any part of that. Never had, and I was almost certain I never would.

I sighed and picked up my phone before I could talk myself out of it. I was just going to give him my number. That was all.

Toby: Hey Whiz Kid

. . .

My thumb hovered over the keyboard, hitting *send* a second later. I didn't miss the flip-flop of my stomach when I did. Somehow, this guy had made me into a huge mess. I shoved the phone under my leg, muttering curses at myself for being so quick to text him.

I tore off a bite of pizza, chewing it longer than I had to, trying to distract myself. Maybe make the seconds tick by faster. I'd gotten through a slice and a half before my phone mercifully buzzed against my inner thigh. Of course. Because I needed to be even more hot and bothered.

Mark: This is either Ethan with a new number or... someone else
Mark: Please be someone else

I laughed. Dammit, that wasn't even funny, but the relief bubbled up out of my chest, making me feel instantly lighter.

Toby: Why on earth would you want to hear from me instead of Ethan?
Mark: You know why.

I pulled in a shuddering breath, letting the air swirl in my lungs. Reading the almost-admission from Mark was like taking a hit from a cigarette—I knew it probably wasn't good for me, but I wanted a second to savor it anyway.

The phone buzzed again.

Mark: You could send me proof. That you're not Ethan.

A smile slowly spread across my face.

Toby: Trying to think of what kind of picture would convince you to come and share this pizza with me

Mark: Ok, pizza? Now I demand proof.

I grinned and balanced the box on my knees, then snapped a picture and sent it, scrunching up my face and waiting. His response came a few seconds later.

Mark: Sorry, try again. Those could be anyone's thighs. How do I know Ethan hasn't taken up swimming and decided to shave?

I laughed and turned the phone on myself. I fluffed my hair on one side and brushed it behind my shoulder on another. I made sure I was showing at least a little cleavage, widened my eyes just a smidge, and smiled the tiniest bit. Then took the picture and sent it.

Mark: That'll work.

I frowned a little. That was all he had to say?

Toby: So what are you up to? It's just me and my Vocal Production homework. And this pizza.
   Mark: And no pants.
   Toby: No pants.

I bit my lower lip, hoping that was all I had to do to get him over here. Any other guy would have responded in an instant by banging on the front door and maybe pinning me up against it when I let him in. But right here, right now, I didn't want any other guy.

I wanted Mark. And I wanted *him*, not this pizza, hot on my legs.

I munched on another piece while I waited for his reply. I read another five pages, stood up to put the pizza away, folded the blanket, sat down again with my tablet, then unfolded the blanket again and tucked it around my legs when I decided I didn't want to get up and go to my room for pants.

My stomach twisted. Every rule in the book told me not to text him again. My fingers, apparently, didn't care about rules and were already typing one more text.

. . .

Toby: **Don't tell me you're already asleep.**

My phone rang, and I nearly jumped off the couch.

"Hey," Mark's voice came through the other end when I answered.

"I cannot remember the last time I talked to anyone on the phone besides my mom." I slid down on the couch, snuggling up under the blanket. Something about his soft, deep voice being piped directly into my ear made me feel warm all over.

"I have this weird eyesight thing that makes texting a pain in the ass. And I wanted to keep talking to you."

There was a silence as I snuggled a little farther down.

"Is that okay?"

"Yeah. Yeah, it's okay." The reading for class could wait, I guessed.

"So, what in the world was on that pizza?"

"Oh. My favorite. Sausage and banana peppers. Second only to ham and pineapple."

"Never had it," Mark said.

"Pepperoni?" I asked.

"I don't like meat on my pizza," he said.

I wrinkled my nose. Of course the normal, basic, plainest guy I'd ever met would eat boring pizza, too. "Are you some sort of vegetarian or something?"

He laughed. "Or something. You have a problem with a guy who doesn't like meat on his pizza?"

"No, guess not. Just find it interesting that Whiz Kid Mark Mahler is keeping secrets from me."

"Don't call me that," he grumbled. It was almost cute.

"What? Whiz Kid? Why not?" He was so easily teased. I kind of liked it.

"Because that's for the show. That's performance. This is real."

"This? You and me?"

"Yeah. Well, I want it to be real, anyway. I think it is."

A lump rose in my throat at the sincerity in his voice, keeping me from responding right away.

"Besides," he said. "I like talking with you, and I don't want to think about Ethan when I'm hearing your voice."

"Well, I can't really argue with that, can I?"

He chuckled again, low and soft. I'd have to figure out how to record it, so different from the way he sounded on the radio.

"So, what are you reading about? I want to know what keeps that beautiful brain of yours interested in...whatever you're interested in."

I propped my feet up on the opposite arm of the couch and grinned. "Well, if you really want to know..." I woke up just as the sun was starting to peek through my windows, the imprint of my phone case etched into my cheek, and a crick in my neck. I'd fallen asleep on my couch, talking to Mark about my Vocal Production homework, his favorite pizza toppings, and a dozen other things, and, as I thought about it while sipping my morning tea, I had zero regrets.

Even though I'd never, not once in my life, even wanted to talk to anyone all night about anything.

The crazy part was, that wasn't the end of it. We talked on the phone every single night after that.

"So, are you sure you don't want to hang out before the show on Friday?" I was scrambling eggs for dinner on Thursday night, embarrassed by my own boring weeknight existence. Hell, I was watching HGTV and staring at a basket of laundry that needed to be folded. I could practically see myself turning into my mom.

"I am absolutely sure. I mean, I want to hang out as soon as I get back. And I am cursing the photo capability of our modern phones, plus your selfie skills, for making me want that even more. But I want to ration my material for the show. Remember? I'm sure yoga is going to take up the whole seven minutes that Shari is giving me. And that—Lion King Yoga—is just too good to leave out."

It had been too good. So good that it had occupied my dreams the last two out of three nights. So good that I had considered showing up at Mark's apartment, picking the lock, and jumping him in bed.

"Besides," he continued, "our schedules have done nothing but clash." One thing I had learned about Mark over the last two days and hours of talking on the phone was that he was really good at closing over the blank spots in our conversation, at not making me feel weird for my tendency to get lost in thought. Lost in overthinking everything was more like it.

"Yeah. I still need to learn more about this job that has you out for brunch on a Saturday, then still out at two in the morning on Sunday. Then out late *again* on Sunday night."

He'd told me about the itinerary for his work trip. With so many meetings and commitments at odd hours, maybe Mark wasn't as basic as I had previously taken him for.

"You'll learn. I'm going to show you. I'm saving it, remember? Date material?"

"Yeah, yeah," I grumbled. Over the last couple days of talking on the phone, I had figured out that what Mark called "date material" was really a series of events that would weave me even further into his life, making it even more difficult for me to tear myself away from him when it inevitably came time for us to break up because I was feeling antsy, or bored, or restless, or just not living the way I really wanted to live. Every guy I'd ever dated had gotten that kind of goodbye. Mark would be the same. It was the order of the universe.

Who knew? Maybe the sound of me chewing scrambled eggs in his ear would be enough for him to run away and never come back.

It wasn't, though. He called again after my Friday morning class and stayed on the phone with me through lunch and an hour's worth of errands, which were filled with awkward interruptions to talk to shop attendants. He only hung up the phone when he had to go to work – something I was biting my tongue to keep from asking him about.

I didn't want him to know he had the upper hand in all this. Hell, I could barely admit it to myself.

That didn't stop me from talking to him every time he called, though. On Sunday morning, his call woke me up bright and early. He still hadn't gone to bed.

Then, I didn't hear from him at all the rest of Sunday, or Monday. Tuesday morning, still nothing. I didn't get a wakeup call from Mark, something I'd had at least twice in the past week, but I went for a run anyway, even though I'd woken up too late. I could go to class sweaty. Whatever.

Forcing myself to leave my cell at home so my stupid thoughts of stupid Mark Mahler couldn't distract me, I headed to my nine o'clock Jazz Styles and Analysis class where I bit off at least two guys' heads in an argument over the influence of Arabic jazz on the contemporary American jazz scene and narrowly avoided cursing at the professor when she scolded me for it. I came home, dropping my bag on the floor, and practically fell on top of my phone, dying to see the message that I was sure Mark would have sent by now. At the very least, I expected a missed call.

Nothing.

"Dammit!" I yelled to my empty house, my voice bouncing off the walls, emphasizing the feeling of cold loneliness seeping its way into my bones.

I needed heat and white noise. I needed a shower.

Sighing, I stalked into the bathroom and cranked the shower on to hot, hoping the steam would calm me down. As I chucked my workout clothes in the washer, I admired how cute my boobs looked, the nipples all puckered from the cold. That gave me an idea—one that might entice Mark to come see me before the Friday taping, after all.

I perched my phone on the robe hook screwed into the bathroom door, which faced the frosted glass doors of the shower, started the video feed, and ducked into the shower.

When it was wet, my hair plastered itself over the full length of my back and down to my butt. Luxuriating in a long, hot shower usually made me feel like a goddess, but the only thing it made me feel today was cranky. The shower felt empty. My still-firm nipples wanted attention from someone that wasn't their owner, and the ends of my hair should be slip-sliding over Mark's fingers while they grabbed my butt.

The ancient water heater in my house meant I only had about six and a half minutes before the shower turned from steamy to lukewarm, and after wrapping one towel around my head and another under my arms, I snatched my phone from its perch and got to work cutting the video down. If Mark wasn't going to come see me in person, then he most certainly wouldn't get any boob shots. But a little frosted-glass shower silhouettes would come close enough to killing him that he'd regret leaving me starved for tactile attention all week. There was just enough detail that you could see my head drop back and my mouth open in a sigh of pleasure at the hot water, and then my hands skate down over my breasts and stomach. When I turned to let the water douse my hair, my nipples stood out clear as day in the glass-door shadow.

If this didn't drive him nuts, nothing would.

Satisfied with the thirty-second clip I'd created, I attached it to a message to Mark and hit send.

Then I settled on the couch with a bottle of lotion, moisturizing my legs and elbows and waiting for his response.

For thirty minutes. Hell, I had almost dried off enough to need another round of lotion.

Nothing.

God, I had never felt like such a loser in my entire life. Or more like crawling into bed, getting myself off, and going to sleep.

But this was fucking ridiculous. I had never let a guy upset me like this before, and I'd be damned if I was going to start now, over Mr. Average, Mark Mahler. I didn't need to mope around. I needed to kick some ass.

Forty-five minutes later, I was suited back up in fresh workout clothes and standing in the middle of a boxing ring, ready for Natalia Ortiz's Krav Maga class.

My mother had put me in Krav Maga lessons as a child. I'd thrown a fit over wearing tights and a leotard for dance classes, begging to do something that was actually fun and that I could wear baggy clothes to. Krav Maga is known as one of the more intense and deadly forms of martial arts, which didn't exactly square with the image my mom had in mind for her sweet little wisp of a daughter. But it was Israeli, which made her happy. If I wasn't going to go to Hebrew school or keep kosher or even learn to speak the language, she said, I could at least do one thing from her home country. From our heritage. I remembered feeling like I'd won something, even though I now knew it was Ima who'd won.

Whoever won didn't matter, though. I loved Krav Maga from the first minute of my first class when I was eight years old, and I'd been kicking ass and taking names ever since.

I still enjoyed going to Natalia's kickboxing classes from

time to time, just to confuse the latest group of gym bros who didn't understand how a reedy woman with bones of a bird had just taken them down in less than twenty seconds.

I'd been to Natalia's class at least a dozen times since moving to Philly. I knew Ethan went to this gym from time to time, but I'd never seen him here. Until today.

He sauntered up to the ring and I tried to look like the badass I knew I was before I said anything to him. "You come here to get your ass kicked?" I managed before he levered himself into the ring with me.

"No, I came here to kick the Whiz Kid's ass."

My heart jumped into my throat. Mark was meeting him here to work out, and I would have to face him.

After he'd ignored my steamy video.

"Too bad he's too much of a pussy to fight me. Texted me five minutes ago that he's too swamped with work to make it over here."

I tried to let out my sigh of relief slowly. Not only was Mark not going to see me makeup-free, but now I knew that if Mark was purposely dodging me and using work as an excuse, I wasn't the only person in his life getting that treatment.

"Now I don't have an opponent *or* someone to test out my lame show jokes on." Ethan shrugged, letting his gloved hands drop at his sides heavily.

"Excuse you," I laughed, "What am I? A wisp? A hologram? A nothing? Fight me!"

"Come again?" Ethan said, his eyes running up and down the length of my body. "Sorry, but I have a hundred pounds on you easy, and I don't want to do permanent damage to the only sound engineer we can afford on The Bro Show."

I narrowed my eyes.

"Uh," he said, "I mean, the greatest sound engineer we've ever had."

I quirked an eyebrow.

"The same great sound engineer who is now royally pissed at me and who I desperately want to make it up to."

I smiled brightly, and just as I was about to open my mouth, Natalia's throaty voice called out from behind me. "You mean you don't want to get beaten up by a girl." She hopped the cords and practically glided across the mat, right to Ethan's side. Immediately, I could practically see his eyes turning into hearts. Natalia bent in and gently bit at his earlobe, brushing a soothing kiss over it when she pulled away.

"My girl here says that she is strongly cautioning me against fighting you."

"I am not your girl," Natalia hissed at him, her voice dark. "And tell her why I told you not to fight her."

"Because she will kick my ass," Mark mumbled.

"She might even kick mine," Natalia said as she stepped up to me and pulled me into a hug.

"If we make it strictly Krav Maga, I will."

"Ha. Whatever you say, soldier. Good to see you back. Are these guys giving you too much trouble on their show? You feeling the need to punch something?"

"Something like that," I said to her with a small, confirming smile.

"Let me get him set up with some bag drills and then we'll see who the better woman is today, huh?"

I grinned. I always beat Natalia. Or, as it turned out, always minus today. And she'd punched a cut onto the corner of my lower lip and what would likely be a pretty sizeable bruise under my left rib.

"What's wrong with you?" Natalia asked as she crouched down in front of me while I clutched my side. "I was just joking about The Bro Show. Is Ethan really making your life that miserable that you come here wanting to beat me up and then fail at it?"

It's not Ethan," I said, wincing as I straightened up. "Shit, I hope you didn't break me."

"Don't be such a drama queen," Natalia said cheerfully, slinging an arm across my shoulders. "When a bone breaks, you almost always hear some sort of crunch. Or snap."

I knew the girl was working at becoming a professional stunt double—she'd already done some impressive work when she lived in L.A.—but it was still damn annoying how excited she could get about how you knew when you were truly pushing the limits of a human body.

"Is Mark giving you problems? He can be cranky sometimes. Not very patient."

I raised my eyebrows. "Mark? Impatient? Really?" My heart warmed when I thought of the admittedly few hours we'd spent together. Mark had seemed openminded and kind, if a little boring. Not a grump.

Natalia's lips spread into a wide grin. "Not bothering you, then," she said, nodding. "I'm guessing the opposite. Maybe have him kiss the rib better?"

My cheeks flushed as she walked away, laughing. Then she put a finger to her lips and snuck up to Ethan, where she spun and kicked his legs out from under him, fast as lightning. We were the only three people on the floor of the small gym on a Tuesday afternoon, and watching the two of them made me feel a little bit like a creepy third wheel. I laughed as Ethan shouted, then rolled onto his back so Natalia was straddling him. When he pulled her down to him for a long kiss, I took that as my cue to leave.

It was almost dark when I got home, and pitch black by the time I got out of my second shower. I was utterly exhausted, and my rib hurt, and I had no desire to text some of the girls I'd met in Philly and ask to go out with them. Besides, I was in grad school now, pushing twenty-six; I was getting close to full-blown grown-up status, and it was time I started acting like it.

Just as I had gotten settled on the couch with an ice pack, my phone buzzed against my palm. This *had* to be Mark. But the screen displayed some random 215 number—probably the pharmacy calling to let me know my face cream had been refilled, bless my California dermatologist. And, probably, bless my mom for checking in with my dermatologist.

I groaned as I silenced the phone and wedged it back under my thigh. Only Jon Snow could improve my mood now.

Sour thoughts populated my brain. What if Mark wasn't interested anymore? I had literally never had to worry about a guy not being interested in me, and yet...here I was. It wasn't rational, and none of this made any sense. Not in my grand plan, not even in the moment. But my heart was still in a knot over fucking Mark Mahler. Or maybe it was just that my lady parts so badly wanted to be...fucking Mark Mahler.

Either way, there was only one thing to say about this whole goddamn situation. It sucked. And I had to end it, as soon as possible.

CHAPTER 18

MARK

THERE COULD HAVE BEEN NO WORSE time for me to drop my phone into a Los Angeles storm drain than in the middle of watching the hottest video I had ever received directly to my cell phone. Toby's shadow twisting and arching under a stream of hot water was sexier than even my fantasies about seeing her naked. Which were pretty damn hot.

So of course, the universe would tear my phone away from me and hurl it directly into a rushing stream of underground city waste water. The phone sailed out of my hand and past the bars of this thing without so much as bouncing or scraping against one of them.

It was like something cosmic wanted to fuck with me.

The especially shitty part of this whole thing was that, on any other day, I could have just gotten myself over to Toby's place and finished what she'd started with the most incredible tease I'd ever been subjected to. But today was the day that my business chose to start taking off, apparently.

That's right. Magnus Gunnar had just won the fucking Grammy for Best New Artist—and my world was about to explode.

I couldn't complain. Obviously. In fact, a giddy sort of pride had taken over my mood. Watching Toby's fuzzy naked form had felt like the cherry on top of what was shaping up to be the greatest weekend of my life. Rather, I couldn't help thinking, it *would* have been the greatest if she'd been there at my side.

My life had been in a bit of a freefall since graduating with my MBA. I was full of anxiety over getting a cubicle job in some nondescript business firm like every other white dude toolbag in Philadelphia, and it was really starting to eat away at me. Hosting The Bro Show was fine, but it couldn't be my main source of money forever. Besides, I'd just about blown through all the seed money I'd put aside to get Mark Mahler Management off the ground.

That was why, after I'd gone to all the parties, sat beside Marcus through all the post-Grammy interviews, done my own interview with Entertainment magazine, and closed out all his bills in L.A., I was happy to head back to Philly, where there was always more work to be done.

A couple hours after getting off the plane, I had some work to do for Cosmick Crew. As annoying as the brother-and-sister musicians who seamlessly blended trance-like dance beats and electric violin could be, we'd had an influx of requests for them in the greater Philadelphia area. A couple months ago, they'd had a gig in a King of Prussia suburb, then another small club way down the Main Line, but more recently, they'd been booked to play in five clubs within fifteen minutes of downtown.

Last night, I'd gotten a tip-off from one of my buddies in the mail room at Rolling Stone that one of their indie reviewers would be in Philly, along with information about what hotel he'd be staying in. All I had to do was haunt the lobby of his hotel that evening, and hopefully I could push him toward Dance Face, the club where Cosmick Crew would be performing live starting at ten.

In other words, the whole future of Mark Mahler Management may very well be on the line tonight.

Yes, my dick was begging me to say to hell with all of it, show up at Toby's house and beg her to repeat whatever it was she'd done on that video, then kiss every inch of her gorgeous, lithe body until she forgot how I'd gotten there in the first place. I was a grownup, though, and I had to think with the brain in my skull. I knew I'd regret it if I didn't do the adult thing tonight and head to work. God, I hadn't even had time to get a new phone.

Thank God I was one of the old-schoolers who still carried paper business cards.

Joey Blake, the Rolling Stone indie reviewer, turned out to be a five-foot-two blonde girl with thick tortoiseshell glasses and a smile so bright it could blind you if you weren't careful.

Turned out that this was my lucky night.

I always wore my lucky tie when I went review-fishing—unless you looked closely, my tie with record albums decorating it would have just looked polka-dotted. But music reviewers were hard-wired to pay attention to shit like that, and I'd struck up conversations with a solid handful of young magazine writers with word counts to fill thanks to that tie.

It was one of the few things I'd kept that Kylie had given me. It was a joke Christmas gift, from two or three years ago, and this record-album tie was somehow more supportive of my career dreams than Kylie herself had ever been.

Joey, the blonde ball of energy that she was, accepted my help calling her an Uber, then invited me to share it. She noticed my tie within a couple minutes, gleefully snapping a selfie of us to show her Instagram followers. By the time she stepped out of the car she was carrying one of my business cards with Cosmick Crew's performance information for that night scrawled across the back.

I had just enough time to get home and change, and on the way there, I tried to figure out what the hell I was going to do about Toby. Our cell phones had been our sole mode of communication. We'd been talking so often the first few days I was gone, and now, because of that damn storm drain, it was all radio silence.

I knew where she lived, but we were nowhere near comfortable enough to stop by one another's places unannounced. The only alternative was to stop by the studio for something slightly less creepy.

God bless Shari's flakiness; her office door was always left wide open. Didn't take too long for me to find her Rolodex—outdated, and the only way she kept track of contact information—and flip to Toby's entry. No phone number, which was fine, since I couldn't text her from Shari's desk phone. There was, however, an email address listed for her.

I logged myself on to my email account and dashed off a quick note, explaining myself and telling Toby I couldn't wait to see her in a couple days. I wanted to see her so badly, and I ached to invite her to my place. The only problem was that I'd be out working for the next day, and I knew she had classes Thursday and Friday morning.

Four hours later, beaming as Cosmick Crew took a break after a solid half hour of whipping Dance Face's dancers into a frenzy, I felt like the luckiest newbie music manager in the world. My mood was only slightly dampened by the fact that Toby hadn't opened my email yet. I told myself it was okay, and focused on appreciating my amazing luck.

Joey Blake was here, as promised. She was perched on the edge of the dance floor at a cocktail table, tapping notes into her phone with fast-flying thumbs. When she finally finished, she looked up and caught my eye. I almost wept with relief when she stuck one of those thumbs up in the air with a big, blissed-out smile on her face.

Those were the smiles music managers lived for. You usually saw them on the faces of dancers or other people in the audience, but seeing one on a reviewer for an international music magazine? This just might be the best day of my life.

I was out until three that night, visiting other clubs and chatting up their talent coordinators. I had enough sense not to dangle Joey Blake's possible review of Cosmick Crew in front of club owners while I was trying to get them booked. Instead, I had them search for videos of other crowds from the week dancing to their music and looking ecstatic.

I knew there was a reason I'd signed them in the first place. Here it was. Real-time dance club crowd reactions didn't lie.

I collapsed into bed after half-assedly running a toothbrush through my mouth, and, for the first time in a very long time, not feeling an ounce of worry for my business.

That didn't stop the blurry shower footage of Toby from leaking into my dreams, though. I tossed and turned and had the greatest sex dream ever—me digging my fingers into Toby's gently swelling hips, her petite boobs jerking and swaying as I lifted her up against the shower wall and buried myself deep inside her. I woke up, sweating, and checked my email app again. I growled when I saw she still hadn't opened the damn thing.

The next morning, I finally got to the cell phone store, where a guy with a too-bright smile told me that he was so, so, so, so, SO sorry, but I wouldn't be able to get a new phone until tomorrow afternoon.

Thursday at nearly seven o'clock, I finally got a new phone. An hour later, it had synced all my contacts and I tapped out a text to Toby.

. . .

Mark: I'm back in town. My phone drowned and I just got a new one. Really want to see you. Please?

To hell with my resolve to keep our time together limited between dates. I was absolutely itching to be near her.

Even though it didn't seem like she felt the same way. I watched that screen for a long time. The reply dots never even showed up.

On Friday, I woke up just in time to be at the studio for our official two-thirty call time for a three o'clock taping, still half-hard from my dreams as I tugged on some clothes, scrubbed my face, and made my hair look somewhat decent before shoving a dry bagel in my mouth and running out the door. By the time I got to the studio, I was dying to see her.

I wasn't prepared to find her waiting for me at the front desk, perched on the edge. As soon as she saw me, she morphed into the picture of anger: arms crossed, chest heaving, and eyes glaring.

"Toby? Are you okay?"

"You tell me, *Whiz Kid*," she hissed, glaring at me in a pretty clear dare to challenge her on calling me that. "Would you be okay if you sent me a dick pic and I never responded? What the hell am I supposed to think? Are we playing some sort of game here, or...?"

Her eyes darted down and to the left, and in that second, I could swear I saw tears welling along the bottom lid.

"Hey," I said in a hushed, but firm voice. "Can we put this on pause? Talk about this somewhere else, where Ethan or Shari won't hear us and make this a bigger deal than it is?"

"How big a deal *is* it, Mark? Because I thought you wanted..."

"Shhh," I said, grabbing her hand and tugging her to her feet. "Just trust me for a sec, okay?"

Parts of Shari's studio, like where we recorded the shows, were new, built within the last ten years, but others were older. The only reason most people would walk into one of the old store rooms would be on a search for a long packed away 8-track or set list from a 90s-era live show.

All three of those old rooms, stuffed in the back hallways of the studio, were musty and dark, but they would work just fine for Toby to lose her shit at me without anyone hearing. I tugged her through the twists and turns of the older part of the studio until we came to one of the old heavy pine doors with a worn brass knob.

"In here," I said, flipping the light switch a couple times before the thing blinked to life.

I took a couple steps into the room, unwilling to get too far away from Toby, whose chest was still heaving and whose cheeks were still flushed and who I wanted my hands and lips on more than pretty much anything else right now. I turned to face her and took in the full picture of her, leaning against the door.

"Did you see it? The video I sent?" Toby looked like she couldn't decide whether she wanted me to have seen the video and ignored it, or missed it entirely.

"I saw it. Drove me crazy for the past five days." Stark honesty was a gamble, but I was willing to pull out as many stops as I had to if it would make Toby less likely to kill me. Or worse, call off our whole arrangement.

"So why didn't you—"

"Because my phone took a nose dive into the runoff drain."

Toby stood and took a slow, tentative step forward, like she wanted to touch me but was afraid of me at the same time. She didn't say a word.

"I was insanely busy the day I got back, and then the next day, when I got to the phone place, they couldn't get me a new one for at least another twenty-four hours. I sent you an email, and then I texted you, but..."

"I never check my email," she said softly. Her lips only moved a tiny bit with the words, like they'd suddenly gone numb. "And I rage-blocked you, like, a day after you didn't respond to the video," she finished, sounding sheepish.

"Right," I said on an exhale, begging her with my eyes to forgive me.

"So, the only reason you didn't reply was..."

"Because of the phone, yeah. I swear to God, Toby, it was a crazy busy night at work but that video was so fucking hot that I still seriously considered saying fuck it all and coming to your place, but then I..." I completely lost my train of thought when I realized that her eyes were fixed on my mouth as it moved.

In the next second, she murmured, "Shut up", fisted my sweater in her hands, pressed her body up against mine, and hauled my mouth to hers. Her lips were frantic but firm, molding mine to her will. Her tongue darted into my mouth and teasingly ran along the underside of mine, only pulling back when she sucked my bottom lip, biting down slightly.

She pulled away and murmured, "I thought you weren't interested" against my lips. "In seeing me naked."

"What do you think now?" I teased, gently kissing her again and running my tongue along the inside of her lower lip.

She let loose a very satisfying groan, and I decided I didn't really need to hear her response. I'd much rather be kissing her. But I wanted to make sure the door was locked while I did. I slid my hand down to her hip, thrilling at the way my thumb notched just-so over the bone jutting out ever so slightly there. It was like we were made to be together, to be doing this. I craned my neck a couple feet over toward the door, and Toby started trailing hot, open-mouthed kisses down my throat, latching onto the spot where my shoulder met my neck and nipping with her teeth. I couldn't keep my hips from jerking forward against hers, and as I reached over to twist the lock shut, she pushed up on her tiptoes, smacking a hard kiss on my mouth with a satisfied grin. Then she hauled me to the side, spinning around so that I was the one pressed up against the wall...right into the light switch.

In half a second, we were plunged into darkness, the only sign of the world outside this room the thin crack of dim light reaching in from the hallway. I was all sensation, and hungry for more.

I pulled away, thrilling in the heavy breaths exchanged in the sliver of air between us.

"Sorry, sorry," I mumbled, kind of glad that she couldn't see the goofy smile spreading across my face at the sudden, forceful realization of how much she wanted me. *Me.* "I'll get the light."

"No," Toby murmured, sliding her hands up my shirt, skimming her fingertips along my lower back and grabbing hard, digging her nails in just under the waist band of my jeans. "I like it like this."

I would have told her how badly I wanted to just look at her after missing her the whole week. I would have reminded her that we only had about twenty-eight minutes until we needed to have our asses in seats to record this week's show. But before I could even get a syllable out, her mouth was on mine again and her hot palms had moved back around to my abs—slightly sore from the extra crunches I'd done this week—and then her nails clicked against the button on the front of my jeans. She brushed one gentle kiss against my lips and then I felt a soft whoosh of air and the loss of her warmth against my chest.

It took my feeble, lust-clouded brain a second to realize she'd gone down on her knees and started tugging on my zipper.

The hot, moist air rushing against the front of my boxers told me that she was doing it with her teeth.

"God almighty," I growled, letting my head clunk against the cinderblock wall.

"Is this okay?" she murmured, clearly not caring about my answer that much, because her thumbs were working their way into my waist band and tugging. Then I was bare-assed with my dick about to poke her in the face, begging for her, and I must have been dreaming because the next thing I knew, she was cupping my balls in one hand and licking a slow trail up the underside of my shaft, following it with the other hand.

"Yeah, I just..." *Please don't let this be the moment my voice cracks or I forget my words.* "I just don't know what to do with my hands," I finished.

She gave a soft chuckle before enveloping the head of my dick between her lips, flicking her tongue against the slit. Holy shit. I had no hope of lasting. She reached up for my hands, and then placed them gently at the back of her head so my fingers threaded through her hair. The feel of strands slipping through my fingers while her mouth took even more of me in, sucking and licking and gliding, was going to put me over the edge in a minute. If I was lucky, it wouldn't be before that.

"God, Toby, I - *ungghh*." I couldn't control the sounds coming out of my mouth or the jerk of my hips. I felt like such an animal, standing here while she took me like this, loving it so much. Every time she slid her lips over my cock, she hummed like she'd never savored anything more than the taste of me sliding over her tongue, and every time she pulled off, she gave a little suck, then a soft sigh, blowing warm air over the wetness and setting every nerve on edge.

"Toby, this is...I mean...I am not gonna last."

For whatever reason, all this did was make her movements, syncopated between mouth and hands, faster, harder, wetter, hotter. I groaned, pulling a hand from where her hair had woven through my fingers and biting down on a knuckle. A deep rumble came from her throat, and a thrill rushed through me—did she like that I'd pulled her hair? Had I even done it right? Holy shit. I had never felt this close to coming this hard before in my life. Once again, Toby Eisen was taking me completely by surprise, turning every sensibility I had about dating and sex and what felt good and the right order for doing things and turned it completely on its head.

And I loved it.

"I'm not gonna last," I repeated as she concentrated her efforts on flicking her tongue against my slit, then taking me in deep.

When she popped off again, she giggled. "Oh, Mark. You're not supposed to."

Oh. *Oh*.

"Just let go. Come for me."

She licked the underside of my shaft once more, then pumped her hand up and down my slick length while sucking hard at the tip. Her hot mouth was vibrating all around me, devouring me, setting me on fire, making me explode.

I banged my head against the cinderblock wall, hoping the pain would distract me from making the ungodly noise hovering in my throat, begging to be let loose. I managed to push it down into my belly, and when I finally came in long, hard spurts down her throat, it sounded more like a deep rumble instead of the shout that had been threatening.

Toby, angel that she was, pulled away a few seconds later, but kept breathing that delicious hot breath of hers over me, still teasing my balls with gentle strokes of her fingertips.

For my part, I was still trying to tame my breaths into any sort of a normal rhythm.

"Okay?" she murmured while gently tugging my boxers

back up over my ass and tucking me back inside. I'd mercifully picked some of my softest today, which offset the sensitivity that I was sure would take forever to wear off.

"That was...you are...I just never—"

"Never what?" Her voice was teasing, but guarded. Tentative. She'd just brought me more pleasure with just her mouth and hands than Kylie ever had in a skin-on-skin lovemaking session, but she was worried I hadn't liked it.

"Nobody has ever done that to me—*for* me—before."

She drew back and smacked me on the chest with her palm. I grunted. "Stop that. You're lying."

"I swear to God. My last girlfriend apologized a few times, but she just...didn't do that. I mean, not the whole thing. I mean..." There was more to the story, but I really didn't want to have a conversation with the sexiest woman I'd ever laid lips on, and, oh my *God*, who'd ever laid lips on me, about a really bad trip my ex had to the orthodontist. Or at least, that was how she'd always explained it.

"Honestly, I was always sort of relieved? Because I was worried about teeth?" I was overwhelmed with affection for her in that moment, for her brilliant mouth, so much so that I reached out, cupped her face in my hands, and laid a firm kiss on her mouth.

She just laughed. "I'm kind of glad you didn't tell me. I would have been worried I'd mess up your first time," she said in a low, sexy voice just before nipping at my bottom lip again, then trailing kisses over to my ear. Holy shit, if she kept this up, I'd be hard and ready to go again with plenty of time to spare before the show. Maybe...

"Too bad we have a show to tape," she whispered in my ear, and her warm breath eddying there gave me a full body shiver. She tugged my shirt down, well past my waistband, and snuck her hands down to give my ass one more squeeze. "I like this," she said. "And these abs...not too shabby. Not at all."

Score one, Couch to 5k.

"But most of all, I like this," she said, moving her lips back to mine and sliding her tongue languidly into my mouth. I could still taste traces of myself in her mouth, and holy shit, I was already reliving the past several minutes in the blessed quiet of this old store room. I was stuck between wanting this kiss to last forever and wanting to kiss her harder, faster, *more.*

Toby pulled back just enough to utter, "I've been dreaming about your mouth, on *my* body. And using my hands is no good substitute."

I groaned again, seconds away from saying fuck the show and taking her right here, in the dark, against the wall, hoping Ethan hadn't stolen the condom from my wallet sometime in the last few months.

But before I could make the next move, she brushed one more kiss against my lips, so light it could have been our first. A question waiting for an answer, an offer of more to come.

Honestly, that was what I really wanted from Toby. I wanted more, not faster. I wanted deeper, not a relationship filled with one-off encounters skimmed off the top of real life.

As amazing as those encounters might be, I wanted more than that.

She pulled away from me and twisted the door handle. A swath of light flooded the room, and she stepped out, sticking her head back in only to say, "Wait three minutes to go in. Break a leg in there."

I tried to reply, but it ended up just a mess of stuttered syllables.

The next three hours were going to kill me.

CHAPTER 19

TOBY

THE POINT of giving Mark a blow job was to make him want more—ruffle his feathers a little bit, make him squirm during the recording of the show, and hopefully follow my lead like the sweet puppy dog he was.

It was crazy how two things I assumed to be true for a decade could just be turned on their head in a couple minutes of sucking a guy's dick. First, that blow jobs were foreplay for guys, a lead-up to the main event, something that would have any guy desperate to have his dick inside me. But, when I settled myself in the control chair on the opposite side of the studio glass, he looked completely sated, like he'd eaten a turkey dinner and was totally content sitting there, basking in the afterglow. Not only that, but he was looking at me with the biggest heart eyes I'd ever seen on a guy.

Okay. That was not the desired effect.

Heart eyes were not the same as hungry eyes. I'd seen enough of both from a variety of guys over the years to be able to tell the difference.

My other lifelong assumption that had been turned completely on its head was, at least, exciting instead of stressful.

I'd always loathed giving blow jobs. First, guys usually felt like they were entitled to them, like they were the king and of course I would want the opportunity to kiss their scepter, so to speak. There was the guy who enthusiastically fucked your mouth and held your head in place while he came. Gross and a little scary. There was the guy who dirty-talked the whole time, which wasn't always awful but usually went bad for me as soon as he decided to call me a "little slut" or "bitch", which happened more often than you might think. And then there was the guy who whined and yelped his way through the whole experience. If was going to suck dick, I wanted to feel like I was doing something sexy, not milking a goddamn goat.

I had literally never given a blow job to a guy who didn't do at least one of those things. And yet, Mark...he hadn't. Not a one. He'd been responsive and respectful, a little tender. The sounds he made were *so* manly. God, I wished I'd recorded the grunts, groans, and growls so I could listen to them again in the dark privacy of my own bedroom. Not to mention that his dick was inarguably larger than average and even smelled kind of nice.

And so, having my tongue all over it wasn't a chore. In fact— and here was the most shocking part—it was a turn-on.

The awful net result of all this was that I spent the next three hours behind the glass watching him shoot the shit with Ethan and obsessing over how I wanted to do it again. As awful as it was to admit, I barely registered half of what the guys were saying. Yeah, I saw Ethan clap Mark on the back and Mark's cheeks turn red as he brushed off whatever mortifying thing Ethan said, but that was de rigueur for these two.

What was not typical was how badly I wanted to blow Mark again. I wanted to see what would happen if I lightly scratched his balls while I sucked, or told him to grab my hair harder. I wanted to see what would happen if I only used my hand and bit down on his neck at the same time, in that spot right under his ear that drove him nuts. I wanted to hear the sound of him coming again, especially, knowing I'd made him feel that good.

And thinking about all that only made me so wet that my panties clung annoyingly between my legs. That just made me think about how I wanted Mark to help me peel them off. With his teeth.

"Toby? Earth to Toby?"

I blinked, hard, and turned my head to Shari, who was tapping the desk in front of me impatiently with the flat of her fingers.

"Hey. Adjust your monitor. This song he's playing sounds like it was recorded on a fucked-up amplifier. If we record the show with it sounding like this, we're either gonna have to go back and do it again or lose a shit ton of listeners because you're daydreaming. Remember, you can always add more reverb or fuzz later but it's a lot harder to take it out after the fact."

"Sorry, Shari. I'm sorry." I scrambled to adjust the controls, commanding my hands to stay steady. It wasn't my headset that needed adjusting so much as my brain. For the first time I was grateful I hadn't spent the week rolling between the sheets with Mark. Instead, I'd done my homework on this internship, reading and re-reading articles and manuals for the studio's equipment. I'd found a couple sites that helped me virtually manipulate the sound boards and the final output. I was quick on the draw, changing the sound this time so that the slight tinge of nails-on-a-chalkboard that was present in the band's electric guitar melted away into something much easier on the ears.

As the minutes ticked by, I was able to focus a little bit more. Instead of drooling over Mark, I was taking advantage of the unique situation of just watching him, observing every little thing he did that it might take me months to catalog if we were just casually dating.

But then, I never casually dated anyone. Every single guy I'd ever dated had a purpose.

What was the point of dating Mark, again? What was he *giving* me?

A chance to piss off your parents, that's what.

Right. It was convenient, that was for sure, with the annual non-negotiable pilgrimage to my parents' holy land, California, for Passover.

Plus, it was the first time I'd ever dated someone I just couldn't pin down my attraction to. That had to be worth something, right? Dating Mark, getting him into bed with me, whenever *that* happened, would teach me something about how to recognize what I found attractive. Now I knew that it was something that couldn't be encapsulated in physical features, a style of dress, or specific hobbies.

Like the way Mark caught my gaze through the studio glass, holding it for a second longer than a casual acquaintance would have, and letting one eyebrow twitch up before he looked away, a small smile tugging at the corners of his lips. I couldn't figure out what he was thinking, and where that once would have annoyed the hell out of me, when it came to Mark, I just wanted more.

I snapped out of my stupor again when that dumb song Ethan had mastered about Whiz Kid Mark Mahler looking for a girlfriend blasted through the studio. Between the first time we met and just a few hours ago, Mark and I had spent enough time together to fill so much more than his allotted eight minutes for the week.

"Week two, dude? Any experiences you'd like to share with us?

"I just want to take issue with the basic premise of this

segment, man." Mark tried to make his voice sound nonchalant and weary, but both Ethan and I knew that this was part of the persona, the guy-talk baiting that would drive this particular part of the show.

Ethan leaned in. "You take issue with me and, indeed, Greater Philadelphia encouraging you to join the world of twenty-something red-blooded American males? What is it, Mark? Do you not *want* to get laid?"

I looked at Mark through the glass with my eyebrows high, a barely suppressed smile on my face. His mouth gaped and then shut again. I snorted.

"I just take issue with the idea that I need your help getting a date."

"Bro, the song specifically states 'girlfriend'. This isn't about hooking you up with dates. As dense as you are, I'm pretty sure even you could work one of those swipe-left dating apps."

Mark groaned theatrically. "Well, whatever. I don't have a girlfriend yet, but I do have something new to report for week two. Unfortunately for you guys, but excellent for my embarrassment levels, it involved yoga." He leaned in and lowered his voice on that last word, prompting Ethan to hover his finger over some of the sound buttons.

"Is that like secret yoga, or sexy yoga, or...?"

Mark leaned back in his seat and cracked his knuckles. Was he seriously nervous to be talking about this? That was...well, kind of adorable.

"It felt a little secret, since we were the only ones in the studio, and yeah, it was sexy. To say the least."

Ethan blew out a long, low whistle. "Bro. Didn't you say she planned the date?"

Mark nodded, stretching his fingers out, like a peacock displaying its feathers. I pictured them digging into my ribs, twisting in my hair, sliding into my—Dammit. There I went again.

Mark was giving the play-by-play of our yoga class, describing our initial half-undressing, then the poses Lisa put us into. I could swear his voice was getting lower with each phrase that passed his lips.

Ethan made a big deal out of fake-fanning himself, which made me roll my eyes. Half the time it was like he didn't even realize none of the listeners could see him. "Sounds, like... primal, or something."

Mark chuckled. "Yeah. We started calling it 'Lion King Yoga'. Part of me wouldn't have been surprised if we'd opened our eyes and we were sitting there, straddling each other in the middle of the waving Saharan grasses. At sunset."

I snorted. His assessment wasn't off.

"Toby!" Ethan called, and I immediately snapped to attention. I piped my voice in. "Yeah?" My heart was beating a mile a minute. Was he going to call me out, right here on the show, live, as being Mark's yoga girl?

"Toby, we've gotta get that sound on my grid. You know the one. At the beginning of the lion movie?"

Relief rushed through me. "On it, bro," I said, hoping my voice wasn't shaking. I scribbled the note to myself and then caught Mark's eye. He was watching me, giving me a soft, beatific smile. Just like that, I felt centered. Calmer.

"Well, that sounds like an excellent date. And because I know you are not the one to kiss and tell, or, you know—something else and tell—I won't ask any questions about the end of the date. Not that we would ever object to hearing about it. Respectfully, of course."

Mark cleared his throat. "Of course, of course. I walked her back to her place, I think there was a little kiss, and then I headed back to mine."

"You *think* there was a little kiss? Okay, man. I mean, this girl sounds pretty hypnotic and all, so I guess if you want to pretend not to remember every time you kissed her, I will pretend to believe you."

Mark just laughed.

"Well, our eight minutes for this segment has nearly run out, so I'll just remind our listeners that this is a weekly segment, and that next week, we've been approved for three more minutes and taking some calls from our listeners!"

Mark caught my eye again. "And I will make sure to get the info on that particular yoga studio up on our show site so you can navigate there right now and check it out. Wonder how many Philadelphians are up for a little Lion King yoga?"

"Indeed, bro. Thank you so much for working so hard for the cause."

Mark blushed red, adorably, which made me laugh. It was contagious, apparently, and "Whiz Kid Mark Mahler" played over the sounds of The Bro Show bros cracking up.

I sat back in my chair, satisfied. Yeah, it was a little weird being the secret subject of a quasi-experiment for the show I was working on, but mostly, I felt surrounded by warmth, acceptance, pride for something I'd fast become a part of. It was almost like family.

And only the teeny tiniest bit like love.

CHAPTER 20

MARK

RECORDING a whole show without distraction had never once been a problem for me—that is, until I had to spend a whole recording session looking at Toby Eisen without a single chance to stop and tug her into my arms, stroke her hair, kiss her.

And this week, after she'd literally been kneeling in front of me just minutes before start time? Well, this was torture.

I was basically jumping out of my skin, dying to touch her, by the time the four of us had confirmed our schedules for the coming week. The next few days would be rough; I already had a full calendar, post-Grammys, and I was hoping to add a couple open mic nights into my schedule. I had a solid handful of EDM acts to scout, too many DJs to count. The sounds of Electronic Dance Music were what had made me so passionate about music to begin with. They blended my original fascination with the technicalities of music—the same thing that made Toby love engineering, probably—with the feelings that music brought out in me. It sounded ridiculous, but that kind of music made me feel grounded, connected to something indescribable. EDM felt like it moved with some pulse of the universe that I could only faintly hear when I was listening.

Some people meditated or prayed. I listened.

But as a talent manager, I wanted to have a big footprint in Philly, understand the market of the entire city and expand my business with more agents to help more artists get their start.

It was a big goal, but dammit, I loved music. All of it. Managing promising new artists felt like the best way for me to help keep it alive and thriving in a world where most people listened in isolation, remotely, away from the artists.

"So, Mark, I want you to find a time to meet up with Toby to go over the specs for the tracks you're including on the Fresh Tracks Friday segment for next week. She should have a chance to be prepared. This week's slip-up is on us for not introducing her to the music beforehand."

I snuck a glance at Toby with guilt rushing through me. Shari was right. Toby was learning a lot from the show, most importantly how to manipulate the output to make each song sound its best on air. I scanned her face, expecting her to look embarrassed, or even angry, but instead, she nodded enthusiastically while scribbling notes.

"Mark, I'd love to go over the final output with you for the second and last tracks we played today."

The stress of adding that to my schedule for the week, not to mention sitting across from Toby and hashing out optimal equalizations for all the tracks without wanting to spread her across the studio sound table, felt overwhelming for half a second, until I realized I had a way to make this into excellent date material.

We left the studio together, waiting until Shari was ensconced in her office and only letting ourselves walk close to each other once we'd cleared a couple blocks, making sure nobody would see us. I stayed quiet, wondering if Toby was going to ask about Ethan's idiot comment early in the show. He'd wanted to know whether I was going to use this weekend's big win to find new girls to date, and I told him I wanted to know if he was ever going to learn to keep his big damn mouth shut. After a short tussle and a sharp look from me, Ethan changed the subject. I'd told him and Shari that I didn't want the whole Grammy thing to be mentioned on the air, or to change anything. I still had a ton of work to do to make this management company into a livelihood. Maybe it was my mother's superstitious genes, but I didn't want to jinx anything.

But Toby didn't ask, and I didn't offer to talk about it. Sure, I was proud of my client's Grammy, but I was more interested in simply being with her than in talking about myself.

A block from Toby's apartment, a gust of wind swept over us, knocking her into my side and sending her hair flying into both of our mouths.

"Oh my God," she gasped, and quickly set to work pulling the strands off my face, gingerly extracting them from between the teeth of my jacket. "I am so sorry. I need to control this mess a little better."

"I hope you don't." I laughed, pulling a few strands away from my face, where they'd gotten caught in the stubble. "I love your hair."

Toby's laughing faded away in just a breath, and her eyebrows curved up over sparkling dark eyes in the most affectionate expression I'd ever seen on her face. "Yeah?"

"Yeah," I said quietly.

The smile she gave me in return was something I'd never forget. Genuine, but relaxed. Safe. Content.

I reached down and threaded our fingers together as we crossed the street. Her apartment was in view. Even though we'd only done this a few times, this part always made me nervous. I'd never been able to predict her behavior before, but for some reason, I really didn't want it to take me by surprise today. So I spoke first.

"I have a plan for a date this week. If...uh...if that's something you still want to do."

One side of Toby's mouth quirked up. "Do you think I want to?"

I stammered for half a second before she squeezed my hand. "Think about what we were doing before the show, Mark."

Oh, hell. I'd be thinking about *that* until the day I died.

"I really, really enjoyed myself," she offered. "Really enjoyed you."

All I could do was gape at her.

"So, yes. I absolutely want another date." She dropped my hand, took a step toward her front steps. "How soon can we do it?"

I shook my head, knocking myself out of my daze. "Can we do...?"

"The date?" Toby giggled.

"As soon as possible. Tomorrow. One o'clock?" I managed. I really wanted to ask if tonight was a possibility.

"Okay. Tomorrow. Text me?" She gave me a warm smile and bounced up the steps. No hug, no kiss, no acknowledgement that she had just basically won the medal in blue-balling. To have her mouth on my cock before the show, and then to not even let me taste her lips after? Ridiculous. This woman was a torturer. Maybe she worked for the CIA in her spare time. Hell, it'd make sense after the way she'd managed to completely confuse and disarm me in just a couple of weeks.

"Uh, yeah," I said, fumbling for my phone. If the idea I had to impress Toby, and our listeners, was going to happen tomorrow, I had to start getting in touch with my contacts now. I ran through some of the logistics in my head. "It'll be daytime, though. One o'clock? You up for it?"

I heard the scrape of her key against the door, the grind and twist it made in the lock. Toby put one foot over the threshold, then threw me another smile over her shoulder. "You're in charge. Whatever you say."

Then, she was inside. Without a suggestion that she'd ever been making advances on me just a few hours ago.

Yeah, she was definitely a torture-specializing super spy.

And I was in really big trouble.

CHAPTER 21

TOBY

LEAVING Mark on the sidewalk outside my apartment nearly killed me. Even as I crossed over the threshold, I was imagining what he might be doing to me if I'd pulled him up the stairs—dragging his tongue over my collarbone, dipping his long fingers past the waistband of my jeans, bending down to pull my heels off and letting his palms skim the soles of my feet. God, a shiver ran down my spine, reverberating against my shoulder blades. If just thinking about him could do that to me....

Whatever. I was sure he was just an itch I needed to scratch. A bad itch, but just an itch. Obviously, he was. It didn't matter that I felt all warm and fuzzy when I was around him, that I sort of adored the way he looked at me like I was more fascinating than a shooting star, and even more rare. Mark Mahler was a mess, albeit a newly well-groomed one. He couldn't even decorate his own apartment, for God's sake, and he'd been far too dependent on a girlfriend for far too many years for me to even want to get close to stepping into that role, however briefly.

And falling in love with him was absolutely, positively out of the question.

I ignored my itchy texting finger and rooted around in my cabinets for any semblance of anything I could make into dinner. I'd played the foodie with Marcus, but hadn't really learned anything more substantive about cooking from him, I now realized, other than how to make eggs six ways. He'd insisted eggs were the most basic of cooking lessons. I'd wanted the most basic of relationships with him, it turned out, and only made it through the lesson on eggs.

That explained why I'd cooked them for myself twice this week and called for delivery the rest of the time.

I sighed as I hung up my bag and took my shoes to my closet, settling them back into their designated shoe box. I wove my hair into a braid and leaned over my sink to scrub the makeup off my face, wiping the sink dry with a towel after I did. I took a deep breath, letting it out slowly. There was a quiet satisfaction in knowing, just for a moment, that my life was in order, and everything was in place. The place designed by me, that was dependent on nobody else. I headed to the kitchen and stood on tiptoes to grab the binder where I kept my takeout menus.

I didn't really have to look up the number for Pu Pu Hot Pot; I'd ordered from them six days ago, and their number was in my phone. Didn't really need to look at the menu, either, but somehow the action of flipping to the plastic-sleeved page and running my finger over the phone number made this all feel more intentional, more centered. More adult. I was in control of my feelings, my identity, my life. Not anyone else. Certainly not Mark Mahler.

"Pu Pu Hot Pot, what's your phone number please?"

I rattled off my number and listened as the guy tapped it into his system. "Oh, hey, Toby," he said brightly. "Beef and broccoli, right?"

"I don't...it's not...what?"

"I'm sorry, Miss, it's just that that's all you've ever ordered from us."

Silence stretched over the line for a couple agonizing seconds. Mr. PuPu Hot Pot cleared his throat. "Should I put the order in, then, Miss?"

I sighed. "Yes, please."

I traipsed into my living room and slumped onto the sofa, no reading material, phone, or TV remote in hand. This was just pathetic. Nothing to do but wait for my Chinese food and, I seriously hoped, the return to my normal self.

Mark was turning my life upside down, and as much as I hated him for it, I really just couldn't wait to see him again.

Dammit.

It turned out that the angst over Mark, an order of beef and broccoli, and one (or two or three) glasses of wine was a deadly combination for me. I woke up with my neck at an awkward angle against the arm of the couch, my face smooshed to the side, and drool trickling down my chin. My underwire dug into the spot where my boob met my rib, and my waistband rubbed uncomfortably against my hipbone. My temples pounded my heartbeat, sending reverberations through my brain.

Holy shit. When had two—okay, three, pretty large—glasses of wine become too much for me to handle?

Maybe when I'd hit twenty-five and grown up. Dammit. This must be the beginning of my descent into old lady territory, when I couldn't handle a night of moderate drinking in my own home.

My phone buzzed insistently, skittering a millimeter across my polished coffee table. I blinked, hard, trying to clear the film over my eyes, then dragged myself to sitting. After a couple seconds trying to adjust my bra so it didn't dig into my skin proved useless, so I just took the thing off, threading it through the short sleeve of my tshirt and letting it drop on the couch. Annoyed at how sloppy it looked, I kicked it to the floor.

Well, that wasn't any better.

It was a text from Mark, letting him know he'd pick me up at one. Which was...oh shit. In fifteen minutes.

How in the world had I slept so hard, so long, in that position? I shook my head to clear it and hurried to my closet. I flicked through the clothes on hangers for a couple seconds,

I tugged on some skinny jeans, then a black camisole to give a little bit of support in place of the bra I would most certainly not be wearing. My breasts were small enough that it wouldn't hurt, and they needed a break. Over that, I layered a cotton tank with fat gold sequins laid like scales all over the front, which was playful, a little fancy, and pretty comfortable all at once, topped with a tailored dark denim jacket. My red-soled black stilettos from yesterday went back on; they were comfortable enough, and I was willing to bet that the wet chill to the air would keep Mark from dragging me through the city on foot.

I didn't have time to curl and volumize my hair like I would have liked, but the braid would be okay with this outfit. I quickly re-wove it, telling myself that the slight messiness of the plait looked sensual, like I just got out of bed.

Yes. Making Mark think of me in bed in as many ways as possible could only help. I was just swiping on some mascara when my phone buzzed again.

Mark: I hope you're ready. We can't be late.

I smiled appreciatively. I liked the little bit of tease factor he had going on. Liked it a lot.

. . .

Me: Are you here?
Mark: Yep. Meet me downstairs.

I stuck an arm in my closet and grabbed the first bag my fingers touched, tossing a tube of lipstick and another of mascara in, along with a couple condoms from my bedside table.

Hey, maybe confidence would take me places today.

Excitement ran through me in a palpable electric buzz as I locked up the house.

I took a deep breath and centered myself before opening the front door of the building. I didn't want to look completely beside myself with excitement to see him.

Even if I really, really was.

There he was, on the sidewalk, face upturned to the door, patiently, gorgeously waiting for me.

Yes, he looked incredible. His dark jeans were expertly cut, slung in exactly the spot on his waist that made me want to unfasten them just so I could see more. His full-zip hooded sweater hugged his shoulders and fit snug to his torso, making me want to snuggle into him and tear it off his body all at once.

God, this was a confusing flurry of emotions. What could I do when he showed up here looking so delicious, with that adorable half-excited, half-shy smile on his face?

But instead of throwing my arms around his neck, jumping on him, wrapping my legs around his waist, and begging him to take me inside, I just slipped my hand into his and returned the smile. I'd promised him this date and he, apparently, had something very specific in mind.

Mark tugged on my hand gently, guiding me down the sidewalk. "It's not a far walk," he said, his eyes slipping down to my heels. "Just a couple blocks."

We walked quietly into the heart of Philadelphia. I used my free hand to pull my jacket closed, trying to tamp down the stubborn shiver working its way through my body. But he noticed. Of course he did. Mark's arm wound around my shoulders and pulled me close to him. He seemed to notice everything about me.

Out of all the guys I'd dated, that was new. The thought made a whole different kind of shiver, gentle and delicious, race down my spine.

We passed the Academy of Music, then the Wilma theater, until the grand windowed arch of the Kimmel Center curved up through the sky.

"C'mon," Mark murmured, leading me down a side street and then turning us into an alley.

We came to a large door with a key code panel, and Mark dropped my hand to pull up a note on his phone. My eyes widened as I realized where this door led.

The Kimmel center was gorgeous inside, with huge arching ceilings and intricate designs. I'd only been inside once, for a symphony concert Liz dragged me to when Jordan got a stomach bug and couldn't use his ticket.

I loved the orchestra, but I had been totally awed by that hall.

He punched in a series of numbers, the panel beeped...and then flashed red.

Mark cursed and tugged on the door, which remained shut. He typed in the numbers again.

He cursed again, pulling up a text window. "Hold on, I just...my buddy must have typed the numbers wrong." He sent off the text and gave me an apologetic smile.

We stood there, the wind tunneling itself through the dark alley, for a couple awkward seconds, and I shivered again.

"Oh, Tobes," Mark murmured, frowning slightly. "Here, take my—"

I waved my hand at him. "Absolutely not. No. You'll freeze." His forehead was so adorable crinkled up in concern like that. I laughed, stepping slowly toward him so he eventually backed up against the alley's brick wall. My fingers reached up and flicked the zipper of his sweater. "I could just..." I said in a low voice as I tugged the zipper down, then plunged my arms inside the thick knitted fabric, sighing as my arms found their spot around his waist. I leaned into him, loving how my heels put my eyes just an inch below his. "That's better," I said against his ear.

He stiffened and let the briefest of groans escape.

"This is nice, isn't it?" I whispered.

"Yeah, but..." He turned his head, checking his phone again. "Of course he's not answering."

Mark's little growl of frustration when he cursed was seriously doing things to me. I wanted to press my body against his, without our clothing in the way. I wanted to make him growl in pleasure instead.

"I've seen the hall. It's absolutely stunning. Looks like the inside of a cello, great acoustics. Whatever."

"But I had this whole...plan." His bottom lip pushed out into the smallest pout, and his eyebrows pulled together. He looked so adorable it made me want to get even closer to him.

It was kind of sweet of him to be so stressed about what apparently would have been a very charming date, but I didn't have much patience for that when the freshly-shaven smoothness of his chin brushed so alluringly against my cheekbone, kicking up the smell of his aftershave and filling my senses with a heady cloud of the woodsy scent.

"We could make a new plan," I said, letting one hand drift to his waistband, teasing up and down the seam running between his ass cheeks. "Maybe at your place?"

Mark laughed, low and sexy, then pushed himself off the wall and standing me up and slightly away from him when he did. "You are persistent," he said, gently pulling my arms out from around him and slipping his hand in mine again.

"Is it working?" I asked, trying to keep the tinge of disappointment out of my voice.

"You know, if it was at all possible for me to reschedule this...but my buddy works sound crew here. Says it's only empty for a few hours on Saturdays. And I had a whole plan..." he repeated.

I couldn't help it. I let out a soft laugh.

His lower lip puffed out a little more and hell if I didn't just want to nip at it. Mark's eyes rolled up to the sky for a moment while he shifted from one foot to the other, like he could somehow find an answer to the problem in the gray clouds. Another gust of wind swept through the alley, and I shivered again. His lip pushed out more when he frowned at me.

"Now that I think about it...we *could* do this at my place. It won't be as cool, but now Kai owes me. We'll come back another time. Maybe he'll get us tickets to something."

God, that sweet frown. It was making him look more delectable with every second that ticked by.

I squeezed his hand. "Your place isn't far. I'm freezing. C'mon, let's go warm up."

Mark caught my double meaning right away. "You are relentless, you know," he said with a sparkle in his blue eyes, dark as storm clouds in the shaded alley.

"That is correct," I said, my chest flooding with warmth.

The walk was short, but filled with easy chatter. Mark had been flooded with work last night, he said, which made me a little embarrassed to describe my night to him. I didn't feel like I needed to leave anything out or elaborate, though. I felt his acceptance of me and my ridiculousness even as I said the words "Pu Pu Hot Pot" and "third glass of wine ."

"You know, I never pictured you as the kind of girl who would eat out of paper boxes or crash on the couch."

I gave him a shaky smile. Neither had I.

CHAPTER 22

MARK

BEFORE I LEFT for our date, I'd told myself I wasn't going to let myself glide my hands over Toby's warm, smooth skin until I'd made her feel something non-physical first. Anything that would connect us on more than a physical level, in a way she couldn't deny.

Why I insisted on torturing myself was a mystery, but the fact that I wanted to see her face light up or tears spring to her eyes before I let myself taste her was a sure thing. I couldn't describe the need, but I knew it was swirling in my gut, sure as I knew my own name.

We didn't talk much as we walked up the stairs. I had to admit, I was a little nervous about sharing this particular aspect of my geekiness with Toby. But she told me she'd gone through a music festival phase in her undergrad years, so I thought she might put up with trusting me for a few minutes.

A shiver went down my spine, watching her step over the threshold of my place and waiting inside for me. I shut the door behind us, looked at her, took a deep breath, and gently placed my hands on her shoulders. I leaned in, placing a kiss on the tip of her nose, and the soft smile she gave me almost froze me in place. But I fought the desire to kiss more of her, letting my palms smooth down over her upper arms and stepping back. "Give me a minute, okay?" I murmured.

She just nodded, her brow wrinkling in a slight moment of confusion.

I crossed to the other end of the room, smiling at the butterfly painting she'd admired the first time she'd come to my place. Hannah had approved the butterflies from Ikea, and I'd wanted an acoustic panel hanging there. It was really the only way to make the room suitable for listening at all. Luckily for me, I had the best sister in the universe. As a "breakup gift," she'd found a company that could print anything on an acoustic panel, making even the biggest sound geeks' rooms look like normal human living spaces.

I went over and tapped it with one knuckle, smiling over my shoulder at her.

"Do you remember that I told you this is an acoustic panel?"

"Oh! Right. Yeah, I do." Her eyes lit up as she made her way over to it. She gently trailed her fingertips over a small section of its surface, and I couldn't help but imagine my skin in its place. She stepped to the side of the panel, leaning in to examine the surface. "Incredible. I never would have guessed the first time I saw it. What pattern is the foam's surface?"

"Pyramid, I'm pretty sure. That's what I told Hannah to order, anyway."

"That's right. It was a gift from her."

I grinned. "You really do remember."

Toby's head dipped into a nod. "Probably not how the artist would have chosen to have it displayed." The smile hadn't left Toby's lips.

"No, I guess not, but it makes music sound a hell of a lot better. Not like it would at the Kimmel Center, but..."

Toby's teeth had caught her bottom lip, her chin had tilted

down, and she was looking at me with so much mischief in her eyes I nearly burst a capillary. "Are you going to show me?" Her voice had gone low, pitching up at the end as she grinned.

"What kind of a music enthusiast would I be if I didn't?"

"One who just wants to get laid."

"Toby, that's not why I—"

"Mark. Relax. I know. You're the one who's been turning me down, remember?" There was laughter in her eyes, but her voice stayed soft. Patient.

Holy shit. How did she always know exactly how to knock me off center? "Not a very good music enthusiast, though, all the same," I said, cracking my knuckles. "Uh...sit."

I gestured to the couch, but Toby just crossed her arms and scanned the room. "No. Help me move this coffee table."

I raised an eyebrow at her, which made her laugh. "Trust me. Based on where your speakers are, and the location of that acoustic panel...just trust me. I'm the sound engineer here."

I had to give her that. We hauled the coffee table over to the wall, running parallel to the couch. Toby found some blankets and stuffed them under the table, then re-oriented herself to the speakers. She grabbed a pillow from one side of the couch and motioned for me to hand her another, then dropped them in the middle of the floor, side by side. I nodded appreciatively. It was entirely possible that all the times I'd thought I'd been hearing amazing sound in this room were all, more or less, shit.

I made sure my phone was connected to the Bluetooth speakers, then turned them most of the way up—one notch below where they were the last time my neighbors had complained about the excessive sound. I adjusted the equalizer to "classical", pulled up the song I wanted, and dragged the slider on the twenty-three-minute track to ten minutes and nineteen seconds in, exactly, the starting point I knew had the best chance of getting a reaction from her.

If this wasn't a real emotional point of connection between us, nothing would be.

The orchestra played a few largo measures, and then a confident baritone started in on German lyrics.

I settled on the floor next to Toby, who was lying on her back, arms relaxed at her sides, fingers half-curled.

"Opera?"

I scooted close enough to her to hold her hand, interlacing my fingers with hers, at which she hummed with a gentle smile. "Close, but no. Just listen. You'll know what it is soon enough."

The voice warbled for a few bars, weaving in and out through a brisk marching pace, until a chorus of voices joined his. I snuck a glance at her, and watched as her face, which she'd let almost completely relax, reacted to the music, her eyelids fluttering at points, her brows twitching in time to the rhythm at others. Her whole body moved gently to the music as the tempo stepped up a bit, moving into a dropping-off point where a lone oboe introduced a brief slowing point. At exactly thirteen minutes, the strings played the first four notes of one of Beethoven's most famous symphonic melodies, and her lips parted in the smallest gasp of realization.

"Oh!" she whispered, clearly assembling all the musical pieces of what we'd already heard. Then the melody dropped away, back to the spare, patient oboe.

And then, after two breath-holding measures, the entire chorus dropped in with bold, sweeping chords to the allegro portion of Beethoven's ninth choral finale – what most people knew as "Ode to Joy ."

I squeezed my eyes tight as she squeezed my hand, and then opened them, praying I'd see what I was hoping to. My heart swelled and a huge grin broke across my face when I saw tears streaming from Toby's eyes, disappearing into her hairline, her lips parted in a small but breathless smile.

The chorus came to that section's resolution a few seconds later, giving way to more instrumentation that would lead to an even grander choral finish. I turned the volume down a notch every second or two, until the room was utterly quiet.

Toby's eyes drifted open, and when she looked into mine, they still sparkled with tears. "I...did not expect that."

I rolled toward her, propping myself up on my elbow, loving the vantage point of viewing her from above while her breath was slightly quicker than normal. Her breasts pushed up the slightest bit over the edge of her camisole, the sequins gently winking with every intake of air, rhythmically rising in a way that made me absolutely desperate to taste them.

She was an angel. A fascinating, sexy, brilliant creature from heaven.

"Didn't expect it in a good way, or...?" My voice was filled with entirely too much hope. I was an open score before her; I had no idea whether she even cared enough to read me at this point, and I didn't really care. For just this moment, I'd worship her for feeling the music in exactly the same way I did.

"Did you know that there's a scientific reason behind the euphoria of the drop? The tears?"

"Seriously?" I said, my voice soft. I reached out with my free hand to brush at a tear track with my thumb, wanting to touch her but also needing her to keep talking.

"It's, uh..." She cleared her throat and turned to look at me. "It's something you find across every culture's musical tradition. Before every drop, there's a breakdown of rhythm, order, melody, whatever, and then a heavy return to it, all at once. In most cases, it's a solid, heavy instrument, like the bass. Obviously, here, it's the chorus. That's the drop."

I knew what the drop was, but didn't see the point in telling her that. She just lit up inside when she was talking music—no need to interrupt her impromptu lecture. When my DJs played

EDM shows, the attendees lived for the ultimate drop. You could feel the anticipation building throughout any set, and when a DJ got it really right, they were on their way to becoming a legend. "Okay, but why the euphoria?" I felt myself leaning closer to her with each word, wanting to be near her just as much as I wanted to hear what she had to say next.

"So, your brain releases dopamine during the, um, anticipation of the return to the established order of the music. It's waiting for a reward, essentially, just like when you're heading to your favorite donut shop and you're in such a good mood because you have this expectation for how delicious it's going to be. Or when you're with someone you really like, and you're all alone, and you are pretty sure they're going to make a move on you. The whole time you're waiting, it's a natural high. It's tension..."

"And release," I finished. God, she was brilliant. And she was beautiful, but mostly the analytical genius with which she listened, and the emotion that impacted her despite her scientific understanding. Yeah, I loved the music, but I knew damn well that all it took was a flick of her tongue or a flash of her eyes to soak my brain in dopamine. I didn't think I could deny how badly I wanted that reward for very much longer.

Her eyes searched mine, and I swallowed hard.

"Mark," she whispered.

"Yeah?" I choked out.

"If you don't kiss me right this second, I think I might die." Her lower lip trembled in what might have become a smile. I thought I saw another tear leak out of the corner of her eye, but I didn't stop to watch it.

After all, I definitely didn't want Toby to die.

CHAPTER 23

TOBY

HE SWOOPED down on me like a hawk on its prey, and I gasped in relief as his mouth devoured mine. I had no idea I wanted to be *ravaged* by Mark Mahler until this moment. When his fingers wasted no time pushing my shirt up past my ribs, a flash of worry hit me that he'd realize how my heart was thrumming mercilessly at the sudden fullness of his touch.

Then anxiety and relief and every other identifiable emotion fled my thoughts as his thumb flicked my nipple while his tongue tasted the inside of my lower lip.

"Mark," I groaned again, completely aware that it was one of a very few words I even felt capable of saying at the moment.

"I want you," he growled into my mouth, sending a shiver down my spine.

"Yes," I answered breathlessly. I chewed on my lip debating whether to push him onto his back and get to work separating his clothing from that body I wanted so badly to be pressed up against, or to let him have his way with me.

To hell with debates, just take advantage of this while he's so willing. God, he was like a suddenly changed man, mouthing at my neck now with teeth and tongue. I pushed up on my elbow, hoping to stun him for a second so I could tug his shirt off and mess up his hair even more.

How many times had I imagined what his sex-ruffled hair would look like? Finally, I was about to find out. My stomach flipped.

He took my shift as a directive, apparently, and pushed up to kneeling, then standing, stretching his hand down to me. I took it. I would have taken his hand if we were about to jump off a cliff at that moment, just as long as I thought there was a reasonable chance at getting him inside me shortly thereafter.

He tugged me to my feet, then planted his palms on my waist and hoisted me into his arms. My legs went around him and I squirmed against the hardness pressing between my thighs, exactly where I wanted it—but there were too many layers of clothes between us.

Mark stretched his neck up to murmur in my ear. "This living room is right above Mrs. Esposito's living room. If we stay here, I'll never hear the end of it from her."

Oh. So he wanted this to be loud. I was most certainly not going to complain about that. "I'm not gonna argue with moving to the bedroom," I said, grinning.

His hand gripped my ass, his fingers digging in even through my jeans, and fire raced across my skin. If he didn't tear my clothes off soon, I'd die. Thankfully, he was already striding toward the bedroom, and within seconds, he laid me down on his bed. I scooted back and he climbed over me, his eyes glowing with something soft and happy. My heart twisted, and I reached up to grab his neck, pulling him down for a hard, decisive kiss. He responded by dotting kisses on each corner of my mouth, then my chin, then down my neck.

The weight of his body lifted as he kissed his way down my torso, and I whimpered, part from the loss of closeness and part from sheer anticipation.

As I tugged his shirt over his head, I dimly registered his bedding, black and gray, masculine, yet soft and smelling like him. Cedar and something warm. The comforter and sheets were all tangled in the spot where he'd slept last night – only one side of the bed, while the other remained completely untouched.

If his lips weren't feasting on my abdomen, his tongue flicking into my navel, I might have surveyed the rest of his room, looking to judge every damp towel flung to the floor or stray sock stuck to the side of his comforter. His hands went to work at my waistband, though, and it was all I could do to close my eyes and try not to moan too loudly.

I wanted to save that for later.

He tugged my pants down over my hips, chuckling at the resistance he met with the tightness of the fabric against my legs. "You know, I thought I loved these jeans..." He chuckled. "But now I think I'm going to hide them from you. Only elastic pants from here on out."

"Oh yeah?" I managed, breathless. "You think you're gonna pull my pants off again, huh?" I hoped he could hear the teasing in my voice. If someone told me we'd never do this again, I'd hiss and bare claws like a cat. There was no way this one time would ever be enough.

Mark rested his forehead on my hip bone, nuzzling in his nose into the skin right inside. His mouth was so close to my...

"Jesus, Toby, you're not wearing panties?"

In fact, I hated the damn things. Too many lines and too much sticking to places that I'd rather let breathe free. I laughed. "Are you complaining?"

"I want to taste you," he said, stealing my thoughts with a deep voice that melted me at my core. His tongue flicked against my skin as his left arm snaked under my leg, his hand wrapping around my thigh so that he could control my entire bottom half.

My left leg, the one that wasn't pinned in place by Mark's shockingly strong arm, spread wider, like my body was answering his request before I could. I covered my face with my hand. "Okay, but you should know that I've never really..."

Before I could finish my sentence, Mark's mouth was on me, covering my pussy and licking into it like it was a dripping scoop of ice cream on a cone.

The "dripping" part was right, at least.

What I hadn't had a chance to tell him was that I was a freak. I'd never come this way before. Though it felt nice when a guy went down on me, ultimately, the stiff, clit-flicking tongue or the slurping, loose-lipped kisses had never been able to take me all the way. I'd enjoyed a lot of sex in my early twenties, and I assumed that the handful of guys that had tried to make me come with their mouths represented the full menu of skill out there.

I'd assumed wrong. So, so very wrong.

His open mouth suctioned between my legs, licking and tasting, tongue penetrating me and then sweeping up to blanket my clit in warm ecstasy in a slow, sensuous rhythm.

"Mark," I managed with a surprised gasp, my arm flailing to the side and eventually reaching up to tweak my nipple.

He raised his head with one eyebrow quirked. "Yes? Were you going to say something?"

"No. Nothing. Just...continue."

"Yes, ma'am," he replied, lowering his head again with a cocky grin.

The telltale warmth gathering at the tips of my toes meant this man had begun to bring me to orgasm. In no more than a minute.

"Mark, I don't...I don't think I'm going to last."

"You're not supposed to," he murmured against me, and I

couldn't help but grin with the repetition of what I'd said to him in the dark studio storage room yesterday.

He guided his mouth a bit higher, his upper lip cupping around the hood of my clit while his tongue went to work flicking. The wet heat of his lips combined with the insistent rhythm of his tongue on that bundle of nerves had my hips desperate to arch up into him, searching for more, harder, but his grip on me was firm. For a second, I wished that he'd held me with both hands, but then I was infinitely grateful that he hadn't. He teased my slit with one finger, and I tensed just the slightest bit. When he thrust inside me, though, it was like my whole body melted down to surround him, welcoming the invasion, begging for more.

He pulled it out, and I whined desperately until he pushed back in with two fingers this time. My breaths were coming fast, noisy gasps and uncontrollable panting. Every second he was winding me up more, filling me with more and more quivering heat, until I was meeting his mouth with a rocking pelvis. I was completely out of control and I couldn't have cared less. This was beyond anything I'd ever experienced.

And then his fingers, buried deep inside me and teasing me with little half-inch thrusts, crooked up, pressing into my upper wall.

He might as well have pushed an ignition button. Whatever fire had been slowly building inside of me suddenly exploded me, and I screamed at the top of my lungs, an uncontrolled noise that I supposed approximated the pleasure wracking my body, its center Mark's incredible, relentless, beautiful mouth.

I dimly registered his fingers sliding out of me, his mouth still hovering between my thighs, not willing to subject me to the cool air just yet. His lips feathered kisses there as the hand that had held me in place for him gently massaged my skin.

It was the sweetest thing a guy had ever done for me after I'd come. It was gentle, considerate. Almost...loving.

I let my head flop to one side on the pillow, then the other, dazed and slow after every one of my nerves had just been temporarily burned out.

Finally, after several long seconds, Mark slid up so that his body was completely flush with mine, and buried his face in the crook of my neck.

"You taste incredible," he said, his hot breath eddying against my collar bone.

"That's..." I said, still trying to find my words. "I have never heard that before." No man had ever used his mouth on me like that, let alone commented on my taste.

Mark's mouth latched onto my neck, where he sucked long and hard, drawing a light moan out of me. I'd have a mark there tomorrow. I didn't care. The opposite. I liked the idea of having something to remember this by, even if it was a hickey. "You are kidding me," he said when he came up for air. "That is a crime. For a woman as delicious as you to never hear it."

I rolled my neck, pressing my lips to his hair.

"Nobody has ever made me come like that before. With their mouth."

"You are fucking *kidding* me," Mark repeated. Mark raised himself over my body, hovering over me for a second before descending on the other side of my neck.

"I just always got the general sense that it was kind of...yucky. Just sort of like something they had to do."

"Thank you for letting me," he murmured between slow kisses from collarbone to ear and back down again. "I couldn't stop thinking about it, ever since the other day."

Mark's right hand slid down my side, his palm resting on my belly and then moving up to cup my breast. His kisses moved downward, thoroughly worshiping my sternum, then my breastbone, before he latched onto the inside of my breast, sucking hard. He dug his teeth in and I gasped.

"I'm going to have a mark there tomorrow," I murmured.

"Hmmm," he said, his brow furrowed in mock concern. "We'd better stay inside, then." I giggled, but it turned to a moan when he leaned back down to swirl his tongue around my nipple, wrap his lips around it, then suck my breast, hard, into his eager mouth. I'd always hated how small my breasts were, barely a handful for most men I dated, but he made me feel like they were luscious and exactly the right size.

Unthinkingly, I reached down and flicked open the button of his jeans. He grunted, and reached down, tugging them off, kicking wildly.

I laughed, full-throated, luxuriating in the fact that this man had just given me an explosive orgasm with the most skilled mouth and hands I'd ever had on my body, yet he couldn't even get his own jeans off.

"Hey, Miss Eisen," he murmured when he returned from that kerfuffle, devouring my mouth with a long kiss. "No laughing at me. It might hurt my confidence."

"Oh, your confidence should never waver again after what you just did to me," I responded, kissing him softly.

In response, his hand slid down my belly, and I arched into him when he pushed two fingers inside. "Still so wet," he murmured. "So fucking ready for me." His words made me shiver with their eroticism. For all Mark seemed to be a typical guy in every other area of life, he was apparently an expert in the finer points of dirty talk and cunnilingus.

A very pleasant surprise.

He was laid out next to me, completely naked, just as I was, his skin touching mine at every possible point, but still I wanted more. I wanted him over me, inside me, surrounding me. I wanted to wrap myself up in him.

In all the ways I'd ever wanted a man, I'd never wanted one like this. I'd wanted a guy's cock pumping into me, or his mouth on my breast, or my lips wrapped around his dick, occasionally. But I had never wanted all of a man, all at once, like I did now.

I was too lost in him to say any of that, though. Instead, I threaded my fingers in his hair, grabbed on, and pulled his head back an inch so I could look into his eyes. "Mark," I said as firmly as I could. "Please."

He kissed me hard then, and arched his back, pulled his fingers from me to reach into his nightstand drawer. He pulled out a small box of condoms, not even opened, and my heart warmed. How long had it been since he'd done this?

He was suddenly shy, his hands shaking just enough for me to notice as he ripped open the packet and positioned the condom at the head. I glanced down, and even in the dim light, I could tell he was impressively sized. Anticipation made a shiver run right to my belly. His fingers fumbled for a second, and I was suddenly overwhelmed at his sweetness, even as I wanted him buried deep inside me.

"Let me," I murmured before kissing him again, then rolled the condom on with careful fingers. There was a slight curve to him, right up at the end, almost like every vibrator I'd ever seen. This man had been blessed by some sex-god, with a cock the perfect combination of length, girth, and g-spot curve. He was almost good to be true. I licked my lips as he positioned himself over me again.

"Please, Mark," I repeated, and as I said his name, every trace of nervousness I'd seen in his face melted away into something determined. Hungry.

I spread my legs for him and he threaded his arms under mine, gripping my shoulders, pulling my body flush with his, like I was something precious.

Then he slid into me in one slow, strong thrust, and I saw

stars. My legs wrapped around him like they were made to fit there, and I clung to him, something warm bursting through me with each rock of his pelvis against mine. He panted into my hair, gripped at my waist one moment, reached up to wrap his fingers around the nape of my neck in the next.

We moved together like we were one person. When Mark pushed into me, I opened for him. When he pulled back my walls clenched, begging him to come back before he'd even really left. We were completely in sync without exchanging a word, our bodies doing all the talking.

The buzz of orgasmic heat started to build again, but slowly, organically, ebbing and then intensifying with each thrust. Mark was inside me, invading every cell and tissue with care and passion, electrifying my skin with each passing second.

He was moaning now, too, breathless and throatier and more desperate with each passing second, his movements growing harder and faster. His body never lifted away from mine. We were doing this together, not doing this *to* each other. We were taking care of one another, not just chasing our own orgasms.

Mark gripped my hair with one thrust that was harder and deeper than any of the others, and let a deep, feral growl rumble out of his throat. God, that was the sexiest noise I'd ever heard, and like the frequency of it flipped a switch inside me, I clenched around him, letting the heady wave of an orgasm overtake me. Seconds later, Mark's thrusts became fast, frantic.

He came, deep inside me, shouting his pleasure against my shoulder.

Long moments later, when his breathing finally slowed, his body slumped over mine.

"Sorry," he murmured, rolling to the side, sending cool air gusting against my overheated skin. I wanted to tell him so many things—that I loved the way his body felt pressing mine into the mattress, that I didn't care that our skin was sticky with a fine layer of sweat, that in the past half an hour he'd given me the two best orgasms I'd experienced in my entire life.

Happy, warm exhaustion flooded me, pinning me to the mattress, leaving me helpless to do anything but lie there panting and watch as Mark eventually swung his feet to the floor and ambled to the bathroom to dispose of the condom. When he came back, he leaned over me, brushing the hair off my face and leaning down to press a slow relaxed kiss to my mouth. "Here, let me..." He tugged the covers out from under me and cocooned me there, then joined me under the soft, cool sheet.

When his body pressed flush against mine again, a sigh escaped me that felt like relief. Mark's arm looped around my waist and his legs tangled with mine.

My memories, and everything I knew was true about myself, screamed that Toby Eisen did not get under the covers, she loathed snuggling, and she never, ever, ever wished she could stay the night.

Apparently, multiple orgasms—the sexual unicorn I thought only existed in romance novels and much-embellished drunken stories from my college friends—were much more powerful than whatever had kept me from doing this before.

Because this was heaven.

My hands wandered over the muscles of his back sleepily, and he hummed with pleasure when I pressed a kiss to his throat.

"Thank you," I managed, my throat full and tense with an emotion I couldn't identify, before the last of my energy left my body, and I fell into a deep sleep.

The warm tones of the setting sun woke me, piercing through a gap in the cheap curtains Mark had hung in this room. My right eye slammed shut again at the invasion of the bright light, and I turned my face right into the warm flesh of Mark's neck. His arms were draped around me loosely, the top one laying heavy across my shoulder. He'd caged me in.

This had happened to me a few times. I'd woken up bracketed by a guy's arms, bolted to the bed by a heavy thigh stretching over my hip, and felt my breath go short and my chest constrict. There was nothing that made me more panicked than being trapped, both literally and metaphorically, by another person.

But this time, instead of feeling my lungs squeeze, cutting off my air supply, I sensed my heart expanding. The sensation pushed the corners of my mouth into a sleepy smile, allowed a slow breath out of my nose as I nuzzled my face deeper into the crook of Mark's neck.

A low hum rumbled from him, making his throat vibrate against my nose, and the swell in my chest moved up, taking me by surprise.

What the hell? Why in the world was there a lump in my throat? Why were tears gathering in the corners of my eyes, again? He wasn't Beethoven. This was no choral drop from the ninth symphony's fourth movement.

Mark Mahler was just a guy. Just like all the other guys I'd ever slept with.

Oh, stop. You know he's nothing of the sort.

Every instinct told me to get out of bed, throw on some clothes, and get the hell out of there.

But something different, something stronger than instinct, insisted that I couldn't just leave Mark. He wasn't like the other guys.

I didn't know how, exactly, yet, but I knew that he was different.

And I knew I couldn't stop thinking about the press of his skin, hot against mine, and the slide of his cock inside me. Couldn't stop wanting more.

I owed it to myself, and probably to him, too, to hang on until I figured out what was really going on between us.

I had just willed the building tension out of my shoulder blades and allowed myself to sink back into the mattress when I heard my phone's alarm chirping in the other room. Mark started to stir, and without another thought, I wiggled my way out from under his arm and traipsed to the living room.

I wasn't ready for him to wake up yet. Wasn't ready to talk to him about what had happened today when I hardly knew myself.

Then I blinked enough sleep out of my eyes to read my phone screen, and gasped.

Calendar: Intro to Engineering exam prep review session: 7:00 PM. (Bring Joey and Hawk's pretzel bites!)

Shit. Shit shit shit. The phone's history showed the alarm had been going off for over an hour. I'd scheduled this study session months ago, when I was writing the syllabus, and proceeded to completely forget about it. Who the hell scheduled a Saturday night study session?

Someone who was planning on absolutely no dating. That was who.

Shit. It was just after six, and I was still stark naked.

I spun in a circle, scanning the room for all my stuff. There was my camisole, tossed over the lampshade, and my shoes, kicked off near the entrance to Mark's bedroom.

Two minutes later, I'd pulled on all my clothing, except for the sparkly tank, which I stuffed in my bag. I shoved my feet back into my heels, thankful that I'd be able to change when I ran back to my place to grab my laptop.

Dammit. I was typically flawless at remembering and keeping appointments. Even when I was seeing someone regularly, like I supposed I was doing now, he'd been just another cog in the machine of my life, clicking into place and staying firmly where he belonged. Mark, apparently, was different. Already he was making me forget things like my own classes and dwell on things like my own future. Whether my future would include him.

I tiptoed back into the bedroom where Mark still lay on his side, now clutching a pillow to his chest where my body had just been. I stifled a giggle. He must have missed me in the few minutes I'd been out of bed.

I didn't want to wake him, but it felt weird to leave him here after we'd done what we'd done.

Which, by the way, I was still trying to figure out. Sex with Mark had changed me, somehow. I couldn't have put words to the feelings bubbling up inside me if I tried.

I could have texted him, but I didn't want the chime to wake him up. I traipsed out to his kitchen, looking for a notepad, and found only a stash of oddly-colored permanent markers. I tore off the corner of a grocery store circular that was nestled in a pile of junk mail on his kitchen counter and jotted down, *Thanks. Toby.*

I frowned at it, then headed to his room where I laid it on the pillow behind his head. I'd taken one step toward the exit when Mark rolled over, crushing the note under his head and taking the Toby-pillow with him. I grinned at the thought of how, if I were still in the pillow's place, I'd be lying flush on top of him right now. That would most certainly have started round two. What a shame.

I still held the marker, and, biting the inside of my cheek, I approached Mark, planning to retrieve the note and return it. But he'd probably just roll over on it again or lose it completely.

At this juncture I would typically decide to forget about it and try to remember to text a guy later. But I hated the thought of Mark waking up and wondering where I'd gone. For a second, I considered, and then realized his pillowcases were a very light gray, the color of concrete. My permanent marker was red.

I bent down over the pillow he held in his arms and lightly scratched out a message:

Went to class.
  See you soon.
  XO Toby

Then I dashed out of there. I would almost certainly be a few minutes late, but it was worth it.

CHAPTER 24

MARK

I WOKE up with a large pillow in my arms instead of the piece of human perfection that had been there last I remembered. A weight of disappointment settled in my chest. I'd guessed Toby wasn't the kind of girl to stick around very long after sex, but I would have bet after today's date that things between us were different than they'd been between her and any other guy. I'd had a respectable amount of sex with a couple women, and nothing had even come close to the connection I'd felt with Toby.

Including with the girl I had once planned on marrying.

Plus, while I didn't know too much about Toby, I knew she was the kind of girl not to fake anything. Not for a guy's sake, anyway. The sounds she made when we moved together, the way she rocked her hips against mine, the graceful beauty with which her back arched in pleasure...that was nothing but one hundred percent sincere, enthusiastic orgasm.

It was early evening. The sun was dipping just under the horizon, and the pillow still smelled like Toby's shampoo. I wondered how long she'd been gone, wondered if her absence had been what had ultimately woken me.

I nudged the pillow aside gently and sat up, blinking the sleep out of my eyes. No note, and all her clothes were gone. I was just about to pat the pillow back into place, my heart sinking, when I caught the flash of thin red ink, right there on the pillowcase.

My whole face split into a grin.

She'd gone to class, which meant she hadn't left because she was freaked out, and she'd said "see you soon", which was better than "thanks" or "take care", or any of the hundred other dismissive things she could have written.

Could be worse. Could be much, much worse, I thought as I plodded to the kitchen, scrounged for something to eat, and shuffled through the latest bit of back-mail sitting on the counter.

But as I sorted through the grocery circulars and junk mail, sifting out one or two bills, my brain was still focused on Toby's note.

It was Saturday night. Nobody had class on Saturday nights. And of course she'd say "see you soon"—she was going to see me on Tuesday.

For God's sake, she was contractually obligated to see me soon.

By the time I'd pitched all the junk mail in the recycling bin and taken my first sip of coffee, my great mood had slowly turned until it was at the edge of sour. Sex with Toby had been beyond words, beyond any expectation I'd had from our various encounters. At least I thought it had been. But she thought it was pretty average, apparently.

Standard. Typical sex, typical morning-after note.

I sighed as I slid into one of the bar stools opposite my kitchen counter. Suddenly, the cheese and crackers I'd pulled out didn't look appealing, and the night stretched out in front of me like a barren wasteland where nothing would be able to take my mind off of her. The last time I'd felt disappointment like this was...

Kylie.

Goddammit, I needed to grow up. Toby was Toby, not Kylie, and we were having a fling, not a long-term relationship. Hell, it wasn't even that serious—technically, we were just fulfilling an agreement. Kylie was Kylie, not Toby, and she had broken my heart. I'd known they were two different women - certainly, two completely different experiences being with them in almost every way. I could not slip into my old ways of attachment.

The only problem was that I knew how to do nothing *but* be attached. In some dense corner of my mind, I'd thought sex would affect Toby as intensely as it had affected me. I'd been wrong. That wasn't the end of the world. It wasn't even the end of the relationship. She'd ducked out of here, yeah, but she'd also signed her note with "xo ." That wasn't ending things. That was normal.

Yes, I wanted to be with her, and badly. But she wasn't here, and if I was going to see her again, I knew in my gut I had damn well better get used to that.

I also knew in my gut that was never going to happen. I wanted someone who wanted to be with me. If I was going to be seeing a girl, I wanted there to at least be the possibility of something more. Toby knew that. But I knew she knew that and didn't really feel the same way.

What in the hell was I supposed to do?

The tune "With a Little Help From My Friends" popped into my head. I punched out a message to Ethan, asking him to meet me for a run. A swig of my room-temperature coffee later and I was lacing up my shoes.

Everything was fine. Hell, everything was great. Or, at least,

I could probably convince myself of that, as long as I stayed busy.

The least I could do for Toby was that.

CHAPTER 25

TOBY

ONE AND A HALF DAYS.

It had been thirty-six hours since I'd heard from Mark. The last communication we'd had was written by me, on a pillow in permanent marker, next to his sleeping face.

It had taken a Monday morning run, way too much coffee, answering every stupid question in every email my students sent me (which I only ever did when Mark had me worked up), and some retail therapy to get through the day without obsessing. I got home, dropping the bags I'd collected from a trendy boutique, H&M, and a vintage shop in front of the full-length mirror in my room. I rifled through them for a moment, then pulled a flowy black polyester jumpsuit from one of them. The shop owner had explained to me that she'd had it forever, but hadn't had anyone try it on who was tall enough to wear it. I didn't even have to try it on—I knew it would fit me like a glove. It was like someone from the past trying to make me feel fabulous. I was in love.

I'd found a pair of strappy gold stilettos in my go-to brand, in my size, and I just couldn't say no. I'd find the perfect occasion to wear the outfit for, I was sure.

I'd checked my phone after that stupid exam review session, which only a third of my students had bothered to show up to. Inexplicably, I'd spent the two hours afterwards on my couch with a stack of papers, halfheartedly grading them, feeding myself the remaining half-dozen pretzel bites piece by piece. I only snapped out of it when my fingernails scraped the thin cardboard walls of the empty box.

So embarrassing, even though I was sitting in my apartment all by myself.

I usually loved sitting in my apartment all by myself. At least, I *had* loved it, the last time I checked. It hadn't felt the same since I met him.

Who the fuck did Mark Mahler think he was, to take away one of the few things I loved doing without fail?

I'd last seen him, dead asleep, on Saturday evening, and after thirty-six hours of radio silence, there was no reason to think I would see him again until a little less than thirty-six hours from now, when we sat across the conference room planning table from each other, in the same place where the biggest hassle of my adult life so far—knowing Mark, and *knowing* Mark—had begun.

The fact that I was counting down the hours was seriously concerning.

I let the pile of papers I'd been holding drop loosely on the coffee table, the sloppiness a reflection of my moodSpare energy was rolling off me in waves. Something was seriously wrong with me.

Before I knew it, I'd pulled the jumpsuit on, reveling in the way the elastic grabbed my waist at the bottom of the deep-V neckline, and stepped into the stilettos. I pulled my hair up in a high ponytail, letting my long hair waterfall down my back, and nodded at my reflection once in the mirror, pleased.

I didn't need Mark to feel beautiful, or to enjoy a night out in Philadelphia.

It was probably good that he still hadn't texted me. I was gorgeous and interesting all on my own, thank you very much. This would be an ideal night to check out that new coffee bar in University City, the Weeknight Buzz. They mixed espresso with artisanal liquor and played EDM. I'd heard some of the other grad students raving about it—a place where you could break up the monotony of work, dance out some of your frustration, and then get back to grading before crashing.

Even though I'd manically worked through all my grading in an effort to distract myself from Mark, I could use a night out with my fabulous self, all by myself. No Mark needed.

It was all working out just fine—an unseasonably warm night in Philly, lots of people out enjoying the weather, and even some people I knew—until I realized that my route to the Weeknight Buzz took me right past Mark's place.

Whatever. It didn't matter. Yes, we'd slept together, but after two days with not so much as a text, that was probably all it was going to be. Forget Lion King yoga. Forget blow jobs in the back room of the studio. It was fun and games, which was exactly what I'd wanted.

Maybe I should knock on his door, though. See if he wants to come along.

No. How many girls had I said this to? If he doesn't call, he's not worth your time. Yes, I'd see him at the studio. No, that didn't mean I had to spend my free time falling all over myself to see him before then.

I'd just gathered the resolve to walk by without even looking up at that freaking loser's window, when the heavy wooden door of his building swung open, creaking on its hinges like just separating from the door frame was an insufferable chore.

Mark's blond head ducked out, followed by a polished shoe and crisply-ironed pants, and that was all it took. I was frozen in place.

Something deeply troubling took root inside me. I didn't even know myself anymore. I didn't recognize this girl who was dying for a glance, maybe a smile, from a guy she'd only slept with once, of all things. It was foreign and terrifying.

But Mark's wide smile as he quick-stepped down the stairs toward me warmed me from head to toe.

"Hey, you. Are you psychic or something?" His tone was maddeningly relaxed. He looked like he'd stepped out of the pages of GQ. His sister, I decided, deserved goddess status for initiating this makeover.

"It's nine o'clock," I said. He stopped right in front of me, closer than someone who was just a friend would dare. I suddenly had trouble breathing normally. *In and out, Tovyah. Get it together.*

"That is a statement of fact," he said, relaxing into his smirk. "Let me try one. You're headed out somewhere."

Hell yes, I was. All by myself, because I didn't need him or anyone to enjoy the city and look fabulous. I should have told him that, but I didn't. Instead I blurted an accusation. "Well, so are you."

Mark laughed. "Good eye. I am headed out. Can I walk you to where you're going?"

God, he was so close, but very obviously not touching me or kissing me. Not even trying. Not even looking at me like he was *thinking* about trying.

With any other guy, it would have been a relief. With any other guy, I might have thought, *we had our fun, now we're done.*

With Mark, I only felt a churning sickness at my center,

confusing my senses and everything I'd ever thought was true about what I wanted from men.

I had no words. I didn't even have clear thoughts. What I did have was tears threatening to spring up into my eyes, so I bit my lip, nodded, and kept walking. I watched my feet as I did. How fucking stupid had it been to wear gold stilettos to this area of Philly? Cobblestone was everywhere.

"I like your shoes," Mark said after several seconds of silent walking, and again, I stopped cold. I wanted to scream. Who the hell did he think he was, not texting or calling after *that* kind of sex and then making a comment about my fucking shoes? When he was so clearly dressed to kill, leaving the house to meet someone who was not me?

"You didn't text," I said in a rush. My cheeks were instantly flaming, but I kept my hands shoved in the pockets of my jumper, thankful that it was dark enough that he probably couldn't tell.

Mark stepped closer to me, close enough to kiss me if he wanted to. In these heels, I was an inch, maybe less, shorter than him. I was glad I could at least still look up into his eyes. Our nearly-even height made me feel capable, confident, grounded. I took a deep breath.

Mark nodded slowly. He put his hands in his pockets, and the way they made his fitted button-down stretch across his shoulders made my head swim.

"You said you liked your space. Figured you wanted it." His eyes told a different story. With his eyebrows pushed gently upward, his intense, unbreaking gaze, he was silently asking for answers.

I didn't say anything. I couldn't. There was a hell of a lump in my throat and if I was going to put words out there, I wanted to make sure they were true.

"I do. I did. Um..." That was all I got out. Mark's lips

pressing into a thin line followed by a single nod of his head spelled resignation, plain and simple. Acceptance of something he'd known and didn't really like.

The thing was, I didn't like it either. Hadn't liked a single second of being so separated from him, and didn't like the uncertainty it stirred up in me.

He turned to start walking again, and I grabbed for his hand blindly, thankfully catching it.

"I *did* like my space. I mean, until a couple days ago. I mean, I still do. Just not..." The terrifying words brought me nothing but relief. I couldn't finish the sentence, but it didn't matter. We both knew where it was headed. I let a shaky smile creep onto my face as he looked back up at me.

"I wanted to text," he said, his voice soft and patient, "or even call, honestly. But I remembered what you said."

How many guys had I kicked out of my life, or just left standing by the wayside, assuming—no, *knowing*—they didn't give a fuck what I wanted? Here was a guy treating me with the utmost respect and care, and because of that, he was keeping his distance. I swallowed hard. Apparently the second sentence in situations like this wasn't easier than the first.

I hated this. Loathed not being in control of my emotions, or even of my body, which had finally allowed a tear to escape and trickle down my cheek.

Mark took one step closer, nearly allowing our bodies to touch. He gently pushed his fingers through my hair, cupping my jaw in his hand, wiping away the tear with the pad of his thumb.

"Are you scared?" The question was quiet, so that only he and I could hear it.

It was exactly the question I needed to answer.

"I..."

"Because *I'm* scared," he interrupted, his words rushed.

"The last girl I was with was Kylie, and it got serious fast, just kind of hovered there for a while, then and crashed and burned. But I really like you. And Saturday was..."

"Yeah," I whispered with a soft, choked laugh.

"I know you don't want anything long-term, but you're helping me learn about dating for the show, like you promised. And I don't want us to stop seeing each other. Do you?"

Fuck no. The only thing I wanted to do in that moment was to kiss him, to let him take me like he had the last time. "No," I whispered, settling for the brush of air that his breaths painted on my lips.

"So...we're both scared, and we both want to keep it up anyway. Right?"

I answered him with a kiss. My thoughts paused on the memory of how long it had taken to paint on my chestnut-to-gold lipstick before I'd stepped out of my place, and how I probably shouldn't mess it up. My brain threw that out in favor of savoring the moment. Mark gently traced the edge of my bottom lip with his tongue. One of my hands snaked around his waist and a thrill shot through me as he groaned in response, subtly pressing his hips to mine.

He slowly pulled away, pulling a hand from my hair to wipe his lip and check for traces of my lipstick. He chuckled and showed the gold sparkles on his finger.

"As much as I wish I could invite you up to my place," Mark said, "I'm meeting someone and I can't miss it."

"Oh," I said, trying to pin back any traces of shock, heavy with disappointment, in my tone. Was he going on a *date* with someone else? What other reason was there for him to be so deliciously dressed on a Monday night? "So..."

"Come with me," he said, reaching down to lace my fingers with his like it was the most natural thing in the world.

Oh. "So it's not...?"

"It's a work thing, Toby. You really think I'd start dating someone else after two days of no communication with you? I'm not that desperate for a girlfriend, no matter what Ethan wants you to believe," he said, a teasing smile on his lips.

I grinned at him, not even trying to suppress any wattage.

For the first time ever, I walked down the street hand-in-hand with a guy, not worried in the least about where we were going or about what it meant. He didn't want to stop, and neither did I, and for now that was just enough.

CHAPTER 26

MARK

I HATED NOT BEING able to just turn around and take Toby back to my place, but it was my client Beth's first time playing the piano bar at Tavern on Camac, and I wanted to be there to make sure she was doing okay. The ten-to-two crowd at Tavern on Camac could be fun, but it also could be a bit rowdy with its calls for artists to play on request. I was very protective of my artists, and this one was new to the city, just out of school from some halfway-prestigious liberal arts college in southern Ohio. I felt almost as concerned about her as I would about Hannah. Maybe more, because while my twin sister lived in New York, Beth had never played in a town with more than half a dozen stop signs.

Toby walked so close to me that it made my body buzz with some cross between reassurance and anticipation. I'd never seen her like I had tonight outside my door—caught off guard. Unsure. Stammering. The Toby I knew didn't stutter, didn't stumble. She knew what she wanted and she went after it. I should have felt satisfied that I knocked her off-balance just as much as she did me, but mostly I just wanted to get the reunion from our short time apart underway.

I explained to Toby that I was here to meet Beth, introduced them, then called a waiter over to get Toby a drink while I worked. This particular piano bar was gorgeous, with old-fashioned wallpaper and polished tables, and the six-to-ten player had gotten the crowd nice and drunk. That usually lent itself to a fairly stress-free environment for the artist playing from ten-to-two; the crowd would pay less attention to her and the technicalities of her playing, and more to the atmosphere she created.

"I hate to tell performers this, especially women," I told Beth, who was trembling, despite having paced and stretched her fingers in the prep room, "but, smile, okay? Here, I'll get you a drink."

One gin and tonic and an introduction from me later, Beth was happy, relaxed, and almost sparkling when she played. She was gifted at playing songs off the cuff, making her a great match for a place like this, where patrons submitted requests. When she started banging out Lady Gaga's "Bad Romance", and the crowd laughed and cheered, I knew she would be just fine.

It was almost midnight, and I gave Beth a little wink and salute when I ducked out the back. I'd have to call her in the morning, see how it had gone, but she looked a lot like the Beth I'd met almost a year ago in that little Ohio town—energized and at peace, doing what she loved. Not many managers would have taken her on to develop her piano lounge player/singer/comedienne act into something marketable, but this was my favorite thing. I'd never been good at performing myself, despite a dozen years of piano lessons under my belt. I was great at making a match between crowd and entertainer, though.

Toby'd had a drink or two, enough to relax her while still letting her walk upright in those gorgeous shoes. She was so tall in them, and talking with her while her eyes were level with mine added a whole new dimension to my attraction to her. The lack of distance between our faces made every word exchanged between us somehow more intimate.

"So, you helped her get set up at that venue?" Toby finally asked after we'd strolled a block or so together.

"More or less, yeah." I didn't really feel like going into the ins and outs of what was involved in running my management company. I'd only been doing this for a year or so, and one thing I'd learned about Toby was that she had no respect for amateurs.

"That's nice of you." She snuggled into my arm. She was tired and tipsy, and it wasn't the time to tell her that Beth was on the low end of my spectrum of artists, at least revenue-wise. I wasn't the kind of guy to brag about my business.

"My brother used to do that," she said.

"Play piano bars?"

"Yeah," she said with a soft smile on her face. How long had it been since Toby had done anything softly? I wondered how many people ever saw her this calm, this gentle. This vulnerable.

"David did it to raise money for college. My parents had plenty of money to send him, of course, but my dad wanted him to learn work ethic. Or something." She wrinkled her nose. "I could give her pointers for next time. He had a list of ten songs he could play flawlessly. Biggest money makers." She yawned.

"What about you? Did you play piano bars for college, too?" The idea of working to save for college didn't seem strange to me at all. In our town, most kids, including me, worked their asses off in high school for good grades in the hope of scholarships, spending their free time at part-time jobs. I'd saved enough from tutoring and babysitting to pay for two years of room and board at Penn.

Toby scoffed. "Absolutely not. Dad just paid for everything for me, without asking. He's a little...old fashioned. Women are to be taken care of," she said in a deep voice, apparently imitating her father.

I felt her stiffen just the slightest bit. Without even thinking, I let my hand cover hers and squeezed it gently. "That's kind of...nice?" I ventured. I knew right away it was the wrong thing to say.

"Yeah, it's *nice*," she said. "If you like being a little China doll in a cabinet that is only good for people to look at, and for being at your dad's beck and call."

My eyebrows shot up, but I kept my mouth shut. Toby'd just shared more about herself with me in the past few minutes after a drink or two than she had in the whole three weeks that I'd known her. Instead of opening my mouth and making her answer questions she wasn't comfortable answering, I just let my arm wrap around her waist, and waited for her to say more. One thing I'd learned about Toby was that she would talk when she wanted to.

After another block or so, I realized we were close to home. I could have walked with her for hours and not realized how much time had passed. "Can I take you home?"

Of course, I was hoping for an invite up to her place, but of all the things I'd learned about Toby, "assume nothing" was one of the most important.

She yawned again. "Only if you stay."

I tried to keep my grin in check. "I'd love nothing more."

There was that soft smile again, that slight, trusting lean farther into my shoulder.

Everything about her was softer tonight, like she'd transformed from lemonade—bright, exciting, and with a little sour kick—to honey—slow and sweet and nearly overwhelming. She got the key to turn in the lock after a couple tries, and I wrenched open the old, solid-wood door, holding it open for her. No sooner had I eased her bag off her shoulder and dropped it on the small table just inside her door than she had plastered her body against mine, pinning me against the door and molding her flesh to mine.

It felt like she wanted to climb me, and I wasn't about to complain. She caught my lips in a slow, intense kiss that had me hard for her in seconds. When she pulled away, though, her eyelids drifted half-shut, then dragged themselves up again, and it wasn't from lust. My heart swelled with affection. My girl was exhausted.

"Toby, honey. Let's get those shoes off."

She slumped against me, not unsteady, but heavy—just exhausted. She nodded, her forehead rubbing against the shoulder of my shirt. She was probably getting makeup all over it, and I couldn't bring myself to care.

We traipsed into her room, and she winced as she plopped down on her bed. Her feet lifted up, and she raised an eyebrow at those goldenheels. I suddenly hated them, however, when I realized they'd left angry red marks crisscrossing her feet. I frowned.

"We've gotta get those off of you."

"They're so beautiful," she whined softly, collapsing back on her bed. I chuckled and looked up, taking in the room. Her huge bed was framed in a tufted headboard, made out of a cream-colored fabric. The sheets and comforter were the same color, accented with a deep blue-green knitted blanket and brown and yellow pillows.

"They are pretty, and I love them, but I love the well-being of your feet more." I got down on my knees at the foot of her bed, puzzled over the tiny gilt buckles at her ankles for a moment, and then got to work removing them. I pulled my palm over the top of each foot, then gently pushed her toes toward the ceiling, digging my thumbs into the arches.

Toby moaned again, and whispered, "So good." I shifted my

legs, partly to adjust my hardening dick to a more comfortable position, partly to wait for further instructions.

"Need any water?"

"No. Need you." Her eyes were drifting further shut by the second, but she lifted her arms up to me. My heart warmed and suddenly all I wanted to do was hold her. But I didn't want to wake up to an upset Toby.

"How about take off your makeup, and brush your teeth?"

"That's the thing about you, Mark Mahler," Toby said as I watched her stomach contract and her upper half pull up from the bed. "You're so *boring*."

I still knelt between her legs, looking up at her, loving the feel of the curtain of her hair tumbling over one shoulder, darkening the space between our faces. "Yep. I'm a boring grownup. And grownups don't go to sleep in their makeup, right?"

She shrugged with a soft smile, and I got to my feet, reaching down to help her stand. The bones in her feet popped when she stood on them.

Five minutes later, she emerged from the restroom in a thin strapped tank top and little sleep shorts, her hair in a ponytail and her face scrubbed clean.

I didn't know whether I wanted to snuggle her or taste every inch of her.

Her eyes were more alert now, and she gave me a dazzling smile. "Still want to stay, now that I'm not all dolled up anymore?"

I just nodded numbly. I'd seen her in sequins and sweats, jeans and stilettos, but this bare-footed, one hundred percent natural Toby was quite a sight. She wasn't more beautiful one way or the other, but seeing her like this felt like I'd just knocked down every wall and pulled back every layer all at once.

I knew right then that I wanted her. Not just tonight, and not just in a sexual way. I wanted her in every way, forever.

I was a goner.

"I left a spare toothbrush on the counter for you," she said. She slid under the covers, sighing as she moved over the smooth sheets. The only time I'd seen her look more ecstatic was when my face had been buried between her thighs.

Huh. Maybe that was why people bothered to make their beds.

"Hurry," she continued. "Don't wanna miss out." She turned her shoulder a bit, as if she was trying to face me seductively, but failing miserably.

I already knew I'd be missing out on the stuff she was thinking I wanted. On what she wanted, too, maybe, in her head. I didn't care one bit.

I unbuttoned everything there was to unbutton on my way to the bathroom, stepping out of my shoes and leaving them outside the bathroom door, slipping my watch inside. My head spun at what I was about to do: get into bed with Toby and stay for the night.

The one thing she'd made abundantly clear since our first encounter was that she didn't do relationships. Didn't even want to try.

I couldn't claim to know everything Toby was thinking, but I was pretty sure one AM snuggles in pajamas would fall under the "relationship" column for almost anyone.

Not that I was complaining.

With my mouth minty fresh, I headed to the bed in just my boxers. I had taken to sleeping naked, lately—who needed more laundry?—but if Toby had put on sleep shorts...

I slid into the sheets and, holy shit, this *was* why people insisted on making their beds in the morning. This felt amazing —the cool glide of the silky surface along my skin, like it was just waiting for me to decide I was done with the stress of the day. I scooted toward her and snaked my arm under her shoulders, pulling her to me. She pressed her body to mine from thigh to chest, nuzzling her face into my shoulder with a barely audible hum.

My heart soared. Soon, I was fast asleep.

CHAPTER 27

TOBY

ON THE WEEKENDS, either sunlight or an alarm telling me to show up at Natalia's gym woke me. This morning, I rolled right into a warm, solid mass of muscle. Mark had slept over.

I'd brought Mark home with me, convinced him to stay, and then *not* had sex with him?

Slowly, the memories of the night before trickled into my brain.

Leaving my house, wanting to get away, do anything but sit home alone.

Running into Mark, who looked impeccable. Assuming he was meeting another girl.

Watching him do something like a real job, not some bro-grade radio show, helping this young artist blossom and succeed, even if it was just in a tiny piano bar...

He'd looked so happy, and assured of himself, so in control of his life and everything around him that I hadn't been able to contain the weird emotion flooding me from every angle—the desire to be wrapped in him, connected to him. I wanted to share breath with him, to press by body against his and settle in there, like I wasn't planning on leaving for a good, long time. Maybe ever.

Last night, I'd been too tired to think about the implications of that feeling.

Mark was the first guy who'd stayed at my place. Ever.

Last night, it had seemed like the absolute best decision I'd ever made, inviting him up.

I instinctively spent a few seconds poking around in my brain for a reason to regret it.

I couldn't find one.

My chest was pressed against his back, my fingers lazily resting on his lower stomach. So close to that cock that had done such incredible things to me. Without thinking, my fingertips started to trace circles on his skin, and I felt him stir. A few seconds later, though he didn't open his eyes, his hand moved to cover mine.

"Dangerous, Toby."

I chuckled softly. "What in the world would be dangerous about something that feels this nice?"

"Because it's going to be very, very difficult for us to stop, and my balls might turn permanently blue. And also, we have morning breath."

"Ever the practical voice in this relationship," I murmured. I rolled slightly away, and Mark whined, a sound that he made into something somehow raw and masculine.

"I didn't say to get out of bed," he said.

"I'm not. Patience." My outstretched hand found a tin of strong mints that I kept at my bedside, a trick I'd learned that one time I'd tagged along with a band on tour. We stayed six or seven to a room sometimes, and if you woke up with rough breath in the middle of the night or early morning, sometimes it was just better to pop a mint instead of disturbing the whole room to go to the bathroom and brush again.

Plus, I'd read somewhere that blow jobs with a mint made a guy's head spin. I'd been meaning to try it for months. No time like the present.

I extracted two mints, placing one in the corner of Mark's mouth and another in mine. My lips found the back of his neck, feathering light kisses there, following the line of his shoulder, brushing over the downy hair. While I kissed his lightly stubbled skin, my fingers snuck under the waistband of his boxers, nudging them down and away from the part of him I wanted most.

Mark made a soft rumbly noise from way down in his belly. That turned my mind directly to things below his belly, and suddenly, I couldn't resist. I slid downward, my cheek moving down the smooth, muscled sculpture of his back. When I bumped up against the roundness of his ass, also deliciously muscled, I turned my head and bared my teeth, nipping it ever so lightly. Mark groaned.

"You're going to kill me," he muttered.

"Just wait," I said.

I liked to take control in bed. I liked to map out the whole process in my head, then let my little fantasy play out on the man I'd chosen to lay out in front of me. Or to lay out under. Having sex with a guy had always been part of the goal of experiencing the guy, but Mark was different.

Our first time had been all-consuming, physically and emotionally. I couldn't remember what had happened between us, from start to finish. What I did have locked away were snippets of memories: gasping moments, a wave of overwhelm, a spinning of my head that I thought would never stop and then suddenly, gloriously ended in the most incredible orgasm I'd ever experienced.

I wanted that again, but in this moment, I craved teasing fun, laughter. Play. Mark made me feel light and confident, and here in my bed, in the barely filtering-in light, with a mint dissolving between my teeth, I wanted to enjoy him.

With my fingertips pressing gently into his hip, I guided him so that he was lying face up on the mattress, pitching a tent with the bedsheets so high that it made my eyebrow shoot up. In the dark of the studio back room, and of his bedroom, it had been hard to imagine what his dick looked like.

I was pretty sure I wouldn't have been able to imagine one this beautiful if I tried.

I nudged his thighs apart and hoisted myself up, arranging myself between them. My head dipped down of its own volition, my lips opening just enough to lay a soft, sweet open-mouthed kiss on the head, my tongue flicking the slit. Mark groaned and his hands fisted into the sheets. One of my hands reached up to intertwine fingers with his, and the other rested on his thigh, which was already tensed, waiting for his release as if he had full confidence that I could make him come in seconds. A wave of affection washed over me, and I reached up to pet his cock from head to base. I kind of loved that he was circumcised, I thought before languidly licking a line along the path my hand had just traveled, admiring the way the lack of foreskin made every single ridge and vein stand out like it was waiting to pleasure me.

"Is that...the mint?" Mark choked out, and I grinned, taking hold of his cock and running the head over my lips like I was applying lip balm.

"How does it feel?"

Mark squeezed his eyes shut. "I don't know." He swallowed hard.

"It's not...bothering you, or anything?" I managed, waiting for permission to take even more of him into my mouth.

"God, no. It's..."

I sucked as much of him as I could inside, and his answering gasp ended in a slight choking yelp that I found absolutely adorable. After a few more seconds of bobbing up and down on him, applying light suction and as much mint-flavored spit as I could manage, his hand let go of the sheets and tugged at my ponytail instead.

"You're a miracle," he murmured. "Toby, you...you have to stop."

I popped off and sat back on my heels, giving him a doe-eyed look of confusion. "Why?"

"Because if you don't, this will be over before it really gets started."

"Or it'll just last that much longer," I said, smirking at his shocked expression and leaning back down to resume my little tasting session. The truth was, I'd been wanting to give Mark head again, and I was reasonably sure he wouldn't need too long to recover enough to fuck me properly. If, for some reason, he couldn't get it back up, well...he was good at oral, too.

That particular memory was seared into my brain. Recalling the way his tongue licked me like I was the most delicious thing he'd ever tasted made me want to make him feel the same way, and before I knew it, I was devouring him. I didn't give a shit about the wet noises or the squeaks of pleasure I was making while feeling his cock sliding against my tongue. I wanted to make him come, and come hard. I wanted him to compare every other blow job he'd ever gotten, ever would get, to the one I was giving him right now.

And I wanted to win every time.

It didn't take long for every one of his muscles to tense up, and then for him to groan, jutting his pelvis toward my lips, spilling over my tongue in hot spurts. I swallowed and kept loving him with my mouth, gently, until he softened between my lips.

I slid back up so that my gaze was level with his, grazing

kisses over his skin along the way, and settled my back against his chest, so that I could feel him still warm and heavy against my ass, brushing the backs of my thighs. His arm wrapped around me immediately, and he buried his lips in my hair, growling in my ear, "I told you that you were going to kill me."

I laughed. "If you're dead right now, it looks—and feels—good on you."

His hand drifted downward, and I lifted my leg slightly to accommodate him. He brushed over the hair covering my mound, which I kept trimmed but not shaved. "Love this," he murmured before licking my earlobe and then biting down on it gently. A warm wave of desire rolled through me. "Never understand why women shave. This makes it so much more... inviting. Like an arrow pointing me in the right direction."

"You are always welcome to visit," I laughed.

"Mmm," he responded. I thought he was delirious from coming, but almost without warning, he pushed himself up off the bed, letting me drop to my back. Instinctively, my arms went up over my head.

"I thought I drained you of all your energy."

"Not all of it."

Mark set to work nipping down my neck, flicking his tongue along the tendons there, moving down and sucking my nipples with abandon, placing huge licking kisses into my navel, and finally putting that gifted mouth of his to work beneath my legs.

I laughed, breathless, delighted, and deliriously happy, giving myself completely over to this man, beyond grateful that I'd given him a second glance.

As he worked over me with his mouth, my thoughts faded into a haze of never, ever wanting this to end.

CHAPTER 28

MARK

TOBY WAS INSATIABLE, as desperate for me as the first day I'd met her. I made her come with my mouth, and then she straddled me again. The way she bent down to kiss me, her hair blessing the space when it curtained on either side of our faces, drove me wild with possessive affection for her, and the way she moaned into my mouth like I was the most delicious thing she'd ever tasted made me want to taste back—everywhere, all at once.

That morning, I learned that she stashed condoms inside pillowcases and just under the elastic corners of her fitted sheets. I learned that she loved being on top, as long as I gripped her hips and helped her set the rhythm. I learned that she could have three—no, four—orgasms in one session, as long as the first one was oral foreplay and the last was teased out with slow, steady fingers in the haze of afterglow.

That morning, Toby Eisen became putty in my hands.

Early that afternoon, I walk-of-shamed back to my apartment. With every step, I tried to ignore that Toby had sent me tumbling head-over-heels for her, and my emotions showed no signs of slowing down.

After that, our relationship fell into a steady, albeit tentative, pattern. Work, sex, hang out, go a couple days without seeing each other, repeat.

We saw each other at Bro Show tapings, of course, but agreed to never let on to Shari that we were a thing. Toby and I took turns scolding each other for any look, any giggle that might reveal that she was the girl I was dating for all my "Whiz Kid Mark Mahler" segments.

Of course, more than once we either waited for Shari and Ethan to leave the studio, and fucked up against the wall of the office, or got back home immediately after the show where we would spend hours in bed, our mouths busy devouring each other.

Somehow, we managed to fit in a few other things, too. I finally rescheduled that visit to the Kimmel Center, but it was to hear Beethoven's 9th Symphony played by the Philadelphia Orchestra. Toby cried again. I was more captivated by her than I'd ever been by any music, ever.

She managed to convince me that Starbucks provided the quintessential coffee experience. I fed her as many of Joey and Hawk's scones, which were the best representation of heaven on Earth in baked-good form, as I could. I watched Toby's eyes roll back in pleasure as she bit into a brussels-sprout and cheddar version, then introduced her to the owners, Joey and Will "Hawk" Hawkins.

I was only hoping to impress Toby with my music-scene contacts—this place hosted local acts often—but they ended up sharing a table with us and telling us the story of how they'd met. Joey laughed when she recounted how much she'd hated her now-husband when they'd first met, and Hawk squeezed her hand when he told us how scared he'd been that she'd change his life forever. She had, he said, chuckling, but it was the best thing that had ever happened to him.

I snuck a glance at Toby during the story. Her brows tented together and a soft smile pulled at her lips. One thing I'd learned about Toby was that she absorbed peoples' stories like they were an elixir of life. It was as if the more she gathered, the more substance her own life story would have. She collected them like some kids collected trading cards. She loved every one, but it was like she'd always be on the lookout for that one life story that would complete her stash.

As if, when that happened, she'd finally know what she really wanted from life.

She didn't hesitate to offer critiques of those stories, either.

"I could never fucking understand Cinderella," Toby groused in my ear while I was on my way to one of Cosmick Crew's gigs. "I mean, sure, she had the memory of her parents to keep alive and whatnot, but after a certain amount of abuse, don't you think she'd just leave that damn house? Hitchhike her way out of there and find a job? Like, what was she waiting for? Obviously, on some level, she was capable of handling her shit that whole time."

"She was waiting for her prince," I answered absentmindedly as I shrugged out of my coat just inside the club's door.

"That's bullshit!" Toby yelled, effectively blocking out any of the club's background noise.

"You're right, Tobes. It is bullshit. But not everyone is as self-assured and driven as you and unfortunately that includes Cinderella. Listen, I gotta go, but—"

"Yeah, yeah. I can hear the bass. Tell your friends good luck, okay?"

My friends. I bit my tongue. What would be the point of mentioning that I was the manager for the biggest up-and-coming act in Philly EDM?

Despite all the time we spent together, I hadn't told her too much more about my work. My instinct was to guard our fragile, tentative relationship from any outside influences. Outside the bedroom, Toby was mostly one big unknown in my life. I didn't want to give her details about my personal life that would make her want to peel herself away, like the plans I had to build up my business, or even the nature of said business.

The fact that she hadn't outright asked about my work made that a lot easier. I tried not to let her disinterest bother me. I was out late lots of nights and had lots of days where I jumped from meeting to meeting and couldn't see her at all.

She never indicated that it bothered her.

She never indicated her feelings at all—toward me or anything that I did. We got along great when we were together, but Toby didn't suggest in any way that she wanted to intertwine our lives any further.

Which, if I let myself think about it, bothered me.

The last thing I wanted, though, was to ruin whatever this thing was between us. So, for the next five weeks, I didn't let myself think about it. Instead, I made sure I was busy.

Seven weeks into the Whiz Kid experiment, I had an opportunity to meet with some record execs in LA, an in from one of my friends from college. I took the week off from the show, counting on Ethan to find a replacement for me since I had to fly out on a Tuesday morning. I watched my phone all day, finally getting a text from Toby at five-thirty, right around when Shari would have been calling the first break.

Toby: Are you okay? Not like you to be a meeting no-show.

. . .

Of course I replied right away. I might have been able to keep myself in the present with Toby, but I couldn't ignore her texts.

Me: Yep. Taking the week off. Traveling for a work thing.
> **Toby: Oh.**
> **Toby: Have fun!**

I bit my lower lip, waiting for her to text again, asking for more information. After ten minutes, I didn't see anything. Not even the little reply dots.

But hell, I really did miss her. *Really* wanted to talk to her.

Me: Call me tonight, if you're not too tired?
> **Toby. Yep. Not the same here without you, whiz kid.**

I didn't respond until she called me at what would have been eleven o'clock her time. I was still wide awake. Then, I answered the phone with, "I told you not to call me that." I hoped she could hear the teasing in my voice.

"Okay, but...what if I called you that...*in bed*?"

"You mean, like, right now? Because you *are* in bed, right?"

"How could you tell?" she laughed.

"I know your bedroom voice," I replied.

"Is that so? Does it make you...think of anything?"

I'd never even considered having phone sex before. I'd also never considered that leaving town for five days would make me want a relationship, a real one, with Toby more than I already did.

Biting my lip as I listened to her come over the phone that night, I vowed to do a better job of keeping my emotions in check and my head in the present, not a future that didn't exist.

CHAPTER 29

TOBY

"DUDE! DID YOU HAVE PHONE SEX?" Ethan stabbed at the *"Let's Get It On"* button again, and I couldn't help but giggle. There was frustration just underneath the surface, though. If only that song was applicable to this past week.

"No, but I talked to this particular lady quite a lot this week."

"Help us out, bro. Is this Lion King Yoga lady?" He punched the "Circle of Life" sound button and snickered as the first couple notes blasted through the studio.

"Yes...it is..." Mark drawled, looking everywhere but at me.

"And her name is..."

"Given on a need-to-know basis."

Mark shot a look at Shari, who shrugged.

"Our producer says that will be fine for now," Ethan said. "What should we call her, though? Girl Number One?"

Shari leaned forward, pressing the intercom on her mic that would allow her to pipe her voice into the recording. I quickly scrambled to make sure her settings were compatible with Ethan's and Mark's. It was much easier to make sure things were right going into the recording than to edit them after the fact. "I don't know, boys, I don't like hearing girls with numbers attached to them. That's kind of..."

I scribbled something on a scrap of paper and slid it her way.

"Dickish?" she read. I giggled.

"All right," Ethan began, "Toby, our sound girl, says that's dickish. And even though this *is* The Bro Show, I'm going to say that numbers won't cut it for a lady you're dating, Mark. Just a tad too misogynist for our liking."

I nodded at that.

"Toby doesn't like it either, dammit. At least give the girl an alias."

The guys chuckled.

"All right, how about we go alphabetical then."

"Like hurricanes," Mark commented.

"Yeah. Give her a name. Any name that starts with 'A'."

"How about 'Ava?'" Shari said. "Like Ava Gardner."

"Ava is perfect," Mark said, gazing at me. I couldn't help but be struck with the possible double meaning of his words. The way he looked at me, so intense and a little dark, it wasn't hard for me to believe that he just might have thought I was. Perfect.

Well, that was a strange feeling.

"So, since I was out of town for work, *Ava* and I spent a lot of time on the phone this week...talking."

"Now, bro, I think a lot of us would agree that talking on the phone to one's girl is a lost art. Texting is like...you can do that whenever. Doing whatever else on the side. You know?"

"Yeah, and I didn't want to do that with her. With *Ava*. It was like every time I tried to text her, the words I typed on the screen seemed...fake. Or shallow, or something. I've texted with other girls, but with her it felt wrong."

"We have a call coming in from Kyle, who lives in—oh! Chicago. Welcome to The Bro Show, Kyle."

"Thanks for taking my call, guys. I gotta say, I mostly just catch this show when I happen to be stuck in traffic, but I like this 'looking for a girlfriend' segment. Made sure to listen this week, and missed you last week, Whiz Kid. Listening to you guys talk about dating and women is like...more realistic than any stupid men's magazine, and less stupid and clueless than talking to your beer-drinking buddies. No offense to them."

"I'm sure there was none taken," Ethan said, beaming. "Thanks for the compliment. I'm sure the Whiz Kid here will learn just as much from you as you can learn from him."

"Yeah, man, I have to tell you, getting back to talking on the phone is something that could have saved my last relationship."

"Seriously?" Mark's question came out a little surprised.

"Yeah. Her job had her traveling a lot, and she wanted to talk on the phone. Like, every night. I couldn't take it, man. I don't know what it was, but I hated having my ear smashed up against the plastic, or something. So, I just texted with her instead, and then, when we could see each other again, there was, like...this gap. Like...I barely remembered her voice. It was like I was so disconnected from her that I couldn't even read her moods anymore."

"Thanks for sharing that with us, man," Ethan remarked, disconnecting the call. "So, Mark Mahler. Experience anything like that? Feel more...connected to her?"

"Well," Mark said, "uh...I mean, I've only really known her for a few weeks, really. But there are things you learn when you talk to someone for hours on the phone that you otherwise wouldn't have."

"Hours?" Shari leaned in and asked. I couldn't help my smile of amusement. I'd rarely seen her this involved in The Bro Show conversations. "How long were you talking to this girl?"

Mark's eyes flicked to me and he grinned. "Longer than she

was talking to me, that's for sure. She fell asleep once or twice. I bet most people don't know she snores."

My mouth dropped open and I was a split second from protesting that accusation before I remembered nobody knew that Mark's mystery girl was me. If Shari knew I was the girl Mark was dating—seeing, fucking, whatever—she might cut it off. I knew for sure and certain that I did not want that to happen.

"She snores? And you still like her, man?" Ethan crowed. "Might just be true love." The strains of Elvis singing "Fools Rush In" blasted through the studio. My heart pounded.

I did *not* snore.

And this was *not* love. I knew I'd let the thought pass my mind at one point or another, but that was just...crazy. I wouldn't let it be love. Couldn't.

Besides, I was sure I did not snore. Someone would have told me if I did.

Except that I'd never stayed the night with any man, before Mark. I liked my own space. Suddenly, the talking on the phone we'd done this week seemed starkly more intimate than any of the things Mark and I had done in bed, or against a wall, or in a utility closet.

How was it possible that knowing Mark had heard me fall asleep felt much more intimate than having his cock in my mouth?

The next caller was a girl, cooing and squealing about how sweet Mark sounded and asking whether he'd consider dating her for a week. My breathing sped up at that, and once again I tamped down the urge to interject and tell her no, he would absolutely *not* date her.

The dude that called after her said that talking on the phone sucked, because you couldn't send pictures. Mark clamped his lips shut, responding with a simple, "Mmm," but Ethan knew him well enough to push.

"Bro. Did you get pictures, too? Like, since you were so far away from each other..."

Mark's eyes flicked to me, and I gave a quick shake of my head. Even though my mishap with the shower video had happened so long ago, I didn't want him talking about it and the misunderstanding that ensued. I had no clue why. Nobody—except Ethan—knew me outside of the show. My name had only been dropped as "the sound girl" once or twice. But it felt too... something. Intimate. And not physically intimate, either. More dangerous than that.

"No. No pictures."

"See, now that's a shame. But whatever. Your thumb is much more effectively used doing something other than texting, man. Texting is literally for pussies," Ethan cracked as he leaned in. Shari glared at him as she marked the time on the recording.

"We have to bleep out that word, you know. Boys."

"Sorry, Shari," they chorused together.

"But please, do not call us boys. This is the week my bro, Whiz Kid Mark Mahler, becomes a man."

"He's having his bar mitzvah?" Shari cracked. Damn, she was enjoying this.

"No, no. Bigger. He's meeting the parents."

"This is still Ava, then? He's meeting Ava's parents, after... what? A week or two?"

Mark cleared his throat. "It's seven weeks. I've only dated one girl this whole time, Shari, despite what a great player you think I am."

"Okay, after only seven weeks?" Ethan's eyes shone, his eyebrows wiggling in a hilarious dance.

"It'll be eight by the time I meet them. But, uh, yeah. Ava.

But I'm doing her a favor. Her parents live far away and she just wanted the company on the plane, I think."

"That's where you're wrong, my friend. A girl talks to you for hours, she's got feelings for you. Serious ones. Hey, are you sure this girl isn't some kind of crazy attachment freak? Like she's not gonna handcuff you while you're at her parents' house and force you to marry her?"

My eyes went wide, my throat dry. I coughed, and Mark didn't miss it.

"Oh, I'm one hundred percent sure she's not going to do anything that even comes close to that." His gaze flicked to mine again.

He was right. Marriage was absolutely, positively out of the question. Forever.

But unlike when we started this experiment, I was seriously hoping I wouldn't be sitting here and listening to him talk about any girl whose name started with a "B."

"It occurs to me that we've been neglecting feelings, Mark Mahler. How are you *feeling* about this whole thing? Nervous to meet her parents?"

Mark's eyebrows flicked up and he leaned back in his chair, like the question was too heavy for him to consider while sitting upright. "Obviously, I want them to like me," he said simply.

Oh. *Oh.* But they would hate him. That simple, obvious certainty had been the crux of Mark's appeal to me since the day I met him. My chest tightened and heat flushed my cheeks. There had to be a way to prepare Mark for all this, to let him know that I fully expected my parents to hate him, but that was just fine with me. Ideal, even.

Hopefully, I could communicate this one simple, yet terribly complicated, concept: that the reasons my parents would disapprove of him had nothing to do with the way I felt about him. They'd been trying to fit me into a mold my entire life. I didn't care that he didn't fit into it, not one bit. I wanted him not to.

Maybe, if I figured out the right way to prep him, I could get him to understand that his goal should be for my parents not to like him, that my parents hating him would be the most promising sign for our future that I could imagine.

Our future. For the first time ever, thinking about any future with a guy, however nebulous, made me smile instead of cringe.

A couple hours later, we were finally wrapping up. Shari was giving me notes, assigning me the first couple hours of the show to edit. I'd have to squeeze it into a shorter week than usual, which was stressful. Anticipating that, I'd scribbled at least a dozen questions in the margins of my show notes, which I asked her while she packed up her stuff and closed down the main computer. I noticed Mark leaving, and hoped I'd get a chance to snag him before he left the studio. Maybe revisit that back room I'd taken advantage of so many weeks ago. God, I'd been sitting for so long, I could use some variety of movement anyway.

But by the time Shari and I left, turning off lights and locking doors behind us, Mark was nowhere to be seen. I hurried off to the train stop, craning my neck down the stairs that led to the platform bathed in sickly yellow light. He knew this was my train. Maybe...

But he wasn't waiting for me there, either. When the train slid into the station, I slumped into a seat, suddenly exhausted, inside and out.

All it took was a buzz of my phone to have me sitting up at attention again.

· · ·

Mark: Hey, beautiful. Sorry I couldn't wait. Had to get to work.

I frowned, checking the time. It was almost ten on a Friday night. I knew Mark made a little money helping local artists, but I'd assumed most of that was studio-based, and that late nights out were a rare occurrence. What in the heck could work want with him this late on a weekend? And why wouldn't he have mentioned it to me before he left me hanging?

I felt full-on petulance start to take over. The sound of him moaning as he came still rang through my memory, and it had been priming me for more all night. I'd really wanted to see him tonight. What the hell?

I shook my head sharply, hoping to knock myself out of this train of thought. I was starting to want him too much...and to assume that he still felt the same as he had about me when I first met him. He'd wanted a real relationship, not just sex. But maybe now he'd changed his mind.

I clenched my fists and took a deep breath, reminding myself of what I knew for sure. Mark was going out with me because it made his life easier on the show. It was obvious that he liked me, which was a nice bonus, but really, I was helping him. Guys like him just didn't go on the prowl, especially not for girls like me. In turn, he was making my life easier by coming home with me to my parents.

This had always been an arrangement. It was never meant to be anything more. Certainly not something to get all heart-twisty and piney over.

Despite what had been building between us the last couple months, I had no right, no evidence, to assume that he'd want to spend any time with me after the terms of the deal had been fulfilled. I had no business acting like he did.

I cradled my phone in my palms, my thumbs poised to type. I thought of what that one caller had said, that Mark's thumbs were better suited to doing different things with me than texting, and felt that surge of arousal between my legs again. Just thinking of Mark's hands, and especially Mark's hands on that particular part of my body, had the power to make me squirm.

I let out a long, slow breath. If this Bro-Show segment, and the impending doom of Passover Seder with my parents, were the only things holding us together, then the only sane thing would be to not put any more thought about the situation on hold until both of them were over.

Two weeks. I could continue to date and fuck Mark Mahler, Whiz Kid in and out of the bedroom, for the next two weeks, without letting myself get hung up on stupid sentimentalities. Feelings. After all, I never had with any other guy. Why should Mark be any different?

Still, as I made my way home, I couldn't escape the feeling that things had already begun to change, and that I had no idea how to stop them. I also didn't know if I really wanted to.

CHAPTER 30

MARK

ONE THING I'd learned about Toby Eisen was that, aside from the occasional frenzy to get in my pants, she was chill and indifferent to all things. At least, that was the outward appearance she'd maintained. Over the eight weeks I'd known her, I'd learned the signs that she was more agitated than she let on. If her knee lightly bounced, if she twisted a long strand of hair around her index finger, if she bit down on the top right corner of her mouth until it turned white, she was anxious.

When we parked the car and walked to our gate at Philadelphia International Airport, she squeezed my hand and smiled.

On the plane, even during the shaky ascent and roaring landing, she sat relaxed, tapping at the edge of her Kindle, flying through the pages at her impossible, but typical pace.

Behind the wheel of the convertible—she'd said we should treat ourselves—she laughed as her hair whipped into her eyes, guiding my hand to the wheel while she tied her long waves up in a messy bun.

When she had control of the car again, I cast my gaze

upward, watching the fat palm leaves as we passed under them give way to open sky a few minutes later. I lifted my head and looked around, finding myself on a pristine stretch of road lined with small mansions, circular drives whirling in front of some, and wrought-iron gates framing others.

"Jesus, Toby. What do your parents do for a living?" It was a rude question, I knew, but my shock pushed it out of me. We hadn't talked about her house, or her parents, or anything that would have hinted at her living in a freaking mansion in a swanky suburb of Los Angeles.

Just one more aspect of her life I knew nothing about.

"Dad's a producer. My mother's a writer, here and there."

"Really," I said, turning fully to her and raising an eyebrow.

"Well, Ima dabbles. She hasn't landed a pilot for...oh, God. Six years now? I don't know what she's been up to since then, just that she's gone on a lot of trips with her friends." Toby wrinkled her nose and looked at me, a little worry line creasing between her brows. "You're not one of those star-struck types, are you?"

I choked out a laugh. After working with Magnus, sitting next to him and his mom when they got the call about his Grammy nomination and hearing him thank me in his acceptance speech, I thought I was pretty immune to swooning over celebrities. "I don't think so. I like to think of myself as a pretty simple man."

"Well," she said, blowing out a long breath, "Dad's the lead producer on *Breathe Free.*"

Now I choked for real. *Breathe Free* was the show Kylie left me to audition for.

Currently entering its thirteenth—or was it fourteenth? – season on one of the three major networks. Centered on the lives of five intertwined New York City families at the turn of the 20th century, it was a fiery, sometimes sexy drama dotted with political and crime-thriller subplots. The show literally had everything any viewer could want, and America had eaten it up, even if I still sort of hated it for pulling Kylie away from Philly. Every celebrity in the country, and many from abroad, wanted to guest on it, and the show had earned dozens of Emmys over the course of its run. I'd sat through God knew how many episodes with Kylie, listening to her sigh over how she'd kill to have just one line on that show.

"Your dad is—"

"Jonathan Kahn, yeah. My brother and I grew up using my mom's last name for school stuff just to keep a low profile, kind of, and I decided to keep using it when I left home. I didn't want—"

"You didn't want it to define you," I supplied. Damn. Suddenly a whole lot of things made sense about Toby.

"Exactly. And I really never had an interest in working on TV, either. So...ta-da! You're dating Jonathan Kahn's daughter." Her mouth stretched into one of those cringy-fake smiles, hiding a nervousness that was obvious to me after all these weeks. We'd pulled to a small booth in front of a gate with the letter "K" woven into the design.

"Hey, Tim," Toby said, pressing her lips together in another fake smile.

"Hey, Tobes! Welcome home! It's been a whole year, hasn't it? Your dad hasn't told me what's keeping you so busy on the other side of the country, but—"

"Thanks, Tim. Good to see you, too."

Tim's mouth clapped shut, like her shortness had taken him by surprise. But I wasn't surprised. Toby was nervous. That much was obvious. But if it wasn't normal for her to feel all shaky when rolling up to her parents' mansion, if Tom wasn't used to her behaving this way, the only thing that could have made this year's visit different was...

Me.

Toby's fingertips—her nails painted an uncharacteristic shade of dark burgundy—drummed on the gearshift. I gingerly reached out and took them in my palm. "I'm really happy to be here with you. I'd be happy about it if your dad was Tim. Or Voldemort."

She didn't respond, her lips still tight, and cruised to a stop at the apex of the circular driveway. Finally, she turned to me. "I'm sorry," she said in a deep exhale.

I reached for her other hand, and she placed it in mine. They *were* trembling. Giving her a soft smile, I squeezed her hands lightly. "I have literally never seen you this nervous about anything. Anything you wanna talk about before we go in?"

"I've never brought a guy home before," she said, her voice barely audible with the engine still running. The ridiculousness of letting the idling car keep spewing fumes into the California atmosphere was too much, and I reached a hand over to turn the key. Her eyes flared wide, looking from the stopped car to me. "We can leave. There are so many things to do around here. We should take a couple days, just for us. Check into a hotel, and..."

"Toby," I said, my voice quiet but firm. "Your parents are expecting you for Passover. Let's just...have dinner tonight and then we can decide, okay? We can skip out first thing in the morning."

"Or we could fly home?" she asked, her voice small.

Home. Whatever the reason for her nervousness, she'd just talked about 'we' and going 'home' in the same sentence and if that didn't mean, at least a little bit, that she was developing real feelings for me like I was for her—hell, like I was falling head-over-heels in love with her—then I didn't know what else it *could* mean.

I let my thumb swipe over the back of her hand. "This'll be fine." She took in a shuddering breath, then we both got out of the car, stretching our legs. I turned my face to the sun. LA really was a breath of fresh air, in some ways.

At that exact moment, the front door creaked open and a tiny, very tanned whirlwind of bronzed skin, large gold jewelry and bright, perfectly-coordinated clothing barreled toward us in a haze of perfume.

"Toby, *bubah,* you didn't even let him drive?" The tiny woman had made it around to Toby's side of the car and swept her into vice-like hug in her sinewy arms, which looped under Toby's. The woman's hands gripped Toby's shoulders from behind, holding her tight as she swayed them both back and forth while crooning in her ear. "It's been more than a year since I've seen you, oh, my baby!"

I would have busted out laughing at Toby's face if I thought there was any chance of her not killing me later. She looked absolutely miserable, yet tolerant of what was happening to her, like a squirrel caught in a tree with a hyper dog barking on the ground, just waiting for it all to be over.

Finally, her mom released her, and Toby let out a soft grunt as her feet were finally allowed to plant themselves completely back on the ground. Her mother couldn't have been taller than five-five to Toby's five-ten, but she clearly possessed a great enough strength to manhandle her daughter. The whole scene was heartwarming and hilarious, and I fought back a grin.

"So?" she said breathlessly, the whiteness of her smile almost as blindingly bright as the patterns on her capris. "You going to introduce me?"

Toby stepped back, scanning her mother up and down. "I don't know. Are you going to swing him around like a wrecking ball, too?"

Toby's mom threw her head back and laughed like she'd

never heard anything funnier. Evidently waiting for Toby to introduce me was just an option. She strode toward me with an arm extended, chunky bracelets clanking against each other. Her hands, I noticed, were exactly like Toby's, if a bit aged— long, delicate fingers, capped with delicately curved nails.

I understood Toby's chipped burgundy polish, now. Her mother's were painted a conventional, flawlessly shiny red. If everything Toby did in her professional life was to set herself apart from her father, everything she did with her appearance was in contrast to her mother.

Her efforts were in vain. She and her mother looked exactly alike. Suddenly I felt a strong connection to Johnathan Kahn, despite never having met him; such gorgeousness was impossible to resist for the both of us. Toby's effortless waves and simple fashion and makeup didn't hide the fact that she was a carbon, if tall, copy of her mother.

"Ima, this is Mark Mahler. I met him doing a radio show in Philadelphia."

She pumped my hand and narrowed her eyes at me simultaneously. This felt like a trap. "Mahler," she said, rolling her tongue around my name. "Radio show."

"Yes, ma'am. Toby's our sound engineer. I'm sure Toby is dying to tell you all about it. She's amazing at what she does."

She dropped my hand, nodding. "Good. Yes, I'm sure she's the absolute best. That's my baby."

Just like that, she turned and walked back to the front door. She spun around on the threshold, looking between the two of us. "Make yourselves at home. There are rooms for you in the East wing. And Mark?"

"Yes, ma'am?"

"No 'ma'am,'" she said, pointing a long red fingernail at me. "*Dina.*"

I just chuckled and dipped my head in a nod.

"Seder is at six, you two." Despite the fact that one of the gold bracelets on her arm was a watch, Dina glanced up at the sky, seeming to assess the position of the sun. "You've got a few hours. Give him the grand tour, *bubah*."

Toby smiled weakly as a young-ish guy in a polo shirt and khakis came jogging from a small building several hundred yards away from the house and reached into the back of the car to pull our bags out.

"We can get them, Kevin," Toby said, but the guy just laughed and hefted our bags into the house.

"I'll just leave these in your room, Miss Kahn," he said, and then he was gone.

I blinked hard to get my bearings. Toby Eisen was the girl I met all those weeks ago, the one I'd taken to bed, the one I'd started to fall desperately for. She had grown up on what might as well have been a different planet from my modest Midwestern childhood, but she was still Toby.

I approached her gingerly, letting my hand rest on the small of her back with the slightest pressure. "Wanna go in?"

"I...yeah," she said with a heavy sigh. "I'm sorry about all this."

"About...?"

Toby swept her hand in a wide arc in front of us, indicating the house and grounds. "All...this. And her."

"She seemed sweet. Like a normal mom."

Toby scoffed. "Okay. When I meet your mom, you can tell me that again."

My heart swelled up so full I thought it might burst. It must have been a slip of the tongue, but it sounded like Toby had thought about meeting my mom. I wasn't rushing into anything —I knew damn well how wary she was about anything looking like commitment—but just thinking about taking further steps with Toby invigorated me. Instead of voicing any of that, though, I just pressed a soft kiss to her temple and said, "Why don't we go get settled?"

This visit hadn't even started, but I already felt like it was going to end very, very well.

CHAPTER 31

TOBY

WHEN MY MOTHER said there were rooms for us in the East wing, she meant that we could have all the rooms in the East wing. That included four bedrooms, two bathrooms, and a living room, which were all separated from the rest of the house by the service kitchen.

Yes, this house had a service kitchen, and it was the one in use today as our chef was busy getting ready for Seder. I knew before we even walked through the front door that I didn't care whether Antoine and his handful of sous chefs he hired for holidays and big dinners heard Mark and I having sex.

Because right now, I needed sex.

Loud sex, with at least one mind-blowing orgasm.

Silently, I hurried up the twisting staircase with Mark in tow, down the hallway that skirted the kitchen, and into the pristine living room. There was a heavy door separating the kitchen hallway from this room. I whirled around, reaching across Mark, and flipped the lock. A few steps further and I finally stopped, dropping his hand and turning to him. Mark glanced around the room, taking in the eighty-inch TV mounted on the wall, the small bar in the corner, the overstuffed white couch that sat on white carpet.

"Toby, this place is..."

I couldn't hear it. Didn't want to hear whatever Mark was thinking about my parents' house, about how I'd grown up, about where I'd come from. About whether he fit in here.

I'd so badly wanted Mark to come home with me because I knew he would stick out like a sore thumb in this place, knew my parents would be disappointed that this guy was my boyfriend. I'd been so focused on wanting to get what I wanted —for them to stop bugging me to find the Ideal Jewish Husband, once and for all—that I'd barely stopped to think about how that disapproval might affect Mark. Hadn't prepared him for it at all.

I could consider other outcomes all I wanted, but deep down, I knew he'd be embarrassed, and sad, and maybe feel guilty. He'd stammer while trying to defend his lack of career. Hell, he probably wouldn't even understand most of their questions about his Jewish upbringing.

Mark was sweet, and wonderful, and brilliant, but my parents wouldn't see any of that, and it would devastate him.

I squeezed my eyes shut. I did not want to be thinking about this. If I thought about it, I'd have to talk to him about it, and if we talked about it, the sense of dread that was slowly creeping over me told me that we might not talk about much else.

We might break up. Might never touch, kiss, or have sex again.

That was a thought I simply couldn't bear.

Instead, I planted a hand on either side of Mark's face and dragged his mouth to mine, plastering his lips with a hot, decisive kiss. When I pulled back, we were both panting.

"Take me to bed," I murmured, having only pulled back enough to let the words out.

"But Toby, we—"

I dove toward him again, this time darting my tongue in between his lips, licking over them and then notching my teeth over his lower one just enough to make him yelp.

If anyone knew how to make Mark Mahler shut up, it was me.

Like I'd pushed a very specific button, his hands went to my ass, his fingers digging in. I jumped, and his hands slid under my thighs, helping me wrap my legs around his waist.

"We shouldn't be doing this," he growled before bending his head to mouth at my neck.

"No," I gasped as my head bent back, giving him better access. "This is exactly what we should be doing. That flight was too long."

He bared his teeth, wiggling them against my collarbone, and I groaned.

"Where?" he sighed, his legs already moving.

"First door on the right. Hurry."

He did. There, in my teenage bedroom, with my parents getting ready for a holiday dinner just a few hundred yards away, Mark Mahler, the random scruffy dude from Philadelphia local radio's Bro Show I'd met two months ago, gave me the two most incredible orgasms of my life.

He muffled my screams with his palm while he breathlessly huffed the sounds of his release into the pillow beside me.

Even without the noise we'd grown accustomed to making, it was the best sex I'd ever had. I couldn't help but wonder if Mark was the best I ever would have—if anyone could ever make me feel the same way he did.

I wished I'd known then, panting beside him on my thoroughly disturbed white comforter, our bodies slicked with sweat, deliriously happy in the afterglow, that it was all about to go straight to hell.

· · ·

Mark had refused to shower with me, saying we'd just get started all over again and then be late to dinner. I couldn't argue with that—there were few things I loved more than Mark, naked, wet, hot, and soapy. I freshened up first, then smacked his ass with a towel when he got in the shower. My hair went into a wet, messy knot on top of my head, and I pulled on skinny jeans and one of Mark's white button-down shirts. No jewelry, and no makeup besides a swipe of concealer on my chin, which Mark's stubble had just impressively chafed.

I knew my casual getup, plus how me wearing Mark's shirt would make it obvious that we just fucked in the East wing on our way to Passover Seder, would drive my mom nuts. That was exactly why I wore it.

It was also the reason I frowned when I saw Mark, dressed and groomed to perfection for Seder. He'd shaved, styled his hair so that none of the short pieces stuck out anywhere, and put on deep gray wool, flat-front trousers and a fine-knit, sky-blue sweater. The worn jeans and slouchy hoodies and plaids I'd gotten used to seeing on him in recent weeks were nowhere to be found.

"Did you dress up for my parents?" I asked, trying my hardest to make the panic in my chest sound like teasing in my words. "Why?" I whimpered, leaning into him. "It's not important to me, you know. That they think you look nice." Nothing could have been truer. I brought him here to do the opposite of impress them, and here he was, pulling out all the stops.

Oh, this was all wrong.

"You said you were going to wear the shirt I got you," I said, fully aware that I was whining. I'd found a vintage Beastie Boys concert tee at one of my favorite shops and picked it up for him on a whim. He'd loved it.

"I am," he said, pulling the collar of his sweater just slightly to the side to show me he was wearing it as an undershirt. "It's my good luck charm."

Good luck. We were both going to need it.

I traipsed downstairs just in time to greet David and Roni at the door. Roni carried two huge totes full of food – something she did every year, despite my mother telling her that Antoine would take care of everything. Roni and I weren't exactly friends, but we both shared in the feeling of ridiculousness that my parents didn't just live in a normal house and have a normal Seder with normally simple food, especially for just the five of us. Bringing the chocolate toffee matzah and homemade charoset was how Roni made sure her two little ones would have a taste of the Jewish upbringing she'd grown up with in the Bay Area. Small and homey. Normal.

How was it possible that Roni hadn't come to Seder for the first time and run screaming away from my brother? She must have really loved him, even back then. Even that first year.

A tiny pit of intense, unidentified emotion settled into my stomach.

She looked exhausted, weighed down by all that food on one arm, and by Leah on her hip. Thankfully—or stressfully—Sarah was walking easily by now, and she skipped, sure-footed, through the front door.

"Tante T!" she squealed in an impossibly high-pitched coo as she jumped into my arms. Her brown, wavy, frizzed out hair was unmistakably a copy of my own.

"Hi, smoosh," I said, laughing as I squeezed little Sarah, despite myself. "Who's been feeding you? You're so big! What are you, three years old or something?"

"I'm four!" Sarah giggled, squirming away from where I was digging my fingers into her ribs. "And it's Mommy's fault, she feeds me the best food."

"Well," I laughed, "I suppose that can't be helped. Now, tell me, is our table all ready for Seder?"

I carried Sarah into the formal dining room, which my mother inexplicably had decorated with a snow-white carpet, where the table was laid with the best china and spotless wine glasses. I wanted to growl in frustration. It was like she didn't even want her own grandchildren here.

"Where are the fwogs?" Sarah asked with an air of four-year-old outrage. "There were fwogs at our Seder at school." She frowned, craning her neck to see between the glinting china and glasses.

"Savta must not have them this year," I said, feigning shock, as though it was a requirement to have toy frogs on one's Seder table. It wasn't, but to my niece, it was part of what made Passover magical. Sarah looked at me in disbelief, her lip trembling.

"Lucky for you, though," I said, letting my smile get wider, "Tante T brought some all the way from Philly." I shoved two fingers in my back pocket, digging out a baggie of tiny plastic frogs, painted in garish colors that would totally disrupt my mother's tablescape, and presented them to my niece, who squealed. She threw her pudgy arms around my neck and squeezed. I laughed and spun her around, then let her run off to show David her prize.

I turned to watch her run through the doorway, only to see Mark leaning against it, the corner of his mouth twitching up.

"What?" I asked, cognizant of the hiss that accompanied my question.

"Nothing. She just looks like you. Kind of crazy to think about what you looked like as a kid."

I hadn't realized that my heartbeat had picked up so much speed in just a couple of seconds until I felt it slowing down.

I knew that at my age, twenty-five, women sometimes

started to feel their biological clocks kicking in. I wasn't even sure if I believed in any of that, but I was sure that I was nowhere near ready for kids. Knowing that Mark had planned to propose to Kylie, the idea that he'd probably been thinking about kids with her was always sort of floating around in my mind.

As much as I liked Mark, and as much as I realized my emotions had left 'like' in the dust and were fast approaching 'head over heels', I was absolutely, positively, in no way close to being ready to even think about having kids with anyone.

Even Mark.

"That's all you were thinking about?" I asked as I walked toward him, unable to resist standing as close to him as I could. Damn him.

He shrugged. "You must have been adorable when you were little. You're cuter now, though."

"Mmmhm," I said, letting my arms wrap around his waist and leaning my forehead on his shoulder.

The short moment of peace was interrupted by the sound of my father busting out in laughter, with David's accompanying chuckles in the undercurrent.

David had worked his way up through the Hollywood production culture, using my dad as a hand-up every step of the way. My brother was a nice guy, but at eight years older than me, and the recipient of every bit of attention from my father at my expense, we'd never been close.

Roni was only five years older than me, and in the ten years since she'd met David, I'd gotten to know her well. I didn't consider her a sister, exactly, but we were close enough that we hugged when we saw each other and even texted sometimes.

"Did I hear my princess is home?" Dad asked, striding into the dining room in dark jeans and a blue button-up. It was what a Very Important Person in Hollywood wore when they wanted to look comfortable and casual, but really were a few steps away from being ready to walk back into the board room. Hell, for all I knew, Dad was going back to the office, or to some studio, as soon as we were done with dinner.

A rush of gratitude that Mark was here washed over me. "Dad, this is Mark," I said, clutching Mark's forearm like a buoy and pulling him along with me.

Mark went willingly, his typical slow, almost dragging steps turning confident and striding. He stretched out an arm, flexing his hand before making it rigid to shake Dad's. I'd learned about that in a behavioral psych class—Mark was subconsciously displaying confidence and asserting dominance with his damn handshake. "Mark Mahler, sir. It's an honor to meet you."

Dad's eyes crinkled at the corners. "Has Toby been bragging about me? Please, don't call me sir. Jonathan will do just fine. When you come to my house for the holidays, you're family."

I rolled my eyes, wondering how many times he'd used that same dumb line on guests who'd come to his house. Family. Dad barely had enough time for his actual family, let alone adding new people do it. I'd been nine years old when *Breathe Free* filmed its pilot, which meant I hadn't really spent any meaningful time with Dad since I was eight.

Still, that little pit that had formed in my belly earlier became heavier, more intense. Dad beamed at Mark like he'd never been happier to see anyone, while I remained at his side, a bystander.

"Thank you for the invitation, s—I mean, Jonathan."

"Of course! When Toby told her mother all those weeks ago that she wanted to bring someone, I was just over the moon that someone was taking care of my little princess all the way across the country."

My cheeks went red, the muscles in Mark's forearm flexed under my hand. He knew this was getting to me, but there was no way he'd say anything. Good. Because I didn't need him to. Never did, never would. "See, Mark, my father doesn't think I can take care of myself. Even though I've been on my own for seven years."

"Sure, baby. I'll just forward those Stanford bills to you, then, okay?" Dad laughed heartily as if that was the best joke he'd ever heard, or made, in his life.

I glanced at Mark, who gave my dad the courtesy of a small smile, even though I knew that look. A muscle at his jaw twitched. He was holding back. I squeezed his arm.

"Sit next to me," I said, acquiescing when Dad pulled me in for a quick hug, pressing my cheek to his jaw when he leaned in and kissed the air.

The sooner we got started, the sooner this would be over with.

Thankfully, Sarah chose that moment to barrel back into the dining room. "Tante T, is that your boyfriend?"

My mouth quirked up at the corner. "He is my very special friend and he is a boy. So, what do you think?"

Her little face screwed up in thought. "That depends. Do you kiss him?"

"Sarah Rivka Kahn!" Roni hissed as she trailed behind Sarah, with baby Leah still on her hip and a basket of toys for Sarah in the other. "I'm sorry, Tobe, that was rude." She glared at her daughter, who kept her feet planted right in front of me. I chuckled softly, not wanting to undermine Roni's parenting, but finding my niece's unflappability hilarious.

I leaned closer to her and whispered, "Yes, I do kiss him. What do you think?"

"I think that's yucky. And I think that makes him your boyfriend."

"Yes, and while I'm happy that Tante T is sitting next to me," Mark interrupted, leaning down to eye level with the little girl, "there is a very empty chair on my other side. Would you take it?"

Sarah regarded him for a long moment, then gave one decisive bob of her head. "Yes, I will."

Mark, smiling, helped her settle in to the seat, which was impractically covered in pristine white fabric, and listened intently as she lined up the little frogs I'd brought her, quizzing her on each of their colors. Dammit, why did he have to be so *good* with her? If I squinted, I could imagine him with his own kid, which would, of course, not be mine.

Because I was never having kids. Because I didn't want an attachment. Because I was not the kind of person who tethered my life to anyone's. Never had been, never would be.

My stomach hurt.

He leaned down and whispered something in Sarah's ear, which earned him a gasp from her followed by a trail of high-pitched giggles, then a high five.

"What are you two planning?" I asked, nudging my shoulder against Mark's.

"You'll see," he said, winking at Sarah theatrically. She giggled again.

In the next few minutes, the kitchen staff came in with the Seder plates, including the orange—a modern inclusion that symbolized LGBT rights and feminism, but which Ima loved for the color and dimension it added to the décor—and a bottle of wine to sit between each pair of adults.

Something snagged at my heart, watching my family gathered around the table. Last year, baby Leah had been so tiny that she'd slept through the Seder in her carrier in the next room. Now, with her babbling on Roni's lap and with Mark in attendance, there were eight of us at the table. Despite the stark white and polished furnishings, the room felt almost homey. Relaxing and happy and brimming with love.

Just thinking that last word made my stomach seize up again. Dammit.

Dad picked up his copy of our homemade haggadot—the books that explained the symbolic foods and told the story of Passover—signaling us to do the same. Ima was no DIY homemaker, but she'd been so proud of these haggadot the first year she'd made them. She'd started with the bare-bones traditional texts, edited to drop the long, snooze-worthy passages. Then she'd liberally peppered the ceremony with poems and readings she loved, plus lines from TV shows and movies she'd written herself. Quotes about love and freedom and acceptance and fighting for what was right first went from her pen to Hollywood scripts, then to the mouths of famous actors and actresses, and only then back to our Seder table.

She never included anything from a script that had failed.

"This is really incredible, Mrs. Kahn," Mark said, thumbing through the pages. "I remember this speech of Layla's in *Next Time, Call Back*. I had no idea you were the screenwriter."

I turned and regarded him, shocked. I had no idea he was a movie buff. My stomach churned again.

"Oh, I was only one of them, darling." Ima waved off Mark's flattery, even though I knew she adored it. "So sweet. And I already said, call me Dina."

Dad led the Seder just like he did every year, reading through it as though it were a script with which he was familiar but to which he was only marginally emotionally attached, and I shot Mark an apologetic glance. He just reached down and squeezed my knee.

Then the time came for the Four Questions, the Aramaic passage my mother had threatened to make me chant aloud all those weeks ago when she'd called about booking my tickets. I was half-ready to rush through them, had even practiced a little in my head because I knew that David would, according to tradition, try his best to mess me up mid-recitation. So, when we flipped to the page, I cleared my throat and said, "Okay, here we go."

"No, Tante T! These are *my* four questions!"

Roni chuckled, adjusting baby Leah on her leg while shoving a spoonful of applesauce in her mouth. "Sorry, Toby, she's been practicing hard." Then she leaned in, whispering to me. "And, honestly, if she messes up, I don't think anyone will care, do you?"

I grinned, and then theatrically announced, "This is such a relief. I was very worried about singing the Four Questions but I just found out that Sarah Rivka is going to save the day and do it instead."

My niece, still so tiny, wiggled on her seat in her giant tulle skirt. She pulled in a deep breath, then blew it out slowly. "Okay," she whispered to herself, before sitting on her hands and singing in a voice as quiet as a mouse, *"Mah nishtana ha laila hazeh..."*

She made it all the way through the first verse, and her eyes were bright while we all applauded. But on the second verse, she stumbled on the fifth word in. Her lower lip started to tremble and she looked around at all of us, taking in her expectant audience.

After two seemingly endless seconds of silence, Mark spoke up. "Oh! We're going around the table, right? It's my turn?"

Without skipping another beat, Mark said, "I don't know how I'm going to follow Sarah's awesomeness, but here goes."

Then he sang the goddamn second question without missing a single syllable or beat. *"She b'chol haleilot, anu ochlin she'ar yerakot..."*

My eyes were wide and my jaw dropped slightly. The

whole table joined in the chorus, *"Halaila hazeh..."* and I was pretty sure my mouth moved, though I couldn't focus on a single thing that came out. It was my turn next, but when I looked down at the page, the letters were a blur.

My dad took over for me, and within a few more seconds, the passage was over.

Dad droned on for a couple more pages, making a big deal out of the one line Ima had written that appeared in a poetry reading in *Breathe Free*, and she beamed.

"Mark, I think your family knows our friends? Beth and Dan Shapiro?"

Mark cocked his head to the side and screwed up his mouth, thinking. My stomach soured. Oh God. I should have seen this coming, all those weeks ago.

"Mayyybe," Mark said. "I grew up right near Pepper Pike, but I might have known her from NFTY youth group stuff. Do they have a kid named Chloe?"

"Yes!" my mother crowed. "Amazing, isn't it? We were friends with that family when they lived in L.A. I think Toby went to a birthday party at their house." She beamed, and Mark gave her a polite smile.

"I met them once, a few years ago. I just have a really good memory for names, I guess. Helps with my work."

He was Jewish. All this time I'd thought Mark's very being violated my parents' number one quality in an ideal boyfriend, he'd been Jewish. Just like they wanted.

I swallowed, hard. We poured a second glass of wine. I knocked it back immediately after the blessing, in one smooth motion.

My head swam.

The recitation of the ten plagues on Egypt was next, and when my father announced them, Sarah began to giggle. Mark extended a fist to her and she took something from it, tucking it between her little legs, buried in the tulle of her skirt, and squirmed in her seat.

Dad started to read the names of each plague out loud, "Blood," he said loudly. "Frog—"

Sarah squealed, then shouted, "Ribbit!"

Mark made a couple low croaking noises, and then the plastic frogs I'd brought for Sarah to quietly play with during our traditionally sedate Passover Seder were flying in the air, falling haphazardly, some with a splat into the charoset dish, others into the flower arrangements. One splashed into the water goblet in front of my mother's plate, and after a split second of staring at it, wide-eyed, she let her head fall back and let out a long, hearty, belly-deep laugh.

"Mark Mahler," my mother said between gasps of air a few laughter-filled moments later, "You did not tell me you were still twelve years old!"

Roni was laughing softly, running her hand over baby Leah's downy hair, which curled over her delicate little ears, and glancing at David, who let out a chuckle beside her.

"I think we all feel like kids at Seder sometimes, Dina. My sister and I didn't even orchestrate frog throwing until we were well into our high school years. You're never too old to be young at heart. I was just delighted Sarah was here so I'd have an excuse to carry on the tradition." He lifted his palm to her and she cracked up as she gave him a high five.

My gut twisted and flipped madly now. I could barely expand my lungs, let alone force a smile on my face, but I did my best. Seder wouldn't last much longer now, just a few more pages before dinner, and then I could excuse myself to deal with the fact that Mark Mahler, the guy I had brought home to piss my parents off with his glaring, obvious non-Jewish status, was Jewish.

How had I not known he was Jewish?

I could have listed on my fingers all the things my parents wanted me to do when I grew up. Live close by, graduate with decent grades from a California college, get a semi-high-profile, semi-corporate career, preferably managing underlings at a high-profile L.A. charity, live close to home, marry someone successful and Jewish.

For twenty-five years, I'd managed to defy my parents on every single one of those things. I'd known from the time I was sixteen years old that nobody was going to dictate my life. I'd gone to Stanford, which was close enough to home, but I'd double majored in anthropology and gender studies, majors which wouldn't even get me close to any kind of job they'd wanted.

I'd left the state the week after graduation, bouncing around the country and working new jobs, taking a steady stream of weird graduate courses, and dating strange men I'd never let them meet for the past three years. I'd done my fair share of those things in college, too, but the years after were when I was really supposed to start acting like a grownup, according to my parents. According to everyone, really.

But Tovyah Eisen did not do what anyone told her. I did what I wanted. I didn't invite, certainly didn't bow to, anyone else's opinion.

My parents wanted me to bring home a nice, successful Jewish boy. Then they wanted me to marry him. Then they wanted me to do whatever he thought was best, over and over, for the rest of my life. They wanted me to find someone to take care of me. They refused to see, refused to believe, that I was capable of taking care of myself.

Mark's hand squeezed my knee, making me jump. "Third glass, Toby." I reached for the bottle mechanically, filling his cup, then watched as he took the bottle from me and filled mine.

The other four adults at the table chatted, and Mark leaned in to whisper in my ear. "You okay?"

"I didn't know you were Jewish," I whispered, feeling my face pale, aware of the blood draining from my lips.

He shrugged and squeezed my knee again. "Long story," he whispered. Like it was no big deal. Like this fact about who he was required no explanation. Like every thought I'd had about him, every decision I made regarding him, hadn't been a complete lie.

Finally, it was time to eat. Mark volunteered to hide the afikomen for Sarah to find—because of course he did—and I stared at a plate of salmon Antoine set in front of me, garnished with roasted potatoes and green asparagus. My stomach was still queasy.

Mark was Jewish. To my parents, it must have looked like I had finally done exactly what they wanted: found an acceptable boyfriend to settle down with, notch directly into the role of Perfect Daughter, get married, have babies, the end.

But I still had one more thing in my arsenal. And really, I thought cheerily, it had been the thing that had made me want to bring Mark home so badly from the start: his floundering, almost non-existent career. I swallowed down whatever nausea the Jewish thing brought, and broke through the small talk between my parents and David to say, "So, I went to one of Mark's gigs with him a couple weeks ago."

"You're a musician, Mark?" Dad's eyebrows furrowed. God, I wished Mark was a musician, but he was really the next worst thing, according to my parents. "No, he co-hosts a radio show."

"Yes, on the side. I've been working on a new business, though, managing artists."

"That too!" I grinned, knowing that Mark occasionally helping his friends find gigs was the bottom of the totem pole in my dad's eyes. By age twenty-six, I knew, my dad would want any guy I was seriously dating to be much more serious about his career. "Mark has been helping out his friends. We went to this sweet piano bar. Beth was just precious. She's right out of college, isn't she, babe?"

Mark quirked an eyebrow at me. I never called him babe. Never called him any pet names, now that I thought of it.

"Uh, yeah, Beth is one of my newer clients. I got her a first gig in Philly, and I have a couple more on the table."

"They loved her," I said, trying to make my voice as effusive as possible. "I mean, she only worked for tips, but Mark loves helping people," I said, plastering a smile on my face while directing the words at my father.

My father didn't give a shit about helping people. He only cared about making money.

"Yeah. Low-earning clients like Beth make my higher-earning clients happy, if you can believe it. The performing—"

"You have many clients, then?" my dad asked.

Here it came. Here came Mark's futile defense of his own rinky-dink 'business', my dad's shaming of him, my jumping to his rescue. I'd piss off my parents by ruining Seder, impress Mark by 'proving how much I cared about him despite him having no real career prospects, maybe spend the rest of the evening in the backyard hot tub with him, making out in full view of my parents.

We'd discuss the Jewish thing later. I was sure my parents were totally thrilled that I'd managed to snag a Member of the Tribe and bring him home to the most Jewish event of the year, but whatever. Being honest with myself for a split second of rationality in all this, I realized that part of me liked that he was Jewish. It meant there was an extra level of understanding between us about holidays, our upbringing, our shared culture. It was nice.

So, I could live with that. What they really cared about was money, and they'd hate a guy who came into my life with empty pockets. Specifically, without career prospects and net worth that came with at least six zeroes after it.

"Yeah, I've expanded my ranks to almost thirty clients, now."

What? I struggled to chew and swallow the small bite of salmon I'd placed in my mouth. I would have sworn under oath that Mark had no more than a handful of friends for whom he occasionally found gigs.

"Really. And how many years have you been in the business?"

"I'm coming up on my two-year anniversary, si—uh, Jonathan."

"And your growth has been good and steady, it sounds like."

"Two years isn't very long at all to have that many clients," David interjected. "I've worked with some music management firms out here, booking artists for pilots and a few other things, and it sounds like you're tearing up the East coast."

"Well, the last few months have seen the biggest growth. And I can't really take credit for that. That was all due to Magnus Gunnar. After his nominations, things really took off for me. Right at the beginning of the year I signed a small handful of artists who are either already high profile, and wanted to leave bad management, or who I think have real potential to break into the upper tiers of the business. The East coast is honestly a really underserved area. People want to live among palm trees, not ice storms in miserable gray concrete jungles."

My dad and brother chuckled, and I mentally transported the whole scene to a vintage men's bar. Gross.

And then, there was that loaded word: *nominations*.

"Nominations?" I repeated, weakly.

"Yeah," Mark said, squeezing my knee again, this time under the approving eye of my father.

I wanted to shake him off. I wanted to run away, down the street, like a petulant teenager fleeing home. God, I hated this. I hated *myself*.

"Not gonna lie, I spent most of the winter riding the coat-tails of that Grammy win. I could have waited to leverage his success, which of course had mostly nothing to do with me, until after he won, but I honestly didn't think he would. Kid hadn't paid his dues, but there he was, holding the statue anyway."

Dad chuckled again. God, it was like nails on a chalkboard. "Isn't that always how it goes, son?"

Son?

Mark dipped his head in apparent agreement. "I did get a few new clients after he floated my name in his speech, but I've learned that my most valuable contacts are the ones I've been with from the beginning. That's why I still set some of my artists up in Philly piano bars."

My mother was walking around the table, filling wine glasses like this was the most normal fucking conversation she'd ever heard. Roni was in the corner singing softly to baby Leah, pausing to give Sarah strict instructions not to break any of my mother's valuables while she was looking for the afikomen.

Mark called Sarah over to him and whispered some clues to the broken matzah's location, and then she was off like a shot. I envied Roni, separate from all this. Hell, I envied Sarah, and she was a fucking four-year-old.

"Don't say you didn't have a hand in that Grammy win, Mark," Ima said in that way she did when she was entertaining an important guest—friendly with a little performance, an edge of flirting. Gross. "I recognize you now. You're Mark *Mahler*. You did that interview for Entertainment in the Grammy preview issue."

Ima was a junkie for Entertainment magazine like other ladies her age were for soap operas or their bi-weekly mahjong game. She memorized every issue, every picture and every word, and from her incessant gabbing, you would swear the obsession was pivotal for anyone who wanted to work in Hollywood. It certainly had never shown through in her career, though. Or at least not that I noticed.

"You cleaned up. You used to dress like a homeless man, with a beard to match."

"Dina," my father scolded sharply and, like a dog who'd been caught raiding the snack cabinet, my mother looked at her shoes, flushing.

"Well, he did. Do we have our Toby to thank for this makeover?"

He chuckled. "No. My sister. We're twins, and we're very close. I'd just gone through a little personal upheaval, and when I started dating again, my sister thought I needed a new look."

"For work reasons," my mother supplied. I shot her a glare, though I wasn't even sure who I was supposed to be defending right now. My plan had been shot to hell, and my body felt like it had been too.

"For various reasons. Honestly, I don't think it hurt my chances with Toby."

"I should think not," my own damn mother simpered at my boyfriend.

The only thing was, now my cheeks burned, too. Because he was right. I would have never in a million years wanted to be seriously involved with pre-makeover Mark Mahler. I knew it was true in the same breath as I was utterly ashamed of it. That was one reason why I'd taken the job with The Bro Show, for God's sake. I didn't want to put myself in the place of knowing I'd fall into bed with whoever I worked with.

And embarrassed that I'd done exactly the same thing,

apparently, my mother would have done. Been tempted by eye-candy Mark, used him for whatever purposes I could.

In this case, sex. Pissing off my parents was the long game.

Somehow, sitting here with my family glowingly approving of the guy I'd brought home for them to hate, I'd lost. Utterly and completely. Which was absolutely positively the worst thing that could possibly have happened.

"So, Jonathan," Mark said, sounding maddeningly like himself even though he was talking to my father—my father!—like they were old friends, "I think I know someone who snagged a role in your season finale."

My dad chuckled. "No offense, son..."

I rolled my eyes. *Son*. Again. This was just getting more impossible by the moment.

"...but I never forget an agent or manager who crosses my show's path. And I'm sure I would have remembered you."

"Oh, she's not my client. Just...a friend. Kylie Pearson? Last I heard she'd gotten cast as a speakeasy singer." Mark leaned back in his seat, but his foot wiggled at the end of his ankle. He could try to look casual all he wanted. I knew he was as keyed up now as he'd ever been.

My dad's face smoothed into an expression of polite indifference. "Yeah, we had to cut the speakeasy scene. It wasn't doing what we needed it to." He waved his hand dismissively. "Kylie was sweet."

Mark swallowed hard, shifting in his seat. "Was?"

"Yeah, and a real talent, too. You know, in an innocent, homey sort of way. Like Judy Garland in her early days, without the little gleam of trouble in her eye. Anyway. She submitted some original songs, isn't that right?"

Mark cleared his throat, then shifted so both his feet were on the floor. I'd never seen him this worked up. Never. "I'm not sure."

"Yeah, I think one of my scouts emailed them to me, just hold on a sec..."

"Jonathan, no phones at the table, especially not the Seder table..." My mother trailed off mid-sentence as soon as it was clear Dad was completely ignoring her. David was doing something with baby Leah, while Roni had been dragged off to help Sarah find the afikomen. I could hear their stomping up and down the polished-wood hallways.

Then the clunky tones of an old piano blasted out of Dad's phone. A sensual voice followed it a few bars later, solid and on-tune, but gravelly at the low notes and fading in and out breathlessly on the high ones. She sounded pretty good. Nothing special, but her voice was so honest, so emotional, that I couldn't help listening to the words.

Let's not forget how good we were
Still those feelings inside me stir
I loved you too deep to know it was there
Oh baby I still love you, I still care.

"I remember her on that day of filming. She really was a sweet girl, sweet song." Dad repeated the assessment—*sweet*—despite the existence of a million other adjectives he could have possibly used. "Sweet song, we almost used that clip."

I knew what it meant when Dad called someone sweet. It meant she had nothing outstanding to offer. Kylie had been cut because she wasn't extraordinary, her voice was forgettable, and my dad waded through dozens of wide-eyed singing rookies looking to fill a few seconds on his show daily.

But the song played on, and Mark looked like he couldn't breathe. Or close his damn mouth. His gaze loosely fixed on my dad's phone, he finally swallowed hard again, then choked out, "Ah, that's, um...that's too bad." He swallowed again.

I wanted to die.

Every horrible circumstance swirling around coalesced into a dark cloud directly over my head, swirling and kicking up wind and blocking out everything else.

My parents adored Mark Mahler, thought he was practically perfect in every way.

He was still in love with his ex-girlfriend. It was obvious from his stunned expression and lack of words and the pain in his eyes at hearing her voice. And those goddamn lyrics. She was still in love with him, too. I would bet she was getting ready to roll up to his front door any day now.

I would bet even more that he'd welcome her back into his life with open arms.

And, last but not least, the worst part of all this. Not only did my whole family love him, I was pretty sure I had fallen in love with Mark, too.

CHAPTER 32

MARK

I'D NOTICED Toby freezing up right after the Four Questions. I'd never recited them as a kid – Hannah and I had learned them when we were fifteen as a surprise for Mom the year after she'd married Alan. She'd teared up when we chanted them, I remembered. I'd always wondered if she regretted never taking us to synagogue or religious school, let alone training us for a bar mitzvah...but we'd never missed it. We'd just always known Mom loved us. It didn't matter to us that we didn't grow up with traditional Jewish celebrations; we knew we were Jewish, and that was what really mattered.

Mom told Hannah and I when we were in our late teens that our father, who wasn't Jewish, had never been supportive of raising us in any religion. He left when we were eight and phased himself completely out of our lives by the time we were twelve. It was a hectic few years for Mom, and she did her best holding our lives and the household together.

Meeting Alan, who was the President of our local Jewish Federation and a board member at a Reform synagogue, turned Mom into an active member of the Jewish community. When they got married a couple years later, we started hosting Seders.

Hannah and I were fourteen, and we never complained. We just wanted Mom to be happy. The truth was we were pretty happy to have Alan in our lives, too.

Toby's dad was insanely knowledgeable about the Hollywood music scene, and he spent the next half hour or so peppering me with questions about my experiences in Philly while the staff carried away dishes and glasses. Soon, David got up to help his wife bundle the girls up to head home, and I realized the only things left at the table were me, Jonathan Kahn, and our wine glasses. When the hell had Toby left? And how much of a jerk was I that I'd let her go?

Luckily, his phone buzzed in his pocket, and he excused himself to take the call. As soon as he was out of sight, I made my way to the East wing.

I found Toby sitting quietly on her bed, its sheets still rumpled from the last time we'd been in this room together.

"Hey," I said softly. Something wasn't right. She was too quiet, too expressionless. Too still.

I didn't touch her. I could tell she didn't want me to, even though I couldn't figure out why.

She just sat there, fiddling with the rings stacked on her fingers, touching them in turn, over and over again.

Finally, she said something, her voice unbearably quiet. "I didn't know you were Jewish."

"It...never occurred to me to tell you. It's not that important."

She turned to me then, her face set with a withering expression. "Of course it's important, Mark."

We'd dated for eight weeks and she hadn't made a single mention of her religion, aside from asking me to come home with her for Passover. There wasn't a bat mitzvah picture or wall hanging with Hebrew letters in her home. Of course, I figured from her name that she was Jewish—Tovyah Eisen left little to wonder about. But she had never given me the slightest indication that Judaism was an important part of her life. "You never asked, Toby. You didn't care."

"Of course I *cared*, Mark, I—"

I threw my hands up in exasperation. "You *didn't* care. You didn't care about my sister, either, but I told you about her. You don't know about my mom, or my parents' divorce, or how I never had a bar mitzvah but am definitely Jewish, which I guess your parents love but doesn't really affect my day to day life, or your day to day life, for that matter, which I know because you never asked, because you didn't *care*."

I'd never even dreamed of speaking to Toby this sharply, but the unfairness of this whole damn thing was starting to bubble up, and almost without warning, it was boiling over.

"You didn't know that Beth is a client I took on as a favor to Magnus Gunnar, whose mom is an alma mater of my mom's school and whose best friend is Beth's younger sister. You don't know that I was actually *at* the fucking Grammys, because you didn't ask, because you didn't care."

"I *did* care, Mark." Toby's deathly quiet words made me believe the exact opposite. She hadn't cared much about my actual day to day life, about who I was, at all.

Then again, if she didn't care, why was she this upset about these revelations? I pressed my lips together in a thin, angry line. Dammit, she was right. She must have cared. Otherwise—

"You know what?" I ground out. "That, I can almost believe. Almost. Because you wouldn't be this pissed off that we're apparently—surprise!—amazing together, if you didn't care." I couldn't keep the sarcasm out of my voice. Couldn't keep my lips from curling into a little bit of a snarl.

"I care about you. I like you. What I don't like is all of this. I don't *want* this, Mark."

"All of what?" For the life of me, I couldn't understand what she was getting at.

"This!" Toby gestured around her. "I spent my entire adult life trying to get away from all this...suburban, Hollywood, fake-ass obsessive *perfection*. To break out of this mold where I have a boyfriend that comes and behaves perfectly at dinner, and just so happens to slot perfectly into my parents' idea of what's perfect for me. God, it's like you came to Seder and suddenly I'm not even here."

"Toby. This is one weekend. You and I are going to go back to Philly and this will not affect our lives back there. I'm meeting your family. We're getting along. This is nice. But it's just a couple of days." I tried to keep my tone calm and measured, even though my heart was beating like crazy. Something was very wrong between us, and I was only beginning to grasp what it was.

"Yeah, well now you practically *are* my family. So." Toby sucked in a breath. It didn't take more than a few seconds for me to realize that her breaths were coming fast and short, and her lips were losing the tiniest bit of color. She was having an anxiety attack.

Suddenly, the anger that had been floating in the air all around me dissipated, and I stepped up to her, cupping her shoulders gently with my hands, lowering my voice. "Toby, are you freaking out about...commitment? Because you and I are not married. Not even close."

She pressed her lips together and shook her head quickly, like she was trying to shake of a fly. I took the hint, and let my hands drop. "I know. But we could be. We could get married, eventually. Because I don't even mind being around you for extended periods of time. And they fucking love you. And suddenly it's like I'm watching the pieces of my life all fall precisely into place but I can't even see *myself*."

I tried not to let my eyes light up too much at the mention of her not minding being around me for long periods of time, just held her gaze while raising an eyebrow slightly. "You really are freaked out by this, aren't you?"

She nodded, biting her lip and looking nowhere.

A deep, empty sadness took root in my chest.

This was the beginning of the end.

CHAPTER 33

TOBY

FUCK YES, I was freaked out by this. Why the hell wasn't he even fazed?

"Okay," I said as I stood up and started pacing the length of the room. "If someone told you that we were getting married... next month. Would that freak you out?"

Mark's mouth quirked up at the corner. "I...plead the fifth."

I flung my arm out as if indicating evidence to a jury. "That's what I'm talking about! You are so damn sure that's what you want—marriage, kids, four questions and frog tossing at the Seder—and I'm so sure it's *not* what I want in the least."

"Right. I know that. That's how we feel right now."

I crossed my arms and glared at him.

"In all seriousness though, I wouldn't freak out," he went on, like what he was saying wasn't insane, "but I'd be super confused as to what changed your mind in just a few days. I'd never want to...you know...do anything related to marriage unless the other person wanted the same thing."

Well, that would have to be a different "other person ." I was not going to want that. Ever. But just the idea of Mark with another woman made a strange shudder roll down my neck. I shook it off. "But you're not terrified. Why would you want to be with me when I am?"

"Oh my God, Toby, who cares? You have been carrying around this attitude that whatever is true now must be true in the future. If someone told you that we were getting married in three years—"

"Mark, don't –"

"Which, by the way, is probably on the inside of a reasonable timeline for that, *if* I was even thinking about that—"

"I don't know why you—"

"Would you break this off? Right now?" He moved toward me, letting his fingertips rest on my hips. My heart stuttered, and I struggled to catch a breath.

"Would you really say 'fuck it' to every awesome moment between us, to being happy for the next two and a half years, because you're afraid of something that might happen in the future but you're not ready for this very second?"

"Mark, I just can't imagine that I'll ever *want* to—"

"Okay. Well, I'll leave myself open to the possibility that you will never change, if you'll leave yourself open to the possibility that you will."

"It's not that easy." My voice broke. Tears welled in my eyes. I couldn't do this anymore.

"I never said it would be easy. But I think it might be worth it. Do you?"

"Yes, all right?" I shouted. "Yes, being with you is worth it. Because I love you. That's why I can't *stand* this!" I shoved my fingers into my hair, nails scraping against my own scalp, wishing I could make him understand. I loved him, but I hated how my parents loved him, and those two things couldn't go together. Absolutely could not.

And there was no way I was going to figure out how to explain that to him and still stay sane.

"Yes, Toby, I love you, too. Alright? Is that the awful thing you want me to admit right now? That's the reason we're going to break up? Because we fell in love?" His chest heaved and his nostrils flared.

"We weren't ever technically together," I said in a low voice.

"Oh. Great. Yes, that helps. This whole thing is fine when you consider we weren't even together. No. We only talked and texted for hours, hung out whenever we had a free moment and had mind blowing sex, but it's okay if all that stops cold because we were never technically *together*? God, Toby. That's deranged!"

"I don't know what to tell you, other than this thing between us is impossible. I can't...it's not...I can't do this. I can't *be* this." I gestured around wildly, hoping that he'd understand. I wasn't going to be just like my parents, perform for them exactly as they wanted. Certainly not for the sake of a guy. Even if that guy was Mark.

"Toby, if this situation is such a surprise to you, if you didn't think your parents would like me, then why in the hell would you want to bring me home in the first place?"

I just raised my eyes to his, not even trying to hide the pain and tears in them anymore.

I could see the moment realization washed over him. It didn't take long. "Oh. Oh. That's *why* you brought me home. Because...because, what? This is how you wanted to break up with me? Using your parents as an excuse?"

"No! Because I wanted them to stop asking me! I wanted to prove to them that I wasn't going to just roll over and be exactly what they wanted me to be, date who they wanted me to date!"

"And I was supposed to be proof of that. The exact opposite of what your parents would ever want for you. That was my value to you. A foil, a tool to troll your parents."

He was absolutely right, which is exactly what made my heart ache. Because he meant so much more to me now than he did when I hatched this plan. I just didn't know how to tell him that in a way that would make him believe it. I softened my voice and looked into his eyes, begging him to understand. "We didn't even know each other when we planned this trip, Mark. We were just...doing each other a favor."

"Yeah, but now we do know each other. You brought me home with you anyway. You didn't even care enough to prepare me for this. For any of it."

It wasn't even a question. We both knew he was right. Weakly, I replied, "That says nothing about how I feel about you, Mark."

"God, you must have thought I was some mega-disappointment to humanity. I gotta compliment your long game, Toby. You've been putting on quite a good act, all for this weekend full of pissing off your parents. I'm really sorry it didn't pay off."

"It wasn't an act," I choked out, my voice almost a whisper.

Mark's jaw clenched, setting so hard into an angle that my instinct was to reach out to touch it. To soothe him.

Fuck it all, I had to get out of here. I had to cry and scream into a pillow and figure out why it felt like my chest was trying to split itself open from the inside out. My heart twisted painfully. I grabbed my keys.

"Tell them I went for coffee or something. I can't...I just can't." I finished as I gestured at him helplessly.

"No, it's fine. I'll go. Please let your family know I loved meeting them. Or...I don't know. Whatever you think is best." He grabbed his suitcase, still packed, and held his hand out for the keys. Numb, I dropped them into his waiting palm.

I caught his hand as he walked past me, when he was just a step away from out of reach. "Mark, I—"

He looked at me with deep, mournful eyes for several long

breaths. I grappled for words, my mouth working open and shut silently. Finally, he squeezed his eyes shut. "Let me know you got home safe, okay?"

Then he was gone. And I collapsed into a heap on the spotless carpet, crying silent tears and not giving a single shit if my mascara was running down my cheeks, dripping onto Mark's shirt and the carpet and staining it all.

CHAPTER 34

MARK

THE HARDEST THING about getting back to my apartment was realizing that Toby hadn't tried to contact me while I was en route. The next hardest thing was dragging myself through the front door, letting my exhausted self in, and being rudely awakened by traces of Toby, everywhere.

Her lip balm carelessly dropped in the bowl where I tossed my keys. A t-shirt from my high school track team that she insisted looked better on her, neatly folded and perched on the arm of my couch. She did look better in it than I did—it barely covered her ass, and when she wore it around my apartment it was with nothing underneath. I knew when I face-planted on my bed that I shouldn't have done it, and the sharp pain in my chest at the hint of her shampoo's scent embedded in my pillowcases was more brutal than I ever would have imagined.

I hauled myself up and slept on the couch. When we sat there together, it usually turned into sex pretty quickly. My pillowcases were the only places she'd really stayed long enough for the scent of her shampoo to seep into the fabric. I knew I'd be sleeping on them tonight, just to feel closer to her, even though I knew it was pointless.

I hated that I'd left Toby crying—felt like an asshole for doing it—but our conversation was going nowhere. The only thing I was ninety percent sure of was that she was dumping me. She was safe, there with her family, and she very clearly didn't want me around much longer.

And, fuck me, I loved her so much that I wanted to make it easier for her.

Besides, she could take care of herself. That was her whole point, wasn't it? She didn't need me to take care of her. Didn't even want me.

It was no use telling Toby that I didn't see her as some kind of Kylie replacement. She'd believed that was how I saw her since the first time we talked.

On the other hand, I'd believed she was genuine about her motives for dating me. Well, that wasn't entirely true. I'd always known she wanted to get in my pants. But that was nowhere near as bad as what I'd been to her the whole time – a tool to use for sex and, ultimately, pissing off her parents.

I rubbed my jaw, grimacing at the stubble that had formed there since I'd last shaved. Maybe it was time to grow out my beard again.

If I still had it, Toby would never have said a second word to me. Maybe in the future, I'd be able to ward off heartbreak with my facial hair.

When there were no messages from her the next morning, I knew there never would be any. I knew it deep in my bones, the way you know Spring has finally come to stay, the way you can sense the person on the other end of the phone has bad news before you've even answered the call.

The funny thing was that when Toby didn't text me, nobody texted me. My phone sat dormant for almost two days, and so did I. I didn't go by her apartment—too stalkery—but I went everywhere else that I ever knew she went. The gym, where Natalia gave me sad looks after I'd been loitering there. The Kimmel Center. Joey and Hawk's, every day.

The Bro Show was the worst. Ethan knew – of course he knew. Natalia knew, and she'd tell him, because as much as she loved punching things, she still had four brothers. She knew what guys looked like when they were hurting. I probably looked worse than every breakup she'd ever seen, all put together.

"You know, man, you were never supposed to date one girl the whole time, anyway."

I shot Ethan a glare, then trained my eyes downward. I was trying not to look at Toby's empty chair. I probably would have shed a tear if I let that particular pit churn in my stomach for too long.

"Yeah, I know. But I can't say I regret it, man. She was incredible. Every day with her was just...the best." I swallowed, hard. I was sure the microphone picked it up.

Sure enough, Shari frowned, gave me a pitying look, and then started scribbling frantically in her notes the way she did when she had to something she'd have to go back and edit. "But, hey," I jumped in, realizing how damn depressing this had to be for our loyal listeners. "It was good while it lasted. The segment wasn't called Whiz Kid Mark Mahler: Looking for a Wife, right?" I chuckled.

"You're right, dude. Real relationships end all the time. Thanks for keeping it down-to-earth here on The Bro Show."

"Always, bro. Always."

Yeah, I was pissed off at Ethan for putting me on the spot like that eight weeks ago, but I meant what I said. Being with Toby had changed my life. I couldn't say how, exactly, not yet. But I was a different person for knowing her. Heartbroken, yeah. I loved her, still. But I'd also learned that work and planning for the future weren't all there was to life—not even close. I'd learned what it meant to fall hard and fast for someone and not give a shit about practicality or making sense of what I was feeling, when I was feeling it. Toby taught me to let go, to dare to envision endless possibilities for my future.

My only problem now was that I wanted her to be part of it.

After the show, Shari reached up to punch me on the shoulder. "You had to date my best sound girl in years, right?"

"How did you –?" I stuttered.

"It was obvious. After a couple weeks, just...the way you moved around each other." She was silent for a minute, watching me. Then she gave me a pitying frown. "She spoiled me, and now I'm scrambling for a new one. You're lucky I like you so much, Mark Mahler, or I'd kill you."

"I don't suppose she...?"

"She didn't say where she was going, just that she'd gotten some interviews and would probably only be coming back to Philly for her finals and graduation."

I cleared my throat. "Right. Right."

I didn't know why that was what made the whole thing with Toby feel truly *over*, talking with Shari like that, but it did.

———

The next day, when my phone buzzed with a text, I basically jumped out of bed to get it. Just because I had a gut sense that our relationship was dead in the water didn't mean I wasn't desperate to hear from Toby again.

It wasn't Toby, but it was someone asking to meet me at Joey and Hawk's.

I combed my hair a little more carefully than usual, hauled

out the iron for my shirt, and made my way to lunch with the first girl who ever broke my heart.

I couldn't have told anyone why I did it, but it was not because I wanted Kylie back. I didn't. In fact, thinking about her felt like thinking about someone I knew well, but distantly...my childhood pediatrician, or maybe not even that well, like one of the anchors of the Today show. There were no hard feelings, but there was no intimacy left, either. I honestly wasn't sure how much there ever had been.

"I wanted to thank you," Kylie said quietly. She blew across the surface of her black coffee, looked up at me with soft eyes. She used to get a slice of pie and coffee with cream and sugar. She was thinner, now. I assumed the changed order, her smaller waistline, and Hollywood living were all connected.

I'd ordered my usual—Hawk's BLTs were to die for—but something about sitting at this table, where I was so used to seeing Toby, now Kylie across from me instead, made me feel like time and space were warping slightly around me. I suddenly didn't think I could stomach any food.

"What for?" I asked, trying to swallow away the odd thickness cropping up in ridges at the edges of my throat.

"I got a call from Kahn Productions back in L.A. They wanted to keep me on retainer for the next season. It's only for a very specific kind of song, and the terms are very narrow, so it's not a ton of money or anything. But it's a foot in the door. They said that Jonathan Kahn asked for me specifically."

Now there was a full-sized lump in my throat. "I still don't get why you asked me to meet you here."

"I hassled Mr. Kahn into telling me about your new girl-friend. It didn't take a ton of internet stalking to figure out she's his daughter."

My mouth went dry. "It's...well, I...we were..."

Kylie's eyes were big and soft, patiently waiting for me to finish sputtering.

"Yeah, I just met him last week," I admitted. Meeting Jonathan Kahn had been surreal, and when I talked with him, my thoughts had gone directly to the one connection we had: Kylie had ditched me for a part on his show. That was the only reason I'd brought it up with him. The fact that it might have bothered Toby didn't hit me until hours later.

Not that it mattered anymore.

She reached across the table and covered my hands with hers. "I know I didn't leave our relationship on the best of terms, Mark. I wanted to tell you I was sorry a hundred times, but I could never find the right words. Or the right time, obviously. We had something good together, and I ruined it."

I pressed my lips together, trying to stave off the rueful smile I knew was forming there, and shook my head. "I got over it, Kylie. I mean, you're great, but...we wanted different things."

She shook her head, too, then squeezed my hand. "It's a shame. You're one of the good ones, Mark."

Before I could stop it, a harsh laugh barked out of my mouth.

"What?" Kylie asked, raising her hand to touch my jaw. "It's too little, too late, huh?"

"Actually, neither," I answered honestly. "I just...it's complicated. Sucks having your heart broken twice in one year, though." My eyes welled with tears, but I blinked them back.

The ever-noisy door banged open, but the sound barely registered until a few seconds later, when Toby stood at our table, her wide eyes darting between me and Kylie, settling on Kylie's hand on my cheek.

Deep purple circles swooped under Toby's eyes. Her mouth was turned down in a slight frown, her hair slightly tangled at the ends. Small things most people wouldn't notice, unless they were in love with her. Like I was.

"I...I'm sorry," she said, then abruptly turned and left, staring at the floor the whole way.

Kylie dropped her hand and I pulled mine away, giving her an apologetic smile. "I've gotta—"

"Yep. Go get her," Kylie said, her voice thin and soft, her smile wistful.

I'd never left a table faster than I did that minute. Toby hadn't made it very far—not even to the intersection. "Toby!" I shouted, hustling after her. I didn't care if people looked. This might be my last chance to talk to her, and I sure as hell wasn't going to waste it.

When she turned around, her cheeks were streaked with tears, her eyes already red.

In a split second, our eyes met, communicated something both of us understood perfectly—I wasn't going to let her go this time without talking.

"I want you to know," she began, "my parents, they're messed up. I never wanted that, so I made myself independent. Whatever I'm doing, it has to be on my own. You get that, right?"

"Not exactly," I admitted. "But enough. I guess." Now was the time for naked honesty. Nothing between us would matter if we only related to each other with half-truths.

Her bottom lip trembled, something that would usually make me want to cover it with my mouth, but the sadness seeping through her every micro-expression just made me want to hold her. I did neither.

"I'm just sorry I didn't become what I wanted before I met you," she whispered, her expression unbearably sad. "I am going to miss you every day."

"Then don't go!" I barely contained the shout that was trying desperately to crawl out of my throat.

"I have to," she said, her brows and lips twisting her face into the most acute vision of misery I'd ever seen. I couldn't wrap my head around it. She was miserable, and I was miserable. Why the hell did we break up? "It's fine." She barked out a rueful laugh. "Well, *you'll* be fine. Everything worked out for you with Kylie, looks like, so that's good. I'm happy for you, Mark." Her tears rolled in fat tracks down her cheeks. "Just do me a favor and don't try to contact me. I already miss you, and I...I don't think I could take it."

Dammit. She was killing me. "You don't have to miss me, Toby. Kylie, she's not—"

She took a step toward me, raised her hand to my chest, fingers loosely curled toward her palm. She paused for a moment, freezing the two of us in a tableau while the sidewalks of Philly kept moving around us. Then, soft as a whisper, she rested her palm over my heart, unfurling her fingers and letting them gently tap at my sternum. She looked straight into my eyes, and I knew that this, if nothing else she ever said, would be her deepest truth. "I'm not what you want, Mark. I'm not *who* you want. I miss you, but I don't want to miss you, because I never wanted to miss anyone."

The last word came out in a wet growl. This was pissed-off Toby. She was angry with herself for wanting me, a realization that sent a lance of red-hot anger through me, because there was not a damn thing I could do about it.

I finally knew, with one hundred percent certainty, there was no way to get her back.

If she was going to come back to me, she had to do that all on her own. Just like every other thing Toby ever did.

It was almost as if she felt understanding dawning over me. Her hand slid from my chest and before I could blink, she'd disappeared, hurrying away from me like she couldn't lose sight of me fast enough.

So I let her go. I watched her walk away, head bent and stiffer than usual, sprained, but not broken.

When I got back to my place, I realized that I also hadn't gone back into Joey and Hawk's where Kylie had been waiting. I sent her a simple text: *Sorry, I had to run. Good luck with everything.*

The little reply dots floated on my phone for long minutes, but I couldn't make myself care about what she'd say. There was no suspense. I couldn't see how I'd ever feel romantically about Kylie when Toby existed, when memories of being with her still lived in my brain.

Finally, a reply came through.

Kylie: I know we have a past, but I'm still looking for a manager. Word is, you're one of the best out there.

I smiled to myself. Kylie really was perfect, just not in the way I'd wanted her to be all those months ago. What seemed like forever ago.

Me: I am. And I'll give you a deep discount.

CHAPTER 35

TOBY

LEAVING Mark outside Joey and Hawk's that day was the hardest thing I'd ever done in my life, hands down. The only reason I'd ever left anyone—my parents, a boyfriend, a room-mate—was that I wanted to. More than that, I'd been crawling out of my skin to leave pretty much every person or situation I'd ever depended on. But not Mark. Mark was patient, brilliant, attentive, and a great match for me.

The problem was, I wasn't really me. I had no real idea who *I* was. Not yet.

Mark made me want to figure my life out in a way nobody else had ever been able to do. Everyone in my life had always been just a stepping-stone in the grand development I always envisioned for myself. An evolution, a becoming, a self-actual-ization that would leave me self-satisfied enough to give myself to someone else.

I couldn't let Mark become that.

He texted me, once. A few days after that day at Joey and Hawk's, telling me I was on his mind, no pressure, no guilt. I'd sobbed when I saw it, hastily tapped out *I can't, I'm sorry*, before blocking him. I told Natalia I'd done it, at the beginning of a workout, and broken down in tears. I hadn't punched anything that day.

She rubbed my back, not questioning my decision, not saying a word about Mark, even though I was sure she knew what he was thinking, feeling, hoping. Ethan was a bigger gossip than any junior high girl I'd ever met. I couldn't imagine he'd keep anything from Natalia, given the gooey eyes he always had aimed at her.

"Maybe it's time to get out of Philly," she said.

I nodded. "Yeah. Maybe it is."

"You know," she said, pushing herself to her feet and reaching down with her half-boxing gloved hand, "I'm looking to start a lease if you're looking to pass one off."

I took her hand with my fingers, the only things peeking out of my own half-glove. "Oh yeah? Moving in with Ethan?"

Natalia threw her head back and laughed. "In his dreams. No, moving out of the apartment above The Knockout. We're expanding."

"Congratulations," I said.

Natalia just nodded.

"Why don't you come over a take a look? I could probably be out in a week."

A week felt like a lifetime. I knew I could be moved out of my place with barely a trace in more like twenty-four hours. After all, I'd built my life around the assumption that, at any given moment, I'd want to leave it. Turned out that still held true.

CHAPTER 36

MARK

I HADN'T BEEN STALKING Toby, but it was hard to miss the U-Haul outside her door that day, one of the tiny ones. One that Toby could drive herself, just a woman on four wheels with all her stuff, free to do and be whatever she wanted. Classic Toby. I couldn't begrudge her that.

A day and a half later, the curtains were changed.

Two days after that, Ethan and I climbed the stairs that used to be Toby's.

"Natalia couldn't pass it up," he said, and I detected a hint of pride in his voice.

"So, are you two official, then? Been dancing around it long enough."

"Nah, man. Nothing in my life is that easy. But I'm working on it." He hefted a bag of groceries he'd just bought on his hip. "I'm cooking dinner for her."

"Oh. Good. That's...good." Suddenly my throat was thick, my head swimming with my own memories of being in that apartment. It hadn't been too much – it was clear Toby didn't really feel at home there. Why hadn't I ever cooked for her there? Maybe it would have helped.

No, it would have cocked everything up even more. Made her feel tied down. She'd have panicked right then and there.

I knew there was nothing I could have done to keep Toby in my life. Still, these thoughts plagued me every day, the maybes and the what ifs. I wasn't over her—not even close. It had been three weeks since I'd seen her. Natalia told me she'd blocked my number. There wouldn't be any more texts or calls. We were done. I had to accept that, *really* accept it.

"Isn't your lease about to be up, man?" Ethan broke my train of thought. "As much as I'd hate to lose you, maybe a change of scenery would be good. Philly isn't exactly a hub of music production. You're starting to get too big for this town, aren't you?"

I shrugged noncommittally. He was right, of course; I was being asked to travel to New York every ten days or so now. But the fact remained that I liked being haunted by Toby's ghost in this city. It hurt, but I didn't care.

Ethan turned to look me in the eye. "You've come a long way since I met you. The career, the look." He put his hand on my shoulder and I chuckled, looking up at him. He was talking about the fact that most days, I decided to shave, and that I'd gotten rid of my worn flannels and baggy pants once and for all. Mark Mahler Management was becoming a serious thing, and as its owner, I knew I probably should look the part any time I might encounter a new contact. That was all the time. "I'd hate to see your broken heart kill you here," Ethan said. "Wouldn't you?"

I shrugged again.

"You've gotta do something. You've gotta move. Forward, or...something. You know?"

I swallowed the lump down. "Yeah. I know."

That night, I started to pack, and I didn't stop until my apartment was as bare and desolate as my heart.

CHAPTER 37

TOBY

EIGHT MONTHS later

I hauled my body out of my twin-sized bed in my shoe closet of a room in my very own L.A. apartment. Well, the apartment I shared with a revolving cast of characters trying to make it in this crazy town, working insane hours as extras, production assistants, and, of course, waiters.

It wasn't like it mattered who I shared the place with. I was never "home" anyway.

I was about to head another eighteen-hour day on the sound crew for *Hell's Handmaidens,* a fast-paced drama about an all-female motorcycle gang that solved mysteries. It wasn't one of my dad's shows, or my mom's, though I'd gotten the contact through my mom. It had just been too good to pass up. Plus, there was some voice in my head that sounded way too much like Mark telling me that if I never had anyone help me through anything, I'd never go anywhere.

They were long, exhausting days. From holding booms, I'd developed muscles that even Natalia hadn't been able to coax out of my skinny arms, and my fingers had even gotten a little calloused from adjusting body mic after body mic. My tan was ridiculously deep, and I hadn't had freckles sprayed over my cheeks or golden streaks through my hair like this since I was little.

This week I was on the boom for an episode that had lots of close-ups, outside. It was going to be a long day on set, and the forecast was calling for freakishly warm December weather. Seventy-five degrees might have sounded nice and cool to most people, but in the California sun, I was going to be sweating my ass off. I pulled on a black tank, cut-off shorts, and a baseball cap to shield my eyes from glare.

Most days, work occupied my mind so thoroughly, and exhausted my body so completely, that I was able to keep myself from thinking about Mark—well, enough to not go crazy, anyway.

For a while I'd thought I just needed time to snap out of it, that I'd be dating and happy in L.A. in no time, carefree and back to life as I knew it before Mark Mahler had sent it into a tailspin. After a handful of failed pickups at bars and concerts that my new roommates dragged me to, and way too many nights of dreams that remembered the brush of Mark's lips over my skin, his unerring fingers working their magic on every part of my body, I knew I'd made a mistake. I still loved him, and probably would never stop. In typical scorched-earth fashion, though, I'd burned every bridge that could possibly lead me back to him. Hell, I didn't even have his phone number anymore.

Today we were filming a climactic scene between the show's token will-they-or-won't-they couple. The director had insisted that we needed a sunny day in the park for the job, symbolizing infinite possibility or the dawn of a new journey for their relationship or some shit like that. I was mostly worried that a sunny December day would bring out way too many rubber-necking onlookers for us to get anything resembling a clean sound sample for hours and we'd spend all day filming a two-minute scene.

I was wrong, it turned out. After shooing away pedestrians and taking care of a couple swarms of gnats, it looked like we'd be filming this two-minute scene for at least *two* days.

That meant that I had to hear, "I don't care if you don't want to hear this, Ellie, because I have to say it. From the moment I met you, I loved you. I always will. Nothing can change that. Ever," from the hero about ten gajillion times before it was time to break for lunch.

My life here in L.A. was going well. I was proud of myself for taking the leap, moving out here, signing a contract that guaranteed I'd be here months, even years from now. I'd even made friends. But none of it could fill the hole I'd dug in my own life when I cut Mark out of it. That part of me wanted nothing more than to hear Mark say the same words to me that fictional Ellie was lucky enough to be hearing over and over, thanks to my boom mic.

Sweat trickled down into the small of my back as I waited in line at the craft services table. I wanted a salami sub, but my body would need good, clean fuel to get me through the rest of the afternoon. Not only that, but meat sweats plus the way white bread made me gassy posed real problems for my ability to work the rest of the afternoon. Ruefully, I stepped up to the make-your-own smoothie station, tossing in two extra spoonfuls of protein powder along with the banana, strawberries, and other stuff that would make the rest of the day bearable, at least on my stomach.

One of the friends I'd made on set, a gangly guy from Seattle who worked in props, bumped hips with me. I grinned up at him. "Picked a bad week to be on boom, huh, Toby?"

I laughed. I loved my job, even if it was sweaty and exhausting. "There's never a bad week to be on boom. And I'm lucky—at least I'm tall."

"Yeah, and your delts have never looked better."

"Bryce, I appreciate your noticing, even if you don't want a piece of all this." I pulled my hat off and massaged the spot where my ponytail had been pulling at my scalp, then yelped in surprise when his sharp elbow stabbed my side.

"Uh, *chica*, don't look now but some producer type has his eyes glued to you from across the lot."

Of course, I looked. My lungs constricted to the size of fists and I had to grab onto the rickety table that held the food when I pitched forward at the sight of him. Tall, blond, and flawless in flat-front pants, a crisp, white button-down, and sleek sunglasses. I knew him even with sunglasses hiding his bright blue eyes. I felt his presence down to my toes when his face broke into a smile, and he begged pardon from one of the producers, making his way over to me.

I had about five seconds to get myself together for seeing Mark Mahler, face to face, on the set of my show, all the way across the country, of all places.

"Toby." He smiled when he reached me, at least giving the semblance of breathing normally. "This is crazy."

"What are you doing here?" I managed to say.

Look happy, dammit. Hide how terrified you are. You might scare him away.

God, that was the last thing I wanted to do. If it was possible, I wanted to freeze time and just keep drinking in the sight of him, somehow more gorgeous and pure and warm than he was in my memories. In my dreams.

He pulled his sunglasses off, tucking them into a pocket, then held his arms out, palms up, relaxed and inviting. "Can I have a hug?"

Could he? I laughed, took three steps toward him and melted into his embrace, squeezing my arms around his ribs, counting out four seconds—not too long and not too short—then letting go. God, he smelled so good, exactly as he always had—cedar and warmth and, despite all the time I'd been away, *home*. It was a balm to me, deep inside, a reminder that, no matter how long it had been or how far I'd gotten, home existed, and it was this man.

When I stepped back from him, I was breathless, looking at him like he was the sun. The smile on his face, though, was undeniably sad.

Oh. Of course. My memories flashed back to the last time I'd seen him. Sitting with Kylie who'd just come from L.A. at the time. He must be here representing her. His girlfriend. Fiancée? *Oh God, please not fiancée.*

I steeled myself and asked, "So did Kylie land a pilot after all?"

"Ky...no. I mean, I don't know. Did she?"

"That's why you're here, right?" I was trying to get the words out without him hearing my voice shake. My hands were doing plenty of trembling on their own. "Mark, I saw you two together in Philly..."

"Yeah, she was asking me to manage her." He was amused; I could tell by the way the corners of his mouth danced randomly. "I tried to find her some jobs, but, ultimately, I didn't have enough contacts with the right people. She found someone else."

"So, what are you doing here?" I blurted.

"Jelian Roth thinks she wants Beth for some indie movie. Says she can already see the Oscar nods." Mark rolled his eyes, which made me laugh. "I think she doesn't even have the budget to hire her. We're here to talk."

"Beth? Our Beth? From the piano bar?"

"Yeah," he said softly, the smile on his lips softening. "Our Beth."

"You don't live here, do you?" I asked in a rush. How ridiculous would it have been for us to be in the same town all this time? My stomach flipped. I didn't know what I wanted to happen next, I just knew I didn't want this to end.

"No. New York."

"You left Philly? You really loved Philly." It was starting to get harder to pull in breath again. I was rambling. He'd moved. Why? Was it my fault?

Mark sighed, his cheeks picking up the slightest tinge of pink. "It was time to let go. It's easiest and best for me to work from New York. The music scene is exploding, in a good way, and besides...I had nothing left to hang onto. Back in Philly." His gaze jerked up, checking mine.

I kept watching him, steady as ever, trying to pour every feeling into that look. There hasn't been anyone else. I haven't even wanted there to be anyone else. Not really. Nothing close to the way I'd wanted him.

"Besides Joey and Hawk's, but, you know," he rambled on. "They're surviving without me. I guess after you and I, uh..."

"Broke up?"

Mark swallowed. "Yeah. I guess I really grew up after that. Turned out you were right. I was letting my old life tie me to a place I'd outgrown, and it wasn't good for me."

That was like a punch in the damn gut. All the time I'd spent this past year trying to depend on other people, form attachments that mattered, add chosen family members to the ones I was trying to see more of...and Mark had been doing the opposite?

"Ethan and I even passed The Bro Show on to new people."

"I know. They kinda suck." I swallowed, hard. This wasn't the time to hide anything from him.

"You listen, still?"

"I missed you, Mark." I felt my own voice break when I said it, felt my heart pour itself into the words. "I knew I couldn't call you, or I'd...not be okay, but I figured I could at least hear your voice."

His eyebrows went up, his mouth dropping open a centimeter before he pulled it shut again.

"I listened once, then again. Then it became like a habit. Until six weeks later, when you were off the air."

"Oh." His jaw worked up and down, once. There were a few more seconds of awkward silence before he stammered, "What are you doing here? In LA?"

"The opportunity was too good to pass up. My mom got me an interview with ABC, and I landed on *Hell's Handmaidens* after paying my dues for a few months on *Looking for Love*. You know, that reality show?"

He nodded.

"I'm on a two-year internship but they already like me. A lot. Like, enough to hire me full time. My supervisor thinks they might promote me early." I was rambling, I knew, but I didn't care. I wanted to fill the space between us with words, make new ties between us that I could maybe, if I was lucky, tighten until we were back to our old selves. Back to having fun and being in love and not caring very much about anything else.

"You're still doing engineering?" His eyebrows tented together, as if he really cared. "Uh, sound?"

"Yeah, I finished the degree," I said, remembering how I'd struggled to get all the work in to my professors while basically fleeing the city. "Um, if you saw last week's fight scene, where it froze into a still and cut together with Latin guitar covers of The Doors? That was me. And some other editors and engineers. Obviously."

Mark just chuckled. "I did not hear it, but now I'm going to go looking for it."

"Thanks. I get to do a lot of on-set stuff, too, which has been good." I bit my lip, trying to keep from filling the tense air with word vomit for a few seconds, at least.

"So, you live here now."

"Here. And, uh, I have a little place in New York, too." He didn't need to know how tiny my place in L.A. was. "I've been trying to develop a show with a friend of mine; the music is heavily electronic. It could be good."

"A show." His eyes narrowed as he breathed out the half-question, half statement.

"On Broadway. Or, you know. Off Broadway. It's much different from TV work, obviously, but I like the challenge, and..."

Mark barked out a laugh and a flash of indignance went through me until he said, "I live in New York mostly, but I have a place here."

"You're kidding."

"Nope. Guess we're polar opposites."

I didn't know what to make of that. I wanted to tell him that opposites attract, but that we already knew that, and that I still wanted him, so much, but the fact that we had probably criss-crossed each other traveling across the country several times in the last month probably meant...something. I just couldn't wrap my mind around what.

"I have a place in Nashville, too," he said with a soft smile.

"I'm thinking of looking for a room to rent in Miami," I quietly supplied. "Club scene there is insane. I might learn to spin."

"Hannah's been saying I should find a crash pad in Chicago."

We were both grinning now, the air between us charged with something.

"Maybe next time we're both in New York, we could grab dinner..."

Mark held up a finger, cutting me off. "Toby, I have three meetings in the next five hours and I'm pretty sure I will lose my chance to manage the next huge teen pop sensation if I don't make it to the third one. But, honestly, none of that matters if I don't know that you'll let me take you out for dinner tonight."

All the breath whooshed out of me, and my knees felt weak. Mark noticed the subtle change in my stance, in the same way he'd always noticed everything about me. His face twisted into something between anticipation and agony, and it was all I could do not to laugh. I stepped closer to him, watching his reaction. When his hand moved up to brush my hair from my eye, the laugh turned to relief, which pushed a tear out. I let it track down my cheek. Tears didn't bother me. Not anymore.

"I think the *only* thing that matters to me right this minute is that you take me to dinner tonight."

"Good." Slowly, his face went from worried to relieved, and he let out a short laugh, too. He stepped in and hugged me again, this time placing a gentle kiss on the top of my head. "Thank you," he murmured into my hair.

I didn't even care that I was dripping sweat and probably stank like a garbage heap. Mark Mahler was back in my life, and life had never felt sweeter.

CHAPTER 38

MARK

I HAD to call five friends and promise auditions to two of them to get this reservation. But it was worth it.

The new rooftop restaurant was the buzz of L.A., protected by ultra-clear glass and offering the best view of the clear night sky possible this close to the city. The twenty-five-minute ride had been, surprisingly, the opposite of awkward. Toby was doing well. She had a little cluster of friends in both New York and L.A., girls—and one very gay man, judging by the way he eyed me at craft services earlier—who had her back and who she could count on.

"I'm sorry we fought," I said in a low voice. "You know, back in Philly. Or here in L.A., at Passover. Whatever. Both, I guess."

I might have found her on set in my cool, collected professional mode, but we both knew what this rambling meant. I was nervous. Our lives seemed even less suited to any kind of relationship now than they had eight months ago, when we just couldn't see a way to make it work.

"Me too. I'm sorry I made you move away," she said. The soft openness of her big brown eyes took my breath away.

I let out a startled laugh. "No, it wasn't you." Reconsidering, I raised an eyebrow, letting a small smile shine through. "I mean, it *was* you. But it was good. it was *time*. I was hanging on to Philly too long. Hanging on to...lots of things too long."

CHAPTER 39

TOBY

MY HEART SANK. God, he was so grown-up, so sure of himself. The Mark Mahler I'd first met could barely get through a date without losing his cool. This wasn't a new Mark, not at all – he dressed the same for work, had the same easy mannerisms and open, patient way of listening to me like I was the only person in the world. But now there was an extra layer, coloring his every aspect, that was so *sure*. So calm and confident.

Meanwhile, I felt like I'd fallen into this new L.A. sound stage life hard and fast. As crazy as it had been, I loved it, but each day had me questioning my choices over and over. Confidence was hard to come by for a sound intern on a big Hollywood set.

"But really, Toby, it wasn't you."

I scoffed. "I basically told you I couldn't see a future with you." I'd replayed my words that day so many times that I remembered them better than most of my actors remembered their lines.

"It wasn't you," he insisted. "I got attached to you without your permission."

I raised an eyebrow at him. How was he so understanding?

"I wasn't asking you to commit to me," Mark continued, "but I was so committed to you, to the idea of not letting you go, that it had the same effect." My heart thrummed wildly. "It was too much. Being there in Philly, knowing you didn't even want to see me anymore. When I realized you hadn't ever really wanted to date me in the first place, I just...I felt..."

"Crushed? Because I—"

"Guilty. I never wanted to burden you. I accepted your help for The Bro Show because it was the easy thing to do. I mean, I was a little afraid of you, but I mostly really liked you. And... then I fell in love with you. Still am, I guess."

My heart dropped into my stomach. Before I could say anything, apologize for telling him I loved him right before stomping on his heart all those months ago, tell him that my feelings hadn't changed, he seemed to realize what he'd said.

"I mean, I..."

I reached across the table and gripped his hand, determined to lay my feelings as bare as I could. I'd spent so long trying to ignore them after I'd walked out of his life, and far too many hours crying into my pillow when I failed. "These past few months have sucked, you know. I never thought a guy leaving my life could make every part of my life so much harder."

My tears were streaming down my cheeks now, half from regret and half from the sheer power of seeing him again. It was like a switch had been flipped inside me. How could I have missed what was right in front of me, not to mention the feelings that had grown for him and only blossomed since he left? "I haven't seen anyone else," I blurted.

Mark cleared his throat, fussed with the napkin in his lap with his other free hand. Dammit, I had no idea how to read him now. With his new confidence came a poker face, a way of masking his feelings to preserve mine. Just the way I'd always done. Finally, he murmured, "I haven't either."

I couldn't help it. A happy laugh burst from my chest, causing a couple tables' worth of diners to look over at our table. I didn't care.

I'd never felt the desire to claim a man as my own, certainly never wanted one to claim me. Yet somehow, over the past year, Mark had become mine and I had become his. Without agreeing to it, we'd left a space open in our hearts for one another.

"It wasn't intentional, exactly, I'm not a monk or anything, but..." Mark's words came faster now, like he was worried that I would think he wanted the same thing I'd rejected from him a year ago. "Nobody's like you, Toby."

There were several things I wanted to do in that exact moment. One of them, obviously, was hauling Mark into the coat check and tearing his clothes off. The other was breaking down into tears. I chose the third option floating through my head.

"It's Chanukah. Fifth night. Tomorrow," I blurted.

Mark looked like he barely held back a wince. "I know," he said, keeping his tone even.

"You said you were here for the next five days."

"I am."

"Would you come for dinner?"

"Can't," he said, his eyes carefully searching mine. "My mom's expecting me. And Hannah, of course. We booked a trip home for their annual party. I have a flight to Ohio and then I'm supposed to fly back on the redeye."

I deflated like an untied balloon. I could practically see myself whizzing around the room in circles and then flopping to the floor.

"If I go home with you for Chanukah," Mark started, and something in me lit up like rays of sun bursting through the clouds, though I didn't show it, "Your family might think we're back together."

I cracked a smile. "I wouldn't mind that."

"Like, together like they wanted us to be together. Last time I was there."

I raised one shoulder in a shrug that I tried to make look casual. "They can think what they want."

Mark pulled his phone out of his pocket, and tapped at the screen, then raised it to his ear. "Hannah? Hey."

God, I loved the smile that spread across his face for his twin sister. There was so much I still didn't know him, so much I was suddenly desperate to learn.

"Yeah," he said into the phone, clearing his throat. "My flight tomorrow morning? For Chanukah? Yeah, I think there's gonna be a storm. Or something. And it'll be cancelled."

A distant, tinny screech came ripping through the phone, and Mark made a show of pulling it back from his ear and cringing. "Yeah. You got me. I ran into Toby. You wanna talk to her?" His lips twitched. "Yeah, you're probably right. Next time."

He hung up and slid the phone back in his pocket, all confidence. Damn. He was still the Mark I knew, and had fallen in love with, just slightly improved by an edge of self-assuredness.

Just as incredible. Even more delectable.

"Looks like I'll need an invite for that dinner after all."

I couldn't stop myself from getting to my feet, walking around the small table, grabbing Mark's hands, and tugging him to standing. I pushed my fingers through the short hairs at the back of his head and pulled him to kiss me. He breathed out a sigh right before our lips pressed together, and we fell easily back into the same rhythm I'd daydreamed about so many times since I'd last seen him. He licked at the seam of my lips, and I met his tongue with mine, whimpering when he gripped my waist and tugged me close to him.

We were interrupted by at least two people loudly clearing their throats.

Mark pulled back, pressing his lips together against a grin. "This is kind of a fancy restaurant, I guess, for PDA."

"Call the waiter," I growled, my mouth still so close to his that his breath skated across my lips. "Call the waiter, and have them pack up the food to go. Or forget the food. I don't really care."

CHAPTER 40

MARK

JUST OVER AN HOUR LATER, Toby was spread out on the mattress in my one-bedroom in L.A., hair splayed around her head in an array of deep chestnut with streaks of gold like a celebration firework. It was shorter now, hitting just below her shoulders instead of down to her butt, and I loved it. Wanted to see how it felt when she was on top of me, bending over me for a kiss. But not this time.

I eased myself over her naked, wanting body. She was perfect. I'd always thought she was perfect, but now it was amplified in a dozen different little ways that I couldn't wait to take my time re-learning. I positioned myself exactly how she liked me, losing my breath at the sensation of her wet heat against my skin.

"You want this," I mused, barely realizing that I said the words out loud until she nodded her agreement. I reached down to feel her, amazed that one strategic brush of my fingertip could still make her moan in the same way it always had.

"Please, Mark," she whimpered, and I couldn't have refused her for the whole world. As I slid into her, she strained up to give me a long, languid, utterly sweet kiss. Then she pulled away just enough to say, "We're not getting married. Ever."

I choked out a laugh, half distracted by the insane sensations racing through my bloodstream and half wanting to tell her that I stopped caring whether I'd ever get married the second the universe decided to give me another shot with her.

"Your dad will hate that," I grunted as I slid in fully to the hilt, in one smooth motion.

"A...Ahhh! Maybe," she gasped as her hips rocked up to meet mine, making me see stars. I put every ounce of energy into remembering to breathe, then repeated the motion. Toby swallowed another moan as her hands scrabbled at my shoulders.

"Your mom will hate me. She'll think I'm refusing to make it official with you," I said, grinding against her, wanting to fill her up, keep her happy, love every single inch of her as long as she'd let me.

"Yeah, she will," Toby breathed, baring her teeth at my neck, nipping at one of the tendons there.

Dammit, she was killing me and bringing me back to life with every second. I gripped her hip, holding it firm to the bed while pushing up on my other arm, giving myself a good view of her. For a few torturous moments, I held myself perfectly still. "I don't give a shit what anyone else thinks. Okay? Nothing matters except you and me, and what we want. I want you. What do you want, Toby?"

"You. Just you," she gasped when I bent down to lick at her neck.

"Good." I started moving again, in slow, thorough thrusts that made Toby's eyelids flutter and her head roll back against the pillows.

"And, um..." she choked out.

I slowed.

"And Chanukah with my family. Seder next year, if you want. Probably this a few more times, too."

"Probably?" I asked. I tried to sound like I was teasing, but even like this, inside of her, I was afraid of losing her again far too soon. Afraid of this being the last time.

She bit her bottom lip and nodded, letting a moan trickle out from between her teeth. I plunged in hard again, held myself close to her, planted a long, bruising kiss on her lips.

"What about a date in New York? Can I take you to dinner there, too?"

"Only if you take me to bed afterward."

EPILOGUE

MARK - ONE YEAR LATER

"I CAN'T BELIEVE this is really happening," Toby said, flopping down on the crisp white hotel bedding with a tiny bag of silver candied almonds in her hand.

"You think it's too soon?" I asked, groaning as I stepped out of my stiff shoes, then loosened my tie. So much formality for an engagement party, but Liz's parents had wanted it.

Toby flipped over to her stomach, and I admired the deep v-cut of the back of her silver dress. Everything about Liz and JJ's wedding was glitz and glamor, even the bridesmaid's dresses for the engagement party. I didn't even want to think of how fancy the actual wedding would be, four months from now. The silver stretched over every one of Toby's curves, but the cutout on the back of her dress laid bare the muscles of her shoulders, the sharp angles of her shoulder blades, and every knob of her spine. Her skin begged me to lick it.

"Let's not make this big of a deal out of everything," Toby groaned into the bedspread. I was sure she was getting makeup all over it, but the meaning behind her words distracted way too much for me to care. "It's too much."

I'd known I wanted Toby in my life forever in the middle of our second first kiss – over a year ago now in L.A. We'd spent the last twelve months living together, and apart, in our various apartments across the country, according to our crazy schedules. Just last week I'd convinced her to give up her lease in L.A., to consider my Hollywood apartment her own whenever she wanted. I wasn't there too much, anyway.

If this was the way she wanted to start to talk about maybe possibly agreeing to marry me, I wasn't going to have any distractions.

I also wasn't going to pressure her. At all. In any way. Not even now.

I cleared my throat softly. "You know, people get engaged without huge parties all the time. We wouldn't have to do any of this."

She lifted her head, turned it to look at me. Her eyes were clear, calm, dead serious as they looked into mine. "Do they get married when they have six apartments across the country and only see each other half the days out of a month?"

My heart did a happy jig in my chest, but I kept my expression calm. "Yes, they do. They do if they're us. We're perfect together, even if we're not normal."

I loved her and she loved me. We said it on the phone and in bed. We showed it in the way we shared our lives, making sure we were together for holidays, hanging around set or back stage with the other if it was the only time we could find. Last month, Toby had gotten someone to cover for her turn in the mixing studio because I had the flu in Nashville, and she decided she had to fly down to take care of me.

Yeah. I loved her, more than I ever thought anyone could love. I was pretty sure she felt the same way. If we never got married, if we never moved in together in more than one city, that was okay. Her love was enough for me.

That didn't mean I wasn't damn happy about this conversation.

"Hmm," I said, loping over to the bed and sliding onto the mattress so that I faced her. I gently wrapped my hand around her waist and tugged her up so she was on her side, "Married with six apartments? I've never heard of that."

"Mmm." The corner of her mouth tilted down, and she stared at the bedspread. "Too bad."

"But remember, we only have five places now. And I have no desire to be just like everyone else. Do you?"

She looked up, her eyes shining with emotion tinged with uncertainty, but steady. "If you asked me," she said in a soft but dead serious voice, "I'd say yes."

I stretched out my free hand to tilt her chin to mine, trying to contain my trembling excitement behind a slow, steady kiss. I jammed my hand into my pocket and pulled out a tiny black velvet pouch.

"You're fucking kidding me," Toby said in an almost-whisper, her eyes wide.

I shrugged with a sheepish smile. "I bought it the day after our second first date. It's nothing fancy—streamlined so you can still run grip work with it on, if you want, and—"

Now it was her turn to maul me with a kiss. I barely managed to slide the ring onto her finger before she tackled me to the bed, straddling me with strong thighs, and tore my shirt off. "I really am keeping my place in Miami," she said when we came up for breath.

"Of course you are," I gasped.

"And I'm keeping my last name," she said right before she sank her teeth into my collarbone.

"I'd be sad if you didn't," I groaned.

"I love you," she whispered, kissing her way up my neck, licking lightly at my ear.

"That's all I'll ever need," I said as I grabbed her and flipped her over, devouring her mouth again.

And this time, I meant it.

The End.

ABOUT THE AUTHOR

Aless is the bestselling author of several steamy romances who swears she was in her twenties yesterday. Since that's sadly untrue, she spends her time writing fun, sexy stories about men and women falling in love under the most unlikely circumstances.

When she's not writing, you can find her with a spoonful of ice cream in one hand and a romance novel in the other, snuggled up with one of her giant dogs.

ALSO BY ALESSANDRA THOMAS

Just Down The Hall: Just Love Series Book One

Descended from Shadows: Book of Sindal Book One

Picture Perfect: Picturing Perfect Series Book One